QUEEN
of
GODS

KATHARINE & ELIZABETH CORR

HOT
KEY
BOOKS

First published in Great Britain in 2023 by
HOT KEY BOOKS
4th Floor, Victoria House
Bloomsbury Square, London WC1B 4DA
Owned by Bonnier Books
Sveavägen 56, Stockholm, Sweden
bonnierbooks.co.uk/HotKeyBooks

A CIP catalogue record for this book is available from the British Library.

ISBN: 978-1-4714-1128-1
Also available as an ebook and in audio

1

This book is typeset using Atomik ePublisher
Printed and bound in Great Britain by Clays Ltd, Elcograf S.p.A.

Hot Key Books is an imprint of Bonnier Books UK
bonnierbooks.co.uk

For our family

The Four Orders of Theodesmioi

Theodesmioi of the order of **ZEUS**
king of the gods, ruler of the heavens and the earth

Battle Wagers ~ fight with beyond-human powers of speed and endurance

Weather Workers ~ control the clouds and wind

Theodesmioi of the order of **POSEIDON**
god of the sea

Sea Singers ~ enhance the speed and strength of ships

Theodesmioi of the order of **HADES**
god of the underworld, ruler of the dead

Soul Severers ~ separate the soul from the body and send it on its journey

Theodesmioi of the order of **HEPHAESTUS**
smith-god and master of metals

Spell Casters ~ bind magic into metal

Note: Houses of the Orders of Zeus, Hades and Poseidon are found in most cities. There are only two houses of the Order of Hephaestus, in Mycenae and Thebes.

Prologue

Sing, Goddess, of rage . . .

That is the poet's request. Yet whose ire shall I make the subject of my song?

The wrath of Deina? Soul Severer, daughter of Hades, demi-god, thief. Tricked, as others have been, by Thanatos, god of death. The seeds he gave her, the seeds she ate that night in Thebes, allowed her to defeat the tyrant Orpheus and save her friends. They also bound her to the Underworld. Now, she makes her way through the darkness to Hades' realm, her heart silenced by the grip of eternity, forced to obey the summons of her divine parent, and fearing that she will never see the sun again.

Or the anger of Theron, true prince of Thebes? Another Soul Severer, and son of Orpheus, slaying his father would have left him lawful prey of the implacable Furies. Instead, he trapped his father's blood-soaked soul forever in the Threshold. He and Deina, Hades' daughter. Only as he lost her did her realise that he loved her. Now he lingers with his companions, hidden in the forest outside Thebes. Listen: he sings a threnody, a song of lamentation, as flames take the body of the betrayer, Chryse.

Within, Theron burns with frustration. He wishes to reclaim Deina from the Underworld, but he knows his duty. He must reveal the truth to the Theodesmioi, the god-marked servants of Zeus, Poseidon, Hades and Hephaestus – the truth of what awaits them after death. Not the joy of Elysium, but the eternal nightmare of becoming a blood hunter. Theron and his friends have evaded their pursuers thus far, and their sights are set on Iolkos, city of broad streets in the gulf of Pagasae – if they can survive long enough to get there.

Perhaps I shall sing the fury of Aristaeus. He is nursing his spite and his injuries in the sumptuous marble and gold surroundings of the Cadmea, the citadel of Thebes, the mighty city of which he now claims to be king. Alone in his chambers, Aristaeus plots his enemies' destruction, sending his spies to hunt them out.

Or shall I tell of the rage of my sisters, the Fates? For this is not how the story should have gone. That night in the Cadmea, Orpheus was to have destroyed his son or Theron was to have slain his father. Either way, Aster and Dendris were to have died. Deina, having watched her friends suffer, was to have been imprisoned in the Cadmea to serve Orpheus or Aristaeus for the rest of her days. This was what the Fates planned. This is what would have happened – if I hadn't stepped in so many years ago. If I hadn't ensured Deina caught the plague and brought her to the point of death. If I hadn't nudged Thanatos into sparing her life. If he hadn't seen the gold bloom around her iris. If he hadn't dared to hope. Shall I tell my sisters for how long their plans have been unravelling and reveal Thanatos's role? I think I should. Even now, the cloud-capped halls of Olympus ring with the clamour of their protests. Once they know the full story, their resentment and bitterness will be beyond all measure.

Yes, that shall be my song. I will even give the poet his opening line.

Sing, Goddess, of the impotent fury of the Fates.

For I am Tyche, goddess of fortune.

And fate means nothing if you have luck on your side.

1

The darkness was suffocating, and Deina felt the weight of it. Like a too tight second skin it squeezed her body, stealing speech as well as sight.

Thanatos's fingers still gripped her left wrist. With every step, he took her further from her friends, further from the future she'd dared to dream of, and nearer to the perpetual imprisonment that awaited her. His touch was so cold it felt like fire. Yet she'd stopped pulling against his grasp. She was terrified that if he let go, she'd wander here forever.

On and on they walked. Until the darkness was displaced by a flaring brilliance that made Deina throw up her right arm to shield her eyes. That too faded, into the ordinary glow of oil lamps.

If you could call anything about Hades' court ordinary.

Deina blinked, looking around as her vision adjusted. Thanatos was next to her, his face impassive; he'd released his grip on her arm. They were back in Hades' throne room. There was the huge obsidian looking glass on the wall, the

sweep of its polished black disc offering Deina a shadowy reflection of herself and her surroundings. There were the two empty thrones, lofty on their dais. There, the lapis lazuli snakes that had attacked her and Theron and the others, ossified and confined to alcoves once more. So much the same – but Deina herself was different. To her dismay, her Severer's robes had gone. Instead, she was wearing the clothes that Hades had conjured her into – briefly – the last time they'd met. A full-length, one-shouldered gown of diaphanous garnet-red silk, secured by a gold belt and a single gold shoulder brooch set with rubies. There were more rubies scattered across the hem. She was shod with delicate sandals made from a fine gold mesh, and – Deina lifted one hand to her head – the dark waves of her hair were confined by what felt like more of the same material.

She turned on Thanatos.

'Is this your doing?'

'No.' Hades' voice echoed through the immense room. 'It's mine.'

Deina spun to see one of the empty thrones now occupied. The god of the Underworld – the god who claimed to be Deina's mother – was wearing the same rich blue gown as at their last encounter. She crossed her legs and grinned. 'Don't you like your new clothes, Deina? I think the colour suits you. And Thanatos approves. Don't you, Thanatos?'

Thanatos blinked at Deina as though just becoming aware of her presence. His eyes widened as he took in her appearance, and a faint flush warmed his pale cheeks. Hades laughed. The sound was chilling.

Deina wrapped her arms tightly around herself. 'Why are you doing this?' she demanded.

The god tilted her head.

'Because I can.' Some invisible force seized Deina's limbs and forced her onto her knees. 'And because you have displeased me,' Hades continued. 'Either Orpheus or Theron was fated to die. One of them should have been down here by now, pursuing the desolate paths of the Underworld towards the place of judgement.' Her voice began to vibrate with anger. 'Instead, what do I find? Theron still alive, free, and Orpheus neither dead nor alive, but trapped in the Threshold – in a place of your making.' She flung out her arm, pointing at Deina accusingly.

Deina couldn't get up; her body was no longer under her control. But she could still speak.

'And I would do it all again.'

'Deina –' Thanatos murmured from behind her – 'you mustn't.'

Deina paid no attention – she would not, could not, conceal her loathing of the being lounging on the throne. If she tried to swallow her hate, it would choke her. 'I'd do all of it, and more. I do not fear the wrath of the gods. And I do not fear you.'

For a moment Hades stared at her. The god's violet eyes glittered dangerously.

'You should be afraid.' She gestured in Deina's direction: one languid flick of her long, beringed fingers. Deina found she could no longer move mouth, tongue or throat. 'You should be absolutely terrified. You are bound to this realm and to me, now, daughter. And I can make you do anything. Even tear out your own hair, should it amuse me.'

Deina's fingers immediately wound themselves in her hair and began tugging against her scalp. The pain brought tears into her eyes. She would have cried out if she hadn't been silenced.

'Or . . .' Hades mulled, as Deina's hands went slack. 'Or I could give you a pin and command you to blind yourself.' A long brooch pin appeared in Deina's left palm. Unbidden – unable to resist, despite the terror turning her stomach – she lifted the pin so that the point hovered just in front of her eyeball. Tightened her grip on the sliver of sharp metal as the muscles in her arm tensed, ready to plunge it into her eye.

'Hades, you have to stop this!' Thanatos demanded.

Hades' head snapped round to stare at the god of death as Deina's arm dropped to her side; she felt faint with relief. The pin rolled away across the marble tiles.

'Have to?' The god raised an eyebrow. 'You dare issue orders to me?'

Whatever spell was restraining Deina's body vanished; if she hadn't put out her hands to brace herself, she would have pitched headfirst onto the stone floor. Quickly, she forced herself to scramble upright; whatever Hades was planning next, better to meet it on her feet. The god's attention switched back to her.

'Tell me,' Hades questioned, 'how do you feel about Thanatos right now?'

Deina gritted her teeth. 'I despise him. He gave me the seeds to eat. He told me they'd make me strong enough to defeat Orpheus, made me think that they'd at least kill me too. But instead, they bound me to the Underworld, and to you.' She turned and glared at Thanatos. 'He claimed to be

my friend. He said he wanted to help me, but all the time he was working for you.' Her voice sank to almost a whisper. 'He betrayed me.'

Thanatos shook his head, the word *no* forming silently on his lips.

A long-bladed knife appeared in Deina's hand.

'Well, then.' Hades smiled. 'Here is a chance to take your revenge. Thanatos may have carried out my orders on this occasion, but I grow tired of his insolence and mischief-making. So do my siblings on Olympus. He interferes and constantly oversteps his authority. If you want to hurt him, I won't stop you.'

The knife was heavy in Deina's palm. Part of her – a large part – wanted to make Nat suffer. She'd thrown a knife at him once before, and he'd just plucked the spinning blade straight out of the air; what if, this time, Hades prevented him from defending himself? The idea of Thanatos writhing in pain at her feet was attractive. Yet Hades *wanted* her to attack the god of death. That alone seemed like a good enough reason not to. Instead, Deina lifted the knife and threw herself at Hades, allowing her rage to drive her forward, bringing up her arm to strike –

The blade slashed through nothing more than air. At the last moment, moving too quickly for her to see, Hades had stepped out of the way and was standing, instead, beside her.

'Don't test me, daughter,' the god warned.

Deina ignored her. Pivoting, she plunged the dagger towards Hades' chest. Again the god moved. Deina snarled. 'Fight me, damn you!' She lunged, slashing the knife through already empty space. 'You – you coward!'

8

Hades raised her hand and dealt Deina a stinging backhanded blow, splitting Deina's cheek open with one of her rings and knocking her to the floor. Blood dripped from Deina's face. With a scream of rage, Deina drove the knife against the green marble, cracking the tile in two and shattering the blade.

Hades was watching her coldly.

'The seeds have made you strong, daughter. But you can still suffer. You can still die. And you can still be forced into obedience.'

Deina felt Hades seize control of her body again. She got up and began to walk towards Thanatos, coming to a halt no more than a hair's breadth away from him. Even while her mind yelled at her to stop, her arms reached up to embrace his neck. She felt herself rising onto tiptoe. Felt her lips curving into a seductive smile – despite the ripple of pain from the wound on her cheek – as her mouth lifted to his and she pressed herself against his muscled torso.

Perhaps Thanatos could see in Deina's eyes the emotions that she couldn't express any other way: horror, despair, fury. Gripping her wrists, he forced her away from him, holding her at arm's length.

'Please, Hades,' he said. 'You've proved your point.'

'Which is?'

Thanatos gazed at Deina sadly. 'That she is not a god.'

'Precisely.' Before Hades even finished speaking the word, Deina was freed again. Thanatos released her and backed away. 'But,' the god continued, 'she could be.'

The statement hung in the air like warm breath on a winter's day.

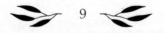 9

'Well?' Hades prompted. 'No clever come back, Deina? No questions?'

'Only one.' Deina turned to face her tormentor. 'You care nothing for my feelings; that much is clear. You've taken my dreams from me. You've separated me from those I love.' An image of Theron reaching out for her, staring in horror as she was dragged into the Underworld, threatened to break what control Deina had left. She fought against the sorrow, determined not to give Hades the satisfaction of seeing her weep. 'So here is my question. You want to keep me here forever, and you want to make me a god – why? It can't be for my benefit. So, I assume that somehow it is for yours.'

A spasm of anger twisted Hades' perfect features. She jumped up from the throne and shifted her shape into the male form that Deina and the other Severers had been expecting when they had first entered the throne room: huge, strong, with thick black hair and a flowing beard, carrying his tall wing-topped sceptre. The god stormed up and down the dais, growling, shoving the thrones out of the way, smacking the end of the sceptre so hard against the tiles that flakes of green marble skittered across the floor. There was some shadow trailing behind him; something older, darker, that spoke to Deina of the corruption of the grave. Without even meaning to, she shuddered and took a step back.

Hades paused in his raging, staring at her. As the god's breathing slowed, he shifted back to his female form. The sceptre became a bangle adorning Hades' wrist. A wave of the god's hand righted the thrones and repaired the floor. She sat down again.

'Why, you ask. And my answer is, why does it matter? When I want something, Deina, I'm used to getting it.' Leaving the throne, Hades stepped off the dais and approached Deina. 'The seeds you ate have taken root within you, binding you ever more firmly to the Underworld.' Smiling, the god flattened her palm against Deina's stomach before lifting her hand to caress Deina's cheek, healing with the lightest touch the injury she had caused. 'Let us not argue like this, daughter. Let me at least show you what your future might be, if you were to accept the divinity you are so quick to reject.'

The throne room disappeared and Deina found herself seated on an ornate chair in a courtyard open to a night sky blazing with stars. The courtyard itself was filled with so much glittering silver it made her squint. Silver ivy wreathed the blue marble columns that marked its perimeter; cloth-of-silver wall hangings shimmered in the glow of oil lamps strung between the columns; pelts of some silvery fur covered the floor and the couches that were scattered about the open space. Some of the couches were occupied by women clad in elegantly draped gowns the colour of ripe plums. More women, identically dressed, were waiting near the throne; some carried wine and platters of fruit, while others sang and danced for Deina's entertainment. Too beautiful to be mortal, Deina guessed they were Lampades, the nymphs of the Underworld said to wait on Persephone and Hecate. And now, apparently, on her. Deina's red gown had been transformed into one of pure white, its folds encrusted with tiny pearls. The golden belt and sandals were now silver, studded with gems she didn't recognise but which flashed with blue fire as she stood, planning to find Hades, to tell the god that none of this would convince her to –

'Deina . . .'

Theron's voice. Shock took her breath away. Shock, mingled with a spark of hope that she couldn't quite extinguish. It couldn't be him. It was impossible. And yet . . .

Deina looked back over her shoulder. There he was, standing just behind the throne, whole and uninjured, smiling at her in that way he had. The kind of smile that, even when she'd hated him, used to make her stomach flip. Now it was enough to send desire pulsing through her. He strolled towards her and caught hold of her hand.

'Come, my love, my divine mistress. It's time for bed, surely?' Theron winked at her. But behind the mischief, his dark eyes were filled with warmth and want. Deina let him lead her out of the courtyard and into one of the adjacent buildings, into a room adorned with brightly coloured frescos and scented with rosemary and mint. Let him lead her towards a huge, fur-strewn bed. Let him stand behind her with one arm locked around her waist while his free hand scooped her long, loose hair out of the way so he could gently kiss the nape of her neck, over and over.

'I've dreamed of this, my Deina,' he murmured. 'We're together now, and we'll never be separated.' The touch of his lips sent a ripple of pleasure across her skin. She sighed and relaxed against him and closed her eyes. 'Do you want me to stop?'

'No . . .'

The sound of her own voice broke the spell. Deina opened

her eyes to find herself back in Hades' throne room, but Theron – Theron was gone. She took a deep, shuddering breath, feeling the empty space behind her as if some part of herself had suddenly been ripped away.

Hades, who was watching her, smiled very slightly. The movement revealed the god's sharp, white teeth.

'You see what riches might be yours, Deina, if you would simply stop this foolish resistance. Give up the human part of you – it's only holding you back. Submit to me, swear to use your power only as I direct you, and take your rightful place as my daughter. Become an immortal goddess.' Hades began to walk around Deina, so close that Deina could feel the heat radiating from the god's form. 'You could have everything you desire and more. No more pain, no more running, no more fighting. You could have Theron. Here. Now. I'd allow you to grant him immortality.' She leaned closer and whispered in Deina's ear. 'He could be at your side forever, ready to do anything you ask of him.' Hades put both hands on Deina's face, forcing her to look at her. 'Don't tell me that you're not tempted. I know what is in your heart.'

Deina wanted to lie. To dismiss Hades' offer with a scornful laugh. But she *was* tempted. More tempted than she could have imagined. After all she had been through – their adventure in the Underworld, Drex's death, Chryse's betrayal, the unforgettable agony that came from eating the seeds Thanatos had given her – the thought of having peace and rest and her friends beside her filled Deina with longing. Her mind cried out for respite even as her body hungered for Theron's touch.

'I could bring them all here? Aster and Dendris, as well as

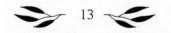

13

Theron? Others from the House?' Deina remembered with a stab of sorrow how much she missed Anteïs.

'Whoever you like,' Hades replied. 'You are my daughter. Obey me, and I will deny you nothing.'

Deina wavered. Giving in suddenly seemed like such an easy choice to make. Her friends would be with her. They'd be safe.

Yes, they'd be safe.

Thanatos's voice, somehow speaking in her head.

They'd also be dead. Oh, Hades might allow you to grant Theron eternal life, though even then I'd make her swear to it first, but as for the others – the gods do not willingly confer immortality on mortals. She'd free the others to be with you here by killing them, most likely. Even if she didn't, you know the living cannot survive in the Underworld indefinitely. Besides, wasn't there something else you wanted? Something I saw in your room one night, not so very long ago? Something that Hades could never truly give you?

An image slipped into Deina's mind: a crude sketch of a ship, its sails straining against the wind, riding wild waves. The picture that had been – still was, she guessed – pinned to her wall, back at the House in Iolkos. Her own personal vision of freedom.

That was what she'd wanted. And what of Theron's wants, and those of Dendris and Aster? Who was she to be deciding for them? Deina's hand went to her neck, to where a spell-cast torc had so recently been fixed. To take their choice away from them would make her no better than the Order, no better than Orpheus, no better than a god –

Which, of course, was the point. She'd become a god, if she took the path Hades had shown her. A god who treated Theron and the others as her playthings, who made them do what she wished and punished them if they refused.

Deina glanced at Thanatos and nodded her thanks for his intervention. A mistake: Hades threw her head back and let out a shriek of rage that made the throne room tremble. The bracelet transformed back into a sceptre and then into a bident, and she jabbed the two dagger-sharp prongs in Nat's direction, hurling the god of death right out of the throne room.

'You will pay for this interference, Thanatos! I will see you strung up in Tartarus, and you will have an eternity of pain in which to contemplate your errors. As for you, Deina, the time has come to make your choice. What is it to be?'

Slowly, Deina shook her head.

'What you're offering me is a lie. If the only way for Theron to be with me is for you or me to force him into it, to take away his choice, or even his life, then –' Deina stood up straighter, defiant – 'then I'd rather be alone. I stand by what I said, Mother: I despise the gods. I will never willingly become one of you.'

Hades' mouth twisted into a snarl. An enormous hammer appeared in the god's hand and she drew back her arm. Deina forced herself to keep her eyes open, to keep her gaze fixed on her mother's face as the god dealt the blow that would surely destroy her.

The blow never fell. The hammer disappeared, and Hades swept back to her throne.

'No. I will not give you death. That is too easy. Instead, you may spend eternity alone, shut away from everyone and everything, with only remembrance of your mistakes to keep you company.'

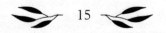

Deina spun, searching for Nat. He owed her – he had to help her. The god of death staggered back into the throne room and reached out one hand towards her.

'Deina –'

Too late. Nat and the throne room vanished. Instead, Deina and Hades were in a small, empty space, no more than four paces by four paces, utterly bare except for a single glowing orb – a faint source of light that served only to emphasise the deep shadows. No windows. No doors. No features of any kind; the floor was indistinguishable from the walls, and the walls were indistinguishable from the ceiling. Yet they were real enough. Deina spun, pressing her hands against the nearest wall. Her palms and fingertips met solid, unyielding stone, as cold and smooth as ice.

Hades smiled.

'Your new home, Khthonia.' The name that Hades had given her; Deina's true name, or so the god claimed. 'There is no time here. You may thirst, you may hunger, but there will be no actual need for you to eat or drink. You will not age. You will not die. No escape through death for you, though I suppose you may go mad, eventually.' The god paused, watching Deina, a faint smile on her face. 'If you want to beg me for mercy . . .'

Dread pinned Deina in place, making her squirm. Part of her wanted to plead, but she couldn't even speak. The horror of never-ending isolation in this place was overwhelming.

Hades clicked her fingers. A small table appeared, set with a stoppered silver jug, rich with jewels, and a matching cup. The god lifted the stopper briefly; a sweet scent filled the room, reminding her of honeysuckle, or a field of wildflowers, or cut grass on a summer's day.

'I do not propose to trouble myself with you any further,' Hades said. 'This is the last time you'll ever see me, or anyone. I am not unkind, however: I will leave you with one final chance. If you do change your mind, your way out lies there.' The god gestured towards the table. 'A sip of the nectar will be enough to start your transformation into a god. If you take that course, I will know about it, and I will release you from this prison. If not . . .' She shrugged.

'Why must I choose?' Deina's voice was hoarse. 'You forced me to kiss Thanatos. Why don't you force me to drink?'

'I suppose I could.' Hades laughed mirthlessly. 'But where would be the fun in that?' The god clicked her fingers again and vanished.

'Wait!' Deina cried out, raising her fists and hammering on the wall. 'Wait! Come back!'

There was no answer.

2

The only damage Deina's fists did to the walls and floor of her cell was to stain them red with her own blood. But she didn't dare stop. Taking the silver cup, she clambered onto the table and hammered the cup against the ceiling, tried to open a crack or even make a dent. Useless; the whole of her prison was constructed of the same indestructible stone. She didn't try to use the glowing globe as a weapon – the thought of being plunged into darkness was even more terrifying. Instead, Deina turned her attention to the table. As strong as she now was, it took only a moment for her to loosen and free one of the legs. There was barely room to raise it over her shoulder; still, she did her best to smash it against the walls. Smashed it to bits in her desperation to escape. She pulled off the next table leg, and the next – until all that was left was the tabletop. Surrounded by fragments of wood, Deina sank to the floor and wrapped her arms and bloodied hands around her knees, hugging them to her chest.

She could not take her eyes off the jewelled jug containing

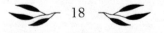

the nectar. The drink of the gods. Her escape, but her death sentence too. If she gave in, whatever humanity she had left, whatever part of her loved Theron and wanted to help her friends, would wither away.

Deina soon lost any sense of how long she'd been sitting, staring at the finely wrought silver. There was no time here. Hades had reminded her of that. Her silent heart offered no rhythm by which she might measure out her captivity. Still, she kept pressing her fingers to her pulse points, feeling – hoping – for some sign that she was still alive, still human – at least in part.

At some point, her attention was claimed by a soft noise: one of the rubies on the hem of her gown tapping against the floor as she moved position. It gave her an idea. Deina ripped the gemstone from the red fabric. The edge was sharp enough to mark the soft wood of the table. Perhaps she could somehow create time in this empty eternity by counting her paces and scratching a line for every thousand steps? She began the experiment – but the room was too small. In a space where the length of each wall was only a little more than her own height, there was more turning than walking.

And all the time – such as it was – the fear of madness haunted her. Deina had seen it, back in Iolkos. After too many rites and too many hours spent walking through other people's memories and regrets, Severers were liable to lose their reason. Their minds broke. Though their bodies were anchored to the present, the rest of them wandered, lost among the Thresholds they had created. There was no recovery – no chance for one; most of those afflicted soon wasted away. Deina suspected the

Severers who cared for them were told not to try too hard to keep them alive. There was no place in the House for those who couldn't work.

Terrified of forgetting that she needed to escape, Deina began to use the gemstones on her gown for a different purpose. Somehow, the two rings she wore were still on her fingers. The plain gold ring given to her by Leida, and the more ornate band holding the agate carved by Drex. Both people she'd loved, both victims of the Underworld and Orpheus. But the rings would only help her remember the dead. She needed to remember the living too. She couldn't write – the letters Drex had taught her had already ebbed from her memory – but she could carve rough images into the tabletop. The sigil of Hades, the same symbol that was on her forehead, to remind her who she was. An arrow, to remind her of Theron, the best archer in the House. A spear for Aster. A tree for Dendris. A wheel with five spokes, representing the rivers of the Underworld, so she didn't forget where she was. And a ship, just like the drawing pinned to her wall back at the House. An emblem of the freedom she'd dreamed of for so long.

Every so often, she slept, more from boredom than exhaustion. While she was awake, she sat next to the tabletop and traced her fingers over the images she'd created, starting again as soon as she'd finished, willing herself to remember. Or she stared at the image Drex had carved of two warriors locked in perpetual combat within the agate of the ring, trying to think of a plan. Because there had to be a way out of here. If she stopped believing *that*, there was no point in resisting any more.

Thanatos began appearing in the cell. At first, she ignored him because she decided he was just a figment of her imagination, a sign that her mind was fracturing. Then, after he'd taken her hand and spoken to her, she ignored him because she was angry with him and hadn't forgiven him for lying to her about the seeds and delivering her to Hades. She ignored him, but she still listened. He spoke of Theron and Aster and Dendris and the Bronze Guards who had helped them escape the Cadmea, the citadel of Thebes. He told her how they'd burned Chryse's body before fleeing the city. How they were trying to reach Iolkos, surviving on meagre rations, theft and ingenuity. Each time he appeared, he let her know they were still alive. That for them, at least, there was still hope.

Until Deina couldn't bear her own silence any longer.

'How much time?' she asked Nat, her voice rusty with dry air and disuse. 'How much time has passed in the mortal world?'

Nat stared at her, then broke into a smile.

'You're still there. I was getting worried that –'

'How much time?'

'It's autumn in Iolkos. The harvest is just over.'

Only a few weeks since that night in the Cadmea. Nat must have seen her confusion. He added, 'The Underworld does not obey the same rules as the mortal world, you know that. Years in the mortal realm may pass here in the blink of an eye. A day there might feel like an eternity in the Underworld.' A snap of his fingers conjured a cup. He crouched down in front of her and offered it to her. 'Water? You must be thirsty.'

'I am, but I'm not stupid. Do you really think I'd accept a cup of water from you?' Deina scoffed. 'Have you forgotten what happened last time I swallowed something you gave me?'

Nat shook his head, as though he didn't want to remember.

'I swear by the Styx that this is water. Nothing more. Please, drink it.'

She was thirsty. Reluctantly, Deina took the cup and sipped the ice-cold liquid inside. It refreshed her a little.

'Are you hungry? I think I can risk a little more . . . acquisition.' Without waiting for her answer, Nat conjured a wooden platter into existence; it was piled with flatbreads, crisp and steaming and drizzled with oil and oregano. 'It's just bread – I swear on the Styx. Someone in the mortal world is wondering where their supper has gone right about now.'

The aroma made Deina's mouth water. She tore off a piece and began to nibble at it, not taking her eyes off Nat.

'Aren't you supposed to be persuading me to give in? I assume that's why you're here. Hades sent you to convince me to drink the nectar.'

Nat shook his head.

'As far as Hades is concerned, I'm back in my cave. Defeated. Humbled. If she looks, she'll see me there – or she'll think she does. What she'll actually be seeing is my twin brother, Hypnos, the god of sleep.'

'Who's helping you because . . . ?'

'Because I've lost count of the number of favours he owes me. There have been innumerable escapades, usually involving severely disappointed nymphs . . .' Nat shook his head, a look of disdain flashing across his face. 'Even for a god, my brother has a short attention span. Anyway, all he has to do is lie there with his eyes closed, which is what he spends most of his time doing anyway.' He sat next to her, stretching his long legs out in front and silently tracing a pattern on the floor with one finger: an all too human gesture. Deina had to remind herself. Despite appearances, Nat was not a mortal.

'You still haven't told me why you're here, Thanatos.'

'Nat. That's what you called me before.'

'That was before you betrayed me to Hades.'

'The seeds worked, didn't they?' he demanded, turning his head to face her. 'You defeated Orpheus. You defeated fate – but only because you ate the seeds. You had no choice, Deina.' He lifted his fingers towards her face; Deina shied away, and he let his hand drop again. 'If I'd told you the truth – if you'd been fully aware of the consequences – you'd still have eaten the seeds. You know you would, because you knew what the outcome would be if you didn't. Theron would have died an agonising death. Your other friends would have been enslaved or killed. And you would be locked up in the Cadmea with a spell-cast torc around your neck and no hope left.'

No hope. But what hope did she have now, sealed up in the Underworld for eternity?

'You could have killed me, after we'd taken Orpheus to the Threshold. I'm a demi-god, supposedly, like Eurydice was. I wouldn't have become one of those blood hunters. You could have killed me and set me free.'

'I'd sworn not to. Hades endowed the seeds with magic and gave them to me, but they were not a gift.'

No such thing as a gift from a god – the Theodesmioi knew that as well as anyone. The best you could hope for was a debt, Deina reflected. If a god gave you something, you'd end up paying for it sooner or later. Nat was watching her, looking almost downcast.

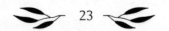

'I am sorry, Deina. I'm not good at apologies, I so rarely feel compelled to give them, but I honestly want to make amends for what I did. To help.'

'Then explain to me why Hades is so desperate to keep me here. And don't try to convince me that she's suddenly been overcome with parental affection . . .'

Nat smiled slightly. 'The gods, old and new, are not noted as being particularly careful or affectionate parents.' He raised his eyebrows and spread his hands wide. 'Truthfully, I have no idea what she wants with you. You'll have noticed that we're not exactly close.' He studied Deina, his dark blue eyes glittering slightly in the faint light cast by the globe. 'The first time I saw you, I knew you were linked to the Underworld. I could sense the power running through your veins, and the – the –' he paused for a moment – 'I suppose the closest word for it would be *taste*, or perhaps *fragrance*, or *colour*, even – it's very difficult to express within the limitations of –'

'Are you saying,' Deina interrupted, 'that I taste or smell of the Underworld?'

Nat hesitated. 'Sort of.'

Deina pulled a face.

'But in a good way,' Nat added hurriedly. 'For gods, the taste of power is like the most intoxicating wine. And I suppose, as human wines from different places taste different . . .' He trailed off, rubbing one hand pensively against the back of his neck. 'My point is, I could tell that some part of you came from the Underworld. But there's also something else there, something I can't quite pin down. Some other sort of power, I think.'

'That tastes different?'

The god pursed his lips. 'Yes. If you like.'

Deina couldn't help laughing.

'I'm so glad I'm amusing you,' Nat snapped, with a flash of his old petulance. 'I happen to be speaking seriously. This other power I can sense within you, that's the only thing I can think of that would make Hades so interested in you. Otherwise, you're just another demi-god, and not even a particularly gifted one –'

'You really are bad at apologies.'

'Sometimes the truth is unpalatable, Hades' daughter.' He smirked and settled back against the wall, staring up at the ceiling of Deina's prison. 'My point is, I wanted to save you, Deina. That's why I agreed when she offered me the seeds. I wanted to save you, and I couldn't think of any other way to do it.'

Deina tore off another chunk of warm bread and began picking at it. Despite everything he'd done, she was finding it hard to stay angry at Nat. He was the closest thing she had in this place to a friend. Or perhaps just an ally. Either way, at least his was a voice she could listen to that wasn't the voice in her head. He could bring her news from the outside and stop her from going mad. Maybe he could even help her escape. Yet from the start, he'd never been honest with her. She studied his profile. All this could be some elaborate charade – part of Hades' deeper plan. How could she know whether to trust him?

'Why did you want to save me?'

Nat opened his mouth to reply.

'The truth, Nat,' Deina added. 'If you're really sorry, tell me the truth.'

Nat paused; she could almost see him weighing up his options. Eventually, he shrugged. 'As you wish. The truth is, you were supposed to die, Deina. Two years ago, or more now, as you'd reckon it. You'd caught whatever plague was ravaging your city at that time. I came to you at night. I was supposed to sever your lifeline and send your soul into the Underworld. I would have done it too, if you hadn't, at the very last moment, opened your eyes. I saw the burst of gold bordering your left iris, and felt your power, and I thought – I thought . . .' He sighed and closed his own eyes briefly. 'I'll tell you what I wanted: not to be the god of death any more. To be free of the Underworld. Free of Hades. Free of the relentless pain and suffering of mortal men. Perhaps because I am so closely entwined with finite mortal existence, I have a sense of infinity that the other gods seem to lack.' His mouth twisted with scorn. 'They are in many ways like human children, and the present moment often fills almost their entire perception. Whereas I have glimpsed the endless vistas of eternity, have felt its crushing weight, and it is monstrous . . .' He shook himself, as though trying to dismiss the remnants of a nightmare. 'When I first saw you, I thought you might have enough of the Underworld in you to take my place as god of death. So, I put my sword away, and let you live.'

Fight harder.

Nat's voice, and the scent of rosemary rising with the night air through the open window. 'I remember,' Deina said. 'You spoke to me.'

He nodded. 'I stayed close to you after that. Watched you, whenever you entered the Threshold.' He gave a short laugh. 'The Soul Severers thought they'd found a way to keep all the gods out of that space, but no human construction can shut out Death.' Thanatos's features darkened, the air grew cold, and frost began to glitter across the wall and floor where he sat.

'I kept you out,' Deina reminded him. 'When I opened the Threshold to imprison Orpheus, I kept you out. Not bad for a not-especially-gifted demi-god.'

'I never claimed you were just an ordinary mortal.' There was a hint of seduction in Nat's smile. 'In many ways, you are extraordinary, as I saw the night I came for you. So, I kept an eye on you. Waited, hoping that as your power grew, I'd discover some way of drawing you further into the Underworld. And then what do I find but you, trying to enter the Underworld as a living, breathing woman . . .'

Deina remembered. After they'd crossed Oceanus and had opened the gateway to the Underworld: Nat appearing in the darkness, guiding her steps, encouraging her onwards. And then he'd appeared again, when she was being deceived by the Dream Children. She'd always known that Nat, whatever he'd claimed, had wanted something from her in return for his help. A dull ache grew in the centre of her chest; Deina swallowed hard. To have her suspicions confirmed . . . Her heart had already been broken by Chryse's betrayal, but if its beating hadn't been stilled by the action of the seeds, she felt that this would have fractured it a little further. 'You were using me.'

Something akin to regret flickered in Nat's eyes.

'At the beginning, maybe. I just wanted to be free.'

Deina recognised the note of desperation in Nat's voice; she could have been sitting next to Theron, or Chryse – she could have been listening to herself. That same note of almost defeated hope. The same recognition that what you wanted was, moment by moment, slipping ever further from your grasp.

Nat brushed his cold fingertips across the back of her hand, making her shiver.

'And then I realised that what I thought I wanted wasn't what I actually wanted at all.'

'What do you mean?' Deina asked.

If Nat had been human, she would have said the glance he gave her was nervous.

'The gods know much of lust – for pleasure, for power – but very little of love. Nothing at all of friendship.' He dropped his gaze. 'I've never met anyone like you, Deina.'

'You're just trying to get me to stay so I can take your place –'

'No – I mean, I want you to stay.' He opened his hand and a purple flame sprang up in the centre of his palm, twisting and flickering. 'I'd like you to stay here, with me.'

'So you are still working for Hades!' Deina shoved him angrily and got to her feet, trying to get as far away as she could despite the tiny dimensions of the room.

Nat jumped up and grabbed her wrists, pulling her close.

'I'm not working for Hades, I swear. Why else would I have helped you in the throne room? Hades is trying to force you into this. I want you to *choose* to stay.' Nat's eyes blazed – with anger, or desire, or both. For a moment, Deina thought he was going to kiss her. Instead, he released her. 'I want you to choose the Underworld and immortality over a few years in the mortal world.' He tucked a loose strand of hair gently behind Deina's ear, his gaze roaming over her face. 'I want you to choose me.'

Deina turned to slam her fist into the wall – but what was the point? Whatever she wanted, the seeds she'd eaten bound her here as tightly as any chain.

'I can't leave the Underworld, you know that. My only choice is whether to stay in this prison as a mortal or leave as a god.' She pressed her palm to the wall, murmuring her fear to its uninterested stones. 'I'm Hades' daughter. If I give in, I'll end up like her. Think about that for a moment. There's more likely to be hatred between us than love. You might even come to fear me.'

She felt Nat's fingers trace briefly across her back.

'I can't imagine a world where I don't want to spend time with you.'

'Nat,' she began, turning to face him.

'I might be able to get you out of here.' Nat rushed the words out. 'It would only be temporary,' he added as Deina gasped and took a step forward. 'I'm not exactly sure how to do it yet and, if I manage it, the magic might not last long. But it would give you a little time to see your friends. To say goodbye, properly.'

'And what do you want in return?' Deina raised an eyebrow. Was he going to make her swear on the Styx that she'd drink the nectar? Did oaths made by the Styx bind demi-gods as well as gods?

'Nothing,' Nat replied. 'I want to help you, as part of my apology.' He waved one hand over the other; a rose appeared, the stem between his thumb and finger, the perfect white petals so translucent they might have been carved out of ice. The flower's perfume filled the air. Nat offered the rose to Deina. 'If you left this space, and joined me in the Underworld, we could

help each other. I can help you remember that you used to be human. You can help me forget that I'm still the god of death. All I ask is that you think about that. About the possibility of us.'

Deina took the rose. Nat hadn't given his beautiful imitation any thorns; perhaps he'd forgotten that the things people desired were sometimes the things that hurt them the most.

'I'll think about it.' Deina tucked the rose into her hair. 'So, how do I get out of here?'

Nat gave her one of his most brilliant smiles.

'I'm glad you asked. There are three problems to overcome. The seeds are actually the easiest. They are like a bow string: if you can find a way out, you can pull away from the Underworld, just as an archer might draw the string away from the bow. Sooner or later, however, the force is too much to resist. You'll be dragged back here with little warning.'

'And what are the other two problems?' Deina asked, not wanting to dwell on the image of being shot back into the Underworld like an arrow into a target.

'Hades will have put a spell on this room to alert her if you manage to escape. That means we need a substitute to fit exactly into your space. Finally, the most difficult problem: how to get you out of here without Hades noticing.'

'Hold on,' Deina frowned. 'There is no way out of this cell, at least not one that I'm likely to discover. She surely won't be expecting me to escape?'

Nat shot her an amused glance.

'Hades is a god. Being paranoid and suspicious goes with the territory. She'll be watching all of the gateways, and the wall of night, which is the way I move between realms.' Deina

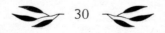

remembered the doorway through which Nat had dragged her from the citadel in Thebes, and the dense, unnatural darkness that had lain beyond it – the same darkness that surrounded Hades' courts in the Underworld. She wondered briefly whether she'd ever really understand the workings of her mother's realm. Probably not, but then she'd rather never have to. 'Once we're in the mortal realm,' Nat continued, 'I can take you wherever you want to go – but we have to get there first.'

'So what alternative way out is there?'

'What's the one place that Hades can't get into and can't control? Think about it.' Nat lounged against the wall and examined his nails. 'I'll give your dull mortal mind a few moments to –'

'The Threshold,' Deina interrupted. 'She can't control the Threshold.'

3

To be a Soul Severer was to spend much of one's life in the Threshold. Created by the very first Severers, the Threshold was a space that lay between life and death. A place that could only be entered by Severers and the souls that they accompanied – or the souls that they forcibly took there to be punished. A place secure from all the gods, except it would seem, from Death. As an apprentice, Deina had first learned how a Threshold could be called into existence by the rites of the Order of Hades. Later, as a novice then an adept, she had mostly entered the Threshold as part of a Severing – the rite to free the soul of someone who was suffering in their dying, to release them from mortal pain and comfort their first steps into the afterlife. Once, she'd summoned the Threshold to carry out the Punishment Rite, where the condemned soul was trapped forever between life and death, forced to relive its crimes eternally. Deina and Theron had used the same rite to trap the soul of Orpheus without first killing him. Each time, the Threshold that appeared was new and unique to the rite, the Severer, and the soul in question. And yet each

Threshold was somehow part of the same space. Anteïs, Deina's mentor, had once tried to explain it: the Threshold was a like a megaron, a huge palace within which lay a labyrinth of rooms. Each time a Severer summoned the Threshold, a new room was added. All the rooms were different, yet each connected with each other. She'd also compared it to a pomegranate, packed with seeds. Each separate, yet part of the whole.

Nat was gazing at her, one perfect eyebrow arched, questioning.

'I'm thinking about the megaron at Iolkos,' Deina told him. 'I only went inside once. Below the great hall were lots of storage rooms and other small spaces, all linked. A servant told me you could go underground from one end of the palace complex to the other, if you knew the right route.'

Nat shot her a look that was part amusement, part irritation. 'I know mortals have a short attention span, but is this really the time to get nostalgic over architecture? We're supposed to be focusing on the Threshold.'

'That's exactly what I am doing,' Deina huffed. 'Each time we summon the Threshold, the space we create is connected to all the other Thresholds. Just like the rooms beneath the megaron.' She offered him a humourless smile. 'I'll give your god-like mind a few moments to catch up, shall I?'

'Fine, I get it.' Nat scowled, giving a marginal shrug of one shoulder. 'I think. You believe you can open a Threshold here, and then . . . ?' He nodded encouragingly.

'And then go through to another Threshold that's being used by another Severer, and then leave that Threshold with that Severer and end up in whatever city they are in.' Deina frowned. 'In theory.'

'And I'm guessing you want to get back to Iolkos, since that's where your friends are going to be. In the unlikely event they survive the journey.'

'Helpful,' Deina commented sourly. 'And yes, I'd want to go back to Iolkos.' She hesitated, biting her lower lip, trying to imagine the different paths she might take and where they might lead her. Perhaps Iolkos. Perhaps not. If only she had room to pace! Moving brought things into focus. 'Can you see what Aristaeus is doing, Nat? Can you spy on him?'

'No. I can see what your friends are doing because they are Soul Severers, already connected to the Underworld through their link to Hades. I have no ability to spy –' Deina could hear the disdain in Nat's voice – 'on Aristaeus or any other mortal who is not a Soul Severer until he is at the point of death. Even if I wished to.' His eyes narrowed. 'What are you thinking?'

'As soon as I've worked that out, I'll let you know.' Deina decided to ignore the tiny dimensions of the room and pace up and down as best she could anyway. 'You – you can get into the Threshold.'

'Yes,' Nat replied, trying to squash himself against the wall to get out of her way. 'We've established that.'

'So, if you can get into it, you can get out again.'

'Obviously, but I can't create the Threshold in the first place, you'd still need to –'

'Yes, I know. I need to summon the Threshold.' Deina drummed her fingers against her thigh. 'Back in the Cadmea, back when I realised what I needed to do with Orpheus, I summoned the Threshold without using the proper rite. I did what I could because I needed the Threshold to include the

Deathless Trees, so I could bind Orpheus's soul there. Now, though, I just need a way in.' She closed her eyes briefly, reaching out with her senses, feeling the power of the Underworld swirling around her like a stream breaking against a rock. Excitement built in her chest despite her stilled heart. 'I think I can do this, Nat.'

'That's good, but not yet – we still need a substitute, remember? Something to take your place.' Nat clicked his fingers.

Nothing.

Deina raised an eyebrow. 'Was something supposed to happen?'

The god of death scowled. 'They're being stubborn. But if they know what's good for them, they'd better cooperate. Quickly. My brother Sleep will do anything for a quiet life, and if I insist that mortals are no longer to be tormented by dreams –'

'Gods!' Deina leaped out of the way as a creature popped into existence right next to her, making the small cell unpleasantly crowded. She'd seen one of these beings before, when she'd been journeying through the Underworld with the other Severers from Iolkos. In shape it was like a tall, stoop-backed mortal, but with pointed ears on top of its head, hands and feet that ended in three claws instead of fingers or toes, and the creature was covered in silvery fur. It hooted at her from its wide blade of a beak, a mournful sound that echoed across the stone surfaces of Deina's prison, but its eyes – two large, black discs – were fixed on Nat.

One of the Oneiroi – the Dream Children. Deina gagged – up close, the creature stank.

Nat beckoned. The Oneiros shuffled closer, radiating unwillingness, and the god murmured something in its ear. When he'd finished, the creature bowed to him, opening its arms to spread its bat-like wings in what looked like some sort of acknowledgement. Nat wrinkled his nose and waved the Dream Child away, though there was no dismissing the terrible smell.

'It agrees to take on your appearance and take your place here, for as long as you can hold out against the pull of the seeds; there's no way of knowing how long that will be, unfortunately.' He frowned. 'Its hardest task will be resisting the temptation to drink the nectar. It has no effect on the Dream Children, but they're addicted to it, so I've offered it something to strengthen its resolve: I'll take it with me when I next walk the earth to bring death to mortals, and will allow it to feast on the fears of those I encounter, to fill their final moments with nightmare.'

If the creature drank the nectar, Hades would return to the cell and discover the switch. Deina needed as much time away from the Underworld as possible to find a way of cancelling the power of the seeds; Nat's bargain appalled her, but she knew herself well enough to know that she wasn't really about to object. Besides, what other choice was there?

'Are you ready?' he asked. 'The Oneiros will need to time its transformation to occur at the exact moment we enter the Threshold. There's no room for error or hesitation.'

'No pressure, then,' Deina murmured. She took a deep breath. Blood was a key ingredient of the Severing rite; the blood of the one dying, used to bind their soul to the Severer carrying out the rite and to open that version of the Threshold that was unique to that moment. There was no soul for Deina to shepherd this time. Still, if she used her own blood, she hoped her power as a demi-god might be enough for her to bend the rite to her will. To open her own personal Threshold.

Somehow, it always seemed to come down to hope.

Deina gritted her teeth, took hold of the brooch that was pinning the shoulder of her gown and dragged the sharp point of the pin across the back of her other hand. Blood welled up, a scarlet line against her skin, and a trickle ran across her fingers and onto the floor. She began to chant the words of the rite, the ancient Song for Severing, as she smeared her blood across palms, breastbone and the sigil that marked her forehead. Some of the words described the Threshold: *space unbounded, hemmed by life and death, created yet eternal sanctuary of suffering* . . . Deina sang the phrases as confidently as she could, commanding the Threshold to open before her, to enfold her. Gradually, the air around her grew chill. It was working.

Nat slipped his hand into hers. As the dim room became dimmer still, the cold grew in intensity, pinching Deina's toes and fingers, making them ache, making Nat's icy touch seem almost warm in comparison. The Dream Child began to alter its shape. Deina's sigil throbbed with pain; the Threshold was nearby. The Dream Child's transformation completed, and for an instant, Deina stared at a more perfect reflection of herself than she'd ever seen.

Then she couldn't see anything at all.

Even before her sight returned, Deina knew she'd been successful. They were in the Threshold. Though the appearance of each version was different, the bones of the place were always

37

the same. She could sense the same underlying harmonics, the same phrases; she could feel the way it was woven afresh each time from the same song. When she opened her eyes, she found herself in a woodland glade: white poplars and oaks, bare branched, interspersed with dark green pines. Though the air smelled faintly of mint, it seemed to be winter here; the dead leaves that lay thick upon the ground glinted with frost. The hushed stillness made Deina shiver. Nat was looking around with interest.

'This is different. Isn't each version of the Threshold supposed to reflect the soul for which it is summoned?'

'Supposedly,' Deina replied reluctantly. 'But I didn't exactly follow the rite.' She waved a hand at the surroundings. 'I don't think this is exactly me.' It couldn't be. This place didn't look alive. It looked . . . preserved, like a dead body one wanted to keep from decay. Like a landscape from the Underworld. Nat's silence was making her uncomfortable. 'Let's get out of here.' She took a step forward; something swung against her thigh. A sandglass was hanging by a chain from her belt. Shiny and black, it looked as if it was made from polished obsidian, and the top bulb was filled with glittering silver dust. It was beautiful – more beautiful than the archon's sandglass in the megaron – but where had it come from? The silver dust was already swirling down, slowly but steadily, into the lower bulb. She held it out to Nat.

'Oh.' He inspected the sandglass. 'Well. That is unexpected.'

'What does it mean?'

'It means the Underworld has made this a game. When the sand runs out, your time is up. The seeds will pull you back.'

Deina tipped the sandglass upside down. The dust continued

to spiral into the other bulb. Shaking it didn't make any difference either. Frustrated, she let it fall back to swing from her belt.

'Do all the gods' realms play games?'

'Only the Underworld,' Nat replied. There was something in his voice that might have been pride, or awe. 'The realms of Zeus and Poseidon are just places. The Underworld seems almost alive sometimes. You must have noticed it.'

Deina remembered the suddenness with which the landscape had shifted during their search for Eurydice. The way dangerous spots seemed to almost sneak up on them.

'Well, at least I'll have some warning of when I'm about to get taken back there.'

'Maybe.' In response to Deina's raised eyebrow, he added, 'The Underworld is playing. Doesn't mean it's going to play fair.'

No change there.

'All the more reason to get going then.' Deina tried to smooth the irritation from her voice. 'Is there anyone dying in Thebes right now?'

Nat frowned.

'Thebes? Why Thebes? I thought you wanted to go to Iolkos.'

'Thebes first.' She looked at him expectantly.

'Obviously there are people dying. Someone is always dying. Particularly in Thebes; it's a mighty city. Many lives, many deaths.'

Deina tilted her head, curious. 'Then how are you here? Aren't you supposed to be off cutting their lifelines?' She mimicked swiping a blade through something. Nat rolled his eyes.

'I am there, or some small part of me is.' He held out his arm for Deina to inspect the lines of tiny, silvery symbols that

seemed to criss-cross his skin like old scars. When Deina looked closer, she saw they were moving – shifting and changing from one instant to the next. 'Every time a mortal is fated to die, the person's name appears here, and some part of my power goes out to claim them.' He frowned, and Deina saw sorrow in his eyes. 'These dancing lines are like a brief memorial of their passing. Hardly a fitting representation of the great weight of so many sundered souls.' Pity moved Deina to lift her hand to his shoulder. Nat shook away his mood and smiled at her. 'I only attend in person, as it were, for certain people. Special people.' He winked.

Deina jabbed her finger into his shoulder.

'Ow!'

'There is no way that actually hurt you.'

'It might have done.' Nat pouted. 'You meant it to.'

'Because you have to stop flirting with me. This is not the time.' She glanced around the sombre glade. 'It's definitely not the place. Can the bits of you that are in Thebes tell us what's going on? We need to find someone who's being taken into the Threshold by a Severer. Preferably someone who is dying in the palace. Someone close to Aristaeus.'

'You've grown very demanding since you realised you were a demi-god,' Nat muttered, closing his eyes. The shadows that always hovered at his shoulders deepened and grew more wing-like. 'Let me see . . .' He paused. 'Many of them are children. Most are poor. No Severers with them as far as I can see.'

Not surprising. Employing a Severer wasn't exactly cheap.

'There's a Spell Caster at the House of Hephaestus who has a Severer with her,' Nat continued. 'A priest, at the temple of

Poseidon. Four men who might be merchants, or officials. Five women who are wives of such men, all dying in childbirth; one of them is within the Cadmea. Oh, and a priestess of Aphrodite.' He opened his eyes again. 'Are you going to tell me why we're going to Thebes?'

'Because I want to know what Aristaeus is up to. Theron is the rightful king of Thebes; there's no way Aristaeus isn't going to keep hunting him down. If I can talk to someone from Thebes, I might get some information. And I can warn the others about whatever Aristaeus is planning.' Deina glanced at Nat. 'My last gift to them, before I have to return here.'

If I have to return here, she added to herself, aware of the new weight of the sandglass.

Which one to choose? The woman in the Cadmea, the citadel of Thebes, was the obvious choice. Yet Deina hadn't forgotten how enamoured Aristaeus was with the Order of Hephaestus, and the creations they'd made for him from spell-cast metal. And Theron had said something once, just after they'd entered the Underworld, about her trusting her instincts . . .

'The Spell Caster,' she said to Nat. 'What's her name?'

'Asthenia.' He blinked. 'She's in the Threshold. You'd better hurry.'

Deina started singing, weaving together phrases from different Songs. Words that spoke of opening, of voyaging, of commanding the Threshold. Lines from the Song used for Severing the soul of a Spell Caster, invoking Hephaestus, and telling of gleaming metals and the heat of the forge. She called on Hecate, goddess of in-between places, and asked for her help to find Asthenia.

The doorway began as a bending and scattering of the light, as if Deina were looking through a piece of ice. A spot of darkness formed at its centre, growing slowly at first, then rippling outwards rapidly. Deina took Nat's hand and stepped into the shadows.

Together, they hurried along a twisting pathway that snaked around and between all the tightly packed Thresholds that surrounded them like bubbles. Every so often one of the bubbles would vanish, but another would appear, or the existing bubbles would move to fill the empty space. Most of the bubbles were filled with swirling cloud, but occasionally Deina caught a glimpse of figures moving around within a Threshold. It was the strangest place she'd ever seen, yet she didn't dare stop to look; it was difficult enough to keep track of the path as it was. The thought of getting lost here sent a prickle of dread across her skin; she clutched Nat's hand more tightly.

'Nearly there,' he murmured. Abruptly, another patch of shadows appeared in front of them; another stride took Deina though the darkness into sudden warmth. Firelight flickered across an encircling hillside of dark rock, studded with glittering crystals and seams of gold and silver; the smoke from the bonfire that blazed nearby rose into a cloudless sky.

'Who in Hades' name are you?' The question came from a man with dark, grey-flecked hair and a startled expression. His forehead was marked with the sigil of the god of the Underworld, he had a bronze torc around his neck and he wore the red robes of an elder of the Order. A glowing lifeline was wrapped around his wrist; the other end was around the waist of a young woman who bore the sigil of Hephaestus. The Severer's eyes widened further as he noticed the sigil on Deina's forehead, before his gaze flicked to Nat. He gasped, took a hasty step back and threw himself awkwardly to his knees.

Nat had grown taller, sterner, becoming Thanatos, god of death. The dark shadows at his back had spread into midnight wings that spanned the space behind them. It was the same way he'd appeared in Thebes, when he'd come to take Deina to the Underworld.

'We're not here to interfere,' Deina said in what she hoped was a reassuring tone. 'I just want to ask Asthenia some questions. And then we'll leave the Threshold with you and return to Thebes.' She slowly approached the Spell Caster. 'I was hoping you might know something of Aristaeus, of what he is planning.'

The woman stared at her for an instant before turning and spitting on the ground.

'I'll not speak that monster's name. He killed me – he had me poisoned, after I'd helped create a new creature for him. A metal bird, an eagle, animated by magic, that can tell all it sees and hears.' Her hands went to her stomach and her face crumpled. 'The pain . . . For days I lay there, sweating blood. It would have gone on if the elders had not sent for a Severer. I was praying for death at the end.'

'I'm sorry,' Deina replied. There was nothing else she could offer. 'Can you tell me what he is going to do with this bird?'

'He has commanded those left in the House to make more of them. They are to be sent out across the Dominion as spies.' Asthenia brightened a little. 'Is it true? Does the monster hunt for Orpheus's heir?'

'Yes, it's true. That's why I want to know what Aristaeus is doing. Is there anything else you can tell me?'

'Only that the monster searches for something else. An artefact constructed by the great god himself, the one who grants us our skill.' She touched the symbol of Hephaestus on her forehead and bowed her head for an instant. 'He has sent out many Spell Casters to search for it, together with some of the thugs he employs at the Cadmea.'

'What does he search for?' Deina asked.

'A torc. I do not even know if it is real, but the monster is obsessed by the works of the god. Our stories tell of a torc created by the god at the suggestion of Eris. It was given to a mortal king beloved of the god, so that he might control all Theodesmioi and use them to defeat his mortal rivals, but the other gods did not approve of one mortal having so much power. In legend, it was broken apart and the pieces hidden.' Asthenia's forehead wrinkled. 'Though surely the gods would have destroyed such a dangerous thing. If it ever existed.'

Eris was the goddess of discord. This torc certainly sounded like something she might have encouraged. Deina turned to Nat, to ask him if he'd ever heard of such a torc, but the Soul Severer interrupted her.

'The gate to the Underworld has opened. Please –' he was still staring, awestruck, at Nat – 'may I – may I complete the rite?'

'Of course,' Deina replied. She tugged Nat forward and gripped the Severer's shoulder with her other hand. 'We'll join you.'

The Soul Severer flinched at Deina's touch. Yet he was an elder, with many years of experience; despite the anxiety

quickening his breath, he knew his duty. 'Do not be afraid, Asthenia. Your path lies that way.' He pointed to a patch of darkness that seemed filled with stars. 'When you reach the place of judgement, you will be sent straight to Elysium, to the paradise that is promised to all Theodesmioi.'

The lie turned Deina's stomach. Altered by the divine power that flowed through them, Theodesmioi became blood hunters after death. Asthenia's destiny was to become a thing of nightmares, not to end up in paradise. But to tell the Spell Caster the truth now would be cruel and pointless.

The Severer chanted the end of the Severing rite and brought his blade down on the glowing white line. Asthenia was swallowed by the gate, and the Threshold fractured and spun away from them. In another instant, they were in a small, ordinary room. She wrinkled her nose. The scent of the herbs hanging from the roof didn't entirely mask the stench of blood and sweat. In the deep shadows next to the window a wasted body lay on a bed: Asthenia, though Deina would have hardly recognised her if she hadn't known what to expect. Two other Spell Casters lingered nearby.

The Soul Severer, drawn with exhaustion, sagged against the wall. Deina could see a new rite-seal forming on his forearm. He opened his mouth, but before he could frame his question, Nat grabbed Deina's hand and snapped his fingers. A whirlwind spun into existence, sweeping Thebes away and depositing them a few moments later outside a run-down building. Deina recognised it. It was the unfinished, already decaying theatre that she'd walked past more times than she could remember.

They were back in Iolkos.

4

Deina looked up at Nat.

They were standing together in a small, narrow street, in Apollo's quarter. The bulk of the citadel loomed in the distance.

'Why did you bring us here? I wanted to go to the House.'

'You said Iolkos. Technically –' Nat held his forefinger up – 'the House of Hades is outside the walls of the city. Though it won't take a moment to get there.' He put thumb and middle finger together, but before he could snap, Deina grabbed his hand.

'No – let's just walk. Whirlwind is not exactly a relaxing way to travel.' They began hurrying along the street in the direction of the gates. Deina got some nervous looks – the combination of her sigil and her mismatched eyes with the finely woven, bejewelled gown seemed to be confusing the townsfolk. Not as many as she'd expected, though. Nat seemed to attract no scrutiny at all. 'Can they see you?' she asked.

'No. You look as if you're talking to yourself right now. It's better for our plan if we keep a low profile, and to be honest,

I'd prefer to avoid the attention. We should sneak into the House, free your friends –'

'What do you mean, *free*?'

'Oh – they were taken into custody as soon as they arrived and are facing trial.'

Deina stopped walking.

'A trial? Why didn't you tell me? We've been wasting time, and – and –'

Nat sighed.

'Because, firstly, it only happened a few days ago, as time is reckoned in this realm, and secondly, we couldn't have done anything differently. We've not wasted time. And I knew that if I told you, you'd get hysterical.'

Deina growled and stamped her foot.

'I am not hysterical.'

'Says the woman talking to thin air . . .'

He was right: there were several people now watching her, uncertain, clearly weighing up whether this was some kind of performance or whether they needed to call the city guards and get her locked up. Several people, but again – not as many as there should have been. Deina started hurrying towards the gate. Something seemed wrong here. It was late morning, as far as she could judge. The streets were quiet for the time of day and the season. The people who were around were moving quickly, and many were glancing up at the sky anxiously. The tension was infectious. Deina and Nat passed a man leading a donkey; he'd left his cloak over the donkey's back, and Deina grabbed it as she went by, not even breaking her stride. With its folds concealing her head and upper body she felt less conspicuous.

It wasn't until they passed through the city gate and were on the path that led to the House that she understood why the inhabitants of Iolkos kept looking skyward. Poised on the top of the city wall that now lay behind them was a pair of huge metal eagles. They glittered in the autumn sunshine. Deina almost took them for two statues until one of them turned its head and fixed its bright black eye on her. She looked away quickly, remembering what Asthenia had told her about the bronze eagle she had helped construct for Aristaeus, animated by who knew what magic. Deina could almost feel the bird's malevolent gaze burning into her back. Reaching the House was a relief.

Or it would have been, if the great bronze gates had not been shut against her.

'This is all wrong,' she murmured to Nat. 'It's the middle of the day.'

Whatever was happening, Deina was sure that Aristaeus was behind it. Neidius too, probably – she hadn't forgotten that the Leader of the House was the one who had betrayed Theron to Orpheus.

'Aren't you going to knock?' Nat prompted.

Deina shook her head. There were no guards patrolling the walls – the incantations on the boundary stones inside the grounds prevented any mortal not marked with the sigil of Hades from gaining entry unless invited in. The room at the top of the bell tower always had a couple of novices stationed there as lookouts, though. Hopefully, with the cloak swathed about her head, they would have taken her for someone from the town, hoping to buy the services of a Severer. Someone who was about to return, disappointed, to Iolkos.

 48

'Let's walk back along the path a little,' Deina said to Nat. 'To where it curves round those rocks.' When they reached the point she'd indicated, out of sight of the bell tower, she stopped. 'Can you click your fingers and land us in the gardens, as far as possible from the main –'

Before she'd even finished speaking, Nat had done her bidding. Taken by surprise, Deina lost her balance and stumbled against him. The god of death caught her. Held her. Even when the dark lines of the maze garden appeared around them, he didn't immediately let go but smiled down at her.

'See how useful I am to have around? Theron couldn't have done that. I have power of which he can only dream.'

Deina wasn't sure that Theron had ever dreamed of having power – not the kind of power Nat spoke of. Yet she couldn't deny that, as she stood with her hands pressed against Nat's chest, with his arms encircling her, waiting for the dizziness to pass, the sudden sensation of being protected, of being safe, was enjoyable. It wasn't a feeling she was used to. It wasn't a feeling she could allow herself to become accustomed to either. She pushed against Nat's arms, and he released her.

'Very useful. Though next time, do you think you can wait until I'm ready?'

Nat grinned at her, but nodded.

'Thank you. Now, I need a weapon.' She turned to assess their position. 'This way.'

Deina set off, Nat just behind her on the narrow path.

'We're going to the armoury?'

'Yes.'

49

'Wouldn't it be better to steal some different clothes instead? You could maybe get in unnoticed.'

'No. I don't want to be unnoticed. I want to use my strength.' Deina felt her mouth twist into a snarl. 'I want Neidius to piss himself with terror when he looks at me.' She glanced back at Nat. 'Besides, I have the god of death on my side. With all his power.'

'You do. And I'm happy to help. I'd just prefer my help to –'

'– go unnoticed?' Deina raised an eyebrow.

'Yes. If possible.'

Deina huffed and hurried onwards.

At least the armoury wasn't usually guarded, though there was always an adept on duty as Weapons Keeper – someone who could write well enough to mark down on a clay tablet what had been taken and by whom. It was the sort of role Drex would have ended up being given, if he'd ever succeeded in becoming an adept. If he'd lived. When Deina and Nat stepped inside, however, the table at which the keeper sat was deserted. The shadows between the shelves were silent. Perhaps everyone had been summoned to witness this so-called trial. Quickly, Deina selected two long knives and tied their leather scabbards to her belt. She thought for a moment, then grabbed a spear and thrust her right arm through the straps of a tall, narrow-waisted shield.

'I'm guessing the trial will be in the great hall.' Even though she'd spoken in a whisper, Deina felt as if her voice had echoed round the armoury like a bell. 'We should –'

'Who's there?' a man's voice demanded. 'I'm not allowed to issue any . . .' The man, slightly built and quite a bit shorter than Deina, trailed off as she turned. She recognised him. Thaddeus had been brought to the House at the same time as Deina. She quite liked him, as far as she'd liked anyone other than Chryse. He'd always been a joker. He'd somehow been able to find humour in almost any situation – but he wasn't laughing now. If anything, he looked horrified. As he took a step back, he bumped into the edge of his table and made the sign to turn away the evil eye. 'Deina? But – but – it's not possible. You're supposed to be dead.' The horror was already fading; Severers spent enough time around ghosts to know the difference between them and the living. 'Where did you come from? How did you get into the House?'

'Long story,' Deina replied. 'It's good to see you again, Thaddeus.' She offered a smile that he didn't return. Instead, his gaze drifted briefly to the weapons she'd taken.

'Who were you talking to, just now?' he asked, looking straight through the currently invisible god of death.

'Myself. Where is everyone? Why are the gates closed?'

'We've been under curfew for the last month or so, since the turmoil caused by the death of the king.' He had to mean Orpheus. 'Gates only open once in the morning and once in the evening to admit those needing our help, and no Severer is allowed out of the House unless on official business. The city is under curfew too, by order of Aristaeus.' Thaddeus scowled. 'You of all people should know this.'

'How so?

'Because it's your fault. Yours and Theron's.'

'What are you talking about?'

'Come now, Deina. Neidius told us what you did. You and

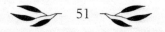 51

the others. You're all traitors; each and every one of you,'
Thaddeus taunted. 'You betrayed this House, and you betrayed
the king. Neidius is in the great hall right now, with the other
Guardians. Judgement is being passed on Theron and Aster
and a female Severer from Mycenae. All three of them are to
be subjected to the Punishment Rite and their bodies burned.
There are volunteers already selected to carry out the rites.'

They'd each earn a year off their indentures if they carried out
a Punishment Rite successfully. Deina was sure there must have
been plenty of volunteers for the elders to choose from. Theron
was popular among the novices and adepts, but not that popular.
Especially if the other Severers now believed he was a traitor.

'And what exactly are we supposed to have done?'

'They say that Theron, having failed in the task of retrieving
Eurydice's ghost, murdered Lord Orpheus, and that the rest
of you helped him.'

'What else do they say?'

'That Aristaeus, defending his master, killed Chryse and
Drex. And you. Though clearly, that didn't exactly happen.'
Thaddeus's expression grew calculating. 'Aristaeus will probably
offer a reward once he realises at least one of you escaped.'
He scanned the shadows between the racks of weapons, as if
half expecting Chryse and Drex to materialise.

Deina wished they would. A stab of grief made her breath
ragged; she tightened her grip on the spear.

'Is that all?'

'And Theron is accused of spreading lies that dishonour the
gods. Lies that are so terrible, Neidius has ruled that those who
repeat them should be stripped of their rite-seals.'

Only death was a more severe punishment. Rite-seals appeared like brands on the skin of Theodesmioi, showing what rites they'd completed, indicating how much time each rite had earned to be set against their indenture. Stripping the seals wiped out the time earned, and it was agonisingly painful. Dangerous too; not all survived. Yet still Deina could hear the curiosity in Thaddeus's voice. He wanted to know what these so-called lies were, despite the risk.

Deina suspected he'd regret his desire once she told him.

'My death is not the only thing you've been wrongly informed about, Thaddeus. Drex died in the Underworld, but Aristaeus stopped us from burying his body. And we did find Eurydice, but she begged us to leave her there. Orpheus was a fiend who'd extended his own lifespan over and over by stealing the lifeforce from others, and he'd been using the queen, herself once a powerful Severer, to help him do it.' Deina tried to keep her voice steady as she felt the anger inside her building. 'Aristaeus murdered Chryse. He forced her onto an altar and slaughtered her like an animal. Theron is Orpheus's son, and the rightful king of Thebes. And the slander against the gods that has supposedly outraged Neidius? We discovered in the Underworld that Theodesmioi don't go to Elysium after death. We're transformed into blood hunters – unkillable monsters, skeletal creatures that scour the dead lands for any trace of fresh blood. We never fully die, and we never find peace.'

Thaddeus's face paled. 'Blood hunters?'

Deina sighed, remembering Eurydice's words. 'Mortal forms are not meant to channel the immortal power of a god.' She paused, allowing her words to sink in, watching the dread bloom in Thaddeus's eyes. 'That's the truth. Neidius knows it, whatever lies he's been spewing. That's why I'm on my way to find him. To force him to admit what he knows, and what he's done. Gods, Thaddeus,' she added scornfully, 'didn't you even wonder why Theron and the others would have come back here, if they were really guilty of the crimes they're accused of? What on earth would they gain by doing so?'

Thaddeus swallowed. His eyes flicked from the point of the spear in her hand to something off to one side: a long rope, hanging down from the rafters. Deina cursed inwardly. She'd forgotten the armoury had a bell in its roof in case the keeper needed aid. She shifted her grip on the spear and levelled it at Thaddeus.

'We're both Severers, Thaddeus. But Theron and Aster and Dendris are my friends. I fought Aristaeus, trapped Orpheus in the Threshold and defied Hades in order to keep them safe. If it comes down to a choice between their lives and yours, I'll kill you without another thought. You know I will. And you know I can.' It wasn't a boast. As apprentices, Deina and Thaddeus had fought in the training grounds, and she'd beaten him every time. Now the seeds had awoken her strength as a demi-god, it would only be easier. Thaddeus's face flushed; Deina knew he was remembering his previous humiliations. 'Why don't we pretend this never happened? That I took what I wanted and slipped out before you returned to your post?'

Thaddeus hesitated, his face a picture of miserable indecision.

'But – but Neidius . . . If he finds out –'

Deina shook her head.

'I promise you'll face no retribution, least of all from Neidius.'
Deina smiled grimly. 'He's about to have a much more serious
problem to focus on than the theft of a few weapons.'

Thaddeus took a deep breath and nodded.

'Go, then.'

Deina turned and hurried towards the exit without once
looking back.

Deina cursed beneath her breath as she hurried through
the gardens, her sandals crunching on gravel, past the training
grounds and towards the great hall. Nat moved silently beside
her.

'Traitors, are we?' She ground her teeth with anger. 'After
Orpheus sent countless Severers to die in the Underworld and
murdered all those who did return. After Neidius helped him
do it. And why did Theron not wait for me? Why take the risk
of coming here alone? He knows what Neidius did. He knows
we were all betrayed. Idiot!'

'He is an idiot. All humans are, compared to gods,' Nat said.
He sighed. 'Yet, I'm forced to remind you that he thought – still
thinks – you are trapped in the Underworld. He had no reason
to wait for you.'

Deina merely grunted in response. She knew Nat was right.
Theron had come back to Iolkos because he believed that was
his duty: to warn those in Iolkos, to tell the truth about Orpheus
and Aristaeus, and about what happened to Severers after
death. And he'd always been reckless. No doubt he thought
he'd never see her again.

*When you think you have nothing to lose, that's when you're
prepared to lose everything.*

But he hadn't lost her. Not yet.

The great hall was just ahead. Deina paused beneath the shadow of a clump of trees. She could hear the murmur of voices through the narrow openings cut into the top layer of the building's stonework. One voice, rather; it sounded as if Neidius was giving a speech.

'Can you get us inside, somewhere at the back of the hall so I won't be noticed?'

Nat grinned.

'I can do better than that: I'll cloak you with my own power and shield you from the mortals' gaze.' He raised one eyebrow, still smiling, and held out his hand. 'Ready?'

Deina took a deep breath, transferred her spear into her other hand, and slipped her fingers into Nat's.

'Ready.'

The trees and the gardens were swept instantly away and the sensation of being weightless, of being suspended in mid-air while the world broke and billowed around her, made Deina's stomach flip. She screwed her eyes shut. It helped a little. When she opened them again, she and Nat were in the gloomy interior of the great hall, right next to the dark wooden doors – currently barred against the outside world. The sunshine that trickled through the narrow openings at the very top of the roof ebbed away long before it reached the ground. Down here, what light there was came from the bronze oil lamps set in niches around the room. There were tiles beneath Deina's feet: white marble asphodel flowers set into black marble pentagons. The edge of each tile was inlaid with an undulating line of blue lapis lazuli. The last time she'd stood here, she'd volunteered for Orpheus's mission to rescue his wife, Eurydice, from the Underworld. Fortune and freedom – that was what she'd hoped for. That was what she'd been promised.

It wasn't exactly what she'd got.

'As long as I'm touching you, they won't be able to see you,' Nat murmured in her ear. Keeping hold of his hand, Deina turned towards the dais at the other end of the wide central aisle, where the eight Guardians of the House, chosen from amongst the elders, had their chairs arranged in a semi-circle. There were eight more chairs arranged along the aisle, four on each side, facing each other. These were occupied not by Soul Severers but by members of the Orders of Poseidon and Zeus, both of which had Houses in Iolkos; all were elders, and Guardians too, Deina guessed. Armed Soul Severer adepts stood behind the chairs on the dais, while those of the other two Houses had brought their own protection. There was also a cluster of heavily armed men standing near the barred door. Lacking sigils and bearing no insignia, they looked more like hired thugs than city guards. All this Deina took in instantly, before her attention was claimed by the four figures kneeling in front of the dais, bound in chains, with four other spear-bearing Soul Severers watching them closely. Theron, Aster, Dendris and one other Deina didn't know. He was marked with the sigil of Zeus; from his stature, Deina guessed he was a Battle Wager rather than a Weather Worker. One of the Bronze Guards she had helped free, perhaps?

Whoever he was, it was obvious that he'd been tortured. All of them bore signs of injury. Theron's face was bloodied and bruised. A deep gash ran the length of his left cheek, and one eye was swollen shut. He looked utterly drained and was staring at the ground with a strange, blank expression on his face. Dendris had been gagged, to prevent her using her power over wood. Aster's lower lip was split and bleeding.

Deina grew rigid as she struggled to contain her rage. Theron and the others had ended Orpheus's murderous reign. They'd risked everything to return to Iolkos. Yet instead of being welcomed as heroes, they'd been treated like criminals. Chained up and beaten like the thieves who were hanged in the square outside the megaron on market days.

Neidius was still on his feet, elaborating on the supposed crimes that Thaddeus had already listed to her. Did the Guardians and the leaders of the other Orders agree with him? It was hard to read their expressions in the lamplight, though Deina could see that Anteïs – her mentor and the only woman to be chosen as a Guardian – was frowning, her lips pressed together as though she was having to bite her tongue.

'And so, in conclusion, although I recognise that this case is beyond the normal remit of the Theodesmioi, I remind you that the new archon has given permission for us to try and execute these criminals ourselves, given the dangerous sedition with which they are charged.' The archon ruled Iolkos in the name of the king; Deina wondered briefly what had happened to the old archon. 'I also remind our guests,' Neidius continued, nodding at the elders of the other Houses, 'that they are here as a courtesy. This decision belongs to the Guardians of the House of Hades alone.' He drew himself up and glared haughtily at the other Guardians seated on the dais. 'I know there are those who counsel mercy. And to those I say that to defy me is to defy the archon, and the king. To defy me is to side with these traitors. To risk sharing their fate.' He folded his arms and waited.

No one rose to defend Theron and the others. No one. Not even Anteïs.

Neidius puffed up with triumph.

'So be it. Let it be known that the Guardians of the House of Hades in Iolkos have found these criminals guilty of the charges brought against them. They are to be taken from this place and subjected to the Punishment Rite immediately. I have Soul Severers already waiting outside to conduct the rite.' He nodded to the guards, who began to drag Theron to his feet. 'These miscreants deserve to suffer eternally for the crimes they have committed.'

A scream of fury rose in Deina's throat as she tore her hand from Nat's grasp. The shock of her appearance rippled across the room. Deina ignored it.

'You're the only criminal here, Neidius. And now it's time for you to pay.'

5

Deina levelled her spear and sent it flying towards the dais. Her aim was true, but a guard leaped in front of Neidius, and the bronze tip of the spear buried itself in his shield. Cursing, Deina drew one of the long knives from her belt and began to run towards Neidius as chaos erupted around her. The handful of Theodesmioi guards hurried to protect their elders, but none ventured to attack. The gang of heavily armed men showed no such restraint. Deina was quickly surrounded, but the power awoken by the seeds made her faster. Stronger.

Someone began chanting her name: Aster. From the corner of her eye, she saw one of the guards strike him backhanded across the face, knocking him to the floor, and her anger blazed hotter. She slashed and stabbed. Thrust others out of the way with her shield. And all the time, she drew closer to Neidius. He couldn't be allowed to escape; she kept her focus on him, even though she could see Theron straining against his chains. Despite the risk, despite the fact that he had been forced low onto his knees, Theron was trying to help, to warn her of attacks, and she loved him for it.

The Leader of the House meanwhile, was screaming at the men, urging them to cut Deina down. Their ranks thinned as she battled her way through them. Yet there were still so many of them. Too many. The circle around her tightened. Deina discarded her shield and fought with two blades. Finally, the few survivors drew close enough to clutch at her limbs, rip the knives from her grasp and pin her at sword point to the ground in front of the dais.

'Cut out her tongue!' Neidius's voice was shrill with fear. 'Cut off her hands and feet and let her suffer before she undergoes the rite!'

Hands hauled Deina onto her knees. One of the men grabbed her jaw, trying to force it open. Deina bit his fingers and he screamed and kicked her in the stomach.

'Stop, all of you!' Anteïs was on her feet. 'This Severer is supposed to be dead, slain by Aristaeus himself. I should like to hear her account of how she comes to be alive.'

'Silence, Anteïs,' Neidius snarled. 'You are merely a woman. How dare you contradict me!'

'I agree with Anteïs.' Deina couldn't see who was speaking. 'We from the Order of Poseidon wish to question this . . . new arrival. Get her to her feet.'

The men who held her muttered, surly. For a moment, Deina thought they were going to ignore the Sea Singer's order, until they hauled her upright and turned her to face the speaker, the points of their blades still pressed beneath Deina's ribs.

The Sea Singer was grey-eyed, grizzled and sunbeaten,

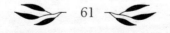

dressed in the dark blue robes of an elder of the Order of Poseidon. He glanced behind her.

'With your permission, Neidius.' It wasn't really a question.

'As you wish, Lysigoras.' Neidius's voice trembled with ill-concealed rage.

Lysigoras studied Deina for a moment.

'Well, Severer?'

Deina spat out the blood that was tainting her mouth.

'Everything Neidius has told you is lies. If Theron and the others have been allowed to speak –'

'They have,' the Sea Singer replied. 'We have heard their claims about Orpheus. About the death of Severers and others at his hands. And about the Theodesmioi, and what happens to us after death.'

'Everything they've told you is true,' Deina hurried to assure him. 'All of it.'

Lysigoras's jaw clenched. He nodded, almost as if he'd been expecting to have the worst confirmed.

'Lies! There is no proof of any of their claims!' Neidius shrieked. 'Would you, Lysigoras, have Lord Aristaeus know that you entertained this – this slander?'

'My concern is the truth, Neidius,' Lysigoras answered. 'As Leader of the House of Poseidon, I have a duty to the king, but I also have a duty to those whom I lead.' He turned his attention back to Deina. 'Well? Have you any evidence of your claims?'

As Deina hesitated, she heard Nat's voice in her ear. He was nowhere in sight, but it felt as if he were standing right next to her.

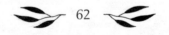

'Call on the gods to judge,' he whispered. 'Ask the gods publicly to slay the liar and spare the one who speaks the truth.'

'But . . .'

'Just do it. Deina.'

Slowly Deina lifted her chin.

'I call on the gods to be my judge. If I am lying, let them strike me down, here and now. If I speak the truth, I ask them to destroy Neidius instead.'

Lysigoras – and others – glanced around the hall.

'Perhaps,' the Sea Singer began, 'the gods do not hear you. Or perhaps they –'

He broke off as Neidius began moaning. There were gasps of fear from those gathered in the hall as his moans became screams. Panic broke out. Theodesmioi of all ranks jostled each other as they tried to get further away from the dais. The men holding Deina let go and raced for the doors. She turned in time to see Neidius engulfed in black and purple fire. His skin peeled and twisted like a piece of papyrus held in a flame as his shrieks of agony went on and on and his body began to disintegrate from the feet upwards. The last thing to disappear was his head, his skinless face caught in a rictus of pain, until that too fell into dust. The flames vanished. Not a mark remained to show that Neidius had ever existed.

The hall rang with a babble of overlapping curses, cries of disbelief, arguments and prayers, until Anteïs finally shouted loudly enough to make herself heard over the din.

'Silence, all of you! The gods have spoken. Deina is telling the truth. Free Theron and the others, quickly.'

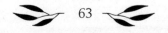

Two of the nearby Severers hurried to obey Anteïs. Another moment, and Deina was face to face with Theron. He lifted his fingers fleetingly to her pockmarked cheek, and she felt him tremble.

'Is it really you?' His voice was choked with emotion.

Deina felt the tears spring into her eyes. She smiled up at him.

'Yes.' She let the back of her hand graze his. 'It's really me.' Deina turned to throw her arms around Aster and Dendris as the tears ran down her face. 'I'm so happy to see you again, my friends.'

'You can't be happier than us,' Aster exclaimed. 'You saved us.'

'Again,' Dendris added. 'Welcome back to the mortal realm, Deina.' She put a hand on the shoulder of the other Theodesmioi, the Battle Wager. 'This is Critos. He is – was – leader of the Bronze Guards.'

The man bowed to Deina and offered a tentative smile.

'We've met before. That night in the secret room at the top of the Cadmea.'

Before Deina could reply she felt a hand take her wrist and draw her away from her friends. Anteïs pulled her into an embrace, bony arms clutching her tightly. 'I thought you were dead. I didn't believe what Neidius said about why you died, but I believed Orpheus had killed you.' She sniffed and blinked away uncharacteristic tears. 'Chryse?'

'Lost,' Deina replied. 'Aristaeus did murder her – that much of what Neidius told you was true.' No need to sully her friend's memory by speaking of the betrayal that had come before. Anteïs was gazing at her searchingly.

'You look different. The Underworld has changed you.' She

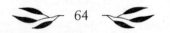

frowned. 'How did you get in?' She gestured to the doors of the great hall. They were standing open now.

'I had help. You look different too.' Anteïs had aged since that summer morning down by the harbour when Deina and the others had joined Orpheus's ship. She was even thinner than she had been, her face more lined. 'Are you unwell?'

The elder shook her head.

'Tired, that's all. And worried. No one here, apart from Neidius, perhaps, was grieved that Orpheus's long reign was finally over, but the world has grown even darker since you and Theron defeated him. Aristaeus rules by terror and magic. The archon died suddenly – too suddenly – and was replaced with another, selected by Aristaeus. The men who attacked you were sent by the new archon to watch our proceedings today. Fortunately, you seem to have injured or killed most of them, despite being so outnumbered.' She paused, clearly waiting for an explanation.

Deina shrugged.

'There were plenty of opportunities in the Underworld for me to work on my fighting skills. I just wish I'd stopped all of them.' It wouldn't be long before Aristaeus learned what had happened and realised that Theron was still alive. She remembered the bronze birds perched, menancing, on the walls of the city, and shuddered.

'Let's go to the herbarium,' Anteïs said. 'Theron and the others have injuries I should attend to, and you'll end up with a bruise along your jaw. I've got some ointment that will help.'

Deina fingered the sore spot where the man had struck her and winced.

Anteïs chuckled a little. 'You always were one for fighting with the boys.' She waved a hand in the direction of the injured and dead that Deina had left in her wake. 'We can leave the others to sort out this. Come, all of you.'

They followed Anteïs from the hall. Deina glanced around, but there was no sign of Nat. As they walked, Theron took Deina's hand. He gripped it tightly, as though afraid she might disappear again.

He didn't let go, even while Anteïs was cleaning and dressing the wound on his face – not until food and drink had been brought in and set at the end of one of the long tables, with benches either side, that ran the width of the herbarium. As the others sat down to eat, Deina drew Anteïs to one side.

'Can we have some time alone? There are things that have happened, since Theron and the others escaped Thebes. I need to talk to them privately.' As Anteïs began to protest, Deina added, 'I'll tell you everything, I promise. I just want a little time to work out some things first. Please?'

The elder sighed.

'As you wish. I must return to the great hall in any case. No doubt the other elders will have questions, and we must discuss how to deal with the archon. You may remain here for now.' Anteïs beckoned to the servants who'd brought the food to follow her out of the room. Deina, Theron, Aster, Dendris and Critos were finally alone.

Deina sat down next to Theron and took one of the flatbreads from the nearest dish. Strange: she could feel pangs of hunger stirring in her guts, and her mouth watered at the sight of a plate of cheese drizzled with honey, one of her favourite dishes, but she wasn't starving. Not like she should have been after the fight she'd just been through. Not like everyone else seemed to be. She stared at the piece of flatbread in her fingers. In the old stories, the demi-gods used to feast and quaff like everyone else. And the bread was certainly appetising. Yet she was pretty sure that, even without eating it, if she'd had to fight again that instant, she'd still have enough vigour to get through. Well, there had to be some advantages to being a demi-god. Unless the numbness of her heart was spreading to the rest of her body . . .

She pushed that thought away, took another flatbread and scooped a generous portion of the cheese on top of it. Everyone else was eating ravenously; they knew she was Hades' daughter, and that she wasn't a normal mortal, but there was no need to remind them of the fact.

Each time one of her friends asked a question, Deina found a way to steer the conversation back to their adventures, asking for more details about their escape from Thebes or their journey back to Iolkos. There was plenty to tell. Racing frantically through the secret tunnels that lay beneath Thebes. Hurriedly burning Chryse's body in a grove outside the city while listening to the shouts of the pursuing guards. Days spent hiding and nights spent hastening along lonely paths, wading through rivers to try to confuse the dogs that had been sent after them, and stealing food from isolated farms. They'd undergone trials that should have made Deina's heart race. Instead, its silence nagged at her like an aching tooth, despite her wish to focus solely on her friends' ordeals.

Not all who left Thebes had survived. Of the six Bronze

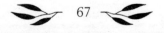

Guards who had escaped the citadel that night, two had asked to be released from their oath to serve the king, and had been set free by Theron before reaching Iolkos, but three had died on the journey. Two were killed by scouts near the city of Gla. The other drowned in the straits between Euboia and the mainland; she fell from a vessel in which they'd stowed away. Critos's voice broke when he spoke of it. Deina noticed the way Aster and Dendris, sitting either side of Critos, reached out to comfort him, and she realised there had been moments of happiness in their journey, as well as grief.

All spoke of unlooked for help from strangers, and Deina could see for herself how a new friendship with Critos had grown up, and how the existing bond between Theron, Aster and Dendris had deepened. The three of them had been marked by their trials, but they were still much the same. Dendris was still plain spoken with a subtle sense of humour. Aster spent almost as much time describing food – or its lack – as he did elaborating the fighting they'd had to do. And Theron had the same lopsided smile and warm, dark eyes that had won him so many friends when they'd both been children here. He even bore a trace of the old arrogance. Yet he, as well as Aster and Dendris, seemed to want to give the others the most credit for their survival. They even laughed at points, remembering some moment of danger or fear that seemed funny with the safety of hindsight.

While Deina was wondering whether she and Nat would – could – ever sit and laugh about getting her out of the Underworld, Theron took her hand again and squeezed it.

'You've still not told us how you came to be here. You

escaped the Underworld, but how? Did Hades relent? Did you defeat Thanatos?'

Deina opened her mouth to answer when she felt cold hands on her shoulders – Nat. The god of death was smirking as he tightened his grip possessively.

'No, she didn't defeat me, son of Thebes, because firstly, that is not possible, and secondly, she needed my assistance.' Nat clicked his fingers. An ornately carved chair appeared at the head of the table; he threw himself into it, dangling one boot-clad leg over the armrest. 'Together, Deina and I found a way for her to leave the Underworld, temporarily, so that she could help you.'

Aster, Dendris and Critos fell silent. The humour drained from Theron's face.

'Temporarily?'

There was an open window nearby; Deina could see the afternoon sun sending long shadows slanting across the herb garden that lay beyond.

'I've not been able to rid myself of the seeds. They will draw me back to the Underworld eventually.'

'When?' Theron demanded.

She held up the sandglass. The thin layer of silver dust in the bottom bulb had already grown thicker.

'I have until this runs out.' She remembered the Oneiros and the nectar. 'Or until Hades finds out I've escaped. And if that happens –'

'You'll be chained up in Tartarus and the key thrown away, I should imagine,' Nat said dryly. 'Me too.'

Aster and Critos were both gazing at her sadly. Dendris was

watching Theron, a worried crease between her brows. And Theron was glowering at Nat.

'This is all your fault.' He ground out the words, his voice hoarse.

'Hardly. And I'd like to point out that you'd have died in the Underworld if I hadn't helped you.' Nat sprang out of the chair and leaned over Theron. 'Let me be clear, Soul Severer. You mean nothing to me, but Deina does. That's why I helped her get here: so she could save your sorry backside. Again.' A scowl still marring his perfect features, he sat back down.

'You came back to stop Neidius, Deina?' Aster asked.

'I didn't know you'd been arrested, not until I got here,' she replied, glancing at Theron out of the corner of her eye. He was glaring at the wine cup clutched between his hands. 'I have some information about Aristaeus, though. That was what I wanted to tell you. You know he hunts you still? He has had the Spell Casters of Hephaestus create great bronze birds as spies. There were two perched on the walls of Iolkos when I arrived.'

Dendris nodded, her expression sombre.

'Aster and I heard the guards speaking of some winged, metal monster. We were held in the cells beneath the megaron before they brought us here today. I didn't think it could be true.'

'It is true. No doubt one of them will soon be on its way to Aristaeus. The news that you have been freed and Neidius killed will reach him quickly. It's not safe for any of you to stay here.'

Aster groaned and sank his head in his hands.

'More travelling. Where shall we go? What shall we do? We can't defeat Aristaeus alone.'

'There's something else.'

'Something worse, no doubt,' Dendris suggested.

'Aristaeus is searching for an ancient artefact spoken of in one of the songs of the Spell Casters. A torc, supposedly created by Hephaestus himself at the suggestion of Eris. The story goes that the torc was broken apart by order of the other gods. Aristaeus is trying to find the fragments. He wants to remake it.' Deina looked at Dendris and shrugged. 'So, yes. Worse.'

The Mycenaean sucked in her breath.

'What does he want with this thing? What could he gain by it?'

'The Spell Casters' song claims that the torc allowed the wearer to control all Theodesmioi. To use them as an army.' Deina didn't feel the need to elaborate. The Theodesmioi were all trained to fight, and all of them drew on the power of the gods. All of them could use that power to kill – or worse. Soul Severers could summon up ghosts, Weather Workers could call down lightning, Sea Singers could unleash a flood . . . The others were just as able as she was to imagine what Aristaeus might do with such an army.

No one spoke. And no one, Deina noted, suggested that Aristaeus was mad to be searching for a fable. Critos had spent the last who-knew-how-many years under a spell. The rest of them had come face to face with legendary monsters, and were now sitting at a table with the god of death. They all knew a myth could be as real as anything from the mortal realm. Just as real, and far more dangerous.

'Hephaestus's torc . . . I was there, you know,' Nat said in a conversational tone.

Everyone looked at him.

'What do you mean?' Deina asked. 'You saw it being made?'

'No. I saw it being destroyed.' He smiled, his earlier bad mood apparently forgotten. 'I'll show you.' A dark orb appeared in Nat's palm, the surface glistening and slightly rainbowed, as if covered in a slick of olive oil. Without warning, he tossed the orb into the air.

The herbarium – apart from the bits of the benches on which they sat, and the end of the table around which they were clustered – vanished. They were at one side of a sort of colonnade. Towering, gilded columns enclosed the space; they sparkled in the sunlight that bathed the colonnade and the gardens and distant hills that lay beyond. The floor between the columns was tiled with glittering white marble. In the centre of the floor was a high dais of the same marble with steps cut into one side and a tall silver pillar at each corner. Some gauzy fabric had been stretched between the pillars to provide shade to the golden couch below and to the large, chestnut-haired man – or god, surely – who was reclining on it. As Deina tried to take it all in, a dark rectangle appeared, hanging in the air in the middle of the courtyard. This, she recognised: the wall of night. Nat stepped out of it – not the Nat who was still sitting at the table with them, but another Nat. A copy. Or a memory. This other Nat approached the being on the couch and knelt.

'You sent for me, glorious Zeus.'

'Yes, Thanatos. You are to end a life for me. A mortal, too

puny for me to deal with, but a king nonetheless, deserving of your personal attention. He has become overmighty. A potential problem. End him, and bring his body to me.'

The scene around them changed. They were on a battlefield now, though whatever battle had waged here was over. Only the dead and dying remained, and there were enough of those that even the most hardened Soul Severer might have been sickened. Deina pressed a hand to her mouth. Bodies lay thick upon the ground as far as she could see. The air was filled with screams and groans and the buzz of flies and the harsh shrieks of carrion crows assembling to feast. And through this field of death walked a solitary figure with a crown upon his head. No armour – Deina guessed this king had others to do his fighting for him. As he drew closer, she could see a torc around his neck, more finely crafted than any torc she'd seen. And she could hear that he was laughing as he looked on the destruction wrought in his name. When the wall of night appeared, and Thanatos stepped out and drew his sword of silent silver flames and severed the king's lifeline, she was glad.

Another scene shift: they were back in the gorgeous, glittering colonnade. Though now Zeus, with Thanatos a respectful distance behind him, was standing next to a table on which the body of the dead king had been laid, and there were other gods present. Two were Zeus's siblings: Poseidon, tall, golden-haired, with a silver trident in his hand, and Deina's mother, Hades, wearing her favourite blue gown. The third – russet-haired, leaning on a crutch, his legs supported by criss-crossing gold bands – was Hephaestus, master smith and nephew to the three Olympians.

'Well, Hephaestus,' Zeus boomed, 'explain yourself. For what purpose did you create this torc? And what possessed you to give it to a mortal?'

'It was Eris's idea.' Hephaestus stretched out a hand and brushed his fingers across the dead man's – the king's – forehead. 'I suppose I shouldn't have listened to her, but I didn't know what he would do with it. I just wanted to please him. He is – was – a beautiful man. Strong. Captivating.' He scowled at the other gods. 'And I'm not the only one of us who has given a gift to a mortal.'

Hades smiled dangerously. 'Traditionally, we give them things like a cursed necklace, or immortality without eternal youth, or an unwanted child. Not gifts they can actually use.' The smile faded. 'What were you thinking, idiot?'

'What was he thinking with, you mean,' muttered Poseidon, chuckling at his own joke.

Zeus shot his brother a withering glance. 'Well, none of that matters now. Remove the torc from the body, Hephaestus. Your workmanship is outstanding, as usual. It might even be the most beautiful thing you've made. I'll enjoy wearing it.'

Hades grabbed Hephaestus's wrist, though she was looking at Zeus.

'Not so fast. That thing is powerful, brother. It can control the Theodesmioi, and the Theodesmioi draw part of our own power. Why should you get it?'

Zeus pointed at his chest. 'King of the gods.'

'But we are all three of us children of Cronos. You, me and Hades,' Poseidon said ponderously. 'Perhaps Hades is right. Hera and the others might agree.'

Zeus's eyes narrowed and a golden thunderbolt appeared in his hand.

'Think of it as safekeeping, Poseidon. If I'm wearing it, the torc won't fall into unsuitable hands.' He glared at Hades.

Thanatos cleared his throat. 'Perhaps I might make a suggestion? Why not destroy it?' He turned to Hephaestus. 'Can it be done?'

'Yes. If I take it back to my forge I can unravel the spells woven into the metal, and melt each strand down.' Hephaestus sighed and leaned over the body on the table, though his attention now was clearly on the torc, not the man wearing it. 'If I must.'

'I'd rather see it destroyed here. Now.' Hades crossed her arms.

'The best I can do is break it apart with my hammer. The spells will linger, but since you won't let me take it away . . .' Hephaestus bowed his head to the three Olympians. 'And which of you will get to keep the broken pieces?' He glanced at Thanatos, and Deina thought she could see a glimpse of humour in the look that passed between them.

There was a moment of uncomfortable silence.

'Perhaps the pieces might be given to another god to hide?' Thanatos suggested.

'You?' snarled Hades.

'Definitely not. I've fulfilled my role in this drama.' Thanatos gestured at the dead body. 'What about the goddess of fortune? You all like her.'

'Tyche?' Zeus raised his eyebrows, considering. 'I suppose that would work. As long as she keeps the hiding places secret from everyone. As long as we each take an oath on the Styx not to search for the fragments.' His eyes darted from one of his siblings to the other. 'Are we agreed?'

There were murmurs of assent from Hades and Poseidon.

'Very well.' In one quick gesture, Zeus plunged the thunderbolt into the body lying on the table and a ball of flame erupted upwards. When it vanished, there was nothing left of the king but a streak of dust and the torc. 'Break it apart, Hephaestus.'

The smith god raised his huge hammer. Before the blow fell, Olympus and the gods disappeared . . .

They were back in the herbarium in Iolkos, with birdsong floating through the window and the shadows falling.

6

Finally, Critos broke the silence.

'I've seen more of Aristaeus's deeds than anyone else here. I know what he is capable of. If he were to somehow find the parts of this torc, if he found a way to put it back together . . .'

He didn't finish the sentence. It was all too easy to conjure an image of Aristaeus, the torc around his neck, striding across a corpse-filled, blood-soaked battlefield, just like that long-dead king.

'But surely,' Dendris said, glancing at Nat, who was rolling the dark orb back and forth across the table, 'surely, it's impossible. Impossible that he should find it, let alone restore its power. The pieces must be hidden too well to ever be found.'

Nat closed his hand on the orb and it vanished. He sat back in the chair.

'The fragments of the torc were divided and one piece hidden in each divine realm: Olympus, the Underworld and Poseidon's underwater kingdom. That should make them almost impossible to find for a mortal. Having said that . . .' Nat pulled a face.

'Mortals are able to enter the realms of the gods, even though they might need help to do so. You Severers are proof of that. And there are those who have stolen from the gods before.'

He meant Prometheus, stealing fire to give it to mortals. But Prometheus was a god himself. One of the old gods, the Titans. Even so, he'd eventually been caught by Zeus and punished. Deina shivered. Spending eternity tied to a mountain with an eagle tearing out your liver every day sounded even worse than spending eternity shut up in the Underworld.

'There's also the possibility,' Nat continued, 'that Tyche might not have hidden the pieces that carefully. Mortals as well as gods know that luck is not to be depended on. Tyche might have treated it as an opportunity for fun, as bit of a game. She's fickle and can be mischievous.' All the Severers around the table nodded at this; games of chance were a favourite pastime. Deina had spent plenty of evenings at the House betting and losing.

'You could tell the gods what he's doing,' Aster said. 'They'd stop him. They don't want a human to have that sort of power. We know that already.'

Nat shook his head.

'What I know is that Zeus, Poseidon and Hades each desperately wanted that torc for themselves. If I tell them Aristaeus was searching for it, each will mutter something about it being amusing to watch him fail. They will all let him look, hoping he finds it, so that they might take it for themselves. And then . . .' Nat held out his hand and a slender black and purple flame burst into life in the centre of his palm. 'You know what happened to Troy.' The flame grew, and an image appeared within it: a great city, burning and crumbling, the remnants of its mighty walls stained red with blood. Deina thought she could almost hear the screams of the dying. 'The Olympians might be a family, but they hate each other all the more for that. They enjoy using humans to fight their battles.' He closed his hand, extinguishing the flame. 'And they never care about the cost.'

Whether Aristaeus gained the torc, or one of the gods, the Theodesmioi would lose.

'We have to stop him,' Deina said, rushing the words out. 'We have to find at least one of the fragments. We have to find it and keep it from Aristaeus. Destroy it, if we can.' No one responded. She saw Dendris and Aster share a doubtful glance. And how could she blame them? They'd already been through so much. Yet Deina could feel how important this was. She just needed the right words, to be able to explain it to herself as well as the others. She took a deep breath.

'Critos, I understand that you must be exhausted. You must want rest, far away from everything that might remind you of Aristaeus. Dendris, I know you must want to return to Mycenae. To finally explore those woods. The ones you could see but never reach while you had a torc around your neck. Theron, I haven't forgotten that you dream of becoming a bard, singing the ancient poems and enchanting huge audiences.' Theron smiled slightly. 'And Aster, you're surely longing to be reunited with Melos.' Aster nodded, and Deina could see the yearning in his eyes. He'd fallen in love with Melos, a softly spoken, dark-eyed novice a year Aster's junior, not long before they left on their quest to the Underworld. 'But you said it yourself earlier.'

Aster frowned.

'Said what?'

'You asked where could we go – what could we do – to either escape Aristaeus or defeat him.'

'Oh.' He nodded glumly.

'And that's the point,' Deina continued. 'The four of you struggled back here because you wanted to tell the other Theodesmioi the truth of what happens to us after death. And I'm guessing you hoped that knowing the truth would somehow . . . would somehow . . .' She threw up her hands and took a few strides across the floor. 'That maybe it would enable the Theodesmioi to stand up to the gods. To abandon the Orders. To be free in life, even if we couldn't change what happened after death. Am I right?'

'Yes,' Dendris replied. 'We talked about what might be possible. We hoped we could make a difference. To start something.'

'Exactly. Freedom for the Theodesmioi. That was why you returned to Iolkos. Yet even knowing the truth, Neidius would have preferred to silence you than have things change.' Deina looked steadily at each of them. 'All the Houses, scattered across the Dominion – each of them might have a Neidius. Someone who would always choose a lie and his own advantage over the truth. Someone who would wade through blood to keep things as they are. Yet even if every House in each Order managed to rise up, all of it might come to nothing if Hephaestus's torc is remade. If it falls into the hands of Aristaeus, or someone like him. The Theodesmioi would just be in thrall to him instead of the gods.' She clenched her fists, hoping she'd said enough to carry them with her. 'Even if we can't use the torc for our good, we have to try to find it. To destroy it, if possible. Otherwise, our dream of lasting freedom will be just that: a dream.'

'She's right,' Theron sighed eventually. 'The only alternative is to run.'

'And to keep running,' Critos added. 'Aristaeus will not stop hunting you.'

Dendris smacked her fist into the table.

'Even if he did it might not help. We are still marked by the gods' sigils. Maybe this torc would enable Aristaeus to simply summon us back.'

'What about the others?' Aster asked. 'What about Melos? I don't want to leave him again.' He glanced at Nat. 'You freed Deina from her torc. Can't you free all the other Theodesmioi?'

'Not quickly enough.' Nat looked slightly peeved at being reminded of his limitations. 'I might get through most of those in this House, but Hades would intervene before I got any further. The rest of the Theodesmioi would still be trapped. And Hades would realise that Deina wasn't where she's supposed to be.'

'There's no other way.' Deina glanced down at the sandglass. 'I've got some time. I can start the search, at least, if you need more time to think, or recover.'

Dendris leaned back in her chair and smiled slightly.

'As if we are going to allow you to attempt this alone. Too much time in the Underworld has made you soft in the head.'

'Exactly,' Aster agreed. 'After everything that you have already sacrificed for us? We won't let you carry this burden alone, Deina. Besides, I don't plan to spend my life hiding from Aristaeus. Where would be the honour in that?'

Theron was nodding.

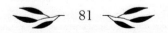

'If there is a way to stop Aristaeus, and even the smallest chance to free the Theodesmioi, then we must take it. Critos –' he stretched out his arm and gripped the hand of the former Bronze Guard – 'I do not ask you to join us unless you wish to. You of all of us have suffered the longest.'

Critos appeared to struggle with his emotions for a moment.

'I am tired,' he admitted eventually. 'I do not remember how many years I was bound and preserved by Orpheus's spells, but I know that I'm older than I look. As the enchantment drains, I can feel my strength fading.' He stared down at one hand, flexing his fingers. 'I would willingly follow you anywhere, Theron. You know I would. It may be, though, that I can best serve you by staying here and doing what I can to help protect the city.'

'We'll miss you fighting by our side, but I understand.' As Theron spoke, Aster and Dendris murmured their agreement. 'But as for the rest of us,' he continued, 'we do this together, or not at all.'

Nat began clapping.

'Not spoken like a king at all. In my experience, they are better at sending others to die than at taking risks themselves. Still, a good speech.'

'I assure you,' Theron said coldly, 'I've no interest in following in my father's footsteps. Despite Critos's attempts to persuade me otherwise –' he smiled warmly at the other man – 'I can't imagine myself ruling the Dominion. I wouldn't trust myself. Kings are no better than any other men, and they are too often corrupted by their power. And I have other hopes and dreams.' He turned in his seat to fully face Nat. 'Speaking of power, you have more than enough to spare. Are you willing to use some of it to help us?'

Nat, stony faced, said nothing.

One by one each of the others seated around the table turned to look at him.

Still the god stayed silent.

Deina sighed, wishing she was able to read Nat's thoughts as easily as he seemed to be able to read hers. 'Nat, you will help us, won't you?'

Nat locked eyes with her. 'I said I'd help you to temporarily leave the Underworld.' He leaned back in his chair and folded his arms. 'But I don't recall making any other promises.'

'I thought that you said that you cared about Deina.' Theron had a mischievous look on his face, one Deina was all too familiar with. 'Even if you're not prepared to do anything for the rest of us, surely that means you'll want to help her?'

Deina did her best to supress a smile. 'It's true, Nat. You did say that I meant something to you.'

Nat shot her a dirty look, then groaned and rolled his eyes. 'Fine. I suppose I'll give what help I can. Until you return to the Underworld. At that point, my involvement ends. And no one can know I'm helping you. I'm not exactly popular in the gold-decked halls of Olympus right now, or in the Underworld.' As he finished speaking, Nat got up, strode towards Deina, took her hands in his and kissed them. His eyes flickered over towards Theron as he pulled Deina closer towards him. 'And for the record, I did mean what I said earlier. I do care about you. Greatly.'

Deina tried to free her hands.

'Nat . . .'

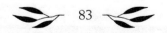

Nat sighed and clicked his fingers. Everything in the room – her friends, the sparrow perching on the windowsill nearby and eyeing up the bread, even the flames of the oil lamps Aster had just lit – froze into immobility. 'No audience now – is that better? Speaking of the Underworld, I need to sneak back in and check on the Oneiros.'

Unexpectedly, Deina felt a stab of unease. She'd become used to having the god of death around. He was looking down at her, humour dancing in his sapphire blue eyes.

'Can it be you're going to miss me?'

'No,' Deina said hurriedly. 'I was hoping you might tell the elders about the blood hunters, that's all. Some of them won't be convinced, despite what you did to Neidius.'

'Right.' Nat seemed to be trying not to smile; he sounded as if he didn't believe her explanation.

'Thank you, though, for saving me.' She brushed her fingers against his. 'I'm guessing you can't destroy Aristaeus in the same way?'

'Sadly not. Neidius was closely linked to the Underworld by who and where he was. I cannot set my flames to Aristaeus's flesh.' For a moment, Nat seemed to look through her, to some distant place or time. 'If you wish divine aid to destroy Aristaeus, you'll need a more powerful god than me.' He half smiled, shaking away whatever vision he'd had, as the shadows clinging to the edges of the room flowed toward him, weaving about his legs like cats. With finger and thumb Nat lifted Deina's chin; she felt the brief, cold touch of his lips against hers, and a shiver of something that might have been anticipation across her skin. 'I'll return before dawn. I'd urge you not to do anything that I wouldn't do, but there are very few things a god can't be tempted to try at least once.' He winked as the shadows rose higher, obscuring him entirely. When they retreated, he had gone.

In the same instant, the others were released from the spell that had kept them still.

'Where did he go?' Aster demanded, looking under the table as if the god of death might have decided to play a game of hide and seek.

'He had things to do,' Deina replied, trying to ignore the weight of Theron's gaze, which was fixed firmly upon her. 'He'll be back later.'

The doors to the herbarium swung open. Anteïs entered, together with the Sea Singer who had questioned Deina in the great hall, and another man whose forehead bore the sigil of Zeus. Anteïs had something in her hand: a small gold box, that Deina had last seen next to Orpheus's throne that night in the Cadmea. It held the teeth Drex had collected in the Underworld; fangs belonging to the serpent slain by Cadmus, founder of Thebes – or so Orpheus had believed. The elder held the box out to Theron.

'Here. The rest of your things – your weapons and bags – are gone, but Neidius had this in his rooms.' Theron took the box silently. 'I supposed he was planning to give it to Aristaeus. You're lucky I was able to get to it before one of the others.'

'What do you mean?' Deina asked.

'Plenty of the elders are afraid of Aristaeus,' Anteïs muttered through gritted teeth, 'and of that new archon he's installed. There's been talk of handing Theron over, or of handing all of you over.' Deina gripped Theron's shoulder. 'Not you,

Deina,' Anteïs continued, 'not after what Theron told us of your parentage. The elders fear Hades. Just not as much as they currently fear Aristaeus. The threat he poses feels much more . . . imminent.'

Aster pushed himself to his feet.

'Then give us some weapons. As tired as I am, I'd rather die trying to fight my way out of here than end up back in those stinking cells, waiting for Aristaeus to devise some new way of torturing us.'

'Sit down,' Anteïs scolded. Aster obeyed instantly. 'A heroic last stand is not required, Aster, at least not today. There is another way. Nothing has been agreed for now. I've been made to promise that you won't pass the gates of the House, but I still plan on getting you out of here. The gates aren't the only exit.' She waved a hand at the men waiting behind her. 'Lysigoras is Leader of the House of Poseidon. Dorias is a Weather Worker and an elder in the House of Zeus. They've both offered me their help.'

Lysigoras stepped forward.

'As you know, the grounds of the House of Poseidon run down to the sea. We keep a small fishing vessel anchored just beyond our walls; you will leave here before first light and make your way to the House, and we will get you on board the boat and away from here.'

Theron stood.

'Thank you for your offer of help. However . . .' He glanced at Deina; she nodded. 'However, there is something we must search for – something we need to find before Aristaeus does. I'm not sure that sailing away from here is the right way to begin.'

'What is this nonsense?' Anteïs asked, turning to Deina. 'We have to get you away from Iolkos.' She dropped into a chair, her face drawn with exhaustion. 'I'm old and tired. I wasn't strong enough to stand up to Neidius on my own. I've no stomach for a fight. The only way I can help you is by speeding your escape. So tell me, what can be more important than saving your lives?'

As quickly as she could, Deina shared with the elders everything she'd learned about Hephaestus's torc. She described it as something she'd heard of in the Underworld, to avoid mentioning Nat's involvement, and she told them of her conviction: that only by finding the torc fragments before Aristaeus could they hope to stop his tyranny and have a chance at offering the rest of the Theodesmioi some sort of freedom.

Dorias was looking at her with concern.

'Is it wise, to place such reliance on a myth? And surely, Aristaeus has no more hope of finding these fragments than I do of suddenly sprouting wings.'

'But if he were to find them, and remake the torc,' Deina urged. 'Don't you see? He'd control us all. We'd be bound to his whim as well as those of the gods.'

To her relief, Lysigoras nodded slowly.

'I am not quick to dismiss ancient stories. They are handed down no doubt because there is some truth in them, somewhere. But you do not know where these fragments might be?'

'Somewhere in the realms of the gods.' Saying the words aloud made it sound all the more impossible. Deina sighed. 'We have to try, even though we don't know where to begin.'

'Well,' the Sea Singer said, 'I might be able to help you.

There is an ancient Song we elders learn. A Song for use when a flood threatens destruction: the Singer may use it summon a sea nymph who will conduct him into the presence of Poseidon, where he might beg for the flood to be averted. It is not a difficult rite, but it demands a sacrifice.'

No surprise there, Deina thought to herself. If there was one constant about the gods, it was their shared insistence on defenceless creatures being slaughtered in droves at their altars. The animal pens next to the temples in Iolkos were kept well stocked even when the city's people were starving.

'There is a lake in our grounds that connects to the sea through an underground passage,' continued Lysigoras. 'We could conduct the rite there. You'd need, however, to know the name of a nymph, and I don't –'

'I can find out a name,' Deina interrupted. Nat probably knew some sea nymphs personally – probably extremely personally, if he was anything like the other gods. 'Should we follow you to the House now?'

Lysigoras shook his head.

'The rite needs some preparation. Certain herbs, and so on. A few hours' work.'

'I'd welcome a night's sleep,' Theron said wistfully. Dendris yawned widely.

'And some more food,' Aster added. 'And I'd like some time to see Melos.'

'You can't tell him I'm planning to get you out of here,' Anteïs warned. 'It's too risky. If the elders think you might escape, they'll lock you up. You can see him, but it's best if you avoid the other Severers as much as possible.' Aster nodded

sadly. 'In fact, don't speak to anyone if you can help it,' Anteïs continued, pushing herself to her feet and wincing slightly. 'You three –' she pointed at Theron, Deina and Aster – 'can sleep in your own rooms, and you can go to the baths, but avoid the refectory. I'll have some more food brought here, and beds for Critos and Dendris. You can spend the evening together. I'll come and wake you when it's time to go.' She paused, frowning. 'Dorias, can you gather supplies, weapons and so on, and meet us at the House of Poseidon tomorrow?' The Weather Worker nodded. 'Good.' Anteïs put her hands on her hips. 'Is there anything else?'

Deina smiled.

'Only that you should have been Leader of the House instead of Neidius. You think of everything, Anteïs. We are in your debt.'

'If you can free us of these things –' Anteïs's hand went to the bronze torc encircling her neck – 'then every one of us will be in your debt. What Theron told us of the fate that awaits us after death . . .' A shadow passed over her face. 'It is too cruel. I'll see you in a few hours.'

When the elders left, no one seemed to quite know what to do with themselves. They went over their plan, such as it was, and spoke a little more about what they'd been through since that night in the secret chamber at the top of the Cadmea. Deina said as little as possible about her time in the Underworld. She already felt separate from the others; excluded, somehow, by their shared experience. By the fact that they were all fully human, with hearts that beat and raced, and she was not. There might have been the occasional troubled glance in her direction, or she might have just been imagining it. Theron smiled at her, but he seemed distant, and made no move to take her hand again. At some point, servants arrived with fresh food and some bedding, and more lamps were lit as the afternoon dissolved into evening. Aster went to find Melos. Dendris went to find the baths. When Theron and Critos began discussing tactics, trying to find ways in which Critos might help Anteïs and start organising some resistance to Aristaeus, Deina took the opportunity to slip away to the gardens.

The moon hadn't risen yet. The lack of light didn't trouble her, though; this was the only home she remembered. Even blindfolded, she could have traced her route among these tracks. As she walked, she let her ankles brush against the rosemary that edged every path and spilled across the paving stones, breathing in the scent it released. The noises of the House faded, and eventually she reached the vegetable beds at the farthest point of the gardens. This was the spot where she and Drex used to meet in secret. Until Orpheus came to Iolkos, she'd been paying Drex to teach her to read. The memory made her insides twist with grief. Deina sat on the wall dividing the beds from the rest of the gardens. Drex should have been there with everyone else. Instead, he was dead. Unburied. And the worst of it was, it had been her actions that killed him. She'd chosen poorly. Drex had paid the price.

Was it guilt, or Hades, that she heard whispering in the back of her mind?

If you were a goddess, you might bring him back . . .

Deina shook her head. If she were a goddess, she wouldn't care about Drex any more. Or about anything but the fulfilment of her own desires. She picked a daisy that was growing in a cleft in the wall and began plucking off its petals, trying not to brood on Theron, or his behaviour, or the vision of him that Hades had conjured in the Underworld, and the way that conjured image had kissed the side of her neck.

She might have returned to her room if it hadn't held so many memories: of Chryse, of her life as it had been before Orpheus's black-sailed ships had arrived in Iolkos's harbour. Besides, she wasn't tired. Better to wander the gardens, to breath in the cool night air and watch the passage of the moonlight and feel the endless expanse of sky above her while she still could.

Hours passed. As Deina walked the grounds, the moon sank back towards the horizon. The night grew colder; the lower part of her gown became damp with dew. It clung uncomfortably to her legs and made her long for a bath. Increasing her pace, she turned her steps towards the main doors. The guards, silent and half-asleep at their posts, didn't question her.

Inside the House, the corridors and courtyards were quiet. The women's bath was empty. Deina undressed next to one of the stone furnaces that served both to heat the bath and to warm the room. She washed quickly and took some clean clothes from the store kept here: a pair of leather sandals, a belt and a plain tunic. Its coarse fabric chafed her skin, but she felt more herself – more real – than she had done in the diaphanous red gown. After folding the gown and its jewelled accessories into a small bundle, she stood for a moment, staring at the sandglass in her hand. Part of her wanted to wrap it inside the gown, to get it out of her sight so she might forget about the Underworld entirely, at least for a little while. But what was the point? The seeds were still inside her. She was still her mother's daughter, as much as she wanted to pretend otherwise. Besides, better to have some warning if the slow spiral of silver sand suddenly sped up. Resigned, she hung the sandglass from her belt and walked silently into that part of the House reserved for novices and adepts. The women's hall was empty, the fire in the central hearth burned to ash. Finally, she reached her room. Pushed open the door. The air was musty. Deina crossed the room and opened the shutters.

'Deina?' a voice asked groggily. 'Is that you?' She spun round. Theron was stretched out on her bed. He'd pushed himself up onto one elbow and was blinking at her.

Automatically, Deina pressed one hand to her chest, even though her heart – which should have been leaping, either from happiness or from shock – was silent, just as it had been since she'd eaten Hades' seeds.

'What are you doing here, Theron?'

'I came to wait for you, but I must have fallen asleep. I wanted to talk to you.' He pushed himself up off the bed. 'I couldn't say everything that I really wanted to say, not in front of the others.' He paused, gazing at her, the expression in his dark eyes impossible to read in the gloomy interior.

Deina waited.

With a shaky laugh, Theron dragged one hand through his hair.

'Ridiculous, isn't it? I've been dreaming about this moment ever since I lost you that night in the Cadmea. Dreaming about it, planning what I might say to you if I ever got the chance, trying to keep my hope alive. And now you're here, and I – I –' He turned away, breathing raggedly.

Deina took a step towards him.

'Theron . . .'

'Before we journeyed to the Underworld, I wasted so much time trying to hate you.' He swung back to her. 'Trying to convince myself that the way I treated you was somehow acceptable. And then to learn that those cursed seeds are still chaining you to the Underworld, that I might lose you all over again . . .' He reached out until his hand hovered a hair's breadth away from her bare shoulder, as if she was some precious thing that might shatter at the slightest touch. 'I've been a fool, Deina, and I don't know how to properly fix things. I don't even know if there's time.'

Deina caught hold of his hands.

'Neither do I. I keep hoping I'll find a way to escape the Underworld, but I've not found it yet. It may not exist. And as for you coming with me, even if that was what you wanted, we know living mortals can't stay in the Underworld for long. The only way for a mortal to stay in the Underworld is to die.' They both knew what that meant. The fate of dead Theodesmioi was to become blood hunters.

They stood there, their fingers entwined, their eyes fixed on each other's face. Deina couldn't help remembering Hades' words: *Become an immortal goddess. You could have everything you desire and more.* Right now, Deina's desire for Theron was a physical ache. But she couldn't give in to her mother. She refused to give up what remained of her humanity.

Theron drew her closer.

'When we got nearer to Iolkos – me and Aster and the others – and you still hadn't come back, I tried to imagine living without you. I thought about falling in love with someone else. Making a life with someone else.' He hesitated. 'Maybe I should try harder? I've seen the way Nat looks at you. He can offer you so much more than me. If that's what you want – if you think that would be the better choice, given everything we're fighting against, I would try to understand.'

Deina lowered her gaze, probing her feelings.

'In spite of everything Nat's done, in spite of all his lies, I can't deny I like him. But I don't feel for him what I feel for you.' She slid her arms around Theron's neck. This close, she could feel his heartbeat and the warmth of his hands on her back. She could smell the scent of the oil used in the baths clinging to his skin. His hair was tousled with sleep. The fantasy-Theron Hades had conjured evaporated in the shadow of the real thing. She reached up to kiss his lips softly. Wanting so much more than kisses. But to let herself fall more deeply in love with him – to encourage his love – when she was bound, as soon as the dust ran out, to be torn from his arms and reclaimed by the Underworld . . .

Deina decided she didn't care. She kissed him again. This time, she tugged his lower lip gently between her teeth.

Theron moaned, caught her into his arms and buried his face in her hair.

'I thought I'd lost you.'

'I thought you were dead.'

They kissed then as though this was both their first and final chance, giving in to pent-up hunger, moulding their bodies together, running hands across skin and through hair as if in these few moments they could map every fragment of each other. As if they could make up for lost time. Until the sound of a cock crowing caused Deina to pull away a little. She looked out of the window.

The courtyard beyond was becoming more distinct as the eastern sky lightened. She leaned her head on Theron's shoulder and closed her eyes, clutching him even more tightly as he trailed kisses down the side of her neck and made her sigh with pleasure.

'I wish we could stay here, in this moment,' Deina whispered. 'I wish I had the power to keep the sun from rising.'

'Maybe – maybe you will have that sort of power one day,' Theron said unwillingly. He didn't want to think about the future any more than she did. 'But you'll still be you. A Soul Severer. A thief. My Deina. Look at me.'

She lifted her gaze to his.

'If the gods offered me the entire world as my stage, if they offered to grant me a voice that could enchant the stars and calm the sea, I would still choose you.' He took her face in his hands. 'I will always choose you.'

Faint colour was bleeding back into the red-tiled roof of the women's hall, on the opposite side of the courtyard. Deina tried to fix this instant in her memory. She closed her eyes as Theron bent his head and began to kiss her again.

Until some shift in the air nearby made her skin prickle. She pulled back and looked over Theron's shoulder.

The god of death was leaning against the wall, his arms crossed, watching them.

7

Deina pushed Theron quickly away from her as Nat grinned – bared his teeth, at least – at their surprise.

'I told you I'd return with the dawn. I trust everyone has had an enjoyable night.' He arched one eyebrow and glanced pointedly at the bed, rumpled from where Theron had slept on it. 'Are you still planning on searching for the remnants of the torc? You seem to have become a little . . . side-tracked.'

'We are.' Deina crossed her arms defensively. 'We'll be leaving here soon and heading to the House of Poseidon. The Leader of the House told us of a rite, a way of summoning a nymph to conduct us to Poseidon's realm. That's where we'll start. There's a place in the grounds where the rite can be conducted.'

'I know it,' Nat said. 'I knew every stone of this city long before you were born, Severer.' Perhaps it was a trick of the light, but his shadowy wings seemed to grow more solid. 'This leader has told you that the rite requires a sacrifice?'

'Yes. And that we need the name of a sea nymph.' Deina raised one eyebrow. So Nat wanted to make suggestive

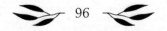

comments about her and Theron? Two could play at that game. 'I'm guessing you must be intimately acquainted with lots and lots of nymphs.'

'Oh, hundreds.' Nat winked, dismissing her attempt to embarrass him. 'They can't get enough of me. And who can blame them?'

'And do any of them still talk to you?' Deina asked sweetly.

'Some.' The god shrugged. 'To be honest, conversation is not generally their strong point.'

Theron muttered something beneath his breath.

Nat laughed.

'Well, this has been fun. I'll see you both at the House of Poseidon.'

The god vanished. Theron exhaled loudly and rubbed a hand across his face.

'Do you suppose if you asked him to knock . . .'

Deina shook her head, remembering other occasions when Nat had just appeared uninvited. 'I don't think he would understand. And if he did, he wouldn't care.' She started to draw Theron back towards her, but a soft tap at the door was quickly followed by Anteïs stepping into the room. The elder's eyes widened slightly when she saw Theron, but all she said was, 'Time to go. Quickly.'

Near the door, there was a rough sketch of a ship still pinned to the wall; Deina had left it behind when she went to join Orpheus's ship. It seemed like another lifetime. She took the picture down and tucked it inside the folds of the red gown Hades had conjured her into, before taking a last look around the room that had been hers for so many years.

Whatever happened, Deina doubted she would be returning here.

From the sleeping quarters, Anteïs led them all swiftly back through the herbarium – pausing only to give each of them a large leather bag – the herb garden and into the maze garden. By the time the sun had breached the horizon and the bell of the House had begun to toll, summoning the Severers to breakfast and then work or lessons, Anteïs had guided them to a small stone hut, overgrown with ivy, in the farthest corner of the maze garden. She lifted some of the ivy to reveal a door so swollen with damp it took Aster's strength to drag it open. Before the sun had fully risen, they were safe inside.

Following the elder's direction, Deina and the others moved the abandoned gardening equipment and rotting sacks and uncovered a trap door. Stone steps led down into the darkness.

'From the bottom of the stairs, there's a path that goes all the way into the city,' Anteïs explained, lighting an oil lamp and passing it to Theron. 'I don't know if any of the other elders know about it, but even if they do, we've got a little time before they start searching for you. I told them I'd bring you all to the great hall after breakfast. I'll come with you to the House of Poseidon.'

Deina hesitated.

'What will you do when they discover you lied?'

An odd expression passed over the elder's face: part sorrow, part triumph.

'Don't worry. They won't be able to do anything to me.' She jerked her head towards the trapdoor. 'Go! Aster, pull the door closed behind us.'

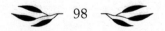

By the time she reached the bottom of the spiral stairs, Deina had lost all sense of direction. She could see, by keeping her eyes fixed on the lamp Theron held, that the narrow tunnel didn't run straight; there were frequent turns and changes in levels, and it seemed to stretch on and on, far further than the length of the path between the House and the city walls. The air was cold and dank. After a while she could hear Anteïs wheezing. She turned to offer the elder her arm to lean on, but Anteïs waved her away.

'Nearly there. Keep going.'

Deina was doubtful; the tunnel showed no sign of rising towards the open air. Yet two more turns brought them face to face with another set of stairs. Anteïs, breathing heavily, pushed her way to the front.

'Now, these stairs come out in an alleyway near the brothel.' She gave Theron, Aster and Critos a withering glance. '*Men*. Still, at least there's not likely to be anyone around at this time of the day.'

The early morning sunshine was dazzling after the confines of the tunnel. Although the alleyway was empty, the roads that led towards the harbour were already growing busy with merchants hurrying to their ships and fishermen returning with their catch. The group hurried towards the House of Poseidon. Every so often, Deina looked skywards, anxiously searching the roofs of the houses, shops and warehouses for any sign of the great bronze birds. She wasn't the only one.

Lysigoras was waiting for them, clad in the dark blue ceremonial robes of an elder of the House of Poseidon. Even though the hardest part of their journey still lay before them,

Deina couldn't help sighing with relief when the doors of the House closed behind them.

'This is Tauredos.' Lysigoras gestured to a heavily built young man with curly auburn hair who was hovering nearby. His brown eyes had a slightly sleepy look, but he already had rite-seals extending down one arm – a lot, for an adept. 'Since this quest is for all the Theodesmioi, not just the Soul Severers, I asked for a volunteer from the small number of our best adepts who are not currently bound to a ship. I've explained what you plan, and have sworn him to secrecy. He understands the danger.'

Tauredos nodded, smiling hesitantly.

'I was due to be bound to one of Aristaeus's warships.' He shrugged. 'I'd rather take my chances with you than drown in the service of that accursed monster.'

The others moved to greet him, but Deina kept watching Lysigoras. He'd taken Anteïs aside and placed a hand on her shoulder.

'You came,' he said in a low voice.

'I said I would.'

'And you're sure?'

'I've made up my mind, old friend.'

Lysigoras nodded, his face grave. Before Deina could ask Anteïs the meaning of the exchange, he gestured for them to follow him.

The House of Poseidon, while it lay within the city walls, had been built as close to the sea as possible. As they approached the furthest boundary of the grounds, Deina realised that at that point the wall of the city and the exterior wall of the

House were one and the same thing. Nothing but sea lay beyond. Lysigoras led them to a large lake, just inside the wall, surrounded by dense thickets of trees. The water level was well below the surrounding ground, and steps, slimy with dark seaweed, led down into the water.

'It's a salt-water lake. Tidal,' the Sea Singer explained. 'The water rises and falls with the tide. There are fissures in the lakebed that connect this place with the sea.'

He beckoned to some figures lingering among the trees. As they drew nearer, Deina recognised Dorias, the elder from the House of Zeus. He was flanked by a man and a woman, both a similar age to Deina as far as she could tell, each carrying three large bundles.

'You have the supplies, Dorias?' Anteïs asked.

'Yes. A few days' worth of food and some waterskins.' He waved a hand and his assistants distributed the bundles. Deina noticed the woman kept one for herself. 'I've brought the weapons you specified too.' Dorias put down the bundle he was carrying and spread it open on the ground. Dendris exclaimed with pleasure as she spotted an axe. There were spears for Aster, a bow and arrows for Theron, knives for everyone and an extra pair of long knives for Deina. She picked them up, checked their weight and balance and stuck them in her belt. Aster caught her eye.

'Almost like old times,' he said with a grin.

'Finally,' Dorias said, 'I would like to present Archis. Critos is claiming sanctuary with us, as is his right as a Battle Wager. In return, I offer Archis, an adept of my House and another Battle Wager, as a volunteer, to represent the Order of Zeus in this undertaking.'

Archis had light brown hair, tied into a long plait, and pale grey eyes. She wasn't gorgeous like Dendris was, with her golden-brown hair and dark skin, but she was tanned and muscled, and her eyes crinkled attractively when she smiled. Similar to the rest of the adepts, her main garment was a plain and rather washed-out tunic. However, Archis had armour too: greaves, guards covering her lower arms, and a moulded breastplate that emphasised her curves and provoked a twinge of jealousy in Deina. Archis drifted over to Tauredos, who was also standing a little apart from the Soul Severers. Two unknowns. It wasn't exactly what Deina had expected, but perhaps it was fitting that at least three of the four Orders of Theodesmioi should have a stake in this particular game of chance.

'Then we are ready,' Anteïs observed. 'All we need is the name of the nymph, and someone to remove the torcs from Tauredos and Archis.' As she turned to look enquiringly at Deina, Nat stepped out of a patch of shadows. Midnight black wings swept wide from his shoulders, casting deep shadows across the lake, and the silvery markings on his arms glowed brightly. Anteïs and the Theodesmioi of the other two houses all dropped to their knees.

Nat extended a hand as if in blessing.

'Your worship is accepted. You may rise. Who is to perform the rite?'

Lysigoras bowed deeply.

'I, my lord.'

'Call on the nymph Ione. She has no reason to love Poseidon.' The god of death surveyed the rest of those

gathered before him. 'And who is to undertake this journey?' Tauredos and Archis stepped forward hesitantly, both flinching as Nat approached them and touched the bronze torcs that encircled their necks with the tip of one finger. The metal shattered. Deina saw the fear in their eyes turn to awe; both touched their necks in wonder as Nat's wings melted to a hint of shadow at his back. Then, to Deina's surprise, he held out his hand to Anteïs. 'And you, Soul Severer – are you ready?'

She let out a long breath and smiled slightly.

'I am, my lord. I just need to say farewell.'

The thing that had been nagging at Deina, the missing element to the scene before her, suddenly crystalised.

Both Nat and Lysigoras had spoken of the need for a sacrifice. Yet there was no animal tied up nearby waiting to be slaughtered.

'Anteïs,' Deina murmured, 'what are you doing?'

'The rite requires a blood sacrifice,' the elder replied. 'A *human* blood sacrifice.'

'How much blood?' Aster murmured nervously. 'A few drops?'

'A death,' Deina said, knowing she was right. She could see it in Anteïs's eyes, in the stoop of her shoulders. She had chosen to sacrifice herself. 'No.' Deina hurried towards her mentor. 'No. There has to be another way. Theron's told you what happens to us after death. You can't –'

'I'm dying anyway, Deina.' She took one of Deina's hands in hers. 'I've been a Severer for long enough to know the symptoms. There's no cure. And though I've prayed to the gods for healing, they've not chosen to hear me.' A flash of anger in her eyes faded into sorrow. 'At least this way I get to die quickly, and for something important.'

Deina struggled to blink away the tears that were filling her eyes. 'No.'

Anteïs lifted one hand to Deina's face and thumbed away the tear tracking down her cheek.

'What would you do instead, Deina? Ask one of your friends to die in my place? They are young and strong, and you need them. Or seize someone from the streets of Iolkos?'

'Yes,' Deina replied. 'Someone unworthy to live. A murderer or – or –'

'Or a thief?' Anteïs said gently. 'No. Aristaeus wouldn't hesitate to make such a judgement, but I do. It has to be this way, child. You have to let me go. Here.' The elder pressed two sealed jars into Deina's hands. 'Some more of the healing ointment I gave you to take to the Underworld, and some more of the tincture to stop your monthly bleed. Dendris has some too.' Deina thanked Anteïs and stowed the jars in her bag while wondering whether the seeds inside her would have the same effect on her cycle as they'd had on her heart. If they did, she could always offer the tincture to Archis. Then she hugged Anteïs tightly, holding her close as she struggled to ignore the voice in her head. *If you were a goddess, you could heal her.*

A bell began tolling in the distance, and Deina felt Theron's hand on her shoulder.

'That's the bell back at the House. They've discovered we're missing.'

Anteïs freed herself from Deina's embrace.

'There's no more time. Critos, you should return with Dorias to the House of Zeus while you still can.'

Another, quicker leave-taking. Critos hugged Deina, Dendris and Aster while Archis and Tauredos waited awkwardly to one side. The former Bronze Guard knelt at Theron's feet.

'I wish I could follow you on this part of your journey, but as I said, I am not the man I was. I'd only slow you down. I am sorry, my king.'

'You have nothing to apologise for, Critos, and you don't ever need to kneel to me.' Theron pulled him to his feet. 'Without your help, we wouldn't have escaped the Cadmea. You've done enough.' He paused. 'I suppose I can't persuade you to leave Iolkos? You'll be safer.'

Critos grinned, shaking his head.

'No more than I seem to be able to persuade you to take your rightful place and rule the Dominion. You know my plan. I'll stay here and do what I can to resist Aristaeus's rule. When you return to Iolkos, I'll be waiting.' He clapped Theron on the shoulder. 'I still hope to see you seated on the throne of Thebes one day.'

'Stranger things could happen.' Theron hugged Critos tightly, raising a hand in farewell as he and the other Theodesmioi of Zeus hurried away. 'Stay safe, my friend.'

'What happens now?' Deina asked, trying to keep her voice steady.

'Anteïs and I will go a little way into the water, and I will sing the rite,' Lysigoras replied. 'The rest of you need to be ready to address the nymph when she appears. At the appropriate moment, I will –' he swallowed hard – 'make the sacrifice.'

'And I myself will sever your lifeline,' Nat added, inclining his head to Anteïs. 'You are deserving of that honour.' The shadow wings took on substance again, and Nat drew his sword. Even though she'd seen it in the memory he showed them, Deina couldn't help taking a step back any more than she could look away from the fierce silver flames that formed the blade. 'As for the rest of you,' Nat continued, 'call on me when you return to the mortal lands.'

'You're not coming with us?' Deina asked.

He sauntered closer to Deina.

'My presence would place you all in danger. Poseidon spends more than half his time away from his realm, lounging around Olympus with the rest of his upstart siblings and their offspring.' Nat's voice was drenched in disdain. 'Yet, wherever he is, if I, a god, try to enter his palace, he'll know about it. *Your* appearance there will hopefully go unnoticed.' Wrapping his wings around her, sealing them into their own private space, Nat bent his head to hers. Despite herself, Deina couldn't resist gazing up at him. 'Anteïs will not suffer long, I promise you,' he said softly, stealing a fleeting kiss before releasing her.

Deina joined Theron by the edge of the lake, ignoring his questioning glance. Lysigoras and Anteïs were already standing on one of the lower steps, knee deep in the brackish water. Things had been laid out on the grass: a bowl that looked to be carved from pine, filled to the brim with some dark liquid; a small, beautifully carved statue of a horse; a knife. Lifting the statue over his head, Lysigoras began singing. Many of the words were unrecognisable – the remnants of some much older language, Deina guessed, fallen out of use and memory. As far as she could tell, the Sea Singer was singing in honour of Poseidon. He reached the end of a phrase and threw the statue into the water; it sank instantly. Taking up the bowl and the knife, he and Anteïs walked further into the lake, until both were submerged from the waist down. He began singing again. This time, though, the tone of the music was darker, full of pain and longing. Over and over, Lysigoras repeated the name of the nymph: Ione, Ione, Ione. There was beauty in this song, despite the Sea Singer's thin, wavering voice. Deina glanced at Theron. His eyes glittered with unshed tears. Lysigoras sang louder, more urgently. He poured the contents of the bowl over Anteïs's head and dropped the empty vessel into the lake. Raised the knife, still chanting. Gripped the back of Anteïs's head and plunged the knife into her belly.

Theron grabbed Deina's wrist, stopping her from running into the lake as Anteïs cried out and fell sideways into the water. In the same instant Nat slashed his flaming blade through the air. The god of death vanished. Anteïs's body spasmed once, twice, and was still.

The bloodied knife was still in Lysigoras's hand. He tossed it into the lake with a grunt and clambered up the steps to stand next to the others.

A figure rose from the centre of the dark waters.

The nymph was beautiful: voluptuous, with dark, darting eyes and pale skin and long silvery hair that tumbled over her shoulders and torso and spread around her like a cloak. She scooped the bloodied water into her hands and let it run through her fingers and trickle down her arms.

'It's been a long time since someone used that rite. Longer than I can recall. You must want to meet Poseidon badly.' She turned her gaze on the Severers. 'It is a pity you chose the wrong moment. He is on Olympus. I cannot conduct you there.' Seizing Anteïs's body, the nymph swung away from them and started to sink back into the lake.

'Wait,' Deina cried out, 'we don't want to see Poseidon. We just want to get into his palace.'

The nymph paused. Turned her head slightly towards Deina. 'Why?'

'We believe there is something within the palace that we . . . require.'

Releasing Anteïs, leaving the corpse floating on the surface, Ione gave her full attention to Deina.

'You mean you want to steal something from the god?' Her dark eyes, curious, flickered to Deina's forehead. 'I thought you one of the Theodesmioi, but you are merely a thief.'

Deina stepped closer to the edge of the lake.

'Yes. I am a thief.' She spoke proudly; why be ashamed of what she was? Sometimes, taking was the only choice left. 'But I am also Theodesmioi. A Soul Severer.'

'Hmm.' Birdlike, Ione tilted her head sharply back and forth, fixing first Deina then the other Theodesmioi with her gaze. 'Wait there. I must take my sacrifice home, but I'll return.' Ione seized Anteïs's body and dragged it beneath the water.

'Farewell, Anteïs.' Aster choked out the words.

Deina couldn't find any words worth saying. She tried to focus instead on the scream of the gulls and the wash of the waves she could hear beyond the boundary wall. When Deina

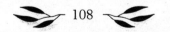

thought of freedom, she always thought of the sea. Freedom was what Anteïs had wanted too, wasn't it? Freedom for all those who, like her, were bound to the will of the gods. Deina ground her teeth together.

No more tyrants. No more torcs.

Ione reappeared and launched herself through the water in one swift movement towards the rim of the lake. She beckoned to Deina. 'Come closer.' Deina obeyed, crouching at the edge. The nymph reached up towards Deina's chest. A look of surprise flashed across her face. 'A thief, and a Soul Severer, and something else besides.' Ione's gaze shifted to Theron, Aster and Dendris, as if she were weighing them all up. 'This thing you want – will Poseidon regret its loss?'

'Yes. If we succeed in our final aim, I believe he will regret it deeply.'

Ione broke into a smile.

'Oh, I should like to see him suffer.' She nodded. 'Very well. I will take you into Poseidon's realm. And if you survive the journey, I'll show you a back way into the palace, past the god's guards.'

If they survived? Deina glanced at the others.

'What exactly does the journey involve?' Theron asked.

Instead of answering, Ione stretched luxuriously. And as she stretched, she changed, shedding her previous appearance like a worn tunic. Her skin took on a bluish hue. What Deina had thought was hair now looked like long strands of dark green seaweed. Horns of red coral twisted up from the nymph's skull. Her hands were webbed, and instead of nails, sharply pointed seashells grew from the ends of her fingers. Only her quick, dark eyes remained the same.

Ione's grin grew wider, revealing small, shark-like teeth.

'Water. Lots and lots of water.'

The nymph sketched out, with very little detail, what they would be required to undergo. She would provide them with temporary gills, though she wouldn't tell them how, and would work a spell that would protect them and their things from the worst of the water. Then, she would summon a fierce current that would draw them through the sea and into Poseidon's realm. If they left the current, they would be lost. If they were attacked, and failed to defeat their attackers, they would be lost. And if they resisted the current, and spent too long in the water, the gills would disappear before they reached the palace, and they would be lost.

'But we can't even swim,' Aster objected. 'How are we expected to fight off something that attacks us underwater? Surely there must be another way?'

Ione shook her head.

'There is no other way. So, what is it to be?' she asked brightly, looking from face to face. 'I have things to do. Any other questions, or shall we proceed?'

'I have a question,' Dendris said. 'I should like to know why you are helping us. Why do you want to punish Poseidon? What exactly did he do to you?'

The nymph scowled. Deina held her breath, ready to reach for her knife – though she was glad the perilous escape from Thebes hadn't altered Dendris's bluntness, she could wish the Mycenaean had waited until *after* they'd reached Poseidon's palace.

Eventually, Ione shrugged.

'He desired me, so he took me against my will. I suppose I should be grateful the crime was not committed in a temple. Even mortals know what happened to my cousin, Medusa.'

Deina's stomach turned. She'd heard the story but had believed it to be myth: Poseidon had raped Medusa in one of Athena's temples. Athena had punished not the god, but the girl, by turning her into a gorgon.

'I'm sorry.'

'Then carry out your plan. Steal this bauble from Poseidon, that he might weep from the loss of it.' She plunged her hands down into the water. 'The tide turns. We must begin. Anyone who does not wish to journey to Poseidon's realm must leave. Now.' As Lysigoras raised one hand in farewell and hurried towards the shelter of the trees, Ione climbed to the top of the steps leading into the lake, faced the water and raised her arms. A deep, inhuman roar issued from her mouth, forcing Deina to cover her ears; if there were words in the nymph's cry, she couldn't make them out. The surface of the lake began to ripple, and the ripples turned into waves that began to spiral around the centre of the lake, faster and faster. Ione had formed a whirlpool. She turned to the Theodesmioi, raising her voice to be heard over the clamour of the water.

'Once you have your gills, you must step into the water immediately. Otherwise you will drown up here.' She pointed at Aster. 'You first.'

He nodded, though Deina could see he was terrified.

'What's going to happen?'

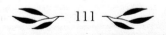

'Some pleasure and some pain. I must kiss you, to give you my breath and protection, and to seal your mouth and nose. And at the same time . . .' She held up her fingers with their sharp seashells.

Aster took a deep breath and walked to where Ione was waiting. She put her hands on his neck, placed her lips on his and dragged her fingertips savagely across his skin. Aster moaned. Yet there was no blood. When Ione released him, Deina saw four gills on either side of his neck – they looked as if they had always been there. Aster's nostrils were strangely pinched together. He started to fight for breath, eyes bulging, his jaw working as he tried and failed to open his mouth. He stumbled forward, fell into the whirlpool and was instantly dragged under the water.

The nymph had already transformed Dendris; the Mycenaean threw herself into the lake. Theron followed her, then Archis and Tauredos. Finally, Ione was facing Deina. She smiled as she reached for Deina's neck. Her lips and her fingers were clammy. Deina tried not to shudder as the nymph kissed her. Pain lanced through her neck, even as her face lost all sensation. Her lungs burned. Desperate for air, Deina fought the impulse to stay on dry land, staggered towards the lake and fell into the heart of the whirlpool.

8

The cold, dark water closed over Deina's head as the current dragged her swiftly down. Panic made her thrash about and sent her clawing at her mouth, trying to tear her lips open, to breath – until she realised that ache in her lungs was easing. She wasn't suffocating. Or drowning. She concentrated on trying to relax, to stretch out her limbs so that she was moving with the water and not fighting against it, like a blade slicing through the sea.

Yes. A knife. A weapon, bringing destruction to the gods . . .

A better image to think about than Anteïs falling into the sea, or Anteïs's blood darkening the water. Gradually the light ebbed, and the shadowy figure of the Sea Singer, Tauredos, just ahead of her in the swift stream, disappeared into the murk. The roar of water in her ears grew louder. Now, she felt rather than saw that the current was sucking her into a tunnel. Stony walls buffeted her and scraped her knees and elbows; she screwed her eyes shut and covered her head with her arms as the current strengthened. The tunnel narrowed further, the rush of icy liquid across her skin grew faster and faster, until finally, when she thought the pressure might crush her, she was shot, like an arrow from a bow, out of the tunnel and into open water.

Deina blinked. It was much lighter here, as if there were a bright, open sky above her. Was she in the sea that lapped Iolkos's coast? The current was still pulling her rapidly along. She could see Tauredos ahead of her again. Nearer at hand were fish, brightly coloured and glittering. She watched them with interest as they darted in swift schools around richly hued corals and boulders thickly crusted with barnacles and seashells and the waving fronds of underwater plants. Sharks and squid and huge crabs, things she'd only seen before as carcasses offered for sale at one of the city's markets. After a while, the water grew colder, and she saw larger creatures still, with groves of plants growing on their flanks and tiny fish grazing on their fins; entire worlds in miniature. There were nameless, glowing terrors with tentacles trailing behind them, longer than three or four ships put together. And in the shadows, other beings lurked. She caught brief glimpses of human faces and torsos tapering into long, powerfully muscled tails: tritons. This was no normal sea. Deina glanced at her waist, checking that her knives were still in their scabbards. Despite the beauty around her, despite the strangeness of her surroundings, she hadn't forgotten Ione's warnings. The prickling at the base of her skull whispered of unknown dangers.

Things passed above her, casting distorted shadows across the rocky outcrop below. Deina twisted onto her back. She squinted, but the rushing weight of water made it impossible for her to distinguish any details. The creatures had wide wings, that was all she could be certain of. Some sort of bird? Confined within Iolkos by her spell-cast torc for almost her entire life, she knew little of seabirds. Besides, given where they were, was it likely the owner of the wings was something as ordinary as a bird? The shadows grew larger as the creature flew downwards until they broke through the surface of the water like a fall of spears. One of the creatures swam back up towards Deina, keeping pace effortlessly with the swift current, and folded its wings behind its body.

Dark wings that glistened as if gem encrusted. Bird feathers covered the creature's lower half too, and it had talons for feet. Yet Deina saw with a shock that its head and upper torso belonged to a mortal woman. A beautiful woman with flowing golden hair and large eyes.

The siren smiled at Deina, opened her mouth and began to sing.

It shouldn't have been possible. The siren's mouth should have filled with water, the sound should have been muffled or drowned out by the rush of the current that was carrying Deina forward. But Deina could hear the song as clearly as if she and the siren had been sitting together in the night-time silence of the great hall back at the House. And she'd never heard anything like it. Not even Theron's voice could compare. A tremor shot through her body, a feeling of such intense longing that she thought her static heart might jolt free of the bonds of the Underworld. The siren sang in no language that Deina recognised, yet somehow she knew exactly what the song expressed: the joy of returning home after long and agonising separation, and finding that you are not only recognised, but have been missed. That you are still remembered, and still loved.

The siren's wings became arms, and she reached out as if to draw Deina into her embrace, and the song changed. Now, the siren sang of peace, and warmth, and safety.

Wasn't that exactly what Deina wanted? She glanced around, suddenly confused. This place – it wasn't where she belonged. Why were they here? The siren must have come to rescue her. To take her somewhere wonderful where she could listen forever to that enchanting music. The strength of the current made it difficult, but Deina stretched out towards the siren's delicate, long-fingered hand. She was almost close enough. The siren's fingertips grazed her wrist.

Something sharp raked across Deina's skin, sending a cloud of blood into the water and a jolt of pain up Deina's arm, and for an instant the siren's appearance seemed to flicker into something else: something with a vicious hooked beak, scale-covered skin and wingtips that ended in claws. Deina remembered. The siren wasn't trying to help her. It was the attacker Ione had mentioned.

The siren smoothed the anger from its face and, beautiful again, sang even more sweetly. This ravishing woman was imploring Deina to leave the current and come with her; the craving her song ignited in Deina's core was almost irresistible. She would have thrown herself into the siren's arms if the ache in her wrist hadn't tethered some part of her mind to where she was. Who she was. Blood was still flowing from the ragged wounds the siren had inflicted. Deina dug her own nails into the gashes. Gouged at her flesh. The hurt was real, and intense enough to change the way she heard the siren's song. Through the veil of her own pain, the creature's voice lost its beauty. It became a wordless howl of hunger – resentful, threatening . . .

As abruptly as it had arrived, the siren swept up out of the water. Had it given up? Deina twisted round, scanning the sky above the water for shadowy wings. Ahead, Tauredos was fighting to free himself from another siren. The creature kicked him out of the current; Deina just managed to grab his hand and pull him into her wake as she shot past him. Claws raked across her back, seizing her and dragging her up towards the surface of the water. Deina thrashed about; the siren dropped her and she tumbled back into the current. It was getting harder to breathe. Touching her neck, Deina found that all but two of the gills had disappeared. She was running out of time. Yet the siren, relentless, was already starting another descent. Deina fought the dizziness blurring her vision and scrabbled to pull one of her knives out of its scabbard. The siren seized her again, talons tangling in her hair and sending a wave of pain across her scalp. Deina fought to free herself, slashing wildly – futilely – with the knife. Up and up through the water the siren pulled her, until they broke the surface. Deina's mouth and nose unsealed as the last pair of gills vanished. Dragging air into her lungs, she reached up, grabbed one of the siren's feathered legs, yanked the creature towards her and with all her remaining strength drove the knife upward. Warm blood splashed onto Deina's arm as the siren let out an agonised shriek and lost its grip. Deina plunged back towards the water, catching a glimpse of a whole flock of sirens. Some were still circling, others flying away towards an island rising out of the sea in the distance. The water closed over her head. The current claimed her, sweeping her onwards. But without the gills she couldn't breathe, and the air she'd manage to gulp before going under wasn't going to last long.

Is this it, Nat? Am I going to die here? Is that even possible, if I'm claimed by the Underworld already?

Deina fought against the urge to open her mouth. It was brighter ahead – if she could just hold on a little longer . . .

The current spat her out, not a moment too soon, onto a small beach of warm golden sand. The others . . . Deina's shoulders sagged. All there, all alive. All injured, though; everyone seemed to be nursing wounds inflicted by the sirens' talons. She could hear Aster cursing. Pulling her bag from her shoulders, Deina checked the sandglass – the dust was still slowly spiralling, but only a thin layer filled the bottom bulb so far – and stretched out on the sand. She caught her breath and squinted up at the blue sky. It was cloudless. Beautiful. Wrong. Too much green in the blue, for a start. Wincing at the pain in her back and scalp, Deina pushed herself slowly onto her feet and saw that the sky was not a sky at all. It was a huge dome, pale teal and smooth, stretching from horizon to horizon. She could just make out shapes moving beyond it; the shadowy forms of immense creatures swimming in whatever sea lay beyond the dome. Within lay a wide expanse of water that lapped the beach on which she now stood. Points of light twinkled among the waves, as though stars had been drowned in their depths. Behind her was a low band of rock; she climbed on top of it and realised that the beach and the rocks curved away from her in both directions, forming a circle. At the centre of the circle, in the distance, stood the island she'd glimpsed earlier. Between the island and the circle of rock was a lake of clear, shallow water. And on top of the island stood a palace.

Too ordinary a word for such a building. Even from here, Deina could tell it was far larger than the megaron that sat at the centre of the Cadmea in Thebes, and it glowed with bright bands of colour.

There was a yelp of pain from somewhere behind her – Theron. Deina jumped down from the rocks and hurried towards him. Dendris, still wrapping a bandage around her forearm, reached him at the same time and hovered protectively next to him.

'What's the matter?' Deina demanded.

'Is it your knee again?' Dendris asked. 'He twisted it badly during the fight outside Gla. I keep telling him to bind it up, but does he listen to me? He does not.' She shook her head and frowned at Theron, but there was no anger in her eyes. Only warmth.

'It's not my knee,' Theron replied through gritted teeth, glaring up at the circle of faces now surrounding him. He shifted position and pointed to something imbedded in the back of his calf.

Aster gave a low whistle.

'What is that – a tooth?'

'Pull it out quickly,' advised Archis.

'No!' Moving surprisingly swiftly for such a large man, Tauredos knelt and grabbed Theron's wrist. 'That's the claw of a siren. If you just yank it out, the poison sack at the end will break open and infect the wound. You'll be dead within

 119

hours. Luckily, I brought my tools with me.' The Sea Singer opened his bag and pulled out a small roll of fabric. Inside were various small bronze and iron implements. Tauredos selected something that looked like a curved needle and held it delicately between thumb and forefinger. 'This is for sails, but I think I can dig out the claw and –'

Theron drew back, pulling his wrist free.

'No.' He shook his head, vehemently. 'Dig it out? I don't think so.'

Tauredos sighed, loudly. 'The alternative, other than letting you die, of course, would be to remove the entire limb. It's your choice, Severer. But I suggest you choose quicky.'

Aster squatted down next to his friend. 'You had better let him do it, Theron.' He looked up at the Sea Singer and smiled at him brightly. 'Besides, I am sure our friend here knows what he is doing.'

'I do.' Tauredos nodded in agreement. 'And I will be gentle. I will even sew you up afterwards.'

Theron grunted. 'Fine. Let's just get it over with.'

Deina rummaged in her bag for the jar Anteïs had given her and held it out to Tauredos.

'Healing ointment.'

'I'll use it afterwards. You look as if you could do with it yourself first.' Deina remembered the gashes on her scalp and back, and they began to throb with pain. Tauredos shooed her, Dendris and Archis away. 'I need an assistant, but not an audience.'

Deina walked along the beach, the other two women trailing after her. The first thing was to wash off as much of the blood – her own, and the siren's – as she could manage. She climbed back onto the rocks and knelt to scoop up some of the clear water from the lake. But something made her hesitate. The hairs on her arms stood up, and the skin at the back of her neck prickled, as if there was something dangerous about the water itself or the coarse grey sand that formed the lakebed. Deina shivered. Returning to the beach, she used a small amount of her drinking water to rinse the wounds instead. As she was applying Anteïs's ointment, she listened to Dendris and Archis, who had settled on the boulders nearby and were chatting.

'. . . so that's when we decided,' Dendris was saying. 'We had to act. Aristaeus is dangerous enough without Hephaestus's torc. And perhaps we can use it to benefit all the Theodesmioi. What about you, Archis? Why did you volunteer for this?'

The Battle Wager gave a short laugh.

'Nothing more selfless than wishing to be freed from my own torc. I've sworn an oath to help find these fragments you seek. Once the task is complete – if we survive – I plan to disappear.'

'Won't your Order hunt you down?'

'They might try, and if they find me, they'll kill me.'

Deina pushed the lid of the jar back on and turned to the others just in time to see Archis grin.

'But they'll have to find me first.' The Battle Wager stood and looked around with her hands on her hips. 'I thought Ione said she would meet us here. I'd like to get this over with.'

'Would you?' a voice asked.

Deina spun round to see Ione striding out of the waves and onto the beach. The nymph hadn't troubled to resume

her more attractive appearance. 'You might regret your wish sooner than you think.'

Deina inclined her head.

'Thank you for getting us this far.'

'You survived the sirens, I see.' Ione looked over to where Theron, with Aster and Tauredos either side of him, was limping towards them across the sand. 'Just about.'

'Will you tell us how to get into the palace now? You mentioned a back way . . .'

'I will show you.' Ione climbed up onto the rocky ridge. When everyone had joined her, she pointed to the island in the centre of the lake. 'Do you see the overhanging rocks just there, on the right? There is a small cave at their base, the entrance to a tunnel that leads down into the palace.'

'Down?' Theron questioned.

'The building you see is only the topmost layer of Poseidon's home. It continues through and below the island. The treasury lies at the bottom. I suggest you begin your search there.' Ione smiled, revealing her needle-like teeth. 'It may take you some time. A few hours. A few days. Maybe longer.'

Deina couldn't help glancing at the sandglass.

The nymph was holding out an orb. It was similar in size to that used by Nat to show them his memory of the torc, but it shone with a pale blue light.

'Something to light your way,' Ione said. 'The palace is lit, but the tunnel is long forgotten. You'll need to watch your steps.' She thrust the orb towards Deina, but Deina shook her head. Her last experience of a magic lamp, the crystal dagger she stole from Orpheus, had not ended well.

'Dendris, you take it.'

The Mycenaean took the globe and held it up before her eyes, examining it curiously. She shook it, and the glow increased a little. 'There's water inside.'

Ione nodded. 'The sea has its own secrets of which even Poseidon knows nothing. I'll leave you now. If you make it back here, throw this –' she tapped the rock crystal globe – 'into the sea. I'll come and find you.' She leaped down from the rocks and began to walk away, pausing for a moment just before she reached the sea. 'I nearly forgot – to cross the lake, you must summon the horses. To touch the grey sand that lies at the bottom of the lake is death, for mortals at least.'

'Wait,' Theron cried out, swearing as he struggled to follow the nymph down onto the beach. 'What horses? Summon them how?'

Ione was already wading into the water.

'Use a sea snail. There should be one around somewhere.' The nymph dived forward, and the waves closed over her head.

Theron looked back up at the others and spread his hands wide. 'A sea snail? What in the name of the gods are we supposed to do with a sea snail?'

Deina summoned the strength to raise an eyebrow.

'In the name of the gods?'

Theron smiled slightly.

'Old habits.' He sighed. 'I don't even know what a sea snail looks like.'

Tauredos made his way down onto the golden sand of the beach and pulled a knife from his belt.

'I'll show you. We have songs of learning as well as the Songs

123

for rites in the Order of Poseidon. Songs to teach charting a course and setting a sail, and some about sea creatures, to help us learn which are dangerous to a ship and which are good to eat. They have drawings, back at the House.' Swiftly, he drew a few lines in the sand. 'That's the sort of shell we need to look for. They're about so big.' He held his palms about a hand's length apart then scratched his head, frowning. 'There was something in one of the songs about how they could be used as a sort of instrument, to warn other boats if you were caught in a fog bank.'

Everyone scattered, searching for something that looked like the Sea Singer's drawing, turning over rocks and poking among the long tangles of seaweed that had been washed up onto the beach. The smell made Deina wrinkle her nose. She was relieved when there was a shout of success from Archis.

'What do we do with it now?' she asked Tauredos.

He brought his roll of instruments out again and – in an unhurried, measured way that made the Battle Wager start tapping her foot on the damp sand – made a hole in the point of the shell. Gingerly, he lifted the shell to his mouth and blew, seeming as surprised as everyone else when a soft note sounded. Quickly, they climbed back up onto the rocky ridge. Tauredos blew through the shell again, more confidently this time, letting the note sound out across the lake. As Theron took the shell to examine it – he never could resist any sort of musical instrument – the surface of the clear water started to shimmer, to ruffle as if a wind was blowing across it even though the air was as still as ever. Higher and higher the waves mounted, and their white caps grew and grew until the foam lifted into the air and spun itself into a herd of horses, whose white coats swirled as if woven from mist. The lake became placid again. The horses trotted forwards. Not towards Tauredos, but towards Deina. When they reached the edge of the lake below where she stood they gathered together, tossing their heads, waiting.

Deina glanced back at the others.

'Does anyone know how to ride?'

'I could steer them,' Archis offered, 'if they were pulling a chariot. Otherwise . . .' She shook her head. No one else said anything.

'I suppose we just climb on and try not to fall off,' Deina muttered, clambering down to the lake edge and reaching for the nearest horse. It was slightly transparent and cold to the touch, but it felt solid enough when her fingers grasped its mane. The horse seemed to know what she wanted; it came close, to allow her to swing one leg over its back and put her arms around its neck. As soon as everyone was mounted, her horse began to lead the others through the lake, racing towards the island, leaping up into the air and dropping down into the water, their movement mirroring the undulation of the waves. Deina bent low, holding on tightly, pressing her cheek against the horse's soft coat. Still, she smiled, despite the risk; it was almost like being back on Orpheus's ship in the storm. The same sense of danger, of being more fully alive. Even though her heart remained stubbornly still.

As they approached the island her horse changed course and slowed, heading for the overhanging rocks Ione had pointed out. There was a small, sloping beach here; the horse trotted up onto the sand and Deina slid awkwardly off its back. It neighed and nudged her shoulder with its muzzle. She lifted her hand to pat it, to thank it, but the horse dissolved into a spill of foam even as her fingertips brushed against it.

Sadly, she turned and craned her neck to look up at the bulk of the palace above as she waited for the others to join her. The outside was covered in bands of shells – white, or brightly coloured in more shades than she could count – weaving their way across arcades, towers and walls. It looked like a place of peace and beauty, until something emerged from one of the archways. The creature was obviously a guard: it was armed with a trident, and a spiral seashell – much larger than the one Tauredos had used – was slung across its shoulders. It was a hybrid, just like the sirens and the tritons she'd seen lurking among the coral reefs. It had the upper body, arms and head of a man. But from the waist down, where there should have been human legs, Deina saw instead the tail, legs and pincers of a giant lobster. She shuddered. The guard lifted his shell to his lips and blew a blast that echoed across the rocky landscape, sending the rainbow-hued lizards basking just above Deina's head dashing into a nearby crevice to hide.

Exactly what we should be doing.

Silently, the Severers shrank into the shadows at the base of the cliff. Dendris pointed; they followed her into the small cave almost hidden behind huge boulders. The cave narrowed rapidly, becoming little more than a cleft in the rock. About two-thirds of the way into the cleft, just as it was starting to get uncomfortably tight, Dendris stopped and held up the orb Ione had given her. Its light revealed the entrance to a tunnel, concealed within an angle of the rock.

'Are we ready?' Dendris asked.

'As ready as we ever are,' Theron murmured, his voice echoing from the cave walls. 'If we survive this, I'd like to spend a long time somewhere really quiet doing absolutely nothing at all.'

As Aster nodded in agreement, Deina followed the others into the damp, airless tunnel.

9

They walked in silence, the floor sloping gently downwards. The roar of the waves crashing against the beach gradually faded into the drip of water. Otherwise, all Deina could hear was the breathing of her companions – punctuated by a curse when one or other of them stubbed a toe on some unnoticed rock – and Theron's humming. Odd musical phrases, that sounded melancholy, and didn't seem to be from one of the rites or from any tune Deina recognised. On and on the tunnel wound. Every so often Dendris, ahead, shook the globe she carried, and the gloom lifted a little. But only a little. They walked for so long that Deina began to wonder if Ione had tricked them. It felt as if they had been walking for hours; Deina found herself checking the sandglass more and more frequently, squinting at the pale glitter of the falling dust. On and on, and Dendris had to shake the globe more frequently. Whatever magic conjured the light, it was slowly fading. Theron stopped singing and no one said much, apart from Tauredos grumbling occasionally about the narrowness of the passage, and Aster complaining every so often about how hungry he was, but Deina could sense the rising anxiety. If they were left down here in the darkness, would they really be able to find their way back out? Deina swore as she wiped another trickle of water from her face. The constant drip of water against rock was setting her nerves on edge.

Dendris stopped so suddenly that Aster, second in line, strode straight into her.

'Ow!' Dendris swore, fumbling to keep hold of the orb. 'That was my elbow!'

'So why did you stop?' Aster asked, rubbing his hand.

'Listen.' Dendris looked back at them expectantly.

Theron frowned and tilted his head. 'Is that –'

'Hammering,' Archis broke in quickly.

Deina strained her ears. Archis was right. Mixed in among the constant plink, plink of water dropping from the tunnel roof was something else, something subtly different. She slid one blade from her belt – if they had to fight in the cramped confines of the tunnel, it would be knifework – and followed Theron onwards.

The sound of hammering grew louder. Faint light showed up ahead, and another twist in the tunnel revealed its source. The tunnel ended immediately below some sort of disc, about an arm's length in diameter, that had been pierced with multiple holes; the light was filtering through the holes, together with the sound of hammering and a murmur that Deina realised was someone singing softly. The disc was set into the roof of the tunnel. Theron, the tallest, stretched up his arm and jumped, but it was too high even for him to reach unaided.

Aster pulled out one of his spears, grasped the iron counterbalance and lifted the spear up above his head. The tip of the bronze, leaf-shaped blade just scraped across the disc. He sighed and let the spear slip down between his hands.

'Not long enough. And it sounds like that disc is metal, so it will be heavy.' He shook his head and huffed. 'I thought after Chalcis, we were done with being stuck in dark, dangerous tunnels. Do you remember? We'll have to tell Critos about this when we get back – he'll be sad he missed it.'

Theron and Dendris both nodded and smiled grimly.

Deina watched them. Despite their surroundings, despite the threat hanging over them, there was something in the way the three of them were looking at each other that sent jealousy stabbing through her. Escaping from Thebes together had changed them and their relationship. Had brought them closer. She realised that she felt excluded, and the realisation shamed her. Archis was watching them too; the slightly wistful expression on her face made Deina warm to the Battle Wager.

'Theron,' she said, 'hoist me up on your shoulders. I'll see if I can push this disc thing up and have a look around.'

'I don't reckon you should be putting extra weight on your leg this soon,' observed Tauredos. 'Despite the quality of my craftsmanship, the stitches might not hold.'

'I'll be fine.' Theron crouched down for Deina to straddle his shoulders. The Sea Singer shrugged and moved out of the way. Theron stood carefully, but he wobbled a little. Deina automatically grabbed his head.

'Gods, Deina – do you deliberately sharpen your fingernails? I'm quite attached to that eyebrow if you don't mind . . .'

'Sorry.' Deina changed her grip. As the other four positioned themselves nearby, ready to catch her, she steadied herself, then reached up towards the disc. Not close enough, not by a long way. She could just about push the disc up with her fingertips – as Aster suspected, it was heavy and wrought from some sort of metal – but she couldn't glimpse what lay above. 'I'll need to get up on your shoulders.'

'But you'll fall,' Theron objected.

'I won't fall.' She paused, then added, 'I won't fall as long as you stay still.'

'No pressure, then,' Aster murmured.

Deina shifted position to get her left foot up onto Theron's shoulder. He grabbed her ankle, grunting in discomfort. Trying to ignore the way his muscles were trembling beneath her weight, she tilted her head back to study the disc. The holes with which it was pierced were large enough for her to slip her fingers into them. If she got up quickly, she could grab the disc as she crouched on Theron's shoulders.

'Right.' Deina tensed her muscles. 'I'm going to push off now –' Surging upwards, she jammed her fingers into the holes and pulled herself up until she had both feet on Theron's shoulders. They both wobbled dangerously. Aster and Tauredos grabbed Theron, trying to steady him. Deina hung there for a moment.

'Are you sure about this?' Theron called up. 'When you push the disc up, you'll be unsupported. It might unbalance you.'

Deina grinned down at him, trying to project a confidence she wasn't really feeling.

'I know what I'm doing. I'm a demi-god, remember?'

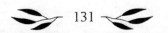

No one laughed.

Perhaps reminding them that you're different isn't the best way of trying to become part of the team again.

She closed her eyes for a moment, trying to bury her irritation and doubt and find the point of balance, and pushed upwards very carefully. As the disc lifted, she glimpsed a large stone block right in front of her and a floor stretching away towards a wall. There was someone – she could only see their legs – standing in front of the wall. Was that where the singing was coming from? With a grunt, she managed to shove the edge of the disc onto the surrounding floor and grabbed the edge of the circular opening with one hand. Braced, she thrust the disc further onto the floor. The noise of metal scraping across stone was loud enough that she was sure someone would come to investigate. But the owner of the legs didn't move. Once she had enough space, she slowly straightened up.

The legs belonged to a man – or something man-shaped, Deina corrected herself – who was standing close to the opposite wall. He seemed to be painting or cleaning the wall; whatever his role, he was obviously consumed by his work and still hadn't paid any attention to Deina's intrusion. His soft, melodious singing was the only noise. She took advantage of his absorption to look around. The walls of the room were covered with paintings of what Deina would have taken for huge but ordinary flowers, if it had not been for the fish depicted darting among the leaves and stems. The floor had been laid with different coloured marble tiles to create the same effect; the metal disc she had just pushed aside was the centre of one huge flower. There were doors at each end of the room and along its length too. Statues had been placed at intervals along the walls; the stone block in front of her was the base of one. Pools of flickering blue-green light were cast by huge crystal globes – larger versions of the orb carried by Dendris – that were set in niches carved into the walls; Deina could see glowing fish swimming about inside them.

'Deina,' Aster called quietly, 'what's happening?'

In answer, Deina pulled herself up through the opening. Strangely, the singing man still didn't react. His single-minded, unswerving focus reminded her of the Iron Guards spellbound within their spell-cast armour. Aristaeus and Orpheus both had found a way to control mortal minds and bodies. And she knew a god could do the same, even more easily. Hades had done it to her. The memory of her own hand, about to plunge a needle into her eye, made Deina shudder.

'I think it's safe,' she whispered down. 'There's someone here, but he doesn't seem to be aware of me. Poseidon must have him under a spell or something.' She beckoned for them to follow her. 'Come on.'

She could hear the others having a muted discussion. Then Aster knelt so Dendris could climb onto his back. Deina stretched out her arms and caught hold of one of Dendris's hands, helping the other woman balance as she carefully stood on Aster's shoulders. Another moment and Dendris was crouched next to her. They both reached down to help pull Archis through the opening. Theron came next. There was a pause – it sounded to Deina as if Aster and Tauredos were arguing over who should go last. She guessed the Sea Singer lost; his disgruntled face emerged a moment later and he heaved himself onto solid ground. Only Aster remained in the tunnel.

'Hold on to my legs,' Tauredos commanded. He shuffled forward until his whole upper body was dangling into the tunnel. Even with four of them hanging on to him, it was difficult. Deina gritted her teeth as she tried to brace herself against the smooth marble floor, jamming her fingernails into a small imperfection in the stone. Still, Tauredos slid forward.

'Hurry!' Theron's voice was strained with effort.

Aster's head appeared. Theron risked reaching forward to grab him and pull him the rest of the way out. Tauredos rolled away from the hole and lay on the floor, gasping.

'What are you made of Aster? Lead?'

Aster laughed softly.

'That, Sea Singer, is the weight of pure heroism. Come on.' He held out a hand to pull Tauredos upright. 'Let's go find some treasure.'

They were presented with their first choice at the end of the decorated hall, where there were flights of stairs leading both up and down.

'Which way?' asked Dendris, peering down the stairwell. 'The nymph said to start with the treasury. The question is, can we trust her?'

Deina realised the others were looking at her. Perhaps she'd overplayed her hand with the demi-god remark. She shrugged, rubbing the back of her neck with one hand.

'We could try the treasury. Remember what Nat said, though?' She added, for the benefit of Archis and Tauredos, 'Thanatos, the god of death.'

'Huh.' Archis gave her an appraising glance. 'You're on familiar terms with this particular deity, then.'

'It's a long story,' Deina replied. 'Thanatos told us the fragments of the torc were hidden by Tyche, the goddess of luck. And he suggested she might have treated hiding the fragments as something of a challenge. Or a game, even.' She sighed. 'We all know how the gods like to entertain themselves. How they like to continually prove to themselves how much cleverer they are than mere mortals, and each other.'

Silence, apart from the faint sounds of singing and metal on stone.

'What would you do?' Theron nudged Deina gently. 'Can you somehow try to think like one of them?'

'But I'm not one of them,' Deina insisted immediately. 'I'm a bit stronger than I was, that's all. I don't know what Tyche did.' She couldn't help feeling as if there was something sceptical in the way the others were looking at her. 'I don't.'

'You are closer to being a god than the rest of us, though. And you've always had a talent for sourcing things.' Theron broke into a quick grin. 'Like when we were apprentices, and Phanius wanted lead, and you stole some from the smithy. Remember? This is the same.'

Deina sighed. Phanius was a nasty and not particularly successful novice who made the apprentices' lives miserable. He'd wanted the lead to conceal in his fists, to give him an unfair advantage in the spring games. Deina had not only found and stolen the lead and sold it to him, she'd also – with Theron's help – convinced the elders Phanius was guilty of the crime and claimed the offered reward. Hardly the same at all, but still – a pleasant memory. She closed her eyes. Theron was right: she was a good thief. And maybe she had inherited something useful from her mother, Hades. Some trait, or some kind of knowledge, that would help them.

What would a god do? What would Hades do? What would I do if I'd been given Tyche's task?

There was no sudden lightning strike of inspiration. Her mind remained stubbornly blank. She groaned.

'This is hopeless. I can't magically –'

'Please.' Theron took her hand. 'We don't know how much time we have, and this place is vast.'

Reluctantly, Deina closed her eyes again. This time, instead of trying to concentrate, she let herself drift on the ebb and flow of her physical sensations. Singing, echoing from a distant hall. The dull metallic thud of hammers. The faint smell of the sea. Cool, damp air against her skin and the solidity of tiles and rock beneath her feet. The taste of salt on her lips. Absorbed by her surroundings, Deina gradually recalled the image of the torc as she'd last seen it in Nat's memory: three strands of metal twisted together and bent into an open circle. Three strands – gold, silver, bronze – each decorated, gleaming in the sunlight . . .

Abruptly, the torc vanished. Deina gasped as it was replaced in her mind's eye by a slender woman with amber eyes and skin the colour of bronze, crowned with an ornate diadem depicting city walls and towers. She gripped Theron's hand more tightly; the image flickered then settled. The detail grew, as if someone somewhere had lit a lamp. The woman – somehow, Deina knew it was Tyche – was standing in a huge, richly decorated room.

The goddess was backing away from her, giggling, and Deina knew with a surge of injured pride that she was not laughing at a joke. She was laughing at her. Or rather, at Poseidon; there was a mirror hanging on a wall behind Tyche, reflecting the goddess's back and the tall, golden-haired god standing before her. When Deina lifted her hand to her face, so did Poseidon. Deina felt herself preening. She was so strong! She had the strength of the sea, the mightiest of all elements! How could Tyche possibly reject her? She decided to give Tyche one more chance to come to her senses, but the goddess had vanished. Her loss. Deina/Poseidon examined her biceps. Time to receive some supplicants. Having people beg him for favours here, in his favourite place, always made him feel better . . .

Someone was shaking her. Theron – his hands were gripping her upper arms tightly.

'What happened? Are you alright?'

Deina's mind was groggy; she couldn't tell if he and the other Theodesmioi were looking at her with concern, confusion or suspicion.

'Hide – hide it in plain sight,' she stammered, feeling the colour rising in her cheeks.

'What do you mean?' Aster questioned.

'That's what I would have done, if I were Tyche.' Deina lifted her chin. 'That's all that came to me: the idea that she'd hide the torc fragment somewhere Poseidon would see it every day without realising it. Somewhere important to him. So – so she could laugh to herself at how stupid he was.' No need to tell anyone she'd actually had a vision, especially a vision in which she'd seen herself as an Olympian.

Slowly, the others began to nod in agreement, though Theron was still staring at her with a slightly troubled expression.

'Upstairs, then,' Aster suggested. 'The throne room. That's usually the most important place in a palace.'

'More likely to be guarded,' Tauredos warned.

'But Poseidon's not here right now, so maybe not.' Archis drew her sword and began to climb the stairs, glancing back over her shoulder and winking. 'I'm willing to take the risk.'

Aster, Tauredos and Theron hurried after her instantly. Deina and Dendris shared a look and set off up the steps together.

The staircase led to another series of long rooms ending in another set of stairs. They climbed these, and the next staircase too, and the one after that; up and up, through seemingly endless galleries. Just like the first room, every space was gorgeous with colour and lit by the same dappled blue-green light. Mosaics made of rainbow-hued stones and shells and glittering jewels were interwoven with intricate wall paintings. Some of the images depicted sea creatures, or branching seaweeds, or glowing corals. Others showed humans, tritons and nymphs engaged in battle, celebration, lovemaking and a hundred other activities. In each room they encountered one or more artists, just like the man they'd seen in the room of flowers, each repairing or adding something to the decoration. All were entirely absorbed in their work. Some were singing or humming softly. Not one was entirely human – or at least, not any more. Most had patches of skin or entire limbs coated in a sheen of iridescent scales or patched with pearl. All had gills. None paid the Severers the least attention. Until Aster, too busy gawping at a painted ceiling, walked into one of them. The artist picked herself up and carried on grinding some gem-like stone into a pigment. Another, however, setting shells into the wall a few strides on, turned from his work as the Severers approached and watched them, curious, until they were out of sight. Deina caught Theron's nervous glance. The same thing happened in the next hall. Dendris, slightly ahead, stopped and beckoned. The Theodesmioi gathered. As Theron got out a waterskin, Aster unwrapped a hunk of dried meat and began tearing off chunks. Dendris cast him a look of mild exasperation.

'Something's obviously changed, thanks to Aster.' She ran a finger thoughtfully along the flat of her axe, ignoring his mumbled protest. 'Do you think we should knock them out? Or tie them up? If they tell those lobster-legged guards we're here . . .'

Deina glanced at the nearest artist. The fixed stare of the man's one remaining human eye – his other eye had been replaced with a large pearl – was unnerving, but his stance wasn't threatening.

'They're not doing us any harm at the moment. I think we should just keep going.'

'I agree,' Tauredos said. 'We should keep moving at a steady pace and avoid doing anything sudden that might draw more attention.'

'We're being too steady, that's the problem,' countered Archis. 'We should go faster and split up – we'll cover more ground that way.'

'No.' Theron glugged down some more water. 'We have to stick together.' He nodded towards the artist. 'As for these poor creatures – we should leave them be. I doubt they chose to be

here, any more than Critos chose to become a Bronze Guard.'
He smiled fleetingly, as if remembering his friend. 'If we had
more time, I'd suggest we talk to them – try to free them even.
As it is, we do need to move faster.' Theron glanced pointedly
at Aster, who quickly shoved the rest of his dried meat back
into his bag. Yet Deina wondered whether he'd noticed her
anxiously checking the sandglass. As they started walking again,
she unhooked it from her belt and hid it in her bag.

More stairs, more galleries. The palace seemed endless.
Finally, just when Deina thought she must have sent them
in entirely the wrong direction, the long room they were in
opened up into a much larger space – a high-ceilinged hall
where huge windows gave views over the lake and the distant
sea. No artists here, but Dendris spotted some guards patrolling.
They had to creep, clinging to the shadows, until they came
to another equally cavernous room with a throne fashioned
from seashells at one end. At the other end hung a huge mirror.

Two more guards suddenly came into view, making their
way along the balcony that ran along the edge of the room.
Deina pressed herself back against the wall, not daring to
move, very aware of the tense stillness of the others around her.
As soon as the guards passed, they all dashed towards a long
table draped with some fine cloth and crammed themselves
into the space beneath. Just in time. Another group of guards
checked inside the throne room before moving on. From under
the table Deina could only see their lobster halves; somehow,
that was even worse.

'That was definitely too close,' breathed Dendris. 'What
now?'

'We won't be able to search the room freely,' Aster whispered. 'Too many patrols.'

'So we need to go straight to the right place.' Archis, Deina realised, was looking at her expectantly. Deina shifted position very slightly, trying to see as much of the room as she could without disturbing the gauzy tablecloth and giving away their location. The walls were covered with the same sort of images they'd seen elsewhere, though here the scope was more majestic. Entire seas were depicted, covered in hundreds of ships, or filled with gargantuan sea creatures. And at the end, behind the throne of seashells, was a depiction of Poseidon himself, reproduced on a grand scale in marble, precious metals and gemstones. The god was shown in a heroic pose: naked, muscular and handsome, emerging from the ocean in a chariot pulled by two hippocamps. These half-fish, half-horse creatures were rearing dramatically as the god brandished a trident in his free hand and mighty waves crashed around him. The image took up the whole height of the wall.

'And I thought Aster was vain . . .' Theron murmured.

Deina concentrated on Poseidon's face, and, suppressing the urge to shiver, stared into the God's grey-blue eyes. His gaze was fixed upon the throne in front of him.

'I'm going to –' Deina broke off as a horn sounded in the distance. Everyone froze. Another guard clattered slowly across the room; Deina had wild thoughts of leaping out from under the table and launching an attack. Finally, the creature disappeared. 'I'm going to try the throne. Wait here.' Leaving her hiding place beneath the table, she made a dash for the throne and ducked behind it, only to find Theron had ignored her command and come after her.

'You don't need to do this all alone. We're a team, remember?' He leaned forward, a little hesitantly, and stole a kiss. 'Let me help you.'

A swell of gratitude made Deina smile. She pointed to the back of the throne, to indicate they should study it more closely. This part of the throne was not covered in seashells at all – instead it was marble, inlaid with precious metals and gemstones. After a few moments, Theron gestured to a picture that ran along the very bottom half: a number of tritons, all gazing up adoring at the representation of Poseidon on the opposite wall. All but one, that was. The expression on this particular triton's face was not what Deina expected. Instead of adoring, this triton looked almost scornful. It was the way his eyebrow curved condescendingly as he gazed up at the god . . .

Deina drew her knife and crouched down to get closer to the triton. This close, she could see that the original eyebrow had been replaced with a curved piece of metal formed of three strands twisted together.

Nice work, Tyche.

It took only moments for her to prise the torc fragment free from the throne. As it dropped into her palm a shiver of something – some slight sense of familiarity – shot down her spine. Experiencing Nat's recollections had clearly affected her. She got up to leave, but Theron gestured for her to wait. Cautiously, he crept round the side of the throne. He held up his hand; Deina shrank back against the throne as the sound of claws on stone signalled another guard patrol. The sound faded. Theron beckoned her onwards and together they raced back to the others. Deina waited, poised, her hand on the hilt of her knife, but there was no indication they'd been seen. She held up the fragment of metal. 'This is it,' she murmured. 'The first part of the torc. It exists. We can do this.' Her words were almost drowned out by another horn blast – closer this time. Aster had taken the fragment and was examining it. He held it out to her, but Deina shook her head. 'It'll be safer with you.' She didn't want to look at the sandglass, gradually sucking away her time, but she knew it was there.

'Are we ready?' Theron whispered. 'We only saw guards on this level. If we can get back down without being seen, we should be safe.'

The throne room and the hall next to it seemed to be clear. Abandoning their hiding place, they raced through the vast rooms and down the first staircase. As far as Deina could tell, they'd not been spotted, but no one seemed inclined to slow down. On they sped across the echoing marble floors of hall after hall. The artists they passed turned to watch them again, but this time their expressions seemed to Deina more hostile than curious. Many of them held chisels and blades. And there was something different about the way they held them. Not threatening – not exactly – yet conjuring up the image of power wanting and waiting to be released, reminding her that a chisel was capable of inflicting brutality as well as creating beauty. And all the time the sound of horns grew louder.

Down and down they went, the muscles in Deina's legs burning, until finally the hall of flowers was ahead of them. As Aster sped past her Deina grabbed his arm and dragged him sideways, forcing him behind the plinth of a statue that lay just beyond the entrance to the hall. The others swerved to follow them.

'Ow!' Aster hissed, rubbing his elbow. 'What did you do that for?'

'A guard – there, at the far end of the hall.' Deina pressed her back against the plinth then peered around its corner.

One of the half-lobster, half-human guards was standing just beyond the far doorway to the hall, blocking their exit. Deina swore and drew back her head.

'We need to distract it. Any ideas?'

'I have a chisel among my tools,' Tauredos said in a low voice. He peeked at the guard and swallowed hard. 'Perhaps I might pretend to be one of the artists. I could gradually work my way along the wall, as if I'm doing something to the decoration, and then when I get close to him . . .' He mimed stabbing the chisel into the guard's torso.

'It's a brave offer,' Aster replied, 'but a chisel alone might not be enough of a disguise. And unless you can silence him instantly other guards could be drawn to the room.'

'And it's too slow,' Archis added. 'More guards might appear in the meantime. We should get his attention and rush him.'

Theron pointed at one of the light-giving globes on the far side of the room they were in now.

'I'm not sure about rushing him, but how easy would it be to smash one of those, do we think? Lobster Legs might scuttle through here to investigate. We could slip into the hall of flowers while his back was turned.'

Deina could hear the fear and uncertainty in Theron's voice, despite his attempt at humour.

Dendris was shaking her head. 'What about the poor fish inside the globe?'

Theron quirked an eyebrow. 'Dendris, I hate to say it, but I really think it's them or us.'

'It's not much of a plan,' Aster muttered, 'but it seems to be the best plan we have.'

It didn't take long for Theron to string his bow and ready his arrow. Deina waited with the others behind the farthest side of the plinth. The first arrow struck the crystal and bounced off. Theron cursed softly.

'Try there.' Archis pointed to what looked like a faint milky streak running through the crystal. 'Battle Wagers are trained to spot weaknesses.'

Were they also trained to be irritating braggarts? Deina had to bite her tongue. Tauredos caught her eye and gave her a quick, understanding smile.

Theron selected another arrow and took aim. The point struck the spot Archis had indicated and stuck fast. Deina held her breath.

A sound like cracking ice, then the globe burst into myriad fragments that clattered across the floor in a rush of water and flapping fish. Deina peered round the plinth. Sure enough, a rattle of claws heralded the arrival of the guard. She tensed, ready to move. Theron had already fitted another arrow to his bow.

Go away, Deina thought urgently, glaring at the guard's back, desperately avoiding looking at the bit where his human body and his lobster body somehow meshed. *Go search the stairs or another room.*

The guard lifted his horn towards his mouth.

'Damn –' Theron loosed his arrow. It plunged into the guard's human chest and cut the horn blast short. Not short enough, though. Another blast sounded in response. 'Run!'

They sprinted into the hall of flowers. Aster dragged the metal disk away from the tunnel entrance. As Theron covered them, his bow bent, Dendris sat on one edge of the hole, gripped the opposite side and swung herself down, followed by Archis, Tauredos and Aster. By the time Deina dropped the final distance to the ground, Dendris had the orb Ione gave them in her hand. She shook it, frowning. The feeble glow flickered uncertainly.

The twang of an arrow being shot was followed by Theron's bow clattering through the hole. Theron himself jumped down immediately after. He hadn't even hit the ground when a muscled arm reached into the tunnel and slashed the air with claw-like fingers.

Aster dragged Theron to his feet and pushed him forward. Everyone hurried to get away, moving as quickly as they could in the cramped confines of the tunnel. Just before they turned the corner, Deina glanced back. One of the guards had got his head and upper body through the hole, but he seemed to be stuck – his lower body, with its huge lobster claws, was not going to fit. No doubt once they found some hammers it would be the work of moments to smash open the roof of the tunnel. Still, it gained them some time.

Up and up they climbed, scrambling through the almost darkness but not daring to slow down, propelled forwards, despite their growing exhaustion, by the thought of what may be coming after them. Theron, weakened by the wound to his leg, was starting to flag when the tunnel twisted a final time and the sudden glare of daylight sliced through the darkness. Deina sped up, racing towards the mouth of the cave and out onto the narrow, sandy beach. Tauredos already had the sea snail shell in his hand. The note he blew set the lake quivering, and the white horses began to form. But the lobster-legged guards on the heights of the palace had spotted them. They began slithering down the side of the island. The arrows they sent flying got closer and closer. As soon as the horses reached the beach Theron dragged Deina out from the rock behind which they'd taken shelter and pushed her towards one of them.

'Quickly!'

The horses started to gallop across the lake, but still the guards were following. Deina looked back and realised with dismay that Poseidon's guards could both swim and shoot their arrows at the same time.

'Faster!' She hoped the horse would understand her and listen. It seemed to; she felt it lurch forward as the wind whipped her hair back from her face. The band of rocks that bordered the lake got closer. They were going to make it. All Dendris had to do was throw the orb into the sea and Ione would rescue them . . .

A cry rang out. An arrow had struck the horse carrying Tauredos, just ahead of her. As Deina watched, the horse dissolved into foam, pitching the Sea Singer into the lake. He struggled to his feet. Deina tried to turn her horse in his direction, holding out her hand so she could pull him up behind her. He started to run towards her until he stumbled, looking down with an exclamation of horror.

Deina gasped.

Tauredos was turning to grey sand. Even as she struggled to reach him, even as the other Theodesmioi cried out in disbelief and fear, his legs crumbled beneath him, pitching him further into the water. The transformation raced like flame up his torso and along his arms. They fell away in chunks. The sand claimed his chest, his neck, his jaw. His body disintegrated and the upper part of his face and head fell towards the surface of the lake. Deina could still see the shock in his eyes as they too dissolved into grey grains that sank from view. Her horse slowed and stopped. Dazed, Deina stared into the clear, harmless-looking water.

'No –' Aster plunged past her to the spot where Tauredos had been standing. For an instant Deina thought he was going to leap from his horse into the sea. Dendris must have thought the same – she roared at him to stop as Deina pushed her mount towards Aster, straining to grab his arm.

'Don't touch the water!'

'Come on, both of you!' The shout came from Archis as she urged her horse forward. Her eyes, as she glanced at the placid shallows, were wide with shock. 'They're gaining.'

Distractedly, Deina turned to look for the others. Theron had wheeled his horse about and was furiously loosing arrows at the pursuing guards. Before Deina could yell at him to stop, to flee, Dendris reached him and began tugging him away from their attackers.

'Please,' Deina heard her say, 'Critos will never forgive me if I return without you.'

She and Theron together drove their mounts towards the rocks bordering the lake.

'Aster, let's go.' With tears in her eyes, Deina urged her horse forwards. Reaching the rocky barrier, she slid from the horse's back and clambered over the ridge of rocks with the others. 'Dendris,' she gasped, 'the orb.'

'They'll be here any moment!' Aster drew his spear.

The Mycenaean hurled the pale blue globe as far as she could into the sea. Ione's green locks emerged from the water and they raced to reach her.

'You're ready to return?' Ione asked.

Deina nodded frantically. An arrow glanced off a rock nearby – one of the guards had gained the top of the ridge.

Ione raised her hand. The whirlpool appeared. Deina yanked Archis out of the way of another arrow as Theron returned the guards' attack and Ione began giving the Theodesmioi gills again. At last, it was Deina's turn. A kiss, a stab of pain, and the nymph pushed her forward into the sea.

Deina's final image of Poseidon's realm, as the waters closed over her head, was of one of the guards launching himself towards her, brandishing a spear in victory at having driven the invaders away.

10

Strong hands grabbed her and hauled Deina out of the water and onto grass half choked with sodden leaves. She looked up into sapphire blue eyes and a mischievous grin. Nat.

'You've been waiting for us?'

'Certainly not – you've been gone for over a month as mortals reckon time, and I do have other places to be. Winter has come to Iolkos in your absence. Winter, and worse.' He ran a fingertip lightly over the gap between her collarbones. 'But we are linked by the Underworld, you and I. I sensed your return to this place.' He jerked his head towards Lysigoras, who was running towards them. 'The Sea Singers have been watching for you, though I think they had begun to despair.'

Deina pushed herself wearily to her feet. The return journey through the sea had been uneventful; no attacks by sirens, and Poseidon's lobster-legged guards hadn't pursued them past the circle of rock. Apart from Tauredos, they'd all made it back to the mortal realm. The others approached. Archis was shivering slightly. Theron was staring at Nat, his mouth flattened into a hostile line.

'My lord . . .' Lysigoras panted, bowing to Nat. 'Soul Severers. I was just informed of your return. Your quest succeeded?'

In answer, Aster pulled the torc fragment from the pouch that hung from his belt and held it out. Everyone, including the god of death, crowded closer.

Archis pointed at some marks etched into the twisted strands of metal.

'Are these symbols, or just decoration?'

'Hmm,' Nat mused. 'Hephaestus took even more of a risk than I realised. This –' he used his little finger to indicate – 'is a script used only by the gods, to inscribe a language spoken only by the gods. To engrave it into an object is to transfer some of one's power into that object.' He picked up the fragment, turning it to examine it from different angles. 'Though I cannot tell whether Hephaestus sought to bind his own power within the torc, or that of someone else.' With a shrug, Nat returned the fragment of the torc to Aster. 'No wonder Zeus wished to keep it.'

Lysigoras glanced up.

'But where is Tauredos?' He looked from one of them to the other helplessly.

'We came under attack, and he was lost.' Deina wished she could say more – that he'd fought bravely – but he hadn't even had the chance. 'I'm sorry, elder.'

'He was an honourable man,' Theron offered. 'Strong. Skilful. And his sacrifice will not be forgotten. We will make sure of that.'

The others murmured their approval, Aster sliding an arm

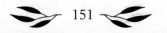

around Dendris as she wiped a tear away from the corner of her eye.

'He was a good man, and this House will suffer for the loss of him . . . But he understood the risk.' Lysigoras shivered and pulled the thick cloak he was wearing more tightly around his shoulders. 'And if songs are ever made about this venture, as I hope they one day will be, perhaps his name will be woven into those tales.' He glanced uneasily at the sky. 'Come. Much has changed in Iolkos in the weeks you've been away. We must get inside and talk.' Aster's stomach chose that moment to rumble. The elderly Sea Singer smiled slightly. 'And eat.'

Lysigoras took them to a small barn that was used to store produce from the gardens. It was dusty and infested with mice, but private. Only the Sea Singer's most trusted assistants knew they were there. They washed and ate, had their wounds tended to, and rested a little, deliberately avoiding any discussion of their quest or the wider war. Critos had risked the journey from the House of Zeus as soon as he'd heard of Theron's return. Theron questioned him further about Thebes, and the Battle Wager seemed happy to help Theron improve his limited knowledge of the city of his birth. Nat sat with them and added his recollections of the city – probably, Deina thought, with the deliberate intention of annoying Theron. Still, though Theron was clearly trying to ignore the god of death, he was obviously fascinated by the first-hand view of ancient events that was on offer. Aster bonded with Archis over a shared love of weapons. He seemed particularly taken with Archis's arm guards, each of which she'd adapted to include a hidden bronze blade controlled by a catch; when she pressed her wrists together, the blades shot out. Deina, meanwhile, had encouraged Dendris to tell her more of their adventures after leaving Thebes. She told herself this was because she enjoyed listening to her friend. That was true, but she knew there was also tiny part of her that had started to wonder whether Dendris felt more than just friendship for Theron, and wanted to test that theory.

Lysigoras's news couldn't be put off indefinitely, though. None of it was good. Aristaeus had descended on the city only two weeks after Deina and the others had left to seek Poseidon's realm. His rage, upon discovering that Theron had not only survived Neidius's trial but had escaped, had been murderous. Holding the House of Hades responsible, he'd butchered the six surviving guardians of the House and several of the elders. Almost a mercy, Deina thought, that Anteïs had died swiftly at the hand of a friend. Most of the city's Sea Singers and Battle Wagers had been conscripted into Aristaeus's army. Critos revealed that he, together with others from the House of Zeus who had escaped conscription, had started planning and implementing a campaign of sabotage, to try to take back some control over the city. That was getting harder, though; not content with the bloodletting, Aristaeus had now garrisoned the city with his own soldiers, both men and Iron Guards, and his warships were drawn up on the sands of Iolkos's harbour. No one was allowed to leave the city without being searched. The garrison was taking most of the food, and people were starting to starve.

'Hence, the somewhat meagre offerings you see before you,'

Lysigoras said, waving a hand at the remnants of their evening meal. 'Our stores are diminishing. Fortunate, perhaps, that there are so few of us left here. I can give you some supplies, however, and some boots and cloaks more suitable to the season.' The five of them, plus Nat, the elder, and Critos were gathered around the table that took up one end of the barn.

'And is Aristaeus still here?' Theron asked. He was sitting with one arm around Critos.

'He went on board his flagship two days ago,' Lysigoras replied. 'A quinquereme that takes up a third of the harbour.' The same vessel, Deina suspected, that had been Orpheus's flagship. 'Whether that means he is planning to return to Thebes, I don't know. We gather what information we can, but . . .' He drummed his fingers on the table. 'It is not safe for you to stay in Iolkos. Not safe for you, and not safe for us either. Aristaeus could send his Iron Guards to search the House at any moment. We dare not bar the gates against them.'

'I wish I were locked in a room with Aristaeus,' Archis grumbled. 'Without his guards, it would be a short fight.'

'One you'd likely lose,' Critos said gravely. 'You're young and inexperienced, and you don't know what you're wishing for. People who underestimate Aristaeus usually end up dead.'

Archis glowered and fell silent.

Nat leaned forward, resting his elbows on the table and his chin on his hands. He'd been watching them eat, and had seemed to enjoy himself as far as Deina could tell.

'What now, Theodesmioi? You succeeded in your quest to Poseidon's kingdom, so the time has come to make your next choice.'

'We have to destroy it,' Aster said instantly. 'That was what we said we'd do.' He paused, frowning. 'We can destroy it, can't we?'

'Surely the Spell Casters of Hephaestus can destroy it,' Dendris suggested. 'It's spell-cast metal, just like all torcs.'

'Not just spell-cast metal,' Nat reminded them. 'It was made by the god himself and is marked with the gods' own language. If I'd known that before, I would have warned you: the Spell Casters will not be able to destroy it. Only Hephaestus can destroy it, and only in his forge, in the dark depths of Olympus.'

'Can you take it to him?' Deina asked. 'Ask him to destroy it?'

Nat threw back his head and laughed. 'Me, enter Olympus uninvited? I think not. Unbelievable as it sounds, given my stunning good looks and sunny personality, the other gods don't seem to relish my company.' His smile faded. 'I'd be discovered the moment I entered and would be ejected just as quickly.'

As she had been before, Deina was suddenly aware of the immensity of the figure who stood before her. This time, though, she could sense the unending vista of Nat's sorrow, the sheer weight of his loneliness, as well as his power. Did the other gods shun him because they feared death? Or because they secretly longed for it?

'Besides,' Nat continued, 'even if I did manage to talk to Hephaestus without being discovered, there's no telling what he would actually do with the fragment. He might destroy it. He might not.'

Theron groaned and rubbed one hand over his face. 'Then we have no choice but to flee. We'll have to keep moving. Keep the fragment safe until Aristaeus is overthrown, or dies.'

Deina could see the despair in her friend's faces. A lifetime of running and hiding lay ahead of them, while she would be back in the Underworld, unable to help them. Or unwilling to help them, if she gave in to her mother and became a god. She still hadn't thought of a way to stop the seeds dragging her back to Hades' realm.

What about the torc?

The words slid into her mind like oil spilling through water.

What if you could not only find the fragments, but reforge them? Recreate the torc and use its power to free yourself from the control of the seeds?

She shook away the whispering voice. Nat was watching her carefully.

It was nonsense. She didn't know how the torc worked or what kind of power it might have other than giving the ability to control the Theodesmioi. She couldn't be certain it would be any use to her at all. And yet, now the idea had blossomed in her head, she couldn't stop thinking about it.

'Could the Spell Casters reforge the torc, Nat?'

The god of death's eyes opened wide.

'Possibly. If one had all three fragments.'

'Deina,' Theron asked, 'what are you thinking?'

'Hiding from Aristaeus isn't the answer. If we have the whole torc, maybe – maybe it could be useful. Maybe the spells carved into the metal could be used to free the Theodesmioi instead of controlling them.'

'How?' Dendris asked, frowning.

'I don't know. But if we had the torc, maybe we could work it out. Maybe it could be used to order the Spell Casters to go to every House and free all the Theodesmioi from their torcs.' There was no need to mention her thought about the seeds, not yet. It was bad enough raising her own hopes without offering false hope to her friends. 'Theron might wear it and command it.' Theron was shaking his head. Well, if he didn't want the torc, she might wear it herself.

'To attempt to usurp the power of the gods is a dangerous path to tread,' Lysigoras said, shaking his head.

'But you've told us we can't stay in Iolkos. Since we have to leave, what do we have to lose?' Deina countered. 'Why not try to find the other fragments while we still have time?'

'I suppose I'd rather do that than simply run away,' Aster said eventually. 'There's no honour in a life spent in hiding.'

'True. The risk, though; what if we succeeded only to have Aristaeus take the torc from us?' Dendris sighed. 'I'm not certain this is a good idea, but we should stick together for as long as we can. If the rest of you agree to do this, I will help.' She glanced towards Theron, seeking his opinion.

'I'm in,' Archis said, draining her wine and slamming the cup down on the table. 'I'd rather fight Aristaeus in the open, but this is the next best option.'

Theron looked at Deina. She could see the doubt in the back of his eyes. She could tell he also wanted to please her, though. He glanced at Nat and seemed to come to a decision.

'I agree. I've no desire to wear the torc, but if we succeed, perhaps we can find someone else suitable to offer it to. I suggest we attempt Zeus's realm next. Can you get us there, Thanatos?'

The god shook his head.

'Olympus is the most closely guarded of all the realms. Deina might gain admission, but mere mortals? Not without changing their nature.'

Theron exclaimed in annoyance.

'That's not what you said before. You said that mortals could enter the realms of the gods. That we Severers were proof of that. If we can't get into that realm then we can't –'

'You do not listen, Prince of Thebes,' Nat snapped. 'As usual. You can enter Olympus. You just have to change your nature first.'

'Now you're talking in riddles,' Theron spat. 'How can we change our nature?'

'I mean, Severer, that you must change your human forms and go in disguise.'

'And can you help us with that, my lord?' Aster asked hesitantly.

'Have I told you, Aster, how much I prefer your deference to Theron's swollen-headed pride?' Nat gave Aster a wink that sent the blood flaming into Aster's face. 'Unfortunately, the answer is still no. I can't. But I know someone who can. Someone renowned in legend and strong in magic. I'll even help you get there. We just need a boat.' He reached across to Deina and slid his hand over hers. 'I know you love the sea. I'd like for you to share that with me.'

There was an unexpected tenderness to his voice. Deina could feel the others watching her. She didn't dare to look in Theron's direction. Instead, she smiled at Nat, though she slipped her hand away.

'Lysigoras, you said the House has a boat.'

The Sea Singer nodded.

'Aristaeus has not requisitioned it. Yet. It's tied up in a small inlet just beyond our walls. The tide will be at its highest a little after dawn; you should rest until then.'

'And you, Critos.' Theron nudged the former Bronze Guard affectionately. 'I thought I was leaving you here to be safe, but Iolkos seems more dangerous than the realms of the gods. Do you want to come with us this time?'

'No. My knowledge of Aristaeus's tactics is valuable to those I am working with in the House of Zeus, and I have promised them my aid; with your leave, my king, my place is here. I do have something for you, though.' Critos lifted a bundle onto the table and unwrapped it. A crown glittered in the lamplight: a narrow circle of golden leaves. Deina heard someone gasp softly. 'The crown of Thebes. I managed to grab it as we left the Cadmea that night. It will be safer with you than here.' As Theron started to object, Critos gently took hold of his hands. He gestured to the thick bands of scar tissue that marred both of Theron's wrists, permanent reminders of how Orpheus had tied his infant son to a stake on a mountainside and left him to be devoured by wolves. 'I know you fear your heritage. I know you fear that taking the throne of the Theban Dominion would lead you down the same dark path that Orpheus trod.' A shiver of pain flickered across Theron's face and sent a surge of sympathy through Deina. 'But you are not your father, Theron – you've already proved that.' Critos gripped Theron's hands tightly and released them. 'Don't let his shadow deter you. Don't let his evil shape the whole course of your life.'

'Critos is right, Theron.' Dendris leaned across the table.

'You could never be like Orpheus. You would be the kind of king the people deserve. Kind and just and merciful.' Her eyes were shining as if she could actually see the future she was describing.

Critos pushed the crown towards Theron. 'At least if you have this, you won't forget to think about it.'

'You're a good friend, Critos,' Theron said with a warm smile, 'and I don't know what I'd do without you. I promise I'll think seriously about what you've said.' He nudged the crown back towards the former Bronze Guard. 'I'd still like you to look after this for me.'

'Very well.' Critos clapped Theron on the shoulder and returned the crown to its wrappings. 'I'll accept temporary defeat. We'll talk more when you next return – soon, I hope. I should make my way back to the House of Zeus; it won't be difficult now night's fallen.'

'And I must return to the Underworld to check again on the troublesome Dream Child,' Nat said, rising.

The thought of Nat leaving made Deina feel suddenly anxious. But perhaps it was the enormity of the task that now lay in front of them that was making her feel so uneasy. They were after all about to break into the realm of Zeus, king of the gods.

'I will join the boat once it is at sea,' Nat continued. 'Lysigoras, I will not see you again until it is time for you to die. Let us hope that is some time from now.' He vanished.

The Sea Singer elder bid them goodnight, and Critos bid them farewell. He spoke quickly and lightly and hurried away, as if there was no risk that this might be their last meeting. As

Aster and Dendris began playing a game of dice, picking at what little remained of the food, Deina picked up the bedding Lysigoras had provided – nothing more substantial than a fur to sleep on and a blanket – and climbed the ladder up to the platform set just below the roof.

'Do you mind if I join you?' Theron was standing halfway up the ladder. He was haloed by the glow of lamplight from below, but it was too dark up here for Deina to see his expression.

'Of course not. I came up here to get away from the mice, not you.' She finished smoothing out the fur, lay down and pulled the blanket over her, staring up at the cobweb-draped rafters and a patch of stars glittering through a small hole in the roof. She remembered the sandglass and sat back up as Theron settled next to her.

'I just need to check . . .' She pulled the obsidian frame from her bag and peered into the bulbs. 'No. No, this is wrong.' She shook the sandglass. 'I had plenty of time left back in Poseidon's realm, but now –' she thrust the thing towards Theron – 'look at it.'

He propped himself on one elbow and stared doubtfully at the sandglass.

'Only a third full. That's – that's not so bad.'

'Nearer to a half.' Even though she knew it would make no difference whatsoever, she tipped the sandglass upside down and banged the flat of her hand against the bottom. The silver dust continued to flow obstinately upwards. Stupid thing. Why? Why had it suddenly filled up?

Oh.

Because while they'd been in Poseidon's realm, time had

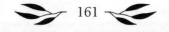

passed more quickly here. So as soon as she'd returned to Iolkos, the sandglass had . . . adjusted. She could almost hear Nat rolling his eyes at her slowness. Deina groaned as she lay back down.

'I'm sorry,' Theron said. His hand found hers. 'I wish I knew how to help you.'

This close, Deina could feel the warmth of his body. She shifted closer.

'So do I.' She stared at the swirling time inside the sandglass. 'This wasn't the future I used to dream of. It seemed so simple when I volunteered for Orpheus's expedition. Find the queen, win the gold, buy out the rest of my indenture. Leave Iolkos forever.'

'The same dream all of us had,' Theron murmured. 'The night before we left, after that banquet, I couldn't sleep. Instead, I spent the time choosing what I would sing for my first public festival once I'd claimed Orpheus's gold.' He laughed softly. 'I was *so certain* I would win.'

'You always were confident. That's why I liked you, back when we were children. I admired your self-belief. I wanted to be the same.'

'And I was drawn to how fierce you were. When some of the children were scared because your eyes were mismatched – even some of the teachers – I saw how they treated you. How they disguised their fear with cruelty. Yet whatever they did, you always came back fighting.'

Thinking over her past, Deina couldn't remember many times when she hadn't been fighting someone. Or fighting for something.

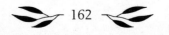

'I always wanted your dreams to come true,' Theron continued. 'Remember? I used to tell you about what I thought it would be like, to sing in an amphitheatre, and you used to tell me how you imagined it would feel to be at sea. That's why I made that sketch for you – the picture of the boat. I – I was surprised to see it, that night I broke into your room. I didn't think you'd keep it. Not after what I did.'

Theron's fist, driving towards her face. Though the way he'd ignored or mocked her afterwards, the way he'd cut her out of his life, that had hurt even more than the physical beating she'd taken.

'Honestly,' Deina replied, 'I don't know why I didn't tear the picture from the wall and throw it away. I hated you enough. But I just couldn't do it.'

'Maybe, deep down, you still cared for me? Or knew that I still cared for you?'

'Maybe.' Or she'd wanted to remember that he had once cared for her. Remembering was important. Dropping the sandglass, Deina held up her left hand and stared at the two rings she wore. Reminders of those she'd loved who were dead. A lump rose in her throat as she remembered the pendant Anteïs had given to her. One of the many things Aristaeus had taken from her. Lost forever, probably. She blinked away the tears that had sprung into her eyes and turned onto her side to smile at Theron.

'We can't change the past, but at least we have the present.' She kissed him softly, one hand pressed against his cheek, and felt his arm go round her waist. It felt right. Good. Safe.

So why was some part of her brain trying to remind her

of how it felt when she'd stood in the shadow of Nat's dark wings, and *he* had kissed her?

Because, perhaps, she could imagine a future with Nat. Not a future she wanted. Still – the possibility was there. Drink the nectar, become a goddess, stay with Nat in the Underworld, and hope to find some solace in his arms for everything she'd lost . . . With Theron, she had the present. The likelihood was they'd share nothing more.

Deina leaned her forehead against Theron's.

'We should get some sleep while we can.'

He tightened his arm around her.

'I'm not tired.'

'Liar. You were yawning your head off over dinner.'

Theron groaned.

'You're right. As usual. Stay close to me, though. I can't bear the thought that I'll wake up and you'll be gone.'

Deina turned so her back was against Theron's chest, snuggling close to enjoy the warmth of his body.

'Do you remember travelling across the Styx, crammed into that box?' she asked.

'How could I ever forget?' He kissed the side of her neck, and it set her skin tingling exactly as she had imagined in the vision Hades had tempted her with. 'Rest well, my love.'

Theron's breathing soon lengthened and slowed; he was asleep. Someone extinguished the oil lamps, and Aster began snoring not long after. Deina waited until Theron had rolled away from her, then quietly sat up and reached into her bag. There was no moon tonight but the starshine was bright enough. She unrolled the sketch of the ship that she'd taken from her room.

The animal hide, old and dry, had split, and the charcoal had smudged so badly the little ship had all but been erased. Most of the dark dust had gathered in the cracks on the surface of the hide. The breeze wandering through the barn blew it away.

Deina pressed a hand to her stomach. It felt as if her future was disappearing even as she watched.

You're being ridiculous. It was a drawing, not a prediction.

There was little point in keeping the square of hide now. Still, she rolled it up carefully and tucked it back into the bag, lay down and tried to sleep.

Voices woke her – they sounded worried. Aster and Dendris talking. Lysigoras too. It was still dark outside, but lamplight was casting strange shadows across the inside of the barn. Next to her, Theron was sitting up, blurry eyed and yawning. Deina nudged him.

'Come on.' She gathered up her bedding and climbed down the ladder.

'. . . not sure she came back at all. Perhaps she's deserted us. Or she's been taken by Aristaeus's forces. We'll just have to go without her.' Dendris was repacking her bag. She handed Deina a fresh waterskin.

'What's happened?'

'Archis is missing,' Aster replied.

'I've sent two Sea Singers to search the grounds.' Lysigoras sounded worried. 'But the tide won't wait.'

'Neither can we,' Theron said, fastening his belt and slinging his bow over his back. 'If she's been captured, she could lead them here.' No one said it, but Deina knew they

were all thinking the same. Aristaeus wouldn't hesitate to use torture to get information. If anything, he'd prefer it. Within a few moments they were ready to leave. Aster blew out the flame of the oil lamp, and they followed Lysigoras into the darkness.

The elder led them in silence along a narrow path that ran through thickets of yew just within the boundary wall of the House. On the other side of the wall, the sea was crashing against the jagged grey rocks that formed its foundation. The eastern sky was turning blue; the start of a fine winter day. Deina pulled up the hood of the cloak Lysigoras had given her and stayed close to the trees. She hadn't forgotten the bronze eagles Aristaeus had sent to spy on the city.

A door came into view. Half overgrown by ivy, it was set in the wall where the stonework turned back towards the city. Lysigoras stopped in front of it, but instead of pulling out a key, he began to sing softly. Deina didn't understand the words, but they had to contain some magic, just like the incantation used at the House of Hades to strengthen the boundary against outsiders: the stones around the door began to glow faintly. There was a click, and the door swung open. Aster and Theron followed Lysigoras onto the headland that lay beyond.

The sound of running caused Deina to spin round. Archis was bearing down on her, but as Deina drew her knives the Battle Wager skidded to a halt, her hands raised.

'It's – it's just me.' She bent over, catching her breath. 'Overslept.'

'Where were you?' Deina demanded.

'House of Zeus. To see a friend I'd argued with. I needed to say sorry. And goodbye.'

Pity muted Deina's annoyance, though Dendris growled something about 'irresponsible' as she lowered her axe and gestured for Archis to go ahead of her. Deina followed the Mycenaean as they hurried to catch up with the others, already halfway down a set of steps cut into the side of the bank. At the bottom was a small inlet. What looked like a large fishing boat was drawn up a narrow crescent of pebbled beach.

Lysigoras was waiting on the final step.

'I cannot go beyond this point.' He gestured at the torc around his neck. Deina understood: if he tried to go further, the spell-cast metal would tighten and eventually strangle him. Even as Leader of his House, he had the same limits placed on his freedom as the youngest Sea Singers fitted with their first torcs. 'These men are fishermen who work for the House. They will take you wherever you wish to go.' He inclined his head. 'I wish you luck, Soul Severer.'

Deina nodded her thanks. They were going to need all the luck they could get.

The sailors were beckoning them forward, clearly in a hurry to leave. Aster and Theron were already in the boat; Theron grabbed Deina's hand and pulled her up over the side of the vessel.

'They want to know what course to plot.'

They needed Nat for that. There was no sign of him so far, but even Deina knew Iolkos was at the furthest end of a gulf. There was only one direction to go.

'Away from Iolkos. Whatever route will keep us clear of Aristaeus's warships.'

The bottom of the boat grated across the pebbles and the last two sailors clambered inside as the waves took the little ship and carried it out of the bay. The four men on the oars began rowing away from the city. This time, Deina didn't look back.

The morning wore on. Sitting in the bottom of the boat, ducked down below the edge of the hull to stay out of sight of anyone who might be watching from the land, there was little for the Theodesmioi to do other than stare at the seabirds wheeling overhead and wait. The promise of the dawn had failed. Clouds now obscured the sun, building into grey towers that threatened storms. The sailors looked anxiously at the small sail, straining against the ropes that held it in place. Aster frowned at the sky.

'We're going to get soaked through, aren't we?'

'Hopefully not,' Theron countered. 'Hopefully we'll be facing mortal danger somewhere entirely different before the rain starts.'

Dendris grinned at them. 'As long as it's somewhere dry . . .'

They began talking in low voices about a village they'd travelled through together, and Deina's mind drifted to Nat. What if he didn't show up? Perhaps the Dream Child had given in to temptation, and his spell had been broken. She wriggled, trying to shed the feeling of tiny claws running across her skin. She'd noticed the sensation not long after leaving Iolkos, and it was getting worse. Was it linked to the movement of the silver dust through the sandglass? She wanted to check, but she wasn't sure she could bear it if the level in the lower bulb had suddenly jumped again. She'd rather ask Nat about it.

Theron was waving a hand in front of her face.

'Oh – what?'

'I said, what are you thinking about?' He tilted his head, his dark eyes suddenly anxious. 'Where did you go, just then?'

'Nowhere. I was thinking about Olympus, that was all. Where we might find the next part of the torc.'

Theron smiled, relieved.

'It would be really helpful if Tyche put each part in a throne room. We'd know exactly where to go.'

'Somehow, I doubt consistency is one of her strong points.'

'Ship ahead!' The call came from the sailor stationed in the prow of the boat. The captain, who was guiding the steering oar, peered across the water as the first spots of rain came down.

'Well?' Deina asked.

'It's a warship,' the man said casually, looking straight ahead as if he was afraid that, even at this distance, someone might be spying on him. 'A big one. Not making for us, but we'll cross its path if we stay on course.'

'Why don't we change course?' Theron suggested.

'That would look suspicious. There's a shallow compartment hidden beneath the fishing nets.' The captain gave a quick, mirthless grin. 'You know how it's been with Orpheus's taxes. A bit of smuggling was all that kept us going last winter. If you can squash yourselves in there without making the boat rock too obviously or showing yourself above the hull, we might just survive this.'

It was an awkward business. They had to edge their way into the compartment one at a time as the ship got closer, and it was barely big enough. And it stank of fish. Deina ended up squashed between the end timbers and Aster. The swell was getting heavier as the weather grew worse. Aster looked like he might vomit.

There were shouted orders from the ship for the fishermen to come alongside, and a shadow fell across the boat. Deina squirmed until she was almost on her back – accidently kicking Aster in the process. There was a gap in the planks through which she could just about see the ship looming above them. From the few words she caught, it sounded like someone was interrogating the fishermen, asking where they'd come from and where they were headed. Deina's attention was focused on a figure looking down from the bulwark.

The rich, purple robe had belonged to Orpheus. The face, however, was that of Aristaeus.

11

He appeared unchanged from the night she'd last seen him in Thebes, when he'd slit Chryse's throat and had tried his best to kill her too. The cruelty of his narrow face was unaltered. She wondered if he still suffered pain from where she'd shattered his ankle. She hoped so.

Someone shouted up to ask him whether the fishermen should be sent on their way or conscripted and their boat destroyed. Deina held her breath.

Tyche, goddess of luck, if you can hear me . . .

Aristaeus waved his hand and disappeared from view. The shadow lifted. Deina heard the fishermen calling out their thanks, calling down blessings on Aristaeus's head, then the swish of oars again as they pulled hard to put some distance between them and the ship.

Deina's relief was mingled with disquiet. Had Tyche heard and responded to her unthinking prayer? On the one hand, they needed all the luck they could get. On the other, owing a favour to a god was never a good idea.

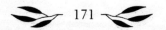

The captain knelt and Deina heard him say quietly, 'We'll be out of sight soon. They've set both sails. Aristaeus must have somewhere to be in a hurry.'

Gradually, the swell subsided. The motion of the boat stilled, and Deina heard a yell of surprise. The hatch slid back. Cautiously, Deina pushed herself up. Nat was standing in the prow. The sailors were on their knees in front of him.

'Deina.' Nat frowned. 'What are you doing down there?' He raised an eyebrow as the others climbed out of the compartment. 'All of you? That must have been cosy.' He smiled sweetly at Theron. 'Hello again, Prince of Thebes. Did you miss me?'

Theron glowered.

'What now?' Deina asked. 'Can you still get us to this friend of yours?'

'Oh, she's more of an acquaintance than a friend, but yes.' He nudged the nearest sailor with his foot. 'That's enough, you can get up now. Here.' He tossed something to the captain. Deina caught a glimpse of overlapping metal cogwheels. 'Slide that over your steering oar. It will get you there and back again. And you'll want to fix up your sail, such as it is.'

'Yes, my lord.' The captain sounded like a man struggling to keep his terror under control.

Nat looked around the small boat with distaste and clicked his fingers. The rank tangle of fishing nets vanished, replaced with a pile of white cushions tumbled across the length of the boat. Archis snatched one up and pressed her cheek against the soft fabric, murmuring with pleasure. Another finger click wreathed the boat in Nat's favourite white flowers. 'Deina, come and sit with me. The rest of you Theodesmioi may relax.' Nat held out his hand.

The imperious note in his voice irritated her, but they needed him. Besides, she knew she would enjoy sitting in the prow and watching it cut its way through the water, and it was only for a little while. Pretending not to hear as Theron murmured her name, she made her way forward to join Nat.

Onwards they went, moving swiftly across the water as the clouds broke and the sun returned. Soon the land she knew was far behind. Nat's course took them west, into an endless afternoon. Deina gazed with delight at the world unfurling before her. They passed through an archipelago of rugged islands, scattered across the water like a handful of uncut gems. Some were gilded with golden sands. Others were green with dense, dark forests. And then even these unknown lands ran out, and there was the just the immense, shifting sea filling her vision, and the wind moving across the water. A warm wind that carried the scent of herbs and honey. Deina removed her cloak and stuffed it into her pack. She closed her eyes and breathed deeply and laughed aloud. Watching her, Nat laughed too.

A rose-gold sunset lit up a bank of pale mist clinging to the horizon. The sailors hesitated, but Nat ordered them onwards, straight into the mist. For an instant the cloud was close about them. The sweetness of the air became so intense it was almost cloying.

They emerged from the cloud into a curved bay. A sweep of sparkling white sand fringed a lush green meadow dotted with trees and bright with wildflowers. The sailors, terrified, barely waited for their passengers to jump into the surf before rowing away again as fast as possible.

173

Nat stood and waved his arm in a grand gesture.

'Welcome to Circe's island. She's probably expecting you.'

'Circe?' Aster exclaimed. 'As in the infamous and legendary witch who turned Odysseus's men into pigs?' He shook his head and started to back away, and for a moment Deina thought he was going to run into the water and try to catch up with the boat. 'This is a bad idea. Very bad. Witches are – are vengeful. Dangerous. She's more likely to curse us than help us. Asking a favour from a witch will not end well.'

'What about asking a favour from a goddess?'

The voice was low and melodious, but Deina could see anger in the eyes of the woman who had suddenly appeared and asked the question. She was stately, with golden skin and hair the colour of honey. Her eyes raked disdainfully over the Theodesmioi and settled on Nat.

'Thanatos.' Her mouth twisted as if his name left a bad taste. 'What are you doing here? Your presence is not welcome. As you know full well.'

Nat was standing next to Deina. Looking down, she saw that the grass around his feet had frozen and withered.

Nat shrugged.

'Your island always was over-sensitive. That's hardly my fault, is it?'

Circe ignored him.

'I am the divine daughter of Helios, and the sun-god's power runs through me and mine.' She spread her arms wide, encompassing the sun-drenched landscape. 'There is no place here for the coldness of death.'

Nat glanced sideways at Deina.

'She's glad to see me really. We're cousins.'

'Distant cousins,' Circe said, narrowing her eyes at him. 'Very distant. Go away.'

'I will go away, and happily so, but only if you agree to help these mortals.' He pointed to the Theodesmioi.

'Help them?' Circe raised an eyebrow. 'And why would you want me to do that? What makes you so keen to lend assistance to mere mortals?'

'Whatever my reasons, cousin, I am not about to share them with you. I have my secrets.' Nat locked eyes with the goddess. 'Just as you have yours.'

Circe glowered at him in response.

'I will listen to their request, if it will get you to leave, but I'll promise no more than that. Or I could find the Fates and tell them you're here.' She smiled sweetly. 'I know they've been waiting for you to emerge from your hiding place in the Underworld. Several of the gods believe you have some questions to answer, apparently.' Circe's gaze, intense and curious, flickered briefly towards Deina. 'Well?'

'Fine, I'll go.' Nat held one finger up. 'Just give me a moment.' He bent close to Deina to whisper rapidly in her ear. 'I'll find you when you escape Olympus. Until then, some advice. Don't eat any of her food, and make her swear to any bargain she offers you. And remember: I can see the minds of Soul Severers more clearly than those of other mortals. Theron begins to dream of the throne of Thebes, and Dendris begins to dream of Theron. You are on a different path.'

'Wait, what path? A path that ends where?' Deina asked.

Nat began to fade.

'In death.' He vanished, leaving his words hanging in the air.

In death? What did that even mean? Was he talking about her death or someone else's? Maybe he meant the death of what was left of her humanity. Or maybe he meant himself . . . Deina realised everyone, including Circe, was staring at her. The sorceress looked her up and down and gave a humph of dissatisfaction.

'Follow me.'

Circe's island was beautiful, no doubt. Deina could hear murmurs of appreciation and gasps of wonder from the others as they were led through groves of trees thick with pale, sweetly scented blossom and past gracefully leaping waterfalls that fed crystal clear pools. The nodding heads of narcissus mingled with glowing sunflowers and fig trees whose branches were heavy with succulent-looking fruit. There were animals too: goats jumping from rock to rock, a herd of horses, and a rainbow of glossy-feathered birds darting through the trees. Yet Deina knew she was walking through this magical landscape almost oblivious. Nat's words filled her mind like a choking fog. She found herself staring at Dendris's back, remembering how the Mycenaean's eyes had shone when she'd urged Theron to take the throne of Thebes. Dendris was gorgeous. Deina bit down on her bottom lip as jealousy, bitter as old wine, left a bad taste in her mouth. Perhaps Theron would decide he did want to be king. Perhaps he would want a queen as mortal as him, one whose heart could race with pleasure at his touch. Instead of one whose heart was slowly turning to stone . . .

Deina tried to shake her mood away. All her hopes were starting to revolve around recreating the torc, so that was what she needed to concentrate on. It was inscribed with the language of the gods themselves. She had to believe it would be powerful enough to free her from the seeds. And to free the Theodesmioi too, of course. And then what? Perhaps she could use it for other things. To make her heart beat again. To make herself fully human.

Or, murmured a voice in her head, *you could use it to make Theron king of Thebes. Use it to send Dendris away. Use it to make him want you, and only you . . .*

'In here.' Circe's voice cut across Deina's thoughts. She realised with relief that they'd reached the object of their walk: a circle of tall grey stones, shaded by oak trees that had been planted between them. Circe led them between two taller stones that had been capped with another stone laid across them, forming a shadowed gateway. Filtered through the leaves, the air within the circle was cool and green. The land was like a steep-sided bowl. A patch of clear blue sky showed where the trees didn't quite meet; below this, at the lowest point of the circle, was set a stone, about waist high, covered with a dark red cloth. A chair draped in the same cloth was set in front of the two stones opposite the gateway. Circe climbed up to the chair and sat, her hands resting on its arms, looking down on the Theodesmioi who stood on the slope below her.

'You must be hungry,' the sorceress observed. A table appeared alongside her chair; it was heaped with glistening fruits and bowls of cream and pastries glazed with honey. Aster's eyes widened and he licked his lips.

'That all looks delicious.'

Deina caught Theron's eye and gave a tiny shake of her head, hoping he'd understand. Quickly, he gripped Aster's wrist.

'Thank you, mighty Circe –' Theron bowed his head – 'for your hospitality, but we must respectfully decline. We seek to enter Olympus, and we do not know how much time we have to – to accomplish what we wish to achieve.'

'Olympus?' Circe drummed her fingernails slowly on the arm of her chair. 'You are not the first who have sought my aid to that end.' Another rattle of fingernails on wood, sharp enough to make Deina wince. 'I am not sure that I am willing to help more mortals enter Zeus's realm. I think I shall turn you into pigs instead. I'm fond of pigs. Or perhaps dogs. Or maybe goats.' A long wooden staff appeared in Circe's hand.

'No!' Deina tried to climb the slope to reach the sorceress, but the air around her thickened to the point she could barely move her limbs. She forced her head round to look at the others. They appeared completely immobilised, pinned into place by some unseen force. Archis was straining, her fingers stretched vainly towards the hilt of her sword. Aster's face was a rictus of pain as he tried to force his hand nearer to his spear. Deina dragged one foot forward. 'I won't –' She pushed herself a step nearer the goddess – 'I won't let you –'

'You can't stop me. You are not a god.' Circe smiled. 'Yet.'

With sickening horror, Deina watched as Circe stood and raised the staff . . .

'One of these trees is ailing,' Dendris said breathlessly, struggling to get the words out. 'It will – it will die, if you do nothing. You – you wouldn't want that to happen, would you?'

The sorceress lowered her staff a little.

'Which tree? Show me?'

Dendris fell forward slightly, as though her legs were still caught fast but her upper body had been released.

'That one.' She pointed to one of the mighty oaks that grew between the standing stones. As far as Deina could tell, it looked as healthy and full of life as its neighbours; she hoped for all of their sakes that Dendris knew what she was doing.

'How do you know?' Circe asked.

'I have dryad blood. I can hear the tree's pain.'

Circe murmured something, and Dendris stumbled forward, suddenly free.

'Tell me what is wrong, and I will spare you and the others.'

Dendris hesitated. Deina could tell she was itching to reach for her axe. She was relieved when Dendris walked over to the tree instead and knelt to place her hands on its trunk. The Mycenaean began to chant a few phrases, over and over, pausing every few moments as if listening. Circe began drumming her fingers again. Deina could feel the sorceress's growing impatience.

'Well?' Circe demanded.

Dendris put her arms as far as she could around the tree's girth before stepping away.

'Something gnaws its roots. Something large and voracious.'

Circe's face twisted with annoyance. 'Again?' She strode over to the tree, pausing about six strides away to plunge her staff into the ground. When she pulled it back up the earth cracked open, spraying chunks of dirt and grass and revealing the head of a huge white worm. Circe's staff was buried in

the creature's neck; blind, it swung its head back and forth, massive jaws open, still searching for something to eat. Circe raised an eyebrow at the Theodesmioi. 'Perhaps some human blood would sate its appetite.' She smiled as a sword appeared in her free hand. Dendris pulled her axe from its harness, but before she could aim it, Circe swung the sword down and lopped off the worm's head. Its body shuddered and was still. Deina fell onto her knees as the spell pinning her in place was finally lifted. She glanced around and saw the others had been freed as well.

'Is – is it dead?' Aster asked. The fanged head had landed just in front of him and the worm's dark blood was trickling across the grass towards his feet. He jumped out of the way.

'Not quite dead enough,' Circe replied. 'I will burn it later and scatter the ashes into the sea. In the meantime, though, I will grant your wish and help you get into Olympus.' She walked briskly down to the cloth-covered stone at the centre of the circle. 'Once you have presented me with a gift.'

'A gift?' Deina questioned. 'Isn't what Dendris did enough of a gift?'

Circe was shaking her head.

'That was given in return for me not turning your friends into animals. This is a fresh bargain.' She tilted her head and gazed steadily at Deina. 'Magic is a form of power, and all power comes at a cost. So you may present me with any of the following. Dendris's power to hear the trees. Aster's strength. Archis's memory of her brother. Theron's ability to sing. Unless you can tempt me with something else. And no, Deina –' Circe held up her hand as Deina opened her mouth – 'I will take nothing from you. A shadow dogs your steps, and I want none of it.' Deina remembered: Hades, in his male form, storming up and down the dais in his throne room. The sense she'd had of an ancient corruption hovering at his back. The image sent a tingle of fear across her skin.

No. I may be my mother's daughter, but I am not that.

Circe laughed maliciously, as if she'd read Deina's thoughts. 'The rest of you, decide quickly. I will prepare.'

The sorceress pulled the cloth away and the clearing was flooded with sunshine, bright enough to make Deina throw up her hand to shield her eyes. The top of the stone was set with a golden disc that reflected the light coming from the gap in the canopy above. Or what she thought was a disc – as she watched, Circe started to cast herbs onto the mirrored surface. They sank. Deina tore herself away to join the others, already huddled at the edge of the circle.

Archis was standing slightly apart from the Soul Severers with her arms crossed.

'I see how it is,' she said gruffly. 'You're friends. You're all from the same Order. You're bound to stick up for each other. But I'm not going to do it. I won't give up his memory. My brother was all I had. I loved him.' Her voice had thickened with emotion, and tears glistened in her eyes. She wiped them angrily away. 'I loved him, and he was taken from me.'

'If you can't remember him, you can't be sad about him,' Dendris argued. 'Besides, you say you had him in your life until last year – do you know how lucky that is? Most of us get severed completely from our families when we're so young we lose even the memories of them.' Deina could hear the bitter envy in Dendris's voice. It raised an answering surge of jealousy in her own breast. She had some memories of her father, restored by her first encounter with Hades, but the handful of years she'd had with him weren't enough. They could never be enough. 'If we're going to get these torc fragments and help the other Theodesmioi,' Dendris continued, 'we're going to need Aster's strength. And my ability has already proved useful. We may need it again.'

Archis shook her head and scowled.

'I told you, I joined this little expedition to get rid of my torc. I'm not that worried about helping the other Theodesmioi, if I'm honest. Most of the elders are only interested in looking out for themselves. Do you really think the adepts or the novices are any different? Look what happened in Iolkos. Half the elders wanted to hand you straight to Aristaeus.' She scoffed. 'You all blame the gods for your woes. I think we get the gods we deserve.'

Aster frowned and put his hands on his hips.

'If you have no interest in honour, at least think of your own life. You want to get back to the mortal world. That means you have to stick with us. My strength and Dendris's dryad blood might help us all get out of this alive. Your memory of your brother won't.'

'And how is the ability to sing going to contribute to our survival?' Archis gestured impatiently at Theron. 'Besides, the king of Thebes doesn't need to be able to sing. Singing is for bards, and they're all a waste of time to start with.'

No one spoke. Theron's skin had flushed darker, and he was staring at the grass beneath their feet. Deina knew she'd mentioned Theron's dearest ambition in front of Archis: to be a bard and sing the great epic poems telling the stories of the ancient heroes – at least, before Orpheus had struck the spark that had led to the mess they were in now. Either the Battle Wager had forgotten, or she didn't care.

And yet, if Theron was indeed to claim the throne of Cadmus . . . Deina looked again at Archis. She was staring defiantly at the other Theodesmioi, her arms folded tightly across her chest. Deina couldn't blame her. She knew she wouldn't be willing to give up one of her memories, even those that caused her more grief than joy in the remembering. She would have fought to hold on to every last recollection of Chryse, Drex, Anteïs or her father, no matter how painful.

'What do you think, Deina?' Aster was looking at her anxiously.

She took a deep breath.

'Our memories . . . they are part of what makes us who we are. It wouldn't be fair to take Archis's away from her. At least, if Circe takes your ability to sing, Theron, you'll still be able to remember what you were once capable of.'

Theron lifted his gaze to hers, disbelief written across his face.

'Don't look at me like that,' Deina said, torn between guilt and anger. 'I was willing to give up everything for you that night in the Cadmea.'

'I know you were, but – but – this is not the same,' Theron insisted. 'You know what this would mean to me.'

'He's right,' Dendris added, edging in front of Theron as if she might need to physically defend him. 'It's not fair to ask this of him. An ability counts for more than a memory, and there's a choice here.'

'So you think I didn't have a choice?' The details of what she went through in the Cadmea were etched into Deina's memory. Chryse – the seeds – fighting her way through the pain – Nat's voice – Orpheus . . . Something that had been trying to get her attention suddenly snapped into focus. 'Wait – what about the heirloom of Cadmus? The – the teeth. Did you bring them with you?'

Dawning understanding sent Theron rummaging in his bag. He brought out the shiny gold box that Anteïs had returned to him. Archis asked what it was.

'Do you think Circe will accept it, though?' Dendris said, ignoring the Battle Wager's question.

'There's only one way to find out.' Theron squared his shoulders and set off down the slope. Everyone followed.

Deina ran to catch up with him. 'Don't give them to her until after she's promised to honour the bargain.'

Theron nodded.

'Great sorceress,' he began, giving Circe one of his dazzling lopsided grins and holding up the box. 'We wondered if you might accept this gift, as an alternative to those you suggested. As you must know, since you know my name, I am the rightful king of Thebes. This box contains the legendary heirloom of the House of Cadmus, the founder of Thebes: teeth from the serpent slain by Cadmus to make a sacrifice to the gods and found the city. You know the story of the Sown Men.'

Everyone knew the story of the Sown Men: Athena told Cadmus to plant half of the teeth, and from the ground sprouted warriors who helped build Thebes.

Circe's eyes were locked on the golden box.

Despite the confidence Theron was projecting, Deina could see the tension in his muscles and tendons, in the carriage of his shoulders and neck. She knew that beneath his tunic his heart would be racing. She could tell the others were scared too. Yet she felt strangely detached from the outcome of their bargaining with Circe. Deina wondered if the ice of the Underworld, that gripped her heart and held it frozen in place, was now spreading its tentacles into the rest of her body. Claiming her, bit by bit. Drawing her irresistibly along a path that would end with her becoming exactly what her mother wanted her to be. How long did she have until it was too late for her to turn back?

Slowly, Circe began to nod.

'I've long wondered what became of the rest of Cadmus's inheritance.' The sorceress smiled. 'It is an acceptable alternative.' She reached for the box. Theron held it out of her grasp.

'Swear by the Styx. Swear if I give you this, that you'll help all of us get into Olympus. Safely. And that you'll give us a spell to get us back to the mortal world.'

'You drive a hard bargain, Soul Severer,' snapped Circe. 'Yet I so swear. Now, give the box to me. The potion for your transformation will not wait.'

Theron handed the box over, as Deina asked, 'What does the potion do? Thanatos spoke of transforming our natures.'

'It will bury your true natures, temporarily. Bury them too deep to be seen. Drink.' One by one, she handed them a small bowlful of something that looked like lava. Deina braced for pain as she swallowed; to her surprise, the liquid was cool and tasted faintly of some herb she couldn't identify. It didn't seem to do anything. Or so she thought, until she looked down at her arms.

'These aren't mine.' These arms belonged to someone shorter, built on a more delicate scale, someone who didn't have callouses on her hands from hours of practice with swords and knives and other weapons. Deina looked up and realised her eyeline had changed – she'd shrunk. The rite-seals that spiralled their way across her torso had vanished. Her clothes were different too. Gone were the boots, dark cloak and plain, homespun tunic. She was clad now in an elegant russet-coloured gown and there were sandals on her feet. The pleated fabric was so fine it skimmed almost weightlessly across her skin.

'Where are my knives?' Deina felt her back. 'Where's my bag?'

'Everything is still there. Just temporarily submerged.' The laughter in Circe's eyes broke out into a broad grin. 'You're all nymphs now, sent from Demeter with a present for Hera.' She handed Deina a cedar wood box.

All of them were nymphs? Deina turned to look at Theron and Aster. Sure enough, not only she and Dendris and Archis, but both men too were now slender, pretty young women wearing identical draped and pleated tunics. Only their colouring remained the same as before. Aster was looking down at himself, horrified.

'What have you done?' Aster's transformed face was a picture of outrage. 'I'm a – I'm a – *girl*?'

'Careful, Aster,' warned Dendris. 'You're outnumbered. And eventually my axe will reappear.'

Theron didn't look much happier than Aster.

 186

Deina covered her smile with her hand and turned back to Circe, trying not to laugh.

'And these disguises will get us into Olympus?'

'They will get you safely through the gates, but the transformation won't last for long. Whatever you seek in Zeus's realm, you'd better find it quickly.'

Deina heard the question in Circe's words and decided to ignore it.

'How do we get there?'

'Leave my sacred circle. You'll find yourself where you need to be.' The sorceress gestured to the opening in the circle through which they'd entered and handed Aster a green glass bottle. 'When you wish to return to the mortal realm, take a sip of this potion and say the name of the place to which you wish the magic to take you.'

'If we get split up, we should all meet in Thebes,' Theron suggested in a quiet voice. 'It's the last place Aristaeus will expect us to be, and if we find the second part of the torc we can asked the Spell Casters of Hephaestus to make a start on reconstructing it.' It sounded like a reasonable plan, but Deina couldn't help wondering what else lay behind Theron's desire to return to the city of his birth.

'Come on,' Aster said moodily. 'Let's get this over with.' He began to climb the slope towards the massive stone gateway, moving awkwardly, as if he was struggling to master his new shape. Deina bowed her thanks to Circe and followed the others, stepping through the darkness into somewhere entirely different.

12

If Deina had thought about her expectations of Olympus, she would have pictured a colonnaded space set amidst open countryside. Instead, she found herself on a road wider than any she'd ever seen. It seemed to curve up the side of a great mountain. Following the road down would lead into a carpet of white cloud that entirely obscured everything that lay below. Following the road up led to a pair of vast silver gates set within an archway of white stone. The gateway seemed to stand alone at the end of the road; no walls flanked it, and, even though the gates themselves were slightly open, nothing lay beyond them but the snowy crags of the mountain. At least, nothing that Deina could see.

There were others on the road, going up to the gates or coming down from them. The scene reminded Deina of that part of the Underworld where they'd found the bones of the minotaur and the hydra and other creatures from myth. Here, though, the myths were alive, and were walking alongside them. Just ahead of the Theodesmioi were four centaurs, their hooves ringing loud on the cobblestones. Passing back in the other direction was a band of nymphs – dryads, Deina guessed. Leafy fronds sprouted from their heads instead of hair, and their voices as they passed sounded like the wind soughing through branches. The dryads were walking swiftly to get away from a gaggle of pans, whose handsome human heads and torsos contrasted starkly with their shaggy, backwards-bending goat legs. Towering above everyone else was a one-eyed giant who was heaving a laden cart towards the silver gates.

As they made their way further up the wide road, Deina realised those approaching the gates didn't actually pass through them. They simply vanished. She hurried to catch up with Theron. His dark eyes were the same, even though they were set in an entirely different face.

'What do you think is happening to them?'

Theron shrugged.

'How should I know?'

'Are you still cross about me suggesting you should give up your singing voice?'

'You need to ask?' Theron replied. There was a distinct edge to his voice. 'You of all people know what it means to me. Besides, had you forgotten that my singing was what saved you from Cerberus?'

'Of course not. I was just trying to be fair, that was all. And memory is important. That's one of the things that scares me. That I'm going to forget who I am. What I am.' She took a deep breath, trying to keep her voice steady. 'And that I'll forget all the people I care about.'

'Even me?'

Deina nodded despondently. 'Even you.'

Theron sighed and slipped his hand in hers. 'I understand,' he murmured. 'I think. And I'm sorry. As you said, you gave up everything that night at the Cadmea to save all of us. I should be prepared to do the same.' He squeezed her hand tightly. 'Except for you, of course – I'd never willingly give you up.'

Deina wanted to tell him that perhaps he should, that perhaps it would be better for him if he did, but they were nearly at the gates; Aster and Dendris had stopped and were both staring up at the massive structure. At first glance, each gate appeared to be embossed with the image of a sphinx: the body of a lion with the head and chest of a woman and the wings of an eagle. The sphinxes were shown in profile, each staring steadfastly at its twin on the other gate. But as Deina studied the silverwork more closely, she realised that the part of each sphinx that protruded from the gate was moving. The feathers of the creatures' outer wings rippled. Their outer feet pawed the air. Their tails twitched. As the giant lumbered past the Theodesmioi, the sphinxes' blank-eyed faces whipped round as if they were sightlessly focussing on him. The giant and his cart disappeared.

'Is that a good thing or a bad thing?' Archis asked. 'Has he been allowed into Olympus, or sent somewhere else?'

'There's only one way to find out.' Clutching the box Circe had given her tightly, Deina marched up to the gate. Before she got close enough to step through the opening, the sphinxes' heads snapped round. Their gaze pinned her in place; she felt their probing like a comb being raked over her skin.

I'm a nymph. I'm a nymph with a present for Hera . . .

The silver gates vanished. Deina found herself in a glittering space. A gold paved floor led past wide-open gold gates into a walled city covering the entire top of the mountain. It was a city filled with lofty stone-built buildings, each like the megaron of Iolkos but on an immeasurably grander scale.

Aster appeared next to her. He held out his hand and sighed disappointedly.

'Still a nymph.'

'Just as well, or we'd be in trouble.' Dendris appeared, swiftly followed by Archis. Deina surveyed the gleaming palaces. 'I guess we want to head for that one.' She pointed towards the white marble columns of the largest palace that sat at the highest point of the city. 'That dominates everything else, so it has to belong to Zeus.' She waited for Theron to materialise then beckoned the others to follow her through the golden gates and up the path that led to the summit. There were statues of gods and goddesses everywhere, many times bigger than life-size, skin and hair and expensive-looking clothes all richly painted on. Some were covered with chryselephantine, the gold and ivory glowing in the bright sunshine. Some were sculpted from polished bronze. Several of the statues turned their heads to follow the disguised Theodesmioi as they passed. The cold gaze of their eyes, crafted from marble and obsidian, sent a shiver down Deina's spine. Up and up, they followed the golden paved path, until it deposited them at the entrance to a vast cloistered courtyard. There were more statues here, all of Zeus. Zeus hurling a thunderbolt, Zeus seated on a throne giving judgement, Zeus half-naked and beautiful. The Theodesmioi huddled in the shadows to one side, out of their sight.

'Which way now?' Dendris whispered. 'Up the steps in through the front of the palace?'

That was where the others who had taken this route seemed to be heading. Presumably it led to the great hall, where you could seek an entrance with the god and deposit the gift that you'd brought with you. But if this palace was similar in layout to the megaron back home, then there would be other doors that led to storage rooms, kitchens and private spaces.

'Shall we find the throne room again?' Theron was playing nervously with the bracelets that were stacked up his arms. He pushed them up and let them drop, one arm after the other, as regular as a pulse. Deina chewed her bottom lip. The throne room would be an obvious starting point, perhaps, but would Tyche have chosen the same hiding place twice? She closed her eyes and tried to let her mind lead her as it had in Poseidon's kingdom, but the only image in her head was the crowd of statues in the courtyard, the physical representation of Zeus's rampant vanity. She blew out her breath in irritation.

'What's Zeus most famous for? Give me some suggestions.'

'Thunderbolts.'

'Overthrowing his father.'

'Marrying his sister.'

'Forcing women into bed, even if he has to change into an animal to do it.' Archis sounded as disgusted as she looked.

Deina tried to reckon up the number of women Zeus had slept with according to the stories, and quickly gave up.

'I think we should find the bedchamber.'

'Really?' Aster said nervously. 'But if he catches us there . . .'

'Don't worry.' Deina spoke more confidently than she felt.

'Between us, we'll figure something out. Let's try this way.' She paused as they turned into a passage leading away from the main courtyard and glanced back at the others. 'And let's try to look like we belong here. We're nymphs, remember, on a mission from Demeter to deliver a gift.' Pointing at Aster, she added, 'Less slouching. More . . . I don't know, skipping. Or something like that.'

Aster scowled and started walking. Dendris choked back a laugh, and no wonder; he'd stuck his nose in the air and was doing something with his hips that an extremely generous person might have described as swinging.

Well. It was a start.

Zeus's palace was a vast, sprawling maze. Unlike Poseidon's underwater home, there was little attempt at artistry. Every available surface was covered with gold: beaten gold, etched gold, gold that had been folded and spun into the shapes of flowers and trees and animals. So much gold that Theron complained the glitter was giving him a headache. Taken on their own, some of the carefully crafted golden fronds and blooms were beautiful, but there was no space to appreciate them. As well as the wealth of gold, each room they walked through was crammed with yet more statues and busts of the god. Everything was too bright, too large, too much. There was nothing comfortable here. Even the servants were automatons. Several times Deina gestured for the others to keep back as a table scuttled by on spindle legs, carrying covered dishes. The palace was a dead space, not a place for living.

Not surprising. Gods aren't really alive.

To be alive, you had to be able to grow and change and learn. Gods were more like insects caught in amber. Deina's mouth twisted and she pressed one hand to her stomach, half-dreading that she'd feel the growth of the seeds bulging through her skin. How long did she have left? She wished she'd thought to check the sandglass before she'd drunk Circe's transforming potion. Preoccupied, she turned a corner and almost walked into someone.

Zeus. The immense power radiating from the being in front of her brought her and all of the Theodesmioi instantly to their knees. That alone would have marked him out as a god, even if they hadn't walked past countless representations of him. Or at least, representations of his favourite appearance. Deina knew from Hades that a god could choose and change their physical manifestation as easily as mortals changed clothes. She bent her head closer to the floor. She was a nymph. She had to remember to act like one.

'And what are you doing here, so close to my private chamber?' Zeus asked. His tone was brisk but not unkind. Deina remembered that Zeus liked nymphs. A lot. 'You may speak,' he added.

'All-powerful Zeus, mightiest of all the gods, ruler over the heavens and the earth, divine wielder of the thunderbolt . . .' Deina went through as many titles as she could recall, her mind racing. This wasn't Hera's palace. They needed another reason to be here. '. . . most glorious of all the children of Cronos, trim-ankled Hera, she of the flashing eyes, has – has sent us to you.'

'Hera?' Zeus sounded suspicious. 'Stand, all of you, that I may see you.'

They obeyed. Deina could tell by the expression in his cloud-grey eyes that the god liked what he saw.

'And why has she sent you to me?' His suspicion had, fortunately, faded.

'We were sent from Demeter to her sister Hera with a gift. Hera commanded that we should offer the gift to you, and that we should place it in your bed chamber.' Deina thrust the cedar wood box in the god's direction. He took it and opened it a little.

Deina held herself very still. She'd not actually checked inside the box. What if it was something very obviously intended for Hera, something Circe had meant as a joke?

Have I just handed the king of gods a 'Zeus smells' amulet?

Zeus smiled. Behind her, Deina heard a faint gasp of relief from one of her fellow nymphs.

'Perfect. Exactly what I need. Hera must have finally come to her senses, and sends me this gift by way of an apology.' He eyed the nymphs lasciviously. 'Along with such *charming* gift bearers. I must go and thank my devoted wife for her thoughtfulness. You may take this into my chamber.' He pointed to a tall pair of doors at the top of a flight of stairs at the end of another corridor. 'Wait there. When I return, I plan to properly enjoy your company.' He handed Deina the box and started to walk away, pausing to pinch Aster's cheek. 'Gorgeous. I can hardly bear to tear myself away. I won't be long, my lovely ones.'

As soon as Zeus was out of sight, Deina raced for the double doors, the others at her heels.

'That – that was too close,' Aster said as soon as they'd closed

the doors behind them. He was trembling, though whether from fear or outrage Deina couldn't tell. 'We've got to get out of here before he – before he –'

There was an exclamation of surprise from Archis. She'd opened the cedar wood box that Deina had dumped on the nearest table and was holding up a hand mirror. The finest mirror Deina had ever seen, offering a far clearer reflection than water or the polished bronze discs that usually served as looking glasses. No wonder Zeus had been pleased.

As they spread out, searching, Deina cast her gaze around the room. It was built out on a precipice; two of the walls were actually no more than rows of columns. One side offered spectacular views over the mountain. Cautiously, Deina held on to one of the columns and leaned over the edge. There was a sheer drop below; if you tried to escape Zeus that way, you'd plunge straight down and through the cloud cover, probably hitting a couple of jagged peaks as you tumbled to your death. Crossing to the other side of the room, she found herself looking down on the city of the gods. Zeus's bedchamber had been built to occupy the highest point on Olympus. There wasn't much in the way of furniture. A golden couch, a couple of golden chairs, five golden tables and a huge bed – with a golden frame – that dominated the space. Oh, and two enormous statues of Zeus flanking the bed. The air was sweet; a table in the corner held a wide bowl full of flowerheads, plus jars of oil and what smelled like honey.

What would Tyche do?

Aster, having failed to lift one of the solid gold chairs, was on his knees peering at the underside. Archis and Theron were examining the bed, running their hands over every segment of the frame. But wasn't this room – the whole palace – more about the exercise of power than the pursuit of pleasure? Not that Zeus likely knew the difference . . . Deina's eyes were drawn to the towering statues of the god that stood beside the bed. She realised Dendris was studying them too.

'You check that one, I'll take this one.'

The statues were the most lifelike she'd seen so far. The polished bronze shone like oiled skin. The chestnut curls of their hair looked soft enough to touch. Real fabric had been draped around the hips and over one arm of the statue in front of Deina. The other statue was clad as a soldier – if soldiers went into battle entirely naked apart from a spear, a shield and a helmet.

'Here!' Dendris exclaimed. She was balanced on the bedframe, stretching up towards the statue's head. The dark-eyed helmet was pushed back so that the statue's face was visible. 'On the front of the helmet, the nose-piece – isn't that it?' She pushed the edge of the helmet with the heel of her hand. 'It's stuck on. I can't make it budge.'

'Let me try.' Grunting with effort, Deina managed to drag one of the tables up to the statue. Climbing on to the table, she grabbed hold of the helmet and pulled, gritting her teeth against the pain as the helmet's edge cut into her fingers. Until the helmet tore away from the statue's head with a crack. Dendris was right; the torc fragment, straightened out, had been stuck to the nose piece. Deina ran her fingers across the twisted strand of metal and sensed the same echo of power she'd felt in Poseidon's palace. The fragment had been bound to the helmet with loops of what looked like fine silvery thread.

'Deina,' Aster pleaded, 'we need to get out of here.'

Deina tugged at the fragment. No good – she'd need a knife or something to cut through the thread. Or maybe a hammer. She tossed the helmet to Dendris and jumped off the table. 'We'll take the whole thing and sort it out when we –'

One of the tall doors swung gently open. Several women hurried in. Not women – more nymphs, Deina realised. About ten of them. They looked a little like Ione had when she first appeared. The sea nymphs stopped short as soon as they saw the Theodesmioi.

Theron grabbed Deina's hand.

'Zeus isn't here right now. We were just leaving.'

He hurried her towards the door. Before they reached it, the nymph standing closest to the door slammed it shut and flattened her hand against it. A large, hairy, scarred hand with dirty fingernails. Deina realised the image of the nymph was rippling, like water disturbed by a thrown stone. The rippling stilled, leaving her face to face with a scowling, beetle-browed man. She recognised him; he'd been in the great hall, watching Neidius prosecute Theron and the others. He was the man who'd tried to force her mouth open to cut out her tongue. Was this what Circe had meant when she'd said they weren't the first people who had asked her help to get into Olympus? The man's gaze darted from the helmet in Dendris's hands to the statue and the table. He grinned.

'I think you've got something we've been searching for. Something Lord Aristaeus needs.'

'I don't know what you mean,' Theron said. 'We are nymphs serving Demeter. If you don't –' His voice cracked. 'If you –'

He sounded like himself again. Deina spun to see Theron standing just behind her. Behind him, Archis was beginning to bulge and distort. Another one of the sea nymphs was transforming back into a mortal man. As he was swaying, disorientated, Deina grabbed the knife from his belt and pivoted to stab it into the stomach of the man holding the door shut. He squealed and bent double. Deina pushed him out of the way.

'Drink the potion,' she yelled at the others. 'Get out of here!' They had all returned to their own appearance now, all had weapons in their hands – but so did Aristaeus's thugs. And they were still outnumbered. Deina pulled her knives from her belt and charged at the man who'd now got Dendris in a headlock.

Her feet slid out from under her, pitching her onto the floor. To her surprise, the tiles beneath her hands were freezing, their surface covered with a slick of ice. Was Nat here? She remembered the circle of frostbitten grass where he'd stood on Circe's island, and the chill of his touch. A gust of icy air enveloped her. Something appeared: not the god of death, but a rectangle of utter darkness, hanging in the air between the bed and the columns that opened onto the mountainside. It was the doorway Thanatos had pulled her through when he'd dragged her from the room at the top of the Cadmea. The doorway to the Underworld.

No. No, not yet –

She scrabbled to drag the sandglass from her bag. Almost all the silver dust had run though. As she watched, the last few grains dropped into the lower bulb. Her time was up.

As the others fought around her, an invisible force seized

Deina and began pulling her irresistibly towards the darkness. She threw herself onto her knees, trying uselessly to get some purchase on the frosted floor.

Theron's hand seized hers. He was holding on to one of the solid gold tables with his other hand. For an instant Deina's progress towards the darkness slowed, but then the table began to move. Theron let go of it as it toppled sideways, and they both shot towards the gaping doorway.

'Deina! Theron!' Aster screamed – he was being pinned down by three of Aristaeus's men. The others had seized Dendris and Archis. Dendris freed one arm and threw the helmet towards Theron. He reached for it. It was too far away.

'Let go of me!' Deina tried to pull her hand free. 'Get the helmet. You have to stop Aristaeus!'

Theron reached once more for the helmet, cursed and scrabbled closer to Deina, wrapping his arms around her.

'No.' Deina fought to push him away. 'It's too dangerous. You have to let me go!'

In answer, Theron crushed her against his chest.

'I love you, Deina. I love you more than my own life. Whatever happens, I'm not losing you again.'

Together, they tumbled into the darkness.

13

The fall – if they were falling – stole Deina's sense of direction. All she could do was cling to Theron, her eyes screwed shut against the terrifying absence of light, until the cell within which Deina had been confined materialised around them and they landed heavily on the stone floor. The impact knocked Deina's breath from her body. Still, despite the shock and dizziness, she forced herself to roll and scramble to her feet, staggering against the wall for support. A loud screeching wail set her head ringing; she covered her ears and cursed, impatient for her vision to return to normal.

'Deina?' Nat's voice. He sounded aghast. 'What are you doing here?'

'What do you think?' she answered, her sight still blurry. 'The seeds pulled me back.' She tried to show him the sandglass, but it had disappeared.

'Perfect. Your timing is terrible.'

'*My* timing?' Her vision cleared, revealing the Dream Child, back in its own form, its leathery wings spread wide and its

beaked mouth open as scream after scream echoed around the small stone chamber. The stench of the creature made her gag. Theron, still dazed, was lying near its feet. The Dream Child spotted him the same moment Deina did; it crouched and seized Theron's head with its claws, drawing back its own head as if it were about to plunge its beak into his skull. Deina still had one of her knives in her hand. She threw herself forward.

Nat caught her mid-stride, seizing her waist with one muscled arm and pinning her against him.

'Let go of me!' Deina yelled through gritted teeth.

Ignoring her struggles, the god of death flung out his free hand, purple and black flames dancing at his fingertips. The Dream Child cowered, releasing Theron, its angry screams faltering into piteous whines.

'Theron is safe! You can stop trying to cut my arm off.' Nat released her.

'Your spell failed?'

By way of answer, Nat picked up the silver jug that had contained the nectar and tipped it upside down. A single drop trickled out and hit the floor.

'Hades will know the nectar's gone, and she'll think you've drunk it. She'll arrive any moment.' Nat tossed the jug into a corner and seized the Oneiros by the scruff of its neck. 'I need to get this out of here.'

Hades. Fear lanced through Deina's core.

'What should I do?'

Nat dragged a hand through his dark hair, more flustered than Deina had ever seen him, and shrugged.

'Improvise.'

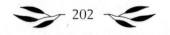

With that, he and the Dream Child vanished.

Deina sheathed her knife and sank to her knees next to Theron.

'Are you hurt?' She ran her hand over his head, checking for blood.

'Deina?' He shuddered and managed to sit up, wrinkling his nose in disgust. 'What on earth was that thing? And where are we?'

'The cell Hades confined me in. That creature was one of the Oneiroi. The Dream Children.' Deina pressed her hands to her temples, trying to massage away the beginnings of a headache. 'I'll explain later. Hades is on her way.'

Theron looked around the tiny room as if hoping for a hiding place.

'What can we do?'

There was nowhere to conceal Theron, that was for certain. *Improvise*, Nat had said. Pretend. Deina drummed her fingers rapidly against the edge of the nearby table. But pretend what?

The silver jug was still lying where Nat had left it, and the cup that she'd tried to use to smash the ceiling. Deina shook her head at her own daring – or possibly, her own foolishness.

Still, it might work. If we're quick enough.

Deina dragged the strap of her bag over her neck and thrust it into Theron's arms. 'Help me. Get out the red gown and belt and brooch and sandals that go with it.' Quickly, she pulled off her tunic and boots – no time for modesty – snatched the red gown from Theron's hands and wrapped its folds around her body. 'Pin the shoulder for me. And give me the belt.' Jamming her feet into the golden sandals, she hurried to lace the glittering cords around her ankles. There was no time to fix her hair; hopefully, Hades would believe she'd pulled it from the golden net while tormented with boredom.

Theron was holding out her old clothes and bag. 'What about these?'

'Put them in your bag. Hurry!' From the way her spine was crawling, Deina knew Hades was nearly there. She snatched up the empty goblet. 'When she arrives, just – just act confused!' Since Theron already looked mystified, she hoped it wouldn't prove too difficult. 'Or pretend you're singing one of the ancient poems, because we're going to be spinning Hades a story.' Last-minute inspiration struck. She twisted her empty hand in the front of Theron's tunic, pulled him closed and jammed her mouth against his.

A flash of colour in the corner of her eye told her that Hades had arrived. With a dramatic gasp Deina broke away from Theron, keeping her grip on his tunic.

The god of the Underworld was watching them through narrowed eyes, her gaze shifting from one to the other, until it alighted on the goblet in Deina's hand. Her eyebrow rose. Deina brought the goblet to her mouth and tipped her head back. Pretended to swallow. Lowered the goblet and ran her tongue over her lips.

Hades' mouth curved into a smile. She picked up the jug and, as Nat had done, tipped it upside down.

'I knew you would not be able to resist.'

'You forced me. I thought I was going mad. You left me no choice.' Deina could remember it well enough; the sense that her life had collapsed in on itself, that she was trapped forever within these unyielding stone walls. She didn't have to force the despair or venom into her voice. 'I hate you. I hate myself. And yet . . .' With a moan of frustration, she tugged Theron nearer again.

'You managed to summon him? The nectar is unusually quick to take effect.' There was a hint of disbelief in Hades' voice. Deina had to convince her.

'I don't know how. After I had drunk . . .' She looked down at the goblet in her hand and threw it away from her with an exclamation of disgust. 'Afterwards, I could feel a new power beneath my skin.' Hades had never been a mortal. She would not know how it would feel to suddenly become immortal.

'Go on,' the god prompted, tilting her head and examining Deina curiously.

'It made me –' Deina closed her eyes, remembering the shame and powerlessness she'd felt when Hades had forced her to embrace Thanatos. The summoned blood flamed into her cheeks. 'It awakened new cravings, deep within my body. I wanted someone to satisfy my cravings. I wanted Theron. And he appeared.' She leaned in close to Theron, as if desperate for his touch. A look of revulsion appeared on his face.

'What has happened to you, Deina?' he asked, his voice sharp with fear. 'What is this place? How did I come here?'

Hades sighed. 'For a prince of Thebes, you're remarkably slow-witted. Deina is my daughter. She has consumed the nectar and has started her transformation into a god. This alone gave force to her desire and brought you here.' The god's eyes lit up with unexpected greed. 'The power she will command once fully altered will be unimaginable.' She held out her hands to Deina. Releasing Theron, who backed away as if terrified, Deina took Hades' hands in hers. 'Now, daughter,' the god continued, 'kneel and swear obedience and loyalty to me. Once you have done that, I will reveal to you my plan, so long in the crafting.'

Deina took a deep breath.

'I will kneel before you. I will swear to obey you. After you've given me what I most desire.'

Hades laughed. 'You already bargain like a god. And do you not have what you most desire?' She gestured to Theron.

Deina shook her head.

'What I most desire is to see Thanatos humbled before me.' She imagined that it was Aristaeus's punishment she was pleading for, and found no difficulty in coating her words with venom. 'He betrayed me, and I want to see him punished for his trickery. I want to watch as he is strung up and left to suffer in Tartarus.' Deina pressed Hades' hand to her breast, ignoring the surprise on the god's face. 'Frozen as it is, my heart burns for revenge. Do this for me, then I'll gladly swear to serve you for eternity. I'll do whatever you want.'

Greed flared again in Hades' face. It was the god's greed Deina was counting on.

'As you wish, daughter. I will summon Thanatos and we may begin his punishment.' Hades raised her voice. 'Come, Thanatos. Show yourself.'

Nothing happened.

'Thanatos!' Hades demanded. 'Do not try me, or your sufferings will be even worse.'

Still, the god of death did not appear.

'Has he escaped us?' Deina asked.

Hades forced a smile. 'Impossible. I will find him in whichever dark corner of the Underworld he is skulking.' Her gaze fell on Theron, still cowering as far away as possible. 'In the meantime, I will return you to the quarters I have prepared for you. You, and your prince. I am pleased with you, daughter. I would not deny you your reward.' The god clicked her fingers.

A door appeared in one of the seamless walls. Hades pushed it open, beckoning Deina and Theron to follow her. Deina found they were back in the starlit surroundings of Hades' courts. The path at her feet, set between silver posts, led to the bone-white palace just ahead. When she looked back, there was no sign of the cell. Just woods and pastures and peace: grazing cattle and a field of barley, its spikes ripe with fat grains of gold. The grass alongside the path was studded with tiny emeralds.

'You see the beauty now,' Hades commented.

Deina remembered first setting foot in Hades' gardens.

'I always did.'

Inside the palace, Hades took them through high-ceilinged halls and across lushly planted courtyards with babbling fountains. In one of these a man was working at a long table, bent over fragments of metal and scraps of papyrus. His concentration reminded Deina of Drex working on carving his agate, though she saw as they passed him that he had coins for eyes, and his clothing was a shroud.

'Is it ready yet, Daedalus?' Hades asked.

The dead craftsman nodded and held up a hand. Something glittered between his finger and thumb: something silvery, pointed at one end and curved at the other, like a giant's teardrop.

'He's nearly as clever as Hephaestus,' the god commented, leading them on. 'I have my own plans for Thanatos – I've finally convinced my brothers that he is more trouble than he is worth – but don't worry. They won't interfere with his punishment.' The next courtyard looked familiar. Hades stopped and gestured to a set of stairs leading to a porticoed building. 'The rooms I had prepared for you. Enjoy them.' Her smile faded into a snarl. 'I'll return once I've located the miscreant.'

Hades vanished. Deina and Theron climbed the stairs. The room they entered was the room she had thought she'd imagined while standing in Hades' throne room. It seemed real enough now: the walls, adorned with vibrant frescos, were solid and cool to her touch.

'Well, we managed to convince Hades,' Theron said, slumping down on a chair. He was trembling. 'Sometimes, I impress even myself.'

Deina, exploring the room, didn't immediately answer him. She sank her hands into the silvery furs that covered the bed in the centre of the room. Ran her fingers across the selection of fresh gowns and tunics – every one a different shade, but all bejewelled – that had been arranged in an open sandalwood chest. Breathed in the scent of the sprigs of mint and rosemary, strewn across the floor, which were crushed beneath her feet as she walked. On a side table a silver jug had been filled to the brim with nectar. A bowl of dark red grapes, still dewed with rain, sat next to it. She plucked one of the grapes and bit into it. As the fruit burst it filled her mouth with sweet juice. It was all as perfect as it had been in the vision Hades had shown her. More perfect.

A ripple of notes made her turn; Theron had picked up a lyre that had been left leaning against the wall and was running his fingers gently across the strings, picking out a tune. Deina recognised one of the fragments of music she'd heard him humming in the tunnel that led to Poseidon's palace and she smiled, warmed by a small spark of happiness. Even being trapped in the Underworld couldn't extinguish Theron's love of music. She sat on the bed and patted the space next to her. Theron joined her.

'What is that? I don't recognise the tune.'

'It's not from one of the rites or hymns. I made it up.' He looked at little embarrassed. 'Do you like it?'

'It's beautiful. Though a little melancholy.'

'It's not finished yet. I haven't worked out all the lyrics, or where the song is going to go – it might be full of happiness in the end. Or acceptance, at least.' He started talking of modes and harmonies. Deina was lost almost instantly – she knew nothing of music – but hearing him speak of something that was nothing to do with the Underworld or the torc or Aristaeus made her want to hug him.

'Don't ever change, Theron. Whatever happens, promise me you'll stay the same.'

He gave her a quizzical look.

'But people have to change. We grow, we learn new things, we hopefully come to understand ourselves better. And the world changes around us.' He took her hand and seemed to study the two rings she wore.

He was right, of course. The gods' inability to learn and grow was one of the reasons she despised them.

'Even since we left Iolkos,' Theron continued, 'the world has changed. We had two pieces of the torc, and we've lost them both. Aristaeus has got the fragments and our friends.'

'You think Aster and Dendris and Archis are dead?'

Theron shook his head slowly.

'No. I feel as if I would know if they were dead. Aster, at least; we grew up together. I hope they're all still alive. Our plan, though –' he shrugged – 'dead in the water. Perhaps trying to find all the fragments was always a bad idea. As difficult as it would be to spend a lifetime on the run with one fragment, it's probably better than whatever the three of them are facing right now.' Theron's face crumpled, and he pressed the heel of his free hand to his eyes. 'Maybe we should be hoping they all died quickly. Maybe –'

He broke off, but Deina knew him well enough to finish the sentence in her head.

Maybe I shouldn't have left them.

It was easy enough to imagine the horrors that Aristaeus might inflict on their friends. He'd probably make Aster into one of his Iron Guards: trapped within spell-cast armour for decades, voiceless, sleepless, barely a person any more. As for Archis and Dendris . . . Deina hadn't forgotten the way Aristaeus had touched her on the journey to Thebes. He'd suggested she give him her body in return for more comfortable quarters. When she refused, her usefulness to Orpheus had saved her from revenge. Dendris and Archis, however, had no such protection.

'We can't give up on them, Theron. We can't give up on them or the torc.'

Theron twisted round to put his hands on her shoulders.

'I know you hoped we could use it to free all the Theodesmioi. It was a good hope, Deina. But right now, I can't see how we can even save ourselves.'

Deina stared into his dark eyes, so full of love and anguish.

'That – that wasn't the only reason I wanted to remake the torc. I hoped – I thought, perhaps, it might be used to free me from the seeds.' Her hand fluttered over her abdomen. 'So the Underworld wouldn't have power over me any more.'

So that you might have power over the Underworld instead. The kind of power you crave . . .

The words rose unbidden into Deina's mind, along with a thrill of desire. For an instant she was back on Circe's island, imagining herself with the ability to stop Theron ever wanting anyone but her.

With the torc, you might do that and infinitely more . . .

She screwed her eyes shut, as if that could block out the voice in her head. She was back in the Underworld, and the chances of remaking the torc were more remote than ever.

When she opened her eyes again, Theron was watching her anxiously.

'I'm – I'm scared, Deina.'

Deina lifted her hands to his face.

'I understand. I'm scared too.' Scared of what Hades might do. Scared of being trapped here. Scared for her friends. Scared of herself. She threw her arms around Theron's neck. 'I'm terrified. But we can't give up. There might still be a way to

save our friends. Nat might find a way to get you out of here, whatever happens to me.'

'You don't really want to see him punished, then?'

'Do you?' Deina asked, pulling away a little.

Theron drew a shaky breath and tried to smile.

'No. Not punished.' He picked at the soft fur beneath them. 'Thanatos being made to look ridiculous, yes. I'd be fine with that.' He cupped Deina's cheek with one hand. 'I won't leave you here.'

'Even if leaving me here was the only way to save the others? To save yourself?'

Theron didn't answer.

'I won't lose another person I love to Aristaeus's blade. And I won't let you throw away your future. Critos was right about you making a good king.' Deina paused. 'You've been thinking about what he said too, haven't you?'

A nod.

'Since our last night in Iolkos, I've been wondering if he is right.' Theron groaned. 'As if I could ever win against Aristaeus. Still . . .'

Maybe he could win, if you had the torc . . .

That voice again, like an insect buzz in the back of her brain. Irritating. Tempting. Deina pinched the bridge of her nose and tried to focus. Get Theron out of here. Save her friends. Find the third segment of the torc. Rid herself of the seeds and escape the Underworld. Free the Theodesmioi. Defeat Aristaeus. A list of ambitions that seemed to become more crucial and less realistic with every passing moment. Dreams and questions, that was all she had, like so many gossamer strands slipping through her fingers. Where was Nat? What was the purpose of thing that Daedalus had made for Hades? What was her next move?

Everything was a game to the gods. If she and Theron stopped playing, the game was over. They'd have lost.

Desperate for a distraction, Deina grabbed the front of Theron's tunic and pulled him towards her.

'Kiss me.'

His eyes widened, but he didn't argue. Just slid his arms around her and drew her against him, pressing his lips to hers and kissing her deeply. His fingers tangled in her hair. They fell sideways into the softness of the bed. Slowly, Theron began working his way down her body, from mouth to neck, from neck to collarbone, his lips soft and warm against her skin. Deina moaned with pleasure. She hooked one leg around him as he slid his hand up her thigh, rucking the fine fabric of her gown up around her hips. Then, in one quick movement, he pushed her onto her back and straddled her hips, straightening up to pull his tunic over his head. Deina gazed at his muscled chest and lifted her hands to trace her fingers greedily over the rite-seals that marked his skin, raking her nails across his taut stomach, drinking in his strength and beauty. He shuddered at her touch. Tore away the brooch that pinned her gown together at the shoulder and bent, trembling, to nuzzle her breasts, making Deina gasp and arch her back. Kissing her mouth again, his thumbs tracing the line of her jaw, Theron smiled down at her. 'I've dreamed of this moment. Of us being together, never to be separated.'

Had he said that before? Memory, ice-cold in its clarity,

tempered Deina's passion. She pictured the pretend Theron that Hades had conjured when Nat had first brought her to the Underworld. Heard him kissing her neck and saying almost exactly the same words . . .

Pushing Theron away, Deina sat up and pulled the remnants of the gown up over her breasts.

'Deina?'

She could hear the hurt and surprise in his voice.

'Did I do something wrong? I thought – I thought this was what you wanted.'

She turned to face him.

'You didn't do anything wrong.' She lifted her fingers to his cheek, then to the sigil that marred his forehead.

'What, then?' He moved to sit slumped on the edge of the bed. 'I thought you wanted me in the same way I want you.'

'I did. I do.' Her body ached for his touch. It would have been so easy to fall back into his arms, to finish what they had started. 'I want you so much, it hurts.' She felt Theron's hand come to rest on top of hers. 'But not like this. Not now. Not *here*.' She glanced at the luxurious surroundings, Nat's question echoing through her mind. *Would it be so impossible for you to be happy here?* If she drank the nectar, she'd be a god, but neither an Olympian nor one of the old gods. Who knew what limits Hades might be able to place on her? Perhaps that was what her mother intended: to keep her here, to use her somehow, to draw on her power like a leech feasting on blood. The idea made every fibre of her body tense in revulsion. Yet still, the honeyed scent of the jar of nectar made her mouth water. If she lost herself in pleasure, if she allowed the thought of staying here with Theron to take root, she didn't trust herself to resist any longer.

'Deina,' Theron murmured, brushing the back of his fingers against her cheek, 'talk to me. Tell me what's in your mind, like you used to when we first became friends. We used to sit in that little ivy-covered shelter in the maze garden. We told each other everything.'

Could she go back to that moment? She imagined describing to him the voice in her head, and the fantasies she'd been having of using the torc – not just to help others, but for personal gain. Maybe he would understand.

Maybe he wouldn't.

She wasn't sure she could stand to see the warmth in his eyes turning to fear. Better to be . . . selective.

'This room, this bed – it's all part of Hades' plan to keep me here. It's not real.' She turned back to Theron and pressed her hand to his chest, feeling the rapid beat of his heart. 'Not like this is real. We can't lose ourselves in the dream, Theron, as much as we both want to. We have to think. Plan. Take charge of the game.'

Theron shook his head, as if the idea of them taking charge was too absurd to be even worth disagreeing with, but he sighed and picked up his discarded tunic from the floor as Deina slid off the bed and walked over to the chest of clothes. One of the folded fabrics, edged with gems that glittered with a strange scarlet fire, was that warm shade of blue that seemed to be one of her mother's favourite colours. Stripping off the torn red gown, she wrapped the blue rectangle around her body, pinning it at the shoulder and securing it at her waist with a silver brooch and belt that she'd found tucked inside. There was a pair of silver sandals next to the chest, and on a nearby table lay a comb and a polished bronze mirror. Someone, either Hades or the nymphs she'd seen in the courtyard the first time she'd been brought here, had thought of everything.

Theron appeared at her shoulder, his face reflected next to hers. Deina put down the mirror and turned to him.

'Well?' he asked. 'What's our play?'

'Find the third part of the torc, if we can.' Theron started to protest, so she added, 'If Aristaeus finds it, then he'll have everything he needs to attempt to remake the torc. It's our last chance to stop him. We have to at least try. And then we have to hope Nat can get us out of here.'

Theron shook his head.

'Hold on – isn't it safer to leave the third part where it is? We only found the other two fragments because we had help from Nat. And you know how dangerous the Underworld is. Say Aristaeus does send his gang of cut-throats to search for the last fragment, what are the odds of them surviving?'

'Yes, we had help from Nat. But Circe helped Aristaeus too – she must have done. And we don't know whether one of the other gods is standing in the shadows, giving Aristaeus aid. We can't leave it to chance,' Deina urged. 'We have to find the third fragment.'

Theron still looked sceptical.

'Do you even have any sense of where to start looking?'

Deina summoned an image of the other fragments: intricately etched spirals of gold, silver and bronze twisted together. Each had been carefully rounded at one end, smashed at the other, suggesting the remaining fragment had to be the central third of the torc. Thinking about it made Deina's fingers itch, just like they used to when she was contemplating stealing a particularly fat purse, but it didn't give her any clue as to the third fragment's location. She thought about Poseidon's throne room, and Zeus's bedchamber, and about what they might have in common.

'Well, we know that Tyche won't have hidden the final fragment in Hades' treasury. And I don't know if my mother is cleverer than her siblings, but I think her ambition is more straightforward.'

'What do you mean?'

Deina tried to put her instinct into words.

'Tyche picks on what the other gods think makes them strong, and shows them up as weaknesses. Poseidon has this image of himself as the all-powerful ruler of the sea – so she put the fragment near the biggest portrait of him she could find. Zeus believes that he's –' she raised an eyebrow – 'irresistible. So Tyche hid the fragment in his bedchamber.'

Theron rubbed his chin thoughtfully.

'So what does Hades consider to be her strength?' he asked. 'That obsidian mirror? It gives her a lot of useful information.'

'But she looks at it all the time. She'd notice if something about it changed.' Deina bit her thumbnail as Theron picked at a fragment of paint flaking off the nearest fresco.

'Nat is in charge of death,' he said eventually. 'Surely Hades' greatest power is what happens after death.'

'She doesn't get to judge souls.'

'No.' Theron blanched. 'But she does get to be in charge of punishment.'

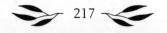

Tartarus. They'd encountered plenty of horrors during their earlier journey through the Underworld, but Tartarus would likely eclipse them all. It was the place of eternal punishment, an inescapable prison where the gods sent those who had offended them.

'If we're right,' Deina said, 'I should go on my own.'

'No. We go together.' Theron pointed at her then back at himself. 'Still a team, in case you'd forgotten.'

Deina gave him a grateful smile.

'Still a team.'

'But please, Deina – if Nat appears and offers to get us out of here, we have to go. Whether we've found the fragment or not.'

'*You* have to go,' Deina reminded him gently. 'While the seeds are still rooted in my stomach, I can't go anywhere.' She sighed as Theron's face fell. 'Now, Hades thinks I hate Nat, so let's go with that. Kneel down. And keep looking anguished.'

Theron took a deep breath and sank to the floor.

'I think I can manage that.'

Deina closed her eyes.

'Lord Hades, can you hear me?'

Instantly the doors swung open, and the god strolled into the room. Her violet eyes lit up as she took in the rumpled bed.

'I see you have been enjoying yourself. Is not my realm all I promised it could be?'

'It is indeed. Has Thanatos been discovered?'

Hades snarled.

'His disobedience is intolerable. Still, he cannot escape. You will not need to be patient for much longer.'

'Don't worry, I've thought of a way to pass the time.' Deina forced herself to sound excited. 'I want to visit Tartarus while you search for him. I want to see the punishments already being inflicted. Then I want to make Thanatos's fate infinitely worse.' She took Theron's chin in her hand and forced his head up. 'Also, though I enjoyed this one, I had to threaten him to make him obey me. I want to show him where he might end up if he displeases me again.'

Hades burst into a ripple of laughter.

'You are far more like me than I had hoped.' Pausing, the god studied Deina's face. 'Very well. I approve your request. You may wait for me in Tartarus.' She waved her hand, and the room, with its graceful furnishings, disappeared. Instead, they were standing on cold black dunes lit by faint starshine. Deina didn't recognise this place, but Dendris had described it, after they'd passed through the wall of night and before Deina had enabled the others to see the beauty of Hades' gardens: a desert of black sand. The rolling landscape stretched into the distance in every direction except one, where the way was blocked by a pair of gates. These, though, were not the bronze gates that Deina had seen before. The gates that faced her now were . . . impossible. Deina advanced warily, until she was close enough to gently touch them. With a gasp she snatched her hand back, her fingertips throbbing with pain.

Ice. The gates were made of black ice, burning with a fierce cold, yet the surface was crazed, scarred by liquid fire that oozed through deep gashes. Deina jumped back as one of the fiery rivulets twisted outwards, forming into a glowing, hissing snake that bared its fangs at her before sinking back into the chasm from which it had appeared. As fast as the fire ran across the ice, it froze and darkened. As fast as the ice formed, a crack appeared, and more fire bled out. And over and over the flaming snakes burst from the doors as if trying to escape. Up close, the gates almost looked alive.

Hades was at her side.

'Tartarus is a realm of extremes. The only true constant is pain.' The god turned to Theron. 'Prepare yourself, son of Thebes. Few of the mortals who enter this place ever leave.'

14

Deina gagged and clamped her palm over her mouth and nose, trying vainly to avoid the stench that saturated the air of the vast cavern in which they now stood. She wanted to do much more: to screw her eyes shut and stuff her fingers into her ears, to bury her head against Theron's shoulder and shut out the horror that surrounded them. Theron hadn't let go of Deina's hand, but he was using his other hand to cover his eyes. Deina couldn't allow herself that luxury. To keep up the pretence of having surrendered to Hades, she had to brave Tartarus and the tortures it contained, to appear . . . interested. She tightened her grip on Theron's fingers and hoped the god would not notice how white her knuckles were.

They were surrounded by suffering. The light in Tartarus came only from huge torches set up on the rocky walls, dimmed by the choking fumes that rose from fissures in the ground. Still, Deina wished it was darker. She could see too clearly the mortal shades, tormented by hunger and thirst, that crowded the banks of the river that ran through the cavern. Every time one of the unfortunate creatures tried to scoop up some water, the rippling liquid instantly turned to stinking mud. Others hovered near blankets on which an abundance of delicious-looking food had been laid out. When Deina drew closer, she saw that every dish became putrid, crawling with maggots, as soon as one of the ghosts tried to grasp it.

'Why are they being punished?' she asked Hades.

'Each has committed some offence against the gods. They are guilty of impiety, or of seeking to thwart the will of the gods, or of breaking some decree the gods hold to be important. Thus, they are punished for bringing dishonour upon those they should worship unconditionally.'

Offences against the gods. Offences against one's fellow humans didn't seem to be so important. Deina dropped her gaze before Hades saw the anger in her eyes.

Hades beckoned to someone standing in the shadows.

'We have visitors, Tisiphone.'

One of the Furies. Deina felt Theron flinch. The figure who approached them reminded Deina of the blood hunters – like something that had been long dead. Mostly bald, a few scraggly hanks of dirty-looking hair clung in patches to Tisiphone's scalp. This, and much of the rest of her skin, was covered in oozing pustules. Her blood-red eyes were lidless, with vertical, reptilian pupils. A forked tongue flicked from between her parted lips. The Fury's costume made a bizarre contrast with her physical appearance: her tunic was so covered in gaudy baubles, sewn on or hanging from her neck, that it was impossible to see the underlying fabric. Snakes coiled around Tisiphone's muscular arms, torso and neck, and there was a scourge stuck in her belt. Each leather thong was tipped with an iron nail. She bowed to Hades.

'My sisters are still searching for the miscreant Thanatos,' the Fury hissed. 'They will scour the very last reaches of the Underworld to retrieve him.'

'I have no doubt. Still, I'm going to join their search,' Hades replied. 'I want to be there when he is dragged from whatever hole he's taken refuge in. In the meantime, show my daughter and her pet mortal whatever she wishes to see. I am making her a gift of Thanatos's punishment, and she desires inspiration.'

'But she is as much to blame as Thanatos. You told us how she shut Orpheus up in the Threshold.' Tisiphone slavered, her clawed hands clutching at the air. 'You promised us Orpheus, Hades,' she whined. 'You promised we could play with him eventually, but now he will never come to us. Never!' Deina's stomach heaved as she tried not to imagine what the Furies' idea of play was.

Hades' bident appeared in her hand and Tisiphone cowered away.

'Enough! You'll have Thanatos to play with and be content!'

'Yes, yes! Content!' Still cowering, the Fury shot a rage-filled look at Deina. 'I hear and obey, Lord Hades.' Slowly she straightened up, moodily eyeing Hades' bident. 'You have a name, Hades' daughter?'

'Khthonia.' The name Hades had given her. The name that, until now, she'd never acknowledged.

'Come then, Khthonia. The suffering dead await your inspection.'

* * *

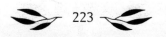

The throng of shades gathered by the riverbank seemed almost without number. For a while, Deina thought the ghosts were oblivious to their presence. Then she realised they were purposefully trying to avoid attracting Tisiphone's attention. When one of the shades did dare to approach, begging for relief, the Fury snarled, raised her whip and brought its lashes down across the ghost's back. The figure shrieked as the iron spikes ripped away its skin, spattering both Tisiphone and Deina with dark, sticky blood.

Deina had to bite her tongue to keep from crying out.

'How – how is that possible? These are ghosts, spirits –'

For the first time, Tisiphone grinned, showing a mouthful of needle-like fangs.

'In Tartarus, their flesh is restored to them, that I may flay it off again to better punish them. Do not be concerned. The creature's skin will soon renew itself.'

Deina gritted her teeth against the bile rising in her throat. Theron threw up. Tisiphone laughed. 'Come. We have much to see.'

The Fury led them on through the dimly lit wasteland of Tartarus. Compared to the other parts of the Underworld Deina had travelled through, this landscape changed only a little. The cavern transformed gradually into a deep valley, hemmed in by sharp, blood-stained peaks. Still, the dull clouds above somehow cast the same ruddy glare as the now vanished torches. Tall pillars of rock appeared, oozing with some dark, foul-smelling liquid, to which condemned souls had been manacled. Tisiphone lashed them as she passed. Down and down they walked, through unrelenting misery. Deina kept hoping for a clue that might lead her to where Tyche had hidden the third part of the torc, but Tisiphone, ever watchful, gave her no opportunity to search properly. The Fury's pace didn't slow until they came upon characters that Deina knew from ancient myth. Sisyphus, condemned for revealing Zeus's abduction of Aegina to her father, pushing a huge boulder uphill for eternity without ever reaching the summit. Ixion, bound forever to a revolving wheel of fire for trying to seduce the goddess Hera. The daughters of Danaus, who murdered their husbands on the orders of their father, doomed to attempt to empty an entire lake using only sieves. Tisiphone pointed out these punishments, although she seemed bored by them. After gesturing for Deina to watch each unfolding scene, she turned her attention to Theron, pale but upright at Deina's side. Perhaps it wasn't surprising; from what Deina had been taught back at the House, Tisiphone never left Tartarus. Theron was likely the only male she'd seen for hundreds of years who wasn't dead and being horribly tortured, though from the way the Fury stared at him, Deina couldn't quite work out whether she wanted to kiss him or devour him, stripping the flesh from his bones. Only when they reached the giant Tityus did Tisiphone show more interest in what was going on around them. As punishment for assaulting the goddess Leto, Tityus was spending the afterlife pegged to the ground, keening like a dying animal, while vultures ate his liver and entrails over the course of each day, only for them to grow back each night. The same punishment inflicted by Zeus on Prometheus – it was obviously one of the Olympian gods' favourite forms of torture.

'This might do for my brother Thanatos,' Tisiphone observed. 'I should enjoy hearing him scream.' She shot Deina a slightly suspicious glance. 'Wouldn't you?'

'I would,' Deina agreed. Sensing that something more was

required, she forced herself to smile at Tisiphone, adding, 'I think I'd find it entertaining to make frequent visits to watch as his innards are slowly pecked and ripped away.' Taking a deep breath, she edged nearer to Tityus's struggling form, as if keen to inspect the vultures' work more closely. The blood-soaked earth sucked at her sandals. Behind her, Tisiphone began interrogating Theron.

'You have a name, mortal?'

'Theron.'

'Are you a good pet? Do you entertain?'

'I – I try.'

'Hm. You're a pretty thing. I like pretty things.'

Deina closed her eyes, hoping to shut out the strain in Theron's voice and Tityus's frantic sobs so she could think. This time, though, there was no inspiration. She couldn't even imagine the goddess of luck somewhere like this; perhaps they were searching in the wrong place. Perhaps she should have asked to visit Charon, to look for the fragment among the detritus the ferryman hauled from the river Styx, but there was no time for second chances. She had to find the torc fragment before Hades returned. She had to find someone to help her. Deina clenched her hands into fists and tried to force her mind to dredge up all the stories she had been told of Tartarus.

Finally, a name floated up through her memories. Deina almost smiled.

Will he help me, though?

He might.

She turned back to the Fury to find Tisiphone running her fingers over Theron's collarbone and chest, while Theron, rigid, sweating, was leaning away from her and averting his head.

Deina hurried forward, resisting the urge to knock the Fury's hand away.

'Tisiphone,' Deina said, carefully disguising the disgust churning through her stomach, 'there is one more sight I should like to see before I make my choice as to Thanatos's punishment. This is amusing enough, but as I understand it, Tityus is only punished during the day. At night, he rests. I want Thanatos to suffer constantly, with no relief. May we visit the old gods – the Titans? I'd like to see what they endure. I'd like Thanatos's agony to be greater than any other inhabitant of Tartarus.'

Tisiphone, barely looking away from Theron, nodded.

'As you wish, Khthonia. Come, mortal.' One of the snakes curled around her arms began to slither onto Theron's shoulders. Seizing him by the hand, the Fury began striding away along the path that led further down. Deina followed.

According to the old stories, the Titans were confined in the very depths of Tartarus, hurled there by Zeus following the Olympian gods' victory over them. It did seem to Deina, as she looked back up the steep path at the circle of dull red sky high above, that she was now at the bottom of a huge well. The walls were no longer rock but solid bronze, cold as death to her touch. The freezing air clawed at her throat, and it was so dark that Deina could see little at first beyond the light cast by the torch Tisiphone carried.

'Which of the Titans do you wish to see?' Tisiphone asked. 'I have most of them within my care.'

Deina tapped one forefinger against her lips, pretending to think. Eventually she answered.

'Cronos, the one they call the Schemer, and the Crooked.

He led the Titans against Zeus and Hades and the rest of the gods. His punishment must be the worst, surely?'

'Cronos talks too much,' Tisiphone hissed. 'But if you wish to see him . . .' She shrugged and jerked her head. 'This way.'

Still holding on to Theron, the Fury led them across the dingy plain. Deina stayed close; she could hear things in the shadows: guttural voices cursing, moans of pain. As her eyes adapted to the gloom, she saw that this part of Tartarus was utterly barren: nothing but empty space, hemmed in by the sheer bronze walls. Large circles had been marked out on the ground with rope; each circle contained a Titan, seemingly unable to step over the slender boundary. Occasionally, one of them called out to Tisiphone, begging her for mercy, or water, or some other relief. Tisiphone ignored them all.

'Here.' The Fury lowered her torch, allowing its flames to leap to the pile of wood set within a huge brass cauldron. The fire caught rapidly, illuminating the scene before them: a large circle of rope on the ground, and within that a table groaning with food and drink, and a figure lying stretched out in the dirt. 'Cronos, you have a visitor. You may talk to him, Khthonia, and hear of his punishment from his own lips. I will look after your pet.' Without a backward glance she tugged Theron away and headed for a boulder a little way off. Deina waited until they were both seated on the boulder, and until Tisiphone was giving Theron her full attention, before turning back to Cronos.

The Titan was standing just the other side of the rope, no more than an arm's length from Deina. She flinched. Cronos grinned.

'Fear not.' His voice creaked as if he rarely used it. 'See?'

He raised his hand, claw-like, and swiped – his long fingernails scrapped against the air between them as if it were a sheet of iron. 'I cannot reach you. I cannot go beyond the rope.' The god's deep-set eyes glittered from beneath matted hair. 'You wish to know the details of my punishment?'

Deina cast a glance at Tisiphone. The Fury was stroking Theron's head and appeared completely absorbed.

'No. I want your help.'

Cronos stared at her for a moment, then burst into wheezing laughter that ended in a snarl.

'You mock me. As if I would help any friend of that night-spawn.' He nodded toward Tisiphone and began to walk away. 'Leave me be, mortal.'

'I'm only half mortal,' Deina said quickly. 'Please, listen to me, grandfather.'

The Titan paused, half-turning his head.

'What did you call me?'

Deina took a breath. Came closer and lowered her voice.

'Grandfather. Hades is your child. She is also my mother.'

Cronos swung back to the rope boundary, coming close enough that Deina could see the dirt encrusted on his skin, close enough that she had to hold herself rigid to keep from recoiling. He looked her up and down. 'Speak.'

'I am Theodesmioi, a Soul Severer of the Order of Hades. I was bound to serve the god when I lived in Iolkos, and now she has bound me to the Underworld. I want revenge. And I am not alone.'

A sneer curled Cronos's lips.

'What can a demi-god, even supported by many mortals, do against a god?'

'Hephaestus's torc. The one that Zeus, Poseidon and Hades forced him to dismember. We have two of the three fragments.' The lie fell easily from Deina's lips. She was betting Cronos wouldn't know the truth. That he, like most gods, only had a dim sense of what truth was in the first place.

The sneer vanished, replaced by a calculating look.

'Well. Perhaps I underestimated you, granddaughter.' The Titan paused, wincing and rubbing his shrunken stomach. 'You search for the final fragment, and you believe it is here.'

'Yes. I need to find it before Hades returns.'

'And what's in it for me?'

'If my friends can get the torc remade, I hope they will be able to use it to attack or at least threaten the three gods who claim dominion over most of the Theodesmioi.'

'Your friends are mortals, no? Dangerous, for a mortal to attempt to usurp the power of the gods. The last one who wore the torc was easily destroyed, from what I've heard.'

Deina hesitated. Telling Cronos too much was risky, yet she had to persuade him – quickly, before Hades arrived and before Tisiphone lost interest in Theron. Or worse, did something to hurt him.

'Thanatos is with us. If I can find the last piece of the torc, I'll give it to my friend.' She nodded towards Theron. 'Thanatos can get him to Thebes, I hope, where the others are waiting.'

Cronos raised his eyebrows. 'Thanatos? As another crooked schemer, I respect his cunning and his deceit, but I wouldn't trust him. Besides, he's a god. He might claim that he's going to help you. He might even believe it, until he gets a taste of the sort of power that torc is reputed to confer. Do you really think then that he'll remember what you wanted him to do? Especially if you're not there to remind him.' The Titan shook his head. 'Dangerous, to pin all your hopes on Death. Remake the torc and then wield it yourself.'

His words reminded her of the voice in her mind, tempting her with whispers of power.

'No. I'm not a god. And I can't leave the Underworld. Thanatos gave me seeds to eat.' Deina's hand went automatically to her belly; she could almost feel the seeds sending tendrils out into her flesh, anchoring her ever more firmly to Hades' realm.

'You're not a god *yet*.' Cronos gave her a sly look. 'I can sense the power in you. More power than you should have. Hades is not like my other children. He never does anything without a deep and well thought-out reason, and that includes seducing mortals.' He leaned suddenly against the invisible barrier between them, rattling his words out as his filthy fingernails scratched at the air. 'I have a better plan.' He pointed down at the ground, and Deina saw that the two ends of the rope circle that surrounded him were knotted together. 'Undo the knot. In return, I'll give you something to drink that will rip those seeds right out of you. Then I'll tell you where the last fragment of the torc is. I'll even help you escape.'

'What kind of a drink?' Deina questioned.

'You wanted to know about my punishment.' Cronos gestured to the table. The delicacies piled on it – ripe fruits, roasted meats, freshly baked breads, flagons of drink – would have made Deina's mouth water if the stench of Tartarus hadn't been so overwhelming. 'Every time I eat or drink, I am forced to swallow some of this.' He held up a stoppered vial, made of some dark metal, that was hanging from a chain around his neck. 'I can't stop myself. This potion, which never runs out, makes me violently vomit up everything I've just consumed. Thus, I am punished for having eaten my children, and having tried to wrest back control of the heavens and the earth from my ungrateful offspring.' He smiled. 'As you can imagine, I try to eat and drink as little as possible.'

Deina stared at the vial. She knew the story of Cronos – everyone did. How he learned of the prophecy that one of his children would be greater than he, and so had swallowed every one of them as soon as they'd been born. Finally, Rhea, his wife, substituted a stone wrapped in swaddling clothes for the baby Zeus. When the younger god had grown to manhood, he emerged from hiding and forced his father to swallow a draught that caused Cronos to vomit up all his other children, still alive in his stomach. There was, she supposed, a certain justice to the Titan's punishment.

'Of course,' Cronos continued, 'the potion would kill you as a half-mortal. But, if I mixed it with some nectar . . .'

Finally, Deina understood. The potion would rid her of the seeds. She'd be able to leave the Underworld without the elaborate magical charade she and Nat had constructed last time. The nectar, though – it would keep the potion from killing her, but it would also start her transformation into a god.

She stared into Cronos's eyes. Had all her choices come down to this? The very thing she'd been trying to avoid. The fate she'd sworn she'd rather die than endure: to become one of those she hated. And yet . . . And yet, to be able to confront the gods as an equal, to be able to use the torc as she wished – that was something. She had a sudden image of Zeus, Poseidon and Hades, all prostrate before her. Of Aristaeus dead at her feet. If she was a god, she could force him to give up the other torc fragments, then she could strike him down. Her gaze drifted to the vial that Cronos was holding out, and then to Theron. Tisiphone was still petting him, running her forked tongue down the side of his face as he tried to recoil.

'Tisiphone has a nasty habit of devouring those she mates with. You could save him, if you were a god,' Cronos murmured. 'You could save all of your friends. As a mere demi-god, you won't even be able to save yourself.'

Caught in indecision, Deina stared at the vial around Cronos's neck.

'Hurry,' the god whispered. 'I can tell Hades will be here soon. Once he returns, all will be lost. Your fate has brought you to this choice, granddaughter. The game is almost played out. You have only one possible move left. If you want to defeat Hades, this is the only way.'

Fate. She'd thought she'd broken free of her fate. It seemed she was wrong. Anger surged through her veins, bitter and fierce and as bright as the sun, before burning away into nothing.

'How long?' Deina asked quietly. 'How long does it take?'

'To come into your full power?' Cronos shrugged. 'Your human blood must be transformed to ichor. A while.'

Theron's voice, strong and melodious, fell across the bleak landscape like rain across a parched desert. Tisiphone must have asked him to entertain her.

'Swear by the Styx,' Deina said hurriedly. 'Swear that after I've drunk the potion, you'll tell me where the last fragment is, and how to get it, and that you won't tell Hades or Tisiphone what I'm planning.'

Cronos looked amused.

'Really, Khthonia? Our interests are aligned. Is an oath necessary?' His smile widened. 'Come. Help me to help you, granddaughter. Undo the knot. You won't regret it.'

'Swear,' Deina repeated. 'And swear to return me and Theron to Thebes.' This was better. At least this way she wouldn't have to risk calling Nat back into the Underworld, and Hades wouldn't know they were working together. And the god of death never seemed to have difficulty finding her.

The Titan made the oath. 'Now, the rope.' He rubbed his hands together. 'Undo the knot.'

The hunger in his voice sent a shiver of anxiety along Deina's spine, but she didn't hesitate. Crouching, she lifted the rope, loosened the knot and folded the two ends of the rope back on themselves to create a tiny gap in the circle. It was easier than she'd expected. A sudden cold breeze whirled the dust into eddies, brushing across her skin and making the hairs on her arm stand up. Almost as if a whisper of something had found its way out of the circle. Or back in.

Cronos let out a long, slow sigh. 'Finally.' He went to the table, poured some liquid from one of the flagons into a horn cup and tipped some of the contents of the vial into it before swirling the two together. He held the cup out to her. 'Here. Drink.'

Theron was still singing, though his voice was faltering.

'Won't Tisiphone notice?' she asked Cronos.

'No. Undoing the knot has already restored a little of my

power. If she sees anything, it will be me demonstrating my punishment to you.'

Deina took the cup and sniffed. The sweetness of the nectar couldn't quite disguise a faint underlying odour; something foul and tainted.

'You should drain the cup, to be sure,' Cronos observed.

Closing her eyes, Deina pictured the sketch of the ship she'd taken from her room in the House. Pictured Aster and Dendris and Archis, struggling to free themselves from Aristaeus's thugs, and the Severers and the other Theodesmioi back in Iolkos, still pinned in place by the torcs they wore.

For freedom. For all of us.

Deina raised the cup to her lips and gulped down its contents. The pain started almost before she was done. A dull ache in her chest which flared quickly into agony, as if blades were being driven between her ribs, over and over. As if her frozen heart was being crushed. Deina dropped the cup and fell onto her hands and knees. Her stomach heaved. Vomit gushed from her mouth and nose, quickly followed by dark red blood. And in the blood, the seeds: somehow whole again, with tangled roots growing out of them, clotted with lumps of torn flesh. All the time the pain grew, until it was almost as bad as that inflicted by Aristaeus's scorpions. Almost as bad as when she'd eaten the seeds in the first place. Almost, but not quite. Deina clung to the thought.

I survived that. I can survive this.

The blood thickened and darkened.

Survive.

Thickened so much she could barely breath.

Survive.

The agony peaked – and subsided. The last drops of blood soaked into the dirt. She pressed a shaking hand to her chest.

Stupid, to still hope for a heartbeat. Gods don't have them.

Dragging her hand across her mouth, Deina pushed herself, trembling, to her feet. Cronos was watching her.

'The last fragment of the torc.' Her voice was barely a whisper.

'She has it.' He pointed to Tisiphone. 'I saw it all. Tyche offered it to her as a bauble to add to her pathetic collection of gewgaws. The Fury does not know what it is, but she hordes her trinkets jealously.' He paused, gazing at Deina as if weighing her strength. Or perhaps her desperation. 'She won't give it to you. She might, though, agree to an exchange.'

There was only one thing Deina had that Tisiphone wanted. She nodded to the Titan.

'Thank you.'

He inclined his head.

'Call on me when you need me.'

Deina could feel Cronos's eyes on her back as she made her way towards Tisiphone and Theron. The Fury seemed to be showing Theron her snakes, making them slither around his arms and legs to either impress or terrify him. She barely looked away from him as Deina approached.

'I've seen all I wish to see,' Deina began, hoping Tisiphone wouldn't notice how weak she sounded. 'I know now how to make Thanatos truly suffer. Has my pet been keeping you entertained?' She patted Theron on the head, ignoring the look of alarm he shot her.

The Fury nodded.

'I want one.'

'There are plenty to choose from, though they are not all the same. Few are as talented as this one.' Deina bent her head to kiss Theron lingeringly on the lips. 'He has many gifts that you've not yet experienced.'

Tisiphone hissed. Her snakes tightened around Theron's limbs, making him gasp.

'I want this one. A swap?' She held her whip out to Deina. 'It's fun, torturing the shades.'

Deina pursed her lips as if considering the offer.

'I don't know . . . Your whip is dull. Like you, I prefer shiny things. Particularly things made from different metals fused together. Don't you have something like that to trade for him?'

'Deina . . .' Theron murmured.

Deina ignored him and waited as Tisiphone pointed out various of her trinkets that fit Deina's description. None was the fragment. The Fury began to grow impatient, hissing at each rejection, until she suddenly brightened and fumbled beneath her tunic. 'This one?'

Slightly curved, formed from one strand of gold, one of silver and one of bronze twisted together, broken at both ends, the third fragment of the torc hung gleaming from a rusty chain.

'Hmm,' Deina mused, trying not to seem too eager. 'Very well. I'll swap my pet for that.' As Deina put the chain around her neck and tucked the fragment beneath her gown, the Fury put her arms around Theron.

'You belong to me now, mortal. Please me. Obey me. Or I'll use my whip on you.'

'Deina,' Theron pleaded, 'what are you doing?' He sounded terrified, but she couldn't explain yet. She forced herself to turn away and start strolling back towards Cronos. 'Wait! Don't go!' Theron wasn't acting now. His voice rose to a scream. 'Don't leave me here! Why are you doing this to me?' Raw fear – Deina could tell he was about to be overwhelmed.

'Stop speaking, mortal!' Tisiphone growled. 'One more word and you'll feel my displeasure.'

Deina kept walking. Theron's frantic, half-stifled sobs made every step feel like a knife through her chest, but if she hurried it would risk alerting the Fury that something was wrong. What if Cronos wasn't able to get them both out of there? She'd drunk the nectar – she'd survive down here, perhaps. Theron wouldn't. She couldn't shake the image of Tisiphone flaying Theron's skin from his body, all the while knowing that his suffering was her fault.

They had to get out of here. A few more steps. A few more steps and it would be over . . .

'Well, my Khthonia.'

Deina was brought up short as Hades appeared right in front of her, a triumphant smile on the god's face. 'Here he is. I hope you have a suitable punishment planned out.'

There, bleeding golden ichor, head bowed, wrists bound, kneeling in the grip of two women so like Tisiphone they could only be her sisters, was Thanatos.

15

If Hades hadn't told her, Deina wasn't sure she would have recognised him at first. His clothes were torn. The lacerated skin of his bare arms revealed the violence of the Furies' lashes. The ropes around his wrists were tight enough to cut into his flesh, and the shadows that usually clung to his back and shoulders had vanished. He looked nothing like the god of death. Nothing like the confident, attractive Nat that Deina had first met. She forced herself to look again at his bloody arms. The silvery chain of names had gone too. It was as if the light that had lain at the centre of his darkness had been extinguished.

Was it an act? Surely, it had to be. Nat was powerful. Older than Hades. He was playing almost dead to mislead Hades and the Furies. What if he wasn't, though? She couldn't just leave him here . . .

Hades was watching her expectantly. Deina forced herself to smile, hoping the god couldn't see how anxious she felt. How weak.

'I'm glad you found him. I've decided exactly what I'd like to be done to him. Exploring Tartarus has been inspiring.'

'I'm glad you've enjoyed it, daughter. So, tell us, what is to be done with this malefactor? Something entertaining, I hope.'

'Very entertaining, I think. May I share it with Thanatos first? I want to whisper every detail to him, to force him to hear me, to make sure he understands exactly what is going to happen to him.'

Hades laughed.

'An excellent idea.' The god waved the Furies aside; they stepped back unwillingly. 'Go ahead.'

Deina put her hands on Nat's face; his eyes were dull with pain. She bent and brought her lips close to his ear.

'I have the final piece of the torc, and I'm free of the seeds. I – I gave in, Nat. I drank the nectar. I had to.' She needed to tell someone, and she wasn't sure Theron would understand. 'Cronos said he could get us out of here.' From where she was kneeling, she could see the Titan, still squatting in his circle, still emaciated and filthy. 'So I hope he gets his power back soon. I'll ask him to send you to Thebes with us.' She paused. 'I can't stand to see you like this, Nat. If this is just an act, please give me a sign.'

'Tell me what he is to suffer,' Hades demanded.

Deina swallowed hard and got to her feet.

'As punishment for his trickery, I wish – I wish him to be chained up right here to the bronze walls of Tartarus, to be inflicted with unending hunger and thirst, and for him to be tormented day and night by – by hundreds of leeches feasting on his naked body. And once every day and once every night he is to be force-fed, then given the same potion that Cronos is compelled to drink.'

Hades nodded.

'A creative plan. What do you have to say for yourself, Thanatos? Any apology to make to Deina for what you've done?'

Silence.

Come on, Nat. Stand up. Snap your fingers in her face. Show her that she's not really hurt you.

Deina glanced at Cronos again. Still no change. If she shouted at him, would he be able to act before Hades and the Furies realised what was going on?

'I'm . . . I'm sorry, Deina,' Nat murmured.

Deina tried to feel relief. He was playing along with the story that she wanted him punished. Any moment now, he'd be back to his old self. Any moment.

And then he slowly raised his head and looked at her, and she realised she was wrong. Fear swept like a frozen blade over her nerve endings. Her gaze went to Hades.

No smile now. The god's violet eyes were cold.

'The Furies can be extremely persuasive. Thanatos has told me everything. How he helped you escape your cell. How he helped you open a path back to Iolkos so that you might save your friends from execution. How he and the Oneiros helped you trick me into thinking you'd consumed the nectar.' Her mouth twisted into a sneer. 'How he did all these things out of love. For you.'

Horror kept Deina silent as Hades advanced slowly towards her.

 241

'I offered you everything, you ungrateful wretch. And this is how you repay me? I suppose I should thank you, though. You've forced me to take a step I long contemplated, but held back from.'

Dark shadows began to gather at Hades' shoulders.

'Whatever power he had is now mine.' Wings burst from Hades' back, black feathers spattered with gold, as if the shadows had been ripped physically from Thanatos's body. 'And now we will put the punishment you've so inventively suggested into practice. Since you seem to care for both Theron and Thanatos, *your* punishment will be watching them endure it, for eternity.' The god flung out an arm, pointing at Theron. 'Seize him.' Vine-like tendrils erupted from the ground. Within the space of a breath, Theron had been dragged to the floor and trussed like a pig about to be roasted.

'No!' Deina cried, throwing herself over Theron as Tisiphone raised her whip, bringing the lashes down upon Deina's upflung arm. The iron spikes bit into her skin and made her gasp with pain. But there was no respite. The other two Furies were upon her, scourging her back and legs, forcing her to her knees and trying to drag her away from Theron, who was struggling uselessly to break the vines that bound him.

'Cronos, help us,' she cried out.

'Cronos?' Hades sneered. 'You think that –'

The god gasped and fell silent. The Furies abandoned their assault and hurried to Hades' side. Deina wiped the blood from her eyes.

'Cronos . . .'

'Never fear, granddaughter. I am here.'

Gone was the emaciated form and matted, filthy hair. Now, standing outside of the rope circle that had confined him, Cronos looked like a man of about thirty, strong, healthy and handsome, clad in a white tunic with a gold belt and a golden diadem set in his curling chestnut locks. He held a golden sickle in his hand.

Hades shrieked with rage and shifted instantly into her male form. The bracelet around the god's wrist became a lethal-looking bronze-tipped bident again. He hurled it towards Cronos as the Titan sent the sickle spinning through the air. The two weapons collided and the bident tumbled to the ground, its ash shaft sliced in half. Hades roared – reared up, transforming again into the huge black-and-blue-scaled snake that had threated Deina and the other Severers once before. As the snake darted at Cronos, the Titan flung out his arms and an invisible wave of power knocked Deina to the ground.

'Be free, my brothers and sisters!'

The rope circles nearby began to twitch as the knots securing them started to pull apart. The Titans that Deina could see were all on their feet. All waiting for the moment of release. Cronos staggered, as if the power he'd expended had weakened him.

'Cronos, get us out of here,' yelled Deina. Nat was still on his knees. 'All of us.'

Hades, back in his male form, bellowed at the Furies as the rest of the Titans, looking like gods once more, charged towards him.

'Stop them! Stop *her*!'

Tisiphone, her face a mask of rage, turned on Deina and began raining down blows. Deina tried to protect Theron and resist

the attack at the same time. She reached for Tisiphone's whip, but the Fury grabbed her wrist and leered over Drex's ring. Without warning, she put Deina's finger in her mouth and bit down through skin – flesh – bone. Deina screamed. Tisiphone released her, holding aloft the severed finger with the ring still attached, and returned to lashing Deina with the whip. All Deina could do was cradle her maimed, blood-soaked hand and moan with the agony of it, and wish for the torment to be over.

I wish I had my knives. I wish I could face her with blades in my hands, not beaten into the earth like a dog –

'No more, sister.' Nat's voice. Deina looked up to find him standing there, broken rope still around his wrists and Tisiphone's whip in his hand. The Fury herself was lying in the dirt some distance away. She hissed at Theron. 'Hiss all you want,' he snarled. 'Come near her again and I'll flay you into pieces with your own lash. Cronos –' he swayed, and Deina thought for a moment he was about to collapse – 'if you're going to help, old friend, it needs to be now.'

Cronos was standing a little back, watching the battle between Hades, the other two Furies and the newly freed Titans. He gave Thanatos a nod. The last thing Deina saw was a wave of darkness rearing up, peaking and crashing down on her, bringing utter silence with it.

'Deina? Deina, can you hear me?'

Theron's voice. There was birdsong too, and the creak of tree boughs being bent by the breeze. The cold wind carried the scent of damp living earth. Surely, unless she was dreaming, they weren't in the Underworld any more.

'Deina?'

Theron's features swam into focus as her eyes fluttered open. Dark eyes, wide with concern. The crooked smile faint and uncertain. Deina smiled back at him and lifted her fingers towards his cheek. A mistake – moving made her conscious of the pain pulsing through her body and brought her injured hand into view.

Tisiphone, biting though my fingerbone –

Her hand was wrapped in bloodied strips of fabric, torn, by the looks of it, from her own gown. The ragged hem now barely covered her knees. There were more makeshift bandages around her arms, and something tied around her left thigh too. With the pain came other memories. Hades snarling at her. Nat, broken and defeated on his knees. Trading Theron for the torc fragment. Vomiting up the seeds. Drinking Cronos's potion mixed with nectar –

What have I done?

The answer came almost instantly: *I did what I had to do.*

Was that true? So much had happened. Deina pressed her uninjured hand to her chest, feeling for the torc fragment; it was still there, hidden beneath her blood-soaked gown. That was something. Yet Aristaeus probably had the rest of torc. Aster and Dendris and Archis, outnumbered, were most likely taken or even dead. And a battle had broken out in the Underworld. What would happen if it spilled over into the mortal realm?

Such an event would matter to her friends. That should have been enough. Yet she couldn't entirely silence the reminder that she was no longer mortal; it wouldn't matter in the same way to her.

I did what I had to do.

Perhaps. Or perhaps the seeds were no more than an excuse, and she'd drunk the nectar because being a god was what she'd secretly wanted all along.

Deina shuddered, making Theron frown with concern as he helped her sit up and rest against what felt like a particularly knobbly tree. His skin was grimy and there were bits of twig clinging to his clothes and hair, but he didn't appear to have been damaged, either by Hades' rage or his encounter with Tisiphone. They were in a wooded clearing. Part of a forest, though at one time it must have been something more. Lumps of carved stone poked out of the undergrowth, their designs long since worn into insignificance.

'Your hand,' Theron said softly, tears welling up in his eyes. 'You should have let them have me. I could hear you screaming and all I could do was lie there, useless, while –' His voice broke and he looked away, dragging the back of his hand across his nose.

'It was just a finger,' Deina murmured. Just a finger. She pushed away the sudden fear that she'd never be able to wield a pair of knives again. 'We all escaped – didn't we?'

Theron pointed mutely across the clearing. Nat was sitting with his back to them a little way away. His shoulders were hunched, and his head was in his hands. As far as Deina could see, his arms seemed to be healing quickly from the torture inflicted by the Furies.

'He helped me bandage you up,' Theron said. 'We needed to stop the bleeding, so we just cut some fabric from your gown and did our best with that and some of Anteïs's healing salve – it was still in your bag. He hasn't said much.' He cast a worried look at Nat, then tried to smile and patted Deina a little awkwardly on the shoulder. 'Are you free of the seeds? Please tell me you don't have to go back there.'

'I'm free of them. Cronos agreed to help. He gave me something that made me vomit them up.' No need to mention the nectar. Not yet.

Theron broke into a relived grin.

'That's the best news I've had for a long time. And you got the third part of the torc, so Aristaeus won't be able to complete it. As adventures go, it could have been a lot worse.' He flushed and glanced again at Nat. For the god of death, of course, it had been a lot worse. In a slightly louder voice than was necessary, Theron carried on, 'Apart from your hand, obviously, and your arms, and one deep gash on your leg, the rest of you wasn't as badly hurt as I'd feared.'

Deina couldn't bring herself to look at her hand; as long as she didn't look, she could pretend it was still whole. Instead, she gingerly turned her attention to her left arm, peeling back the top edge of the makeshift bandage and bracing herself to meet the sight of mangled flesh and bloody gouges.

'Oh . . .' Her skin was raw, criss-crossed with deep scratches and caked with blood. Still, not as bad as it should have looked. Not as bad as it would have been if she was still mortal. She pulled the bandage back over the wounds, determined to conceal the truth from Theron for as long as possible. 'I've seen worse. Anteïs must have added something new into the salve.' A surge of grief caught at her throat, and she changed the subject. 'Do you know where we are?'

'Just outside Thebes. You can see the city from beyond those trees, a few hours' walk away. I don't know why we ended up here.'

'I asked Cronos to send us to Thebes. That's where we agreed we should meet if we got separated, remember? Before we left Circe, before everything went wrong, we said we'd meet at the House of Hephaestus in Thebes.' Deina shrugged slightly. 'I thought we should come here first, in case Aster and Dendris and Archis somehow escaped and were waiting for us.'

There was pity in the look Theron gave her, but all he said was, 'Sensible of Cronos to send us somewhere quiet, rather than have us appear in the middle of the city.'

'Cronos sent us here to make a sacrifice.' Nat pushed himself to his feet and slouched over to bit of rock near the middle of the clearing. 'See the sickle carved here? Cronos's symbol.' Nat sounded tired. Bitter. 'This used to be a temple dedicated to Cronos. I remember it.'

'Are you sure, Nat?' Theron asked. 'Why does he suddenly want a sacrifice?'

'Surely, mortal, you can't really be as stupid as you look?' Nat snapped, making Theron's skin mottle with humiliation. 'Every sacrifice strengthens a god's power. That's why we demand them.'

'We?' Theron taunted. 'Hades took your power. Aren't you one of us now?'

'Theron . . .' Deina murmured.

Nat seethed with anger. For a moment, she thought he was about to launch himself at Theron. Instead, he groaned and threw himself back onto the forest floor.

'I've no heartbeat. I don't know *what* I am any more.'

He sounded . . . despairing.

Deina glanced at Theron. He huffed and gave her an incredulous look. Yet he still helped her up and went with her to sit near to where Nat was slumped.

'Is there anything we can do?' Deina asked.

'No. Not unless you can break whatever spell Hades used to steal my powers.' He turned his head slightly to glance at Deina. 'Look at us. Neither of us what we want to be any more. I'd laugh if it wasn't so . . . pathetic.' He spat the word. 'I don't know how to be mortal, if that is indeed what I'm becoming, and you have absolutely no –'

'We should find something to sacrifice,' Deina interrupted hurriedly. 'The daylight is fading.' She started to get up, but Theron put his hand on her shoulder.

'I'll go.' He pulled Deina's bag from inside his own and got one of her knives out. 'Wait here. I may be a while.' He nodded at her and strode off into the woods.

Nat stopped glowering at a nearby clump of frost-withered ferns long enough to say, 'You should tell him you drank the nectar. It will become obvious eventually.'

'I will tell him,' Deina replied. 'Just not yet.' She nudged Nat gently. 'Thank you, by the way, for stopping Tisiphone.'

'You're welcome. You would have done the same.'

He was right, she realised. She would have.

'What if Hades loses?' she asked. 'She was outnumbered by the Titans, even with the help of the Furies. If Cronos defeats her, then surely you'll get your powers back. Perhaps all the Severers will be freed too.'

'The Titans won't win. They have had no sacrifices, no real belief, for many lives of men. They are weak compared with even one Olympian.' Nat plucked one of the fern leaves and started ripping it apart. 'You saw how Cronos was standing to one side, allowing the others to fight? He will have fled, leaving them to be subdued and re-imprisoned.'

'If he's free, then he can help us.'

Nat snorted. 'You'll have to find him first.' The brief flash of humour faded. 'No. Hades will not have been defeated. She may be tired. She may retreat, briefly, to tend her wounds and nurse her injured pride. But soon she will come for us. I managed to avoid telling her about your search for the torc. Still, she will come. I feel . . .' He dragged a hand through his long hair. 'I think I'm scared, Deina.'

His words fell like a shadow across Deina's heart. As Nat watched, she held out her uninjured right hand and tried to conjure something: a flame, or a spark of lightning, or a sprinkling of frost. Nothing, and she didn't even know where to begin. She tried to grasp her knife in her strongest hand, her left, and almost wept with pain and frustration at the weakness of her grip.

'I don't know what we're going to do, Nat.'

'We?' Nat echoed. 'You forget. I have no power.'

Deina leaned closer to him.

'You said you didn't want to be god of death anymore. At least you're free of that responsibility. Perhaps – perhaps you could learn to be happy as a mortal?'

'Perhaps Hades has given me a gift, you mean?' Nat squinted up at the sky. 'No such thing as a gift from a god. You know that.' His shoulders drooped. 'I said I didn't want to be god of death. I never said I didn't want to be a god. How could anyone wish to be this weak and powerless?'

Deina had no answer for him.

'Whatever happens now,' Nat continued, 'I can no longer help you. I can't even help myself.' He wrapped his arms around his legs and sank his head onto his knees.

Deina lay on her side and tried to rest. She'd lost track of time when Theron finally returned. He was holding a rat by the scruff of its neck.

'The cursed creature bit me,' he exclaimed.

The animal was squirming and hissing. Deina felt sorry for it.

'A rat?' Nat said. 'You cannot offer Cronos a rat.'

'It's a rat or nothing,' Theron snapped. 'I lost my bow back in Olympus, and this is all I could catch. Where shall I make this sacrifice?'

Nat got up and beckoned Theron to follow him to a lump of stone nearer the centre of the clearing. 'This was the altar. I can still feel echoes of power here.'

Deina stayed where she was. The sudden silence told her Theron had dispatched the struggling creature. He offered up a prayer to Cronos and she shuddered, knowing that he would be smearing the rat's warm blood across the altar stone. Old gods and new, all alike, seemed to thrive on death. The sun dipped below the treetops and the light dimmed. Either dusk came quickly here, or the shadows of ancient sacrifices were crowding out the sun.

'There's a shepherd's hut at the edge of the forest.' Theron

pointed in the direction he'd come from. 'It's getting colder. I think we should rest there tonight and head to Thebes tomorrow. There may be patrols sweeping the area, and neither of you look up to marching though the dark.'

Deina nodded her agreement as Theron helped her up. Nat said nothing, but he got to his feet.

'Right, then.' Theron's tone was pleasant, but Deina could see he was gritting his teeth. 'This way.'

The shepherd's hut was still in use. Someone had swept the floor recently enough that only a few leaves had blown in beneath the door. The contents were limited: a stack of firewood for the firepit just outside, a bar for the door, a broom and a long-handled spade. The only piece of furniture was a crudely constructed bed with a stained, wool-stuffed mattress, wide enough for a couple of people to rest on without getting too intimate. Theron set about starting a fire. Deina wanted to help, but he made her stop after realising that she was trying to avoid using her maimed hand. Nat, despite Theron's muttered comments and narrowed eyes, didn't offer to do anything. Instead, the former god of death sat against the stone wall of the hut, staring moodily at his feet.

It was pleasant at least to feel the warmth of the fire. To sit quietly, without having to steal or defend herself from anyone. On the other hand, the tension between Nat and Theron was more than Deina wanted to deal with, and she wasn't hungry. After a while she left Theron to finish his meal – a flatbread and some dried meat and water from their provisions – and went into the hut. The darkness was almost a relief. She stripped off the remnants of the blue gown and put her tunic and cloak back on, struggling to manage the brooches. Tomorrow she would have to check the stump of her finger and clean it again. Anteïs had taught her enough about wounds going bad for her to know that she couldn't avoid dealing with it for long. Right now, though, even though she was supposedly turning into a god, she just wanted to sleep. She wrapped herself in her cloak and lay down on the mattress. The door opened and Theron stood, silhouetted against the night sky. He grabbed the spade.

'I'm going to bury the fire. We don't want to attract any attention during the night. Hey –' he prodded Nat with the spade – 'come inside. We should bar the door.'

Deina heard an unwilling groan, then Nat appeared in the doorway. He immediately stumped over to the bed and lay down next to her. She opened her mouth to protest – but he'd been through so much. The earth floor was cold and hard, and the bed was big enough.

Theron came in. She heard him bar the door.

'Huh. So where am I supposed to sleep?' It was too dark for Deina to see his face, but the tone of his voice was clear enough.

'Just lie down next to Nat. There's plenty of space if he moves up.'

There was a faint snigger from Nat.

'I'm happy to be in the middle.'

'No way. I'm not sleeping next to him. I'd rather sleep on the floor.'

'That's your choice,' Nat replied.

Theron swore.

'And what if I choose to drag you off there and kick your now powerless backside outside?'

 253

Nat pushed himself up onto his knees.

'Oh, you can try, you feeble –'

'Stop it, both of you!' Deina yelled. She felt close to tears. 'Haven't you both got enough enemies without behaving like brainless, strutting cockerels to each other? I just want some rest.' She prodded Nat. 'Move over. I'll lie in the middle.'

After a moment's hesitation, he obeyed.

Deina shifted position. 'Now there's space.' She lay on her back, angry with both of them, angry with herself. She'd traded her mortality for power, so where was it?

'I'm sorry, Deina,' Theron murmured.

'So am I,' Nat added quickly.

Theron, lying on his side, slipped an arm across her waist. A few moments later she felt Nat's fingers brushing against the back of her uninjured hand.

No power. Just an ever-increasing number of problems.

As soon as it began to grow light, Deina slipped out of the bed – noting with a grim smile how Theron and Nat both rolled together into the space she'd left – and went outside to inspect her injuries. The gashes on her arms had mostly healed, looking as if they'd been inflicted weeks ago, not hours. The stump of her missing finger was still bloody and oozing, bad enough to make her wince and bring tears to her eyes. Perhaps there was something in Tisiphone's spittle that was preventing it from healing as quickly. She washed it in the icy stream that ran near the hut and had rebandaged it by the time Nat and Theron appeared. They set off for Thebes soon after. Avoiding the road and hiding from a group of guards on horseback added at least a couple of hours to the almost silent journey. Flurries of snow slowed them further. The sun had slipped beneath the horizon by the time they reached the massive, boulder-built outer walls of the city. They paused to go over their story – tricking their way past the guards seemed a better bet than attempting to force their way in – and carried on up the ramp that led towards the outer gate.

But the story wasn't necessary. When they turned the corner, they discovered the gates of the city standing wide open. No one challenged them, and no guards waited, watchful, on the walkway that topped the thick wall into which the gates had been set. From the first gate, they passed into the passageway between the inner and outer walls that led to the second gate. No guards on the overlooking defences here either, and only corpses in the second passage leading to the third gate. That was open too. Thebes was, apparently, undefended. The three of them walked unheeded into the streets of the city.

Though there was no one in sight, the wind carried the sound of raised voices and weeping. Deina's gaze swept up the slopes of the city towards Thebes' heart: its citadel, the Cadmea on its proud peak, protected by the famous seven-gated wall. She frowned. Rubbed her eyes, uncertain of what she was seeing. A glance at Theron's face confirmed her fears. He was open-mouthed with shock.

The Cadmea had been utterly destroyed.

16

The palace, the whole of the citadel, was gone. Burned into ruins, no more now than an empty shell. Smoke still rose from the smouldering rubble. The gates that they could see had been torn down entirely or hung drunkenly from their hinges.

Deina rested her hand on Theron's shoulder. He'd not been born in Thebes. He'd not known, until Hades revealed it, that he was Thebes' prince. Yet the city was his birthright. It was in his blood. Its citizens were his people.

'I'm sorry.'

'Aristaeus?' he murmured eventually. 'Yet he'd claimed the throne. Would he really destroy his own palace?'

'He would if it gave him some advantage,' Deina replied. Aristaeus had been Orpheus's willing accomplice, and revelled in cruelty. 'Perhaps he wished to punish the city, if the people would not accept him as king. Or maybe Aster and Dendris and Archis escaped his thugs, and this is the result of his fury.' The thought gave her comfort, though it seemed too much to hope that Aristaeus had been destroyed along with the Cadmea. 'We should find the House of Hephaestus. It sounds as if there is at least someone left in the city who might show us the way.'

Deina relaxed a little as they picked a path cautiously through the broad streets towards the Cadmea. There were fewer corpses than she'd feared, and more people than she'd expected hiding within their houses. Rapping on the barred doors produced no result; no one dared emerge. Gangs rampaged as darkness fell, undeterred by the cold, but they made so much noise that she and Theron, trained by the House of Hades, were easily able to evade them. Nat still seemed to melt into the shadows, despite the loss of his power. By the time they found someone willing to talk to them they were almost at the foot of the steeper slope leading to the Cadmea. Close enough for the lingering smoke to catch in Deina's throat and make her cough.

Theron was talking to the child that they'd found rummaging through the smashed and looted remnants of a baker's shop.

'He says he'll show us, but only in return for food. I'll give him my rations. We'll still have yours.'

Deina took in the child's shrunken belly and parched lips.

'Give him all of it. They'll have food at the House, I'm sure.'

Theron turned back to the boy and handed him a waterskin and a small bundle.

'This is for now. You can have more once you've taken us to the right place. Do you understand?'

The child nodded and drank greedily from the waterskin. Then he wiped his mouth with his arm and set off at a brisk pace, beckoning them to follow. Deina had to concentrate not to lose sight of him as he slipped through the narrow, shadowy streets. Still, the glowing, smoking ruins of the Cadmea drew her gaze just as often, a constant background worry. The breeze was strengthening; if it fanned the flames back into life, and they spread to the rest of the city, what then? The homes and the temples were almost all built of wood. The people of Thebes wouldn't stand a chance.

The boy led them past a temple of Apollo, its courtyard dark and deserted, and came to a halt in front of a pair of tall doors set in a high stone wall. 'Here. House of Hephaestus. Where's the rest of my food?'

Deina stared at the doors until she found what she was looking for: a symbol, carved into the old, pitted wood, and set with a strand of gold no thicker than a hair. The sigil of the Order of Hephaestus.

'We're in the right place.'

Theron handed over the rest of their rations and the boy took off, disappearing back into the night as Deina raised her fist and hammered on the door.

There was no response.

Picking up a rock from the ground nearby, she tried again, pounding the wood until the noise echoed through the stillness. She stopped, and the echoes died, and there was still no answer.

'Have they left, or are they hiding?' Theron asked.

'You're wasting your time,' Nat muttered. 'We should leave this place.'

Deina ignored him and peered at the top of the wall, trying to judge its height. It was hard, in the hazy darkness, but she thought she could do it. They had to get in somehow.

'Theron, get ready to boost me. I'll take a run up.'

He nodded. She ran back a little along the lane that led to the house. When she turned, Theron was ready, crouching by the wall with his hands out. Deina took a deep breath, sprinted and leaped up to land with her left foot on Theron's hands. He grunted and pushed her upwards through the air and she reached out for the wall – slammed into it and got her arms onto the top of it as her toes scrabbled for purchase – hung on long enough to swing one leg up, and haul herself, gasping, onto the jagged, upright slabs that formed the wall's top layer. Despite the discomfort, Deina rolled onto her back and lay there for a moment, catching her breath. Her maimed hand throbbed; she felt like it had started bleeding again. No matter – there would be a herbarium within the house, and if she was really lucky, someone as skilled as Anteïs to dress her injuries.

'Deina!' Theron called up softly. 'Are you hurt?'

'No. Hold on.' She crouched on top of the wall and peered over. The House itself lay at a distance, separated from the gate by an expanse of grass dotted with wells and bisected by a winding path. Lights were burning somewhere inside; someone had to be hiding within. Nearer at hand, at intervals along the inside of the wall, were little piles of rubble. Deina puzzled over them for a few moments until she realised they were the remains of boundary markers, similar to those back at the House of Hades in Iolkos. She hadn't known that Houses in other Orders had them. But what could have happened to them? They were strengthened with spells, designed to keep out anyone from outside the Order. What kind of power could have destroyed them so entirely? Lysigoras's words came back to her: *Aristaeus could send his Iron Guards to search the House at any moment. We dare not bar the gates against them.* Had he known something else about the Iron Guards, about the sort of power they wielded? Too late to ask him now.

'Deina,' Theron called up, 'what's going on?'

'I'm trying to work that out.'

It was a long drop to the ground. Deina stood and scanned the space, spotting a cart pulled up against the wall a little further along. She crept carefully across the uneven edges of the slabs to reach it. From there, it was easy enough to let herself drop onto the cart and jump down to the grass. She ran back to the wooden doors and unbarred them to admit Theron.

Nat lingered outside the doors.

'I wish you'd listen to me,' he said. 'There's nothing for you here.'

Deina managed to wind her irritation down a notch by recalling what he'd been through. 'We're going in anyway, Nat. Come if you want to. Or stay here. I don't really care.'

Nat scowled, but as she and Theron hurried towards the house, she could see from the corner of her eye that he was following them.

They arrived at the main doors of the house. Deina reached for the bell rope to summon the door keeper, but Theron grabbed her wrist.

'It's open.' True enough, the door swung wide at his touch. In the entrance hall a large oil lamp was burning in a niche, but there was no sign of the one who ought to be attending it. Theron glanced at Deina, one eyebrow raised. She shrugged, dread growing in the pit of her stomach. They plunged onward into the silence.

The House was not large, and it didn't take long to find the great hall. There was firelight shining from around the edges of its closed doors. Deina's hunched shoulders dropped a little. No surprise, given the state of the city, if all the Theodesmioi of Hephaestus had taken refuge together in the centre of their house. She pushed on the doors, expecting to find them barred, but they opened quickly and Deina half-stumbled forward into the relative brightness.

The smell told her what she'd discovered even before her eyes adjusted.

They'd found the Spell Casters of Thebes.

Every single one of them was dead.

The huge, colonnaded room was heaped with corpses. Bodies were strewn across the tiled floor as if they'd fallen where they'd died. Others were piled one on top of another, limbs and faces contorted, casting monstrous shadows in the flickering firelight. Flies crawled across waxy skin. Deina turned away from the horror. Turned on Thanatos.

'You knew?'

'I suspected. I may not be the god of death any more, but I've spent too long ending mortals' lives not to recognise death's bitter-sweet tang.' He frowned. 'This place is too full of ghosts. You should spread the fire from the hearth to the bodies and let them burn. There's nothing else you can do for them.'

Theron lunged at Nat, pushing him backwards and pinning him against the wall.

'Is that all we are to you – animals to be sacrificed? What was their crime, other than serving their god? Where was

Hephaestus when they were being slaughtered?'

Nat snarled and shoved Theron away.

'How should I know? This murder is recent. I was trapped in the Underworld, busy losing everything to save you from Hades, remember?'

Theron bellowed and lowered his head to charge. Nat raised his fists.

'Stop it!' Deina jumped between them and threw her arms wide. 'Stop, both of you! You can tear each other apart later. But not here. Not now.' Theron was breathing hard. Both men were scowling, teeth bared. Deina drew her one remaining knife. 'You'll not dishonour the dead further by brawling over their corpses.' The fear she'd been holding at bay surged back. 'Dendris could be lying among them. Or Aster.' With a sob, she shoved her knife back into her belt, hurried to the nearest pile of bodies and began heaving them onto their backs, searching the darkness for her friends' familiar features.

A hand gripped her shoulder. She looked up into Theron's drawn face.

'Deina . . .'

'We have to find them –'

'We will. We'll search for them together – tomorrow, when it's light, I promise. Not now, though. You're injured. You should rest.' He glanced back at Nat with a sigh. 'I expect he needs some time too.'

The former god of death was leaning against the wall with his head buried in his arms.

Theron held his hand out to her. 'Come. I'm thirsty – let's find a well and somewhere safe to sleep.'

Reluctantly, Deina nodded and let him lead her out of the great hall. As they passed Nat, Theron nudged him.

'Come along. Unless you want to stay here.'

Nat muttered something under his breath, but he followed them.

They spent the night in one of the many workshops that were clustered around the main buildings of the house. The space was warm and dry, and there was a well of clean water just outside. Nat offered to keep watch and neither Deina nor Theron objected. Deina, however, found the sleep she thought she needed eluded her; she finally gave up the idea of drifting into blissful, thoughtless slumber when she heard birdsong and realised the glow beneath the door was the grey light of dawn. Theron was snoring next to her. She reached over to shake him.

'Theron, wake up.'

He groaned softly.

'It's morning. We need to search for the others.' Around her neck, she could feel the weight of the torc fragment she'd taken from Tisiphone. If by some chance the others were still alive – if they'd managed to fight off Aristaeus's thugs and keep the other two pieces – there was no one left in Thebes who could put it together. They'd have to go to the only other House of Spell Casters that existed. 'How long do you think it would take to get from here to Mycenae?'

Theron sat up, yawning. 'No idea. All I know is it's the opposite direction from Iolkos, more or less. My ability to follow a map is as bad as it ever was, unfortunately. Dendris and Aster and I got back to Iolkos mostly through luck.' He rubbed one hand over his face and gave her a rueful smile. 'If Drex were here –' He broke off, wrinkling his nose. 'Something's burning.'

Deina sniffed. Her nostrils filled with the unmistakeable acrid smell of burning flesh. 'Oh, gods, the bodies –'

Together they hurried from the workshop into the bright winter morning. A thin layer of snow covered every horizontal surface. No sign of Nat, who was supposed to be keeping watch outside, but there was a column of smoke rising from the other side of the cluster of buildings around the great hall. Deina started running. The first two turnings she took were dead ends, but finally she found her way into a courtyard bounded on three sides by high walls, pierced with dark doorways, and on the fourth side by the painted columns of a temple. Theron came pounding in just after her. Somebody – Nat? – had built a huge pyre in the middle of the courtyard, in front of the altar. Fierce red flames rose from the pyre, devouring the bodies that had been arranged on top of the wood. Nat, a corpse cradled in his strong arms, was standing next to the pyre. As she watched, he threw the body into the flames, as casually as a child tossing a ball.

'What are you doing?' Theron yelled. 'Stop! We have to make sure Aster and Dendris aren't here, and you don't know what attention the smoke might attract.'

'Oh, enough with your complaining,' Nat retorted. 'I've not found your friends.' He gave a slight shrug and gestured to a pile of bodies waiting to be cast onto the pyre. 'I think I'd remember them, even though dead humans all tend to look alike to me. Besides, what would you have me do? Leave them unburied? You've seen the shades waiting on the banks of the Styx. Is that what you want for them?' He scowled up at the sky. 'Human corpses don't bother me, but their ghosts do. And there are too many here,' he muttered, as he picked up another body.

Deina bit her lip and watched him work. How could he still see ghosts if he'd lost his power? Maybe he was going to end up as a mortal, but as slowly as she seemed to be turning into a god. The stump of her finger was aching. She still felt weaker than she had done before she'd drunk the nectar, and she still hadn't told Theron what she'd done . . . From the corner of her eye she caught a flash of movement. Holding herself still, glancing sideways, she saw a figure emerging from behind one of the brightly painted temple columns.

Archis.

The Battle Wager raced down the steps towards them.

'You're alive! I thought you were gone forever –' She stopped a few paces away, her gaze flicking uncertainly between Deina, Theron and Nat. Her hands, arms and face were flecked with blood, and her armour was dented. 'It is you, isn't it?'

'Yes,' Deina replied. 'It's us. We lost some stuff in the Underworld. A finger –' she held up her hand, then jerked her head towards Nat – 'and some divine powers, but we're still here. Still in the game.' Just about. 'Where are the others?'

Archis drew a long breath and pressed the heels of her hands briefly to her eyes.

'That's what I've been waiting to tell you. We don't have much time. Aster and Dendris have been taken by Aristaeus.'

Archis led them to the kitchens. Even here, sitting around a wooden table that was covered in scratches from the blades

of knives and cleavers, they could smell the pyre burning. The smoke, and the hiss and crackle of the flames, made a suitable counterpoint to the Battle Wager's grisly tale. Aristaeus's henchmen had been lucky; even though Circe's transformations wore off, they were able to get the three Theodesmioi out of Olympus and use the potion to return to the mortal realm. Archis and the others had been taken to Thebes. They'd found themselves in a city that had descended into civil war.

'We were held in a cell in the Cadmea,' Archis said. She was whetting her knife, running a stone along the blade, over and over. 'But we could hear the guards talking about it. How the people were fighting each other, some supporting Aristaeus, some calling for the return of the true king.' She shivered. 'They spoke of foxes eating corpses in the streets.'

'And what happened here?' Theron asked.

Archis stopped her sharpening and gripped the stone and the hilt of the knife very tightly.

'Aristaeus brought us here, with the two torc fragments. He wanted the Spell Casters to start remaking the torc. He thought that even if the torc was incomplete, that the two fragments fitted together might give him some amount of power.' She glanced up at Nat. 'He seemed to know something about the symbols incised into the metal. Anyway –' Archis shrugged slightly – 'the Spell Casters refused. The Leader of the House said something about power – I couldn't hear it properly – something about the Theodesmioi and the Iron Guards. He said they would rather die. So Aristaeus . . . Aristaeus –' Suddenly Archis drove her knife down into the wooden table, half-burying the blade and splitting the plank in two. 'He had the Iron Guards pen the Spell Casters up in the courtyard. Then they brought them a few at a time into the great hall and strangled them. Sometimes they didn't die quickly. There was one . . .' Her voice faded and she took a sip of water. 'One of the Iron Guards broke his neck then threw him on a pile of corpses and just left him there, begging for death. It didn't care. None of them cared. The Iron Guards were ordinary people once, all of them. Mortals, with families who loved them. And Aristaeus made them into monsters.'

Theron groaned and covered his face with his hands. Nat, a slight frown creasing his brow and his head tilted, gazed at him as if trying to work out why he was so upset.

'Where is Aristaeus now?' Deina asked. 'Where are Aster and Dendris?'

'Aristaeus set fire to the Cadmea and left for Mycenae, taking Aster and Dendris and the torc fragments with him. I escaped; they left us with only a few human guards, and there was a distraction.' She coloured slightly. 'I saw an opportunity and I took it.'

'Then what are you still doing here, Archis?' Theron demanded. 'Why didn't you run away? I can't believe you abandoned them. Did you even try to help them escape?'

'You left them first, remember?' Archis snapped angrily. 'If I'd lingered, I'd be in Mycenae now too.'

Theron scowled in response. Deina understood why he blamed Archis, but the Battle Wager was right; Theron did feel guilty about choosing to go to the Underworld with Deina rather than staying with Aster and Dendris. And he probably hadn't forgotten that Archis had wanted him to surrender his ability to sing to Circe. She put her arm around his shoulders.

'It's better Archis is here. At least she was able to tell us Aster and Dendris are still alive, and where we need to go to rescue them.'

'I'm not without honour,' Archis said coolly. 'Of course I'm going to help myself first. I'm Theodesmioi, and that's what we do.' She pulled down the top of her tunic so they could see her rite-seals. 'Make the kill before another Battle Wager does, or he'll be earning time off his indenture instead of you.'

Deina nodded in recognition, and from the corner of her eye she saw Theron do the same. Self-interest was built into the way the Theodesmioi worked, and was as hard to overcome as any long-ingrained habit.

'Still,' Archis continued, 'I said I'd help you find all the missing fragments, so I decided to wait. To see if you showed up here, since we'd agreed this was the meeting place. To see if you still needed my help. And it looks to me like you do.' She pulled her knife out of the table and stuck it into the scabbard hanging from her belt and glared at Theron.

Theron sighed and lowered his gaze.

'I apologise.'

'I understand. You love them, and that's a powerful thing. Almost as powerful as hate.' Archis jerked her head at Deina. 'You told me what you lost in the Underworld. Did you gain anything?'

'Yes,' Deina confirmed. 'We found the final part of the torc. I have it safe.' She thought about lifting the chain from beneath her tunic to show Archis, and decided against it. It felt . . . personal. Like the fragment was some precious possession that she needed to keep from the whole world. Something that was hers and hers alone.

Theron stood up, went to the shelves, and started sweeping more food into his bag.

'We need to get to Mycenae as soon as we can – we don't know how long Aristaeus will keep them alive. When did they leave?'

'Ten days ago,' Archis replied. 'Maybe more. I've not slept much and it's difficult to keep track. He had horses and carts, and ships waiting at Aulis, from what I heard. We should go the same way.'

'I agree.' Theron started ransacking another shelf for some fresh waterskins. 'We need to finish burning the bodies of the Spell Casters –'

'Oh, so now he admits I was right,' Nat said in a sullen undertone.

'– then we should leave at first light tomorrow.'

'There's no point, Prince of Thebes. You won't catch him.' Nat picked at a spot of grease on the table. 'You're on foot. And you can't take the more direct route. Those mountains will be covered with deep snow by now.' He glanced up at Deina. 'The mortals will freeze.'

'Then what do you suggest, O Being Formally Known as the God of Death?' Theron jeered. Deina was relieved that his anger blinded him to Nat's comment about mortals. 'If you're so clever, tell us how we can get to Mycenae before Aristaeus kills our friends.'

Nat deliberately turned his back to Theron.

'I told you, Deina, I can't help you any more. And if you can't yet –'

'There must be someone you could call upon for a favour,'

Deina interrupted. Nat seemed determined to force her into telling Theron about the nectar. 'Someone who owes you something.' She walked round the table and sat down next to him, and when his hands gripped her shoulders, she didn't try to shrug them away. She looked back at him as he stared into her eyes, his gaze so intense it felt as if he were trying to read her soul.

'Please,' she murmured.

The ghost of one of Nat's old smiles flickered across his face.

'Fine. I know someone who might be able to help us.' Nat gently took her injured hand in his hand. Was it her imagination, or was his touch less chilling than it had been? 'We need to find the – the . . . what do you call it? The herbarium. There's a rite I'll need to perform.'

'I know where the herbarium is,' Archis volunteered. 'I've been exploring. There was nothing else to do.'

Wasn't there? Couldn't she have started doing what Nat had been doing? Couldn't she have tried to give the Spell Casters some sort of burial?

Deina stood up and stretched. Maybe pain and anger and resentment were just making her unreasonable.

'I'll come with you, Nat. I could do with clean bandages.' Theron looked as if he was about to argue about this, to insist on accompanying her, but Deina couldn't stand the thought of the two of them bickering. She moved closer to him and lowered her voice. 'Could you find us some more weapons? I don't know if I'll be able to fight with a pair of knives again, but I'd like to try.'

Theron dragged his gaze away from Nat and gave her a reluctant smile, cupping her cheek in his hand.

'Of course. I'll see if I can find the treasury too, in case Nat fails and we do need to buy horses or passage on a ship. I'll return here when I'm done.' He dropped a kiss on her forehead and strode away.

The herbarium was much like that back at the House in Iolkos. Although larger, it had the same sweet, grassy aroma. The same kind of drying racks hung from the ceiling – some empty, some heavy with herbs. The same kind of shelves lined the walls, filled with similar terracotta urns, all marked with symbols that Deina still couldn't read.

'Do you want me to stay?' asked Archis.

'Yes.' Nat was strolling along the shelves, studying the urns. 'I'll need someone to perform the rite on. Ah – this is it, I think.' As he pulled an urn from the shelf and tipped its contents into one of the bowls stored beneath the tables in the centre of the room, he gave Archis a weary smile. 'Don't worry, the effect is temporary. Now lie down on here and close your eyes.'

Deina watched Nat add some more ingredients into the bowl: different herbs, wine and some of his own saliva. He mixed the contents of the bowl into a sort of mud. Some of this he smeared on Archis's eyelids and lips. The rest he moulded into five small spheres that he placed around Archis's body. To Deina's surprise, Archis began to snore. Nat nodded, pleased.

'Now, since I can't produce my own fire any more, can you find me a flint?'

Deina went to the door and found a flint and a striking stone

kept, as usual, on a handy shelf. Nat struck sparks and set the little moulded spheres burning; they gave off intense green flames, steady and bright even in the daylight that poured into the herbarium from its garden.

'What are they for?' Deina asked.

'The god I'm summoning has a predilection for wine, and for this particular combination of herbs. Apparently, it reminds him of a nymph he once had a long-lasting and passionate relationship with.' He pursed his lips. 'Long-lasting for him. Now, if you can just stand back into the shadows a little . . .'

Deina obeyed. Nat began to sing.

It didn't sound as she would have expected it to sound. His voice seemed strangely high-pitched, almost as if it wasn't his voice at all.

The air near the table began to shimmer and coalesce. A figure appeared, gradually becoming more distinct as if it were walking towards the table from some distance away. Deina began to hear a voice too.

'Nomia, is that really you? Do you wish for me again? Have you finally forgiven me?' The figure became distinct: a mortal male in appearance, though the silvery wings, flickering in and out of existence at his shoulders, betrayed his divinity. The god peered at the table, then rapidly drew back. 'Nomia? Have you changed your form? Not that this form displeases me. In fact, the armour is actually rather erotic.' He paused and yawned widely, then leaned closer to the sleeping Battle Wager, as if he was about to kiss her.

Nat stepped out of the shadows.

'Hello, brother.'

17

The god's white tunic was crumpled, his dark hair dishevelled, and his blue eyes bleary. Still, he was so like Nat that Deina kept looking from one to the other in surprise, as if the former god of death had suddenly doubled himself.

Hypnos, the god of sleep, scowled.

'This isn't really Nomia, is it? You did her voice again.' He glared at Nat, but then his anger seemed to dissipate, his expression becoming almost grave. 'I heard what Hades did. Are you mortal now?'

'I don't know what I am.' Nat moved swiftly to stand in front of Hypnos. He grabbed the front of his tunic. 'But I'm still stronger, more devious and more remorseless than you, brother. Just remember that.'

Hypnos's eyes swivelled as if he were seeking an escape.

'I could just leave. If you've no power, you can't stop me.'

'True.' Nat released his brother's tunic. 'Yet, if you leave, and then I get my power back . . .' He raised an eyebrow. 'Your choice.'

The god of sleep gulped.

'What do you want, then? You always want something. It's never just, "Hello, dear brother, why don't we spend some time together, and how about a nice cup of nectar?" Hypnos's voice rose into a whine. 'I'm going to tell our mother exactly how you treat me one of these days.'

'You do that,' Nat retorted, 'and see if she cares. But first, you can help us with something.' He beckoned Deina forward. 'Deina, this is Hypnos, my brother. Hypnos, Deina, daughter of Hades.'

Hypnos's sleepy eyes opened wide. 'Daughter of Hades? Then why are you with him?' He jerked his head in Nat's direction.

Deina shrugged.

'It's complicated.'

'So,' Nat said, 'now the introductions are over, I'll explain why I summoned you.'

Hypnos bristled at the word *summoned*, but he didn't dare object.

'We need to get to Mycenae as soon as possible. Deina and I, and two mortals.'

'Oh . . .' Hypnos pursed his lips. 'Transport. And for four of you.' He got up onto one of the other large tables and lay down.

'Hypnos . . .' Nat growled.

'I think better on my back.' The god of sleep put his hands under his head and stared up at the ceiling for a while. 'Hades' chariot is clearly out of the question. That leaves Helios or Eos.' A slight smile crept onto his lips. 'Eos. She owes me several favours.' Hypnos pushed himself up on one arm. 'And she's angry about what happened to you. A lot of the older gods

are. They're fed up with the Olympians acting as if they're the only gods, even though we were here first.' He lay back down with a yawn. 'I'm not that bothered about what Hades did to you, obviously.'

'And why does Eos owe you favours?' Deina asked. 'I know she's the goddess of the dawn, but we were never taught her stories at the House.'

Hypnos sat back up again. 'Eos is a Titan, one of the ones that didn't end up in Tartarus, and she has a taste for attractive young mortals. Her preferred style of courtship is abduct first, explain later. I've helped by putting her, um –'

'Victims,' Nat muttered.

'I prefer the term "chosen ones", thank you,' Hypnos snapped. 'I simply put them into a deep sleep while the actual abducting is going on. Anyway, I think she'll lend me her chariot. Shall I go call in a favour?'

Nat nodded.

Just as his brother had a habit of doing, Hypnos vanished.

Deina went to check on Archis. She seemed to be sleeping peacefully and naturally.

'Shall I wake her?'

'No. Her sleep tethers my brother here; I'll wipe away the herbs and rouse her once Hypnos has done as he is told.' Nat wandered over to some jars set on their own on a bench. He took the lid off one and sniffed the contents then peered at the letters incised into the clay. 'This one says it's for cuts. Let me see your injuries.'

Unwillingly, Deina held out her arms and Nat stripped off the old bandages. The deep gashes inflicted by Tisiphone's whip had already healed to pink scars that had a faint golden tint. Even the stump of her missing finger had scabbed over. The scab had a golden sheen too. Still, Nat spread some of the ointment on it and bandaged her hand up again. His touch was gentle.

'You'll have to tell Theron. When he sees your arms, he's going to realise that something has changed.'

'Then I'll keep wearing my cloak. I can't do anything godlike yet. Maybe the nectar didn't work properly. Hopefully I won't turn into a god in the end.'

Nat gazed down at her.

'Hopefully? Then why do you sound disappointed?'

Deina swung away from him.

'You saw the bodies in the great hall. You heard what Aristaeus did. You suffered beneath the whips of the Furies and watched Hades flaunt your power. And yet you still have to ask.' She almost laughed. 'I want to end this, Nat. I want to take on the gods and win. I want to drive a knife into Aristaeus's heart and throw my mother from the peaks of Olympus –' She broke off as a wave of heat swept across her skin, making her gasp and shudder. For an instant, she felt as if flame might burst from her fingertips – but the sensation faded as rapidly as it had appeared, leaving a taste of ash behind. She sat down and rested her head in her hands, waiting for the nausea to pass.

'You crave power,' Nat observed.

'Yes. I mean, I suppose I do. But only so I can help my friends and free the Theodesmioi.'

'Really? Are you sure?' He moved away and started putting the jars of herbs and ointments back on the shelves. Pointless, since there was no one left in the House to use them. 'You didn't actually mention either of those things just now. Why won't you admit that you want to be a god because you want the power?'

'What do you know about what I want? Until that day in the Threshold, you didn't even speak to me. You – you know nothing about me.'

Nat slammed down the jar he'd been carrying, marched over to her and pulled her up into his arms.

'But I do know you, Deina. I've walked with you through days and nights, through your waking hours and your dreams. I've watched you plan, and steal, and hope for a way out.' He lifted a hand to her face, his fingertips just skimming the skin of her cheek. 'I've felt the anger burning in your soul, and I've run next to you in the last laps of a race and tasted the delight flooding through your body. From the moment I spared your life until the moment you ate those cursed seeds, I felt every beat of your heart as if it were my own. And with every beat, I loved you more.'

He bent his head and kissed her. Not a light brush of his lips against hers, but long and passionately. Deina felt her body mould to his as desire flooded through her. When the kiss ended, he cradled her against his chest.

'Embrace what you're becoming, Deina. Slay Aristaeus and break the torcs of the Theodesmioi and put Theron on the throne of Thebes. Overthrow Hades and give me back my power. And let me love you, let me worship you, until time ends and the stars are put away.'

Deina could see the future Nat was describing. She was

seated on a throne with Nat beside her and the gods of Olympus prostrate at her feet. And she knew that she ruled all the realms with wisdom and benevolence, and that gods and mortals both feared and adored her.

See? This is the future you deserve. The future you've always wanted.

Maybe the voice in her head was right. Yet hadn't there been another future she'd dreamed of once? Something smaller and warmer. A ship, and someone's hand in hers.

'Nat . . .' Hypnos's head appeared, hovering at an angle in mid-air as if he was leaning out of an invisible cupboard. 'Oh. I do hope I'm interrupting something,' the god said with a suggestive wink.

'Well?' Nat said coldly. 'Does Eos agree?'

'Yes. I'll be there with the chariot at sunset, just inside the main gates. That gives you a few hours to kill, and I'm sure you'll think of some way of amusing yourselves.' Another wink. Nat muttered something beneath his breath. 'In the meantime, if you don't mind . . .' Hypnos nodded towards the flames burning around Archis's sleeping form.

Still muttering, Nat waved a hand in the direction of the burning spheres of mud; he was, Deina realised, expecting them to be extinguished. Nothing happened. She felt him stiffen.

'I'll do that.' Deina bent over the spheres and began blowing out the flames as Nat picked up a linen cloth from the pile on the table and started cleaning the mud from Archis's eyes and mouth. The Battle Wager stirred a little.

'Thank you, brother. I'll see you later.' Hypnos vanished again. Archis's eyelids fluttered open.

'What happened?' Archis asked, pushing herself up to a sitting position and rubbing her eyes with the heels of her hands. 'Did whatever it was work?'

'It worked,' Deina replied. 'We're leaving for Mycenae at sunset.' There was a fountain bubbling in the garden next to the herbarium; the noise of the water splashing against the stone surround made her aware of how grimy and sticky her skin felt. 'We've got a few hours to spare. Once we've told Theron what's happening, I'm going to find the baths and see if they're usable. And we do need to finish burning the bodies.'

'Exactly why I built a pyre,' Nat said to no one in particular.

As they left the herbarium, Deina fell into step beside him.

'You said something earlier about too many ghosts. What did you mean?'

'Can't you sense them?' Nat replied. 'The ghosts of the dead Spell Casters. They linger. I can taste their rage. Their despair. The air is tainted by it. I thought that giving them some sort of burial would begin to disperse them, but so far, it hasn't helped.' He fell silent, frowning. Deina slowed and glanced back down the dark corridor along which they were walking. If she were not a Theodesmioi of the Order of Hades, she might dismiss as imagination the shadows that seemed to be following close on her heels. Perhaps, even as a Soul Severer, she would have done so had she not herself been to the Underworld. As it was, she could almost see the disembodied dead. Could almost hear their murmuring and feel their wraithlike fingers reaching out for her. She shuddered and hurried after Nat and Archis.

They spent the next few hours piling the corpses of the Spell

Casters onto the pyre and waiting for them to burn and melt away. As Soul Severers, Deina and Theron knew the funeral rites. They took turns enacting them, in the hope that the souls of the dead, thus commemorated, would pass more easily into the Underworld. All of them, including Nat, grew more and more filthy, their skin and clothes stained with blood and worse. Theron seemed especially worn down by their gruesome duty; he'd received the news about Eos's chariot without comment and had barely spoken all afternoon other than to sing the words of the rites. Even when he and Deina and Archis were washing in the large baths – still steaming, thanks to a hot spring – he kept a careful distance. Deina told herself it was because Archis was there, but she couldn't quench the doubt that kept nibbling at her peace. It was a relief to get into a clean tunic, strap the knives Theron had found to her waist and return to the main gate of the House. Nat met them there, still wearing his customary black, though he'd cleaned himself up somehow too.

The rim of the sun began to bleed into the horizon. A burst of dazzling light made Deina throw her hand up to shield her eyes. When the light dimmed a little, she saw four white horses, two abreast, stamping and snorting and tossing their heads just in front of the House. They were harnessed with bronze chains to a large, two-wheeled chariot, apparently made entirely of ornately crafted gold. It shone against the white snow. Hypnos was standing in the chariot, the reins in his hands, yawning.

'Are we ready? Eos told me to follow in Helios's train as he travels west so that he's less likely to notice us. You know what a gossip he is, Thanatos; if he sees us, it will be all over

Olympus before morning. Hades' daughter, you may stand beside me. Something tells me you're not afraid of heights. The rest of you can sit at our feet.'

'I'm perfectly capable of standing,' Nat growled.

'Maybe so, but you'll unbalance the chariot. Eos gave me a lesson on how to steer this thing, not you, brother.' Hypnos wagged a finger at him. 'So do as you're told.'

Nat muttered something beneath his breath, but once Deina had climbed into the chariot, gripping the front edge, he got in behind her and sat down on the chariot's floor, wrapping his arms around his bent legs.

'Now, if we're all quite comfortable . . .' Hypnos cried out something in a language Deina didn't recognise as he flicked the reins. The horses trotted along the ground for no more than a moment before rising smoothly into the air. Higher and higher they raced, wheels spinning and hooves drumming against the air, while the chariot stayed absolutely steady, and the wind that should have ripped them from the sky remained no more than a strong breeze. Thebes became a city in miniature, then a smudge in the dusk while Eos's team rushed away from it. Deina kept a tight grip on her cloak but relaxed her hold on the rim of the chariot and grinned at Hypnos as the speed and the height sent delight bubbling through her veins. Hypnos, who seemed to be enjoying himself as much as she was, smiled back.

'You were born to the wrong realm, Hades' daughter. You should have been Zeus's child, with your love of the sky.'

Onwards the four horses sped, following the sun as it sank into the west. Night swallowed the lands behind them.

'Now,' Hypnos said, 'Eos told me we have to turn south

for Mycenae, and travel faster, and hope Helios doesn't notice our passage.' He flicked the reins again and cried out another instruction to the horses, who veered to the left, gathering speed as they went.

Someone tapped Deina on the leg – Nat. He was pointing behind them.

Deina caught her breath. They were travelling along the division between day and night – dusk to one side, the clouds still lit by the setting sun, and inky darkness to the other. A trail of gold and silver dust streamed out behind the chariot. Deina wondered about the people watching them from far below and seeing the golden chariot with its shining train, a glittering band across the twilight sky. She wondered about the stories they might sing to explain what they had seen.

'There – Mycenae.' Hypnos was pointing to a bright spot a little ahead. 'I remember when those walls were being built.'

They drew closer, and Deina realised the brightness was firelight. Torches were burning on the high, boulder-built walls and around the citadel. The city was at least as large as Thebes, set atop a steep hill between two mountain peaks dominating the plain below. Hypnos steered the chariot around in a long arc, finally coming to rest in a glade somewhere beyond the city. There was no snow here, but the air was still freezing.

'Follow that track.' He pointed to a narrow path. 'The citadel has two gates, as far as I remember; I think the track will lead you swiftly to one of them.'

'Thank you, Hypnos.' Deina bowed to the god and clambered down from the chariot, stumbling slightly from a momentary wave of dizziness.

'You're welcome. I'm sure you'll be able to repay the favour soon enough.' Of course – no such thing as a gift from a god. Hypnos yawned. 'Thanatos, can you come with me?' As Nat started to refuse, the god of sleep added, 'Just for a bit. Some of the old gods would like to discuss what happened to you, and what should happen next.'

Nat grabbed Deina's hand.

'No. If they're planning a revolt, they can do it without me. I've lost enough.'

'Who said anything about a revolt?' Hypnos replied blearily. 'A chat, that's all.'

'You should go, Nat,' Theron said. The sullen edge to his voice surprised Deina. 'They might agree to help us. Unless you're too scared, of course.'

'Fine,' Nat huffed, giving Theron a suspicious stare before climbing back into the chariot. 'I'll go and have a chat. What are the rest of you going to do?'

Deina scuffed the dirt with the foot of her boot. They hadn't actually discussed what to do beyond getting to Mycenae.

'Well, we need to get into the palace. We need to steal back the other two bits of the torc and take them to the Spell Casters here. I just hope Aristaeus hasn't slaughtered them as well.'

'You mean, we need to get into the palace to free Aster and Dendris,' Theron said.

'Of course. I meant we could search for the rest of the torc after that, if we can.' Deina hoped the lie wasn't obvious to the others. She'd actually forgotten Aster and Dendris for a moment. A brief flutter of panic unsettled her stomach. How long did she have before her transformation into a god became impossible to conceal?

'Let's just get inside the city for now,' Archis suggested. 'In the morning, we can go to the Houses of our own Orders. I'm sure they'll help us.'

'Will you be able to find us, Nat?' Deina asked.

He nodded.

'I'll always be able to find you.'

As Nat raised his hand in farewell, Hypnos called out another loud command to the horses that sent them sweeping back up into the sky. The chariot and its occupants shrank, until Deina lost them among the myriad stars.

Perhaps, Deina reflected, it wasn't surprising that Hypnos's definition of 'swiftly' was not the same as that of three mortals – or two mortals plus whatever she was at that moment – on foot. The glade turned out to be much further from the city than it had looked from the sky, and the forest and the outlying areas took longer to walk through than any of them expected. It wasn't an enjoyable expedition. Rain set in – a cold, steady downpour that turned the path to mud and soaked them through long before they reached the city. Both Archis and Theron were silent, lost in their own thoughts. They took a couple of brief breaks to eat and drink, but even then Theron seemed unwilling to speak. He just sat and ate, while Deina, who had no appetite at all, talked a little with Archis about her time in the House of Zeus in Iolkos. The past seemed a safer topic than the shifting sands of the future. By the time they arrived at the gate, set in a courtyard between the wall and an outflung bastion, it was just about to close for the night. They hurried through, beneath the gaze of the guards on the rampart above and the lionesses carved into the heavy stone lintel, keeping the hoods of their cloaks up to conceal their sigils. There was a tavern not far beyond the gate. Theron went in to negotiate for a room. When he returned, he beckoned them round to the back of the building.

'The tavern keeper didn't like the look of me enough to give us space inside, but there's a room out back they keep as extra space for when the festivals are celebrated. I'm glad I took plenty of coins from the Spell Casters' treasury, because he's charging us enough for it.'

The room turned out to be one half of a stable. It was furnished with four mattresses, and an oil lamp hung from a chain in the roof. Someone had built a wall to divide this space from the stable, but it wasn't tall enough to keep out either the noise or the smell of the horses tethered on the other side. Despite the fug, Theron stomped straight inside, lay down on one of the mattresses and pulled his hood low over his face.

'I might sit outside for a bit,' Archis said quietly. 'It's cold, but it's a clear night now it's stopped raining.'

Deina thought for a moment about trying to talk to Theron, but he'd made it clear he didn't want to be disturbed. She followed the Battle Wager outside and sat on the damp ground next to her.

Archis ate some of the rations they'd gathered in Thebes. Deina sipped her water and tried to recall when she'd last eaten – the grape she'd had in the Underworld, probably – and wondered whether she'd ever feel hungry again. All she felt at the moment was slightly sick.

'I never thanked you,' Archis said, interrupting Deina's pondering.

'Thanked me for what?'

'For sticking up for me when we were on Circe's island. When the others wanted me to give up my memories of my brother.'

'Oh.' Deina knew gods remembered things – Hypnos had spoken of remembering the building of Mycenae – but did memories mean the same to them as to mortals? As far as she could tell from the old stories, if a god lost a human lover, it was very much a case of mourn briefly, create a commemorative plant, and move on. Nat might be different, but she doubted that most gods dwelt on their memories the same way mortals did. It made her want to hoard her memories, to hug them to her in the same way she'd seen children hug their toys. The idea of losing them as she changed from mortal to immortal scared her. Her memories of people she'd loved: Leida, Chryse, Drex. Her memories of her father, especially; the memories Hades had reawakened. The one gift her mother had given her that Deina actually wanted to keep. Since her first encounter with Hades, Deina had been able to recall images from her early childhood that she'd thought lost forever, and almost all of them involved her father. Him playing with her or comforting her or cooking her dinner, stirring a pot balanced on the fire with one hand, while his other arm held her secure on his lap, safe from the flames. If she concentrated, she thought she could even remember the sound of his voice singing her to sleep.

'What was he like, your brother?' she asked Archis.

'He was my twin, and he and my parents still lived in Iolkos. That's how we didn't lose each other even when I was taken to the House and he wasn't. The elders didn't like us spending time together, but they found it difficult to stop us, even before I was old enough to be allowed out on my own.' She grinned. 'I found a place in the wall where one of the stones had cracked and partly fallen away. My parents were too scared of the Order to try to see me, but he wasn't. He used to sit on the other side of the wall and tell me about our home, trying to stop me from forgetting.'

Deina felt a pang of envy and wondered what she would have given, or done, to have grown up with someone who knew her almost as well as she knew herself.

'What happened to him?'

Archis grew very still.

'He was chosen to become an Iron Guard.'

Horror made Deina shiver, despite the warmth of her cloak.

'By Aristaeus?

'By the elders of my House. When one of Aristaeus's scouting parties came, looking to abduct strong young men, they told them where he lived. They wanted to stop him being in my life. They knew exactly what fate awaited him.' Archis's voice became venomous. 'When my brother disappeared, I made one of the elders tell me what they'd done. He was old and sick, and he thought I wouldn't dare to hurt him. He was a fool.' She turned her head, and Deina could see her eyes glittering in the starlight. 'Theodesmioi have to look out for themselves. I know you know that. Trust no one but yourself. Rely on no one but yourself. Take your chances when you can.'

Archis wasn't wrong. Severers were expected to compete against each other from the start. Friendship was discouraged.

And yet, it didn't have to be that way. Deina remembered how she'd watched Theron, Dendris and Aster laughing together after her first escape from the Underworld. The happiness they'd found, their delight in each other's company – it lit them up. She'd never seen Severers that happy at the House in Iolkos. No doubt it was the same in Mycenae, and in all the Houses. How could Theodesmioi be joyful when they were forced into endless competition? She'd envied them. She realised she didn't wish for her friends' closeness to diminish, though. She just wished that all Theodesmioi could share their freedom.

Archis had gone back to staring at the stars.

'I know we've only got one fragment of the torc, but I hope we can change things, Archis.'

Archis made a low sound that might have been a laugh.

'Don't worry. Things are going to change. I'm going to make sure of it.' She pushed herself to her feet. 'Time to rest.'

Deina lingered outside for a little longer, gazing at the sky and wondering where Nat was. Where Hades was. How much time she had before her mother came for her. She didn't like waiting. But right now, there was nothing else for her to do.

Deina barely slept at all, and the little rest she did snatch seemed to be nothing but dreams and nightmares. It was early morning when she finally struggled free of them and sat up, groaning and cursing whatever one of the Dream Children had been tormenting her. Archis's mattress was empty. Theron was sitting cross-legged on his, devouring some flatbreads.

'You're awake then,' he said.

'As you can see.' Deina rubbed her hands over her face. Either the day was darker than it should have been, or something was dimming her vision. And her skin felt itchy. Too tight. She wondered whether the mattress was infested with lice. Maybe sticking her head in a bucket of cold water would help. Throwing off her cloak – it seemed to have suddenly warmed up – she got up and headed for the door.

'Wait,' Theron called out. 'Can we talk?'

Deina hesitated.

'You didn't seem to want to talk yesterday.'

'Because we weren't alone. I don't know where Archis is but I'm sure she'll be back soon.' He dropped the rest of the flatbread back into the leaves that served as a wrapping and held out his hand. 'Please?'

Deina turned back and sat down next to Theron.

'What do you want to talk about?'

'When you and Nat and Archis were doing the rite, in the herbarium in Thebes . . .' He blew out his breath slowly. 'I poked my head in to see if you were done.'

Deina froze, waiting for what might come next.

'I saw you and Nat kissing. I saw the way you kissed him. So I left. That's why I've been quiet. I'm angry with Nat, but not with you. I've no right. We're not promised to each other.' Theron gazed at her steadily. 'I'm not blind, Deina. I already knew you have feelings for Nat. I can even understand why. But now you're free of the seeds that bound you to the Underworld, now we might actually have a future together, I suppose I thought you'd choose me.' He dragged a hand through his short black curls. 'I hoped, at least.'

Deina didn't know whether to laugh or to cry. Theron had

seen her and Nat kissing, but it didn't seem as if he had heard what they'd been taking about. He didn't know about the nectar. He still didn't know what she truly was.

Perhaps I should tell him. He's going to find out eventually.

Theron reached out to brush Deina's loose hair back from her shoulder.

'You know I love you.' He gave a slight, rueful smile. 'I've loved you for years, despite my best attempts at persuading myself and everyone else that I didn't. I'll keep on loving you whatever you decide – there's nothing you, or I, can do to change that. But if you want Nat . . .' Theron leaned forward and kissed her gently, lingeringly, one hand resting lightly on her cheek. When he drew back, Deina could tell from his expression that he was expecting something – for her to reassure him or kiss him back. She tried to summon the same burning desire she'd felt back in the Underworld, when they'd fallen onto the bed in a fevered tangle of limbs; yearning flickered briefly, but it was only a shadow in comparison. Dismayed, Deina seized Theron's shoulders and kissed him forcefully. It felt . . . amusing. Nothing more. Nothing deeper. She closed her eyes, telling herself that she loved Theron while hunting through her memories to find something she still craved.

Nat.

Want rose through her like a warm tide.

Yes. I want Nat. I want to make him beg for me the same way Theron is begging. And I want the torc.

Fierce longing made her gasp. She opened her eyes to find Theron staring at her, his eyes wide with worry.

'Deina? Say something, please.'

Archis burst into the room.

'I've found someone – someone who knows how to get into the palace. Come.' She looked from one of them to the other. 'Quickly.'

'Archis,' Theron said, his voice tense, his gaze not leaving Deina's face. 'Deina and I are in the middle of something. Can this wait? Just for a few moments?'

'No, it can't wait,' Archis exclaimed, putting her hands on her hips. 'Do you want to have a chance at saving the others or not?'

Deina, relieved to have a way out of the conversation, to have time to think about what was happening to her, laid her hand briefly over Theron's. 'There's so much at stake right now.' She could feel the weight of the torc fragment around her neck, its twisted strands warm against her skin. 'We will talk – but let's find the others first.'

Theron sighed, nodded and got to his feet, holding out his hand to pull Deina upright.

'Well?' he said to Archis. 'Who is this person?'

'He's waiting for us at the House of Zeus. I went there as soon as I woke.'

Another Battle Wager? That made sense. In Iolkos, Battle Wagers had made up the elite core of the city guards, chosen to protect the archon and the megaron. They were bound to know ways in and out of the palace that were kept secret from ordinary citizens. Deina smiled at Archis. 'Good idea. I thought for a moment you'd left us, after what you said yesterday.'

'No.' Archis started tapping her foot impatiently as Theron struggled to jam his things back into his bag. 'No. I have to see this through. Whatever it might cost. Are we ready?'

Archis led them swiftly through the city streets. Even though it was still early, Deina was surprised at how quiet Mycenae was. There were few people about, and those she did see were hurrying, eyes down, focused on getting to wherever they were going as quickly as possible. Not that it was easy. Archis took a wrong turning more than once; the new day had swathed the city in a dense low cloud that left a fine layer of water droplets on their cloaks. Buildings loomed menacingly from the mist, and the city's higher reaches were all but invisible. It was a relief to finally find themselves standing before the imposing entrance to the House of Zeus.

The gates opened into a vestibule decorated with mosaics of battle scenes. They were clearly expected. An elder greeted them, and as he led them across an open courtyard six younger Battle Wagers – adepts, by their clothing – fell into step around them. Deina exchanged a glance with Theron. This could be an honour guard; perhaps the House here had decided to support Theron's claim to the throne. And Deina felt weak and hot, as if she was running a fever, so maybe that was making her jumpy. Maybe. She rested a hand on the hilt of one of her knives. Through the House they wound, until the elder stopped outside a pair of double doors. He pushed them open.

'After you.'

The interior of the room was dimly lit, but Deina recognised the smell. It was the same expensive scent that Orpheus used to drench himself in. She grabbed Theron's arm.

'Something's wrong.'

The six Battle Wagers behind them had drawn their swords from beneath their cloaks.

'I'm sorry,' the elder murmured, 'but you have to go inside.'

Deina looked at Theron and Archis. Theron shrugged. He was right – they had no choice. She stepped into the gloom.

Eight Iron Guards were waiting for them.

Behind them stood Aristaeus.

18

Deina drew her knives and lunged towards Aristaeus. One of the Iron Guards got in her way; she slammed into the creature, knocking it to the ground. Another seized her from behind, linking its arms around her waist, holding her tight even as she plunged her knives through its sides. Or tried to. The blades broke against the spell-cast armour.

'Enough,' Aristaeus yelled, 'unless you want them to tear him apart.'

Theron was being held spreadeagled between two Iron Guards. A third was poised with his hands around Theron's mouth and throat, as if he was about to twist Theron's head from his neck. Deina stopped struggling.

'Better,' Aristaeus observed. He was wearing one of Orpheus's robes, just like he had been on the ship, and leaning on a cane. 'There's no point. Every time you fight, you lose.'

'Wrong,' Deina spat. 'We didn't lose last time. Orpheus is trapped forever in the Threshold, reliving his crimes for eternity. And how's your ankle? Painful, I hope.'

Aristaeus laughed.

'A minor inconvenience. The important thing is that I will soon have the torc. And I could not have done it without your help.' He grinned at her. 'Once again, you trusted the wrong person, Severer. Once again, you have been betrayed.'

Betrayed? Deina's mind was racing. He was speaking of Chryse. But there was no one else amongst her friends who would ever do what Chryse had done. No one.

'Archis,' Aristaeus beckoned, 'you may approach.'

The Battle Wager came and stood near Deina, in front of the wall of Iron Guards. She bowed to Aristaeus and turned to stare at Deina, her hands on her hips.

'How could you?' Deina murmured. 'After what you told me?'

'Revenge and freedom. You of all people should understand, Deina. His majesty King Aristaeus has already burned Iolkos to the ground and slaughtered the elders who sent my brother to Thebes. In return for delivering you, and the final piece of the torc, I get money and slaves and free passage out of the Theban Dominion.' She shrugged. 'I wasn't lying. Everything is going to change for both of us. Just not in the same way.'

Deina struggled fruitlessly against the guard's grip to get to Archis.

'Where are the others? Where are Aster and Dendris?'

Aristaeus lifted a finger and the Iron Guard clamped one hand over Deina's mouth.

'Your friends are alive, for now,' Aristaeus answered. 'You, Soul Severer, are going to watch all of them die.' He turned his gaze to Theron. 'A public execution, I think, to put an end to the rumours. The people of Mycenae, at least, will be able see the truth: that the so-called true king is nothing more than a pathetic boy. I think I'll return your ruined body to the ruins of the Cadmea, for the rats and crows to feast on. It seems only fitting. Now, where is the third fragment of the torc?'

'Deina carries it on a chain around her neck,' Archis said instantly. 'I saw it when we were bathing.'

'Remove it,' Aristaeus ordered. One of the Iron Guards ripped open the front of Deina's tunic and snapped the chain holding the torc fragment as easily as breaking a loose thread. 'And where is Thalius?'

'Here, Your Majesty.'

A large, grizzled man edged forward. His arms bore the scars of old burns as well as many overlapping rite-seals, and the sigil of Hephaestus was etched into his forehead. He took the torc fragment reverently from the Iron Guard.

'Thalius is the Leader of the House of Hephaestus here in Mycenae. The only house of Spell Casters now left in existence. And if you're thinking that perhaps these Spell Casters will also refuse me their aid, they will not. I brought the Leader of the House in Thebes with me to Mycenae. He gave the Spell Casters an eyewitness account of the executions there, then I had him dismembered. Most of Thalius's people are currently locked up in their own great hall. They won't be released until their leader has reforged the torc and handed it over to me. How long will that take, Thalius?'

'I am not entirely sure, Your Majesty. I have never worked on something wrought by the great god himself.'

Aristaeus waved him away impatiently.

'You'd better start, then. The Iron Guards that escorted you here will be watching you. If you try to deceive me, they will tear you to pieces. Slowly.'

Thalius bowed.

'I will not deceive you, Your Majesty.'

'Good. I hope you will not fail me, either.' Aristaeus turned to one of the guards. 'When the work is finished, send word immediately, then escort Thalius straight to the megaron. As for these two, strip them of their weapons and gear and carry them there now. If you cause any trouble, Soul Severer, I will have the guards break both Theron's legs. Archis, you may walk behind my litter.'

Deina's knives were pulled from her belt, her bag ripped from her back. She was picked up by her guard and thrown over the creature's shoulder. She didn't dare resist.

Thankfully, it didn't take long to get from the House of Hephaestus to the Megaron, but Deina's hope that she would be set on her feet once there came to nothing. From her uncomfortable upside-down position, she caught glimpses: a building, much grander than the megaron at Iolkos. More Iron Guards than she could count. Human guards whose boar-tusk helmets bore the symbol remembered from her brief incarceration in the Cadmea of Thebes: the mark of the House of Cadmus, the royal family of Thebes. There was no evidence of the megaron's previous inhabitants. The Iron Guards were issued with further orders and she and Theron were jolted down into the labyrinth of rooms beneath the megaron. As the daylight faded, the smell of the stale air grew worse: sweat, blood, shit and decay. Finally, the guards carrying them threw her and Theron into a cell and secured the metal grating that served as a door. The guards trudged away, taking their torches with them, and plunging the cell into almost complete darkness; a missing or broken stone in the ceiling allowed a trickle of daylight from the floor above.

'Deina – Theron – is that really you?' Aster's voice, cracked with thirst. Deina felt his hand, and then his arms were around both of them, pulling them close. 'Thank the gods,' he exclaimed, adding, 'If any of them are still on our side.' His hand moved to Deina's forehead. 'What's wrong?' His touch was cool against her skin. 'You're burning up. And you're trembling.'

'Don't worry about me. Where's Dendris?' Deina asked.

'She's here.' Aster guided them to the corner of the cell nearest the door. Dendris was sitting on the floor, leaning against the wall. Deina, Theron and Aster sat down around her.

'How did you get here?' Dendris asked. She sounded exhausted. 'We thought you were trapped in the Underworld – we hoped, but . . .' She gave a faint laugh. 'We should have known you'd find a way out. You have more luck than anyone has a right to.'

Deina tried to smile. The last thing she felt right now was lucky.

'Has he hurt you?' She leaned close to Dendris; the other woman looked haggard.

'Dendris was injured,' Aster replied. 'I'm just hungry.'

Dendris pulled down the neck of her tunic to reveal a gash just below her collarbone, black with dried blood.

'A scratch, that's all.'

Aster tsked.

'For a scratch, it bled a lot. I was worried. We needed poor Tauredos here to stitch her up.'

'Aster exaggerates, as usual,' Dendris said weakly. 'And he's been keeping me entertained at least, counting his press-ups and jumps and lunges and –'

'Hey,' Aster protested, 'it's important to stay strong.'

They both spoke lightly, and Deina remembered the morning on Orpheus's ship when Aster, still distrustful of her, had suggested she count his exercises. Yet Deina could hear the strain underlying their words. The humour faded from Dendris's expression. 'They took everything, Deina. Both parts of the torc, our packs.' She tried to clasp Deina's hand and gasped, flinching, as she noticed Deina had lost a finger. 'What happened to you?'

Deina flexed her maimed hand, the ghost of her missing finger still taunting her.

'I had a disagreement with a Fury. She wanted Drex's ring.' Sorrow at the loss of her only memento of Drex brought a lump to Deina's throat, but it was swiftly swallowed by a surge of rage.

Once I'm a god, I'll make Tisiphone rue the day she attacked me. I'll flay her with her own whip. No – I'll give the whip to the ghosts of Tartarus, and let them take their revenge, let them scourge her until she's nothing but blood and bone.

Imagining Tisiphone's screams was a pleasant daydream; a question from Aster seemed like an irritation in contrast.

'What?' Deina said, frowning.

Even in the almost-darkness of the cell, Deina could tell Aster was taken aback by her tone.

'I just asked if you could tell us more of what happened to you in the Underworld. Are you sure you're well, Deina?'

'I'm well, honestly.' Deina's gaze drifted to Theron; he was smoothing Dendris's hair back from her forehead and smiling down at her. 'Do you want the long version or the short version of our adventures in the Underworld?' And Dendris was looking up at him tenderly, with so much affection. Deina knew she had absolutely no right to feel jealous. And wouldn't it be for the best? Surely, it would be better for Theron if he could love Dendris instead of her. The fever burning through her body was burning away what was left of her mortality, she was sure of it. As much as she told herself she loved Theron, she didn't seem to desire him in the same way as she had done. She might soon forget about him altogether. Despite the heat, despite the trembling, despite the fact that her vision had become dim, she felt a storm building inside her. A storm that would eventually consume her.

'I'll tell you the long version.' It wasn't as if they had anything else to do. Deina leaned back against the wall and stretched her legs out in front of her. 'From the beginning. From when we were attacked in Olympus, and then Theron and I were taken to the Underworld . . .'

The telling took a while. Both Dendris and Aster had questions: about Tartarus, and Tisiphone, and Cronos. About what she and Theron had seen in Thebes and what had been done to the Spell Casters; Aster and Dendris had seen nothing but the inside of a wooden crate in which they were transported to Mycenae. Apart from drinking the nectar, Deina described almost everything, up to and including their most recent encounter with Aristaeus. Aster seemed very struck by Nat's behaviour and went on for a while about how honourable he had turned out to be. Deina didn't reply; she hoped that her silence, combined with Theron's lack of response, would suggest to Aster that the topic had better be dropped. Yet Aster carried on, telling them how glad he was to find that Thanatos's good looks were backed up by something more substantial.

'You think he's good looking?' Theron asked, his voice flat.

'Of course. He's well-built and handsome of face. His eyes, framed by those long eyelashes, are a rare shade of blue, and as for that lustrous dark hair . . .' He trailed off into a reverie.

Despite their predicament, Deina almost burst out laughing. Aster never had been able to read a room; she remembered his poor choice of words when they first encountered Hades, and again when they met Circe.

'Archis told us that Iolkos has been destroyed,' Theron said, with just a touch of venom in his voice.

'Destroyed?' Aster gasped. He dropped his head into his hands.

Deina put her arm around his shoulders and shot Theron a disapproving look. It was too dark for him to have seen her expression, but he obviously thought better of his words.

In a softer tone, he added, 'Try not to worry, Aster. I'm sure Melos is safe. The House is outside the city, remember, and even constrained by their torcs the other Severers could have made it a little way into the hills.'

'What about Critos, though?'

'There are places to hide within Iolkos. Critos has long

experience of Aristaeus's tactics and he and the other Battle Wagers he is fighting with might have had warning of the attack; if anyone can escape Aristaeus, it will be Critos. And cities can always be rebuilt.'

Aster sniffed.

'I hope you're right.'

'If I ever get my hands on Archis,' Dendris said grimly, 'it will not go well with her.' She made a motion as if snapping something in half.

'You'll be behind me in the queue,' Theron replied. 'But somehow I doubt either of us will get the chance. The Spell Caster may well fail, but if he doesn't, Aristaeus will have the torc soon.'

Mention of the torc flooded Deina with a fresh wave of longing. She reached out for it with her mind, and as she did so an image danced in front of her eyes: the torc reformed, a glittering, gorgeous thing, singing with power. It called to her.

You belong to me . . .

Her voice, or the torc's? All she was certain of was that Thalius had succeeded in putting the torc back together again. He had awakened the power that had slept within the fragments. A distant scream jerked her attention towards the metal grating; Aristaeus's guards torturing someone probably.

Deina's hands clenched and opened over and over; she couldn't just sit here any longer. Recalling what she'd seen of her mother's powers, she tried to imagine what it might feel like, to turn into a snake, or summon a wave of darkness. Unfortunately, imagining didn't make the power appear. She would have to find another way to escape.

'The grate's the only way out,' Dendris said as if reading Deina's mind. The Mycenaean sat up a little more, wincing. 'I tried to find some wood when we first got here. Tree roots in the floor. Something like that. I thought I'd be able to break us out, but this cell is all metal and stone.' She tilted her head. 'You're still a demi-god, though, aren't you, Deina? Are you strong enough to prise the grate free?'

Deina groped her way over to the metal grating and gripped it. 'Maybe.'

'Then we can get out of here.' Theron sounded excited.

'Or we can try to get the torc,' Deina suggested.

'No.' He came to stand next to her. 'I know you don't want to hear it, but this fight for the torc is over, Deina. Nat lost his powers, and you lost a finger and we've all almost died searching for the fragments of that cursed thing. You don't need it any more – you're free of the seeds. And I'm willing to bet that the Spell Caster won't be able to put it back together properly. It was made by a god. What are the chances that a mortal will be able to resurrect its power?' He glanced back at Aster and Dendris. 'We should escape while we can. Regroup. Maybe go back to Iolkos and see if we can find Critos.'

Frustration made Deina tighten her grip on the grate.

'Hades is going to come for me, Theron. For you too, probably.'

'Not if the Titans deal with her. Please, Deina – we need to escape. Now.' He rattled the grate then touched her forehead. 'I think you're getting ill. We need to get out of here.'

Deina knew he was wrong. The torc's voice was growing clearer: a song of power and craving, just on the edge of her hearing.

But Theron's right in another way, isn't he? Searching for the torc now will just put the others at risk. Aster's weak and Dendris is wounded – badly, for all I know.

Deina gritted her teeth and fought against her own desire.

'Fine. Let's escape.' Planting her feet more firmly, she and Theron together began to tug the grate away from the wall. The metal bars started bending as the hinges shrieked and fragments of stone rattled across the floor. The first bolt sprang loose.

Torchlight shone and grew, and one of Aristaeus's thuggish soldiers, backed by a cohort of Iron Guards, appeared in front of the grate. She'd hesitated too long.

Deina's strength was useless in the face of the soldier's threat to torture her friends. She had no choice but to submit to having her wrists bound in front of her. Dendris was gagged too – Aristaeus hadn't forgotten her powers and wasn't taking any chances. The four of them were herded along the corridor and up a set of steps into an upper level of the megaron. In the light, the shadows that hovered in front of Deina's vision were more obvious. It was like looking through gauze. Accompanied only by Iron Guards they were marched into a colonnaded room. A fire burned in the central hearth, and at the far end on a dais stood a silver throne swathed in furs. A luxurious space as far as Deina could tell, though the wall paintings were partly obscured by a huge collection of metal objects that had been lined up somewhat haphazardly against the walls. Weapons, and other things.

The door at the other end of the room opened. Aristaeus, accompanied by even more Iron Guards, enough that they surrounded him like a moving wall, strode in and sat down. He was wearing a golden breastplate over a long robe. Archis followed and stood outside the ring of guards. Deina and the others were pushed forward and forced onto their knees.

'Do you know why I've brought you here, Soul Severers?' Aristaeus demanded. 'Do you know the significance of the objects you see around you?'

No one answered.

'Hephaestus made all of them. I am a devoted admirer of the smith god, and I have made it my life's work to obtain as many of the god's creations as I can. Not even Orpheus knew the extent of my collection.' He got up from the chair and began to point to different things. 'See there, the shield made for the mighty Achilles. There, the net constructed by Hephaestus to trap Aphrodite while she lay in the arms of Ares. And at the end there, the cursed necklace of Harmonia. Another heirloom of the House of Thebes.' He grinned nastily at Theron. 'Though you appear to be cursed enough without ever having possessed it.' Aristaeus sat down again. 'I've had word that my torc, which will be the jewel in my collection, has been reforged. The Spell Casters are on their way here now. Since you obtained the fragments, I thought it only fair for you to see what you have lost before you die. I have ordered the nobles of Mycenae, the priests and the Theodesmioi of the Orders of Zeus, Poseidon and Hades to assemble in the courtyard outside the megaron. They shall witness the agony of your punishment and execution. We will have no more threats of disobedience or revolt.' He paused. 'Oh – and there is one more thing I wish to show you.' As soon as Aristaeus clapped his hands, human servants hurried through the door behind the dais, carrying something in their arms. Pieces of iron armour. They set their burden down on the floor. Aristaeus gestured to the piece on the top of the pile: a helmet with a face plate, pierced with eye holes but with no perforations for mouth or nostrils. 'Do you see that, Deina? That is for you.' Deina couldn't tear her gaze away from the mouthless iron helmet. 'Once you have watched your friends die, you will be sealed within this spell-cast armour to become one of my Iron Guards, trapped, forced to serve me for the rest of your long, long life. Thalius will carry out the transformation before I allow him to return to the House.'

Fear suffocated her. All Deina could do was whisper, 'No,' as she stared at the expressionless blank face of her future.

Aristaeus laughed.

'Why so sad, Severer? Don't you want to be virtually immortal?'

Deina heard a voice somewhere behind her. 'Majesty, the Spell Caster has arrived.'

Aristaeus waved a hand at the Soul Severers. 'I wish them to have a good view. Move them to one side, but hold that one separately.' He pointed at Deina; she was pulled away from the others. One of the guards held a knife to her throat.

The Iron Guards obeyed. Now Deina was able to see as Thalius processed along the centre of the room, an iron box held tightly beneath one arm. He was wearing leather gauntlets and sweating profusely, even though his skin looked clammy with cold. Behind him walked two others, both wearing the long, metal-woven robes of Spell Casters, hoods pulled low over their faces. Deina had to bite her tongue as they drew level with her. One was a boy. Despite the robes, she could tell he was almost rigid with fear.

The other was Nat.

A burst of relief made Deina realise that she'd half expected the former god of death to abandon them. To her eyes, Nat's poise, and the strength she could sense within him, still marked him out as different. Perhaps, however, the loss of his powers was continuing to change him, just as drinking the nectar was continuing to change her. He gave no sign of recognition and Deina quickly looked away, anxious not to draw Aristaeus's attention to him. If Nat was starting to think like a mortal, he might be made to suffer and die like one too.

'Well, Thalius?' The clipped tone of Aristaeus's voice suggested he was struggling to control his greed for the torc. 'Did you succeed?'

'I believe so, Your Majesty.' Thalius swallowed hard and bobbed his head. 'The torc . . . It is like nothing I have ever seen.'

Aristaeus leaned forward eagerly.

'And what have you learned of its power? What exactly does it do?'

'I have not had time to study it fully, but I believe the spells engraved into the metal, as far as I can read them, speak of control.'

'Control?' Aristaeus snapped. 'Control of what?'

Thalius waved his empty hand, an expression of misery on his face, his fingers fluttering uncertainly.

'I could not understand all of what I saw, but I believe – I believe the wearer of the torc will at least be granted the power to control all spell-cast metal.'

Aristaeus's eyes narrowed as he gazed at the Spell Caster.

'So, if I wear the torc, and I order one of those spell-cast spears –' he gestured at the weapons leaning against the wall – 'to hurl itself into someone's body, the weapon would obey me? If I were to have spell-cast torcs made and fitted to the neck of every inhabitant in the Dominion, then order those torcs to tighten and strangle the wearers, they would obey me?'

Thalius nodded.

'I believe so, Your Majesty. Yes.'

Aristaeus leaned back again, resting his elbows on the arms of the chair and steepling his fingers. He closed his eyes and a smile spread across his narrow face.

'So much power. I would only have to utter a word, and every man, woman and child in a rebellious city would die instantly.' His eyes flew open. 'I will lace spell-cast quicksilver with corroding poison and order it to fall as rain. No kingdom in the world will dare stand against me.' Aristaeus was gripping the arms of the chair. 'Bring me the torc. Now.'

Thalius hesitated, reaching up to rub the back of his neck.

'There was one symbol etched into all three strands, Your Majesty. The sigils of the Orders of Zeus, Poseidon and Hades combined, surmounted by the sigil of Hephaestus. I – I do not know for sure, I am not certain –'

'You grow tedious, Thalius. Speak plainly.'

Thalius straightened up.

'I believe the symbol marks this object as the property of the gods. It may be that a mortal cannot wield its power. Or that a mortal should not dare attempt to do so.'

'All these things were forged by Hephaestus,' Aristaeus replied, nodding at his collection. 'If the god was going to act against me, he would have done so by now. Show me.'

Thalius nodded and opened the box. The three engraved strips of gold, silver and bronze had been reunited into an undulating spiral, but it looked more like a banded snake than a thing forged of metal. It wriggled in his grip. Deina shuddered. A snake that was blindly hunting for something.

A shadow of doubt crossed Aristaeus's face.

'I will wear this thing around my wrist.' He held out his arm. 'Give it to the nearest guard, Thalius.'

The Spell Caster thrust it towards one of the Iron Guards. His shoulders sagged with relief as soon as the torc was out of his hands. The Iron Guard draped the torc around Aristaeus's wrist. The metal curved and tightened around his arm. It didn't settle, though. Undulating and waving, it started crawling slowly up and down Aristaeus's arm.

'What is happening, Thalius?' Aristaeus demanded. His confidence faltered. 'Why does it not stay still? And do not tell me you don't know.'

The Spell Caster dragged a shaking hand across his balding head.

'There is something, Your Majesty, in one of our ancient songs.' He gulped. 'It has never been clear, but I believe now that it might be speaking of the torc.' Eyes closed, Thalius sang a few words. Old words, their meaning worn away by time but their shape still recognisable. 'It means, *slaughter to seal, sacrifice to secure.*'

'Ah.' Aristaeus nodded. 'Then I shall sacrifice one of them now. The other female. Bring her here.'

Deina tensed as Dendris was dragged into the centre of the room. She caught Nat's eye, wondering whether he was planning anything. She hoped he was. The heat coursing through her body was so intense now that her legs were shaking with the effort of staying upright. If the guards hadn't been holding her arms, she might have fallen.

'This one fought with an axe, if I remember rightly, so she shall be beheaded with her own choice of weapon.' He held up his wrist and smiled at the slithering torc. 'Plenty of blood for you to bathe in.'

Two of the Iron Guards forced Dendris to lie down with her head on the bottom step of the dais. A third brought an axe from the weapons piled around the edge of the room.

Now, Nat. Do something, please.

'Your Majesty.' The interruption came from Archis. 'Wait.'

Aristaeus glared at her.

'If there is no good reason for your interruption, I will reconsider our bargain, Battle Wager.'

'There is a good reason.' Archis's voice was tense and strained. 'This is an important moment. This sacrifice will secure your power over the whole Theban Dominion. Should you not be wearing the crown which you claim? The crown of Thebes?'

'The crown was stolen,' Aristaeus snapped.

'And I stole it back.'

From the corner of her eye, Deina could just see Archis bring something from her bag. Something golden.

'No! Where did you get that?' Theron tried to twist away from his guards, earning himself a punch to the gut that left him doubled over in pain.

'I took it from Critos, of course,' Archis replied. 'I followed him when he left the Sea Singers. Drove a knife into his back and took the crown.'

'I'll kill you,' Aster yelled, his voice dissolving into a sob.

Aristaeus laughed.

'Truly this is a day of triumph. And you, Archis, have proved your loyalty.' He hesitated. 'Come. Lay down your weapons. Then you may approach me and present me with the crown. You have earned that honour.'

Archis unbuckled the sword belt from her hips. Lifting the crown high, she approached the dais.

'Don't do it, Archis. Please,' Deina murmured as the Battle Wager walked past her. Archis glanced briefly in Deina's direction.

'I have to, Deina. I told you. I have to make sure things are different.' On she went. The Iron Guards surrounding Aristaeus parted to let her through. Archis knelt and offered the crown to Aristaeus. He took it, lifting it slowly towards his head.

Archis pressed her wrists together. The narrow bronze blades shot out of her arm guards and she drove them straight into the unprotected flesh above Aristaeus's breastplate.

'That's for my brother, you bastard!'

Aristaeus cried out, dropped the crown and fell forward.

'Seize her!' he wheezed.

Archis grabbed the torc from Aristaeus's wrist.

'Deina – catch!' She hurled the twisting metal towards Deina and raced to reclaim her sword as the Iron Guards converged on her.

From the corner of her eye Deina glimpsed Theron and Aster struggling to free themselves from their guards – heard Theron

shout '*No!*' – but she couldn't drag her focus from the arc of the torc as it spun closer. Nat barrelled into the guard that had been holding the knife to her throat and Deina, gritting her teeth, broke the ropes binding her wrists. She leaped. Grabbed the torc from the air and draped it around her neck. The warm metal tightened. The ends prodded the skin around her collarbone as if looking for a way in. For a fraction of time Deina was petrified: after spending her whole life dreaming of freedom from the Order's torcs, she'd willingly secured another around her throat. But then –

But then, as Archis had predicted, everything changed.

It was like being bathed in light. She'd never seen with so much clarity before. The etched blades of the spears lined up against the wall – she could see every detail of the decoration just as clearly as the hair on her own forearm. The heat that had been consuming her from the inside had vanished, leaving behind a feeling of such strength it made her laugh. Two swords arced lazily towards her; Nat was raiding the hoarded weapons. Deina caught the hilts easily. The grip of her maimed hand was just as strong now as it had ever been. Her finger was still missing, but her body no longer seemed to register any weakness. She swung round and sliced the blades through the midriffs of the nearest Iron Guards. The spell-cast, god-wrought bronze smashed through the iron casing as if it were no more than an eggshell. Nat was hurling spears with unerring accuracy into the Iron Guards surrounding Theron, Aster and Dendris.

'Stop them,' Aristaeus moaned. He slipped from the throne onto the floor, smearing blood across the grey furs. 'Kill them all!' The guards still surrounding him began to swarm towards Nat, Theron and the others.

No. No more.

Deina raced towards the throne, moving faster than she'd ever done, slashing through the Iron Guards who barred her way like a farmer scything down wheat. She reached Aristaeus, dropped the swords and bent over him. There was no pride, no triumph in his face now. Just terror. Deina smiled. She grabbed him by his injured neck and hauled his body upright. Made sure he saw the torc around her neck.

'Looks like you trusted the wrong person, Aristaeus. And now you've lost. Now and forever.'

'No . . .' The word rattled in his throat. The torc shifted and shivered. It wanted blood, did it? Deina tightened her grip on Aristaeus's neck, digging her nails into his skin until beads of his blood dripped from her fingertips and the knife wounds inflicted by Archis gushed. Aristaeus's face purpled. His eyes bulged and turned up in his head. Someone nearby screamed, but Deina focused on her task. Tighter and tighter she squeezed, until she heard his spine snap. His head lolled, lifeless.

'Deina!' Theron yelled. She turned to see an Iron Guard behind her, an axe in its raised hands. She remembered Thalius's description of what he thought the torc could do.

'Stop –'

To her astonishment, every Iron Guard in the room obeyed.

19

The sounds of battle ceased. The Iron Guards stood immobile, at attention, their weapons lowered. Yet someone was moaning with pain.

Deina dropped Aristaeus's body and pushed her way through a knot of Iron Guards to find Archis lying on the floor in their midst. She was shaking. The shaft of a spear protruded from her torso, blood gushed from a deep gash on her scalp, and her sword arm had been hacked off. Deina put an arm around the Battle Wager's shoulder and lifted her head a little and wiped some of the blood away from her eyes.

'Archis, can you hear me?' The other woman's gaze flitted to Deina's face, but there was no recognition. 'Archis . . .' The spear had been thrust clean through her body. And there was so much blood flowing from what was left of her arm that a pool was forming on the floor. What could be done? The Iron Guards were weapons; even if they continued to obey her, Deina could think of nothing she could order them to do that would help. She gripped the torc with her free hand.

Heal her. Make her whole.

Archis kept bleeding. Kept dying.

'Dei . . . Deina . . .' Barely a whisper.

'I'm here.' Deina glanced up; Theron, Aster, Dendris and Nat were all standing nearby. 'We're all here.'

'Had to kill him. Had to –' she gasped with pain – 'kill him myself. Dreaming of it . . . years. Swore to avenge my brother.' Her lips twitched into a brief smile. 'Maybe . . . maybe I should have told you.'

Maybe she'd have been able to, if Theodesmioi were taught to trust. Deina rested her hand on the side of Archis's face.

'Critos . . . didn't mean to. Meant to – to knock him out. Thought I judged the blow. But he fell.' Archis's breathing became more laboured. 'Accident.' A spasm of pain made the Battle Wager scream.

'Hush – don't try to talk any more. Aristaeus is dead, Archis. It's over.'

'No. Not over.' Archis focused on the torc. 'Use . . . use it. I don't want to be . . . blood hunter. End it, Deina.' She twisted her remaining hand into the front of Deina's tunic and pulled herself up, ignoring Deina's plea for her to stay still, to rest. 'Promise me,' she gasped. 'End it for all of us.'

'I promise: if I'm able to end what happens to us, I will.'

Archis's grip relaxed. She slumped back into Deina's arms. No breath, no heartbeat. Deina laid the Battle Wager's body down and closed her eyes. She stood, wiping her bloody hands on her tunic.

In the silence, softly, his voice breaking, Theron began to sing. An old song from one of the funeral rites; the melody filled Deina with a great sadness. A tear spilled down her cheek. Whether Theron was singing for Archis or Critos – whether she wept for the dead, or for herself – Deina wasn't sure.

They pulled out the spear and placed Archis's body, and her severed arm, on a pile of furs on the dais. Aristaeus's corpse was dragged into a corner. Now the Theodesmioi and the two Spell Casters were sitting around the fire. Everyone apart from Nat – he was prowling around the room, frowning up at the ceiling – seemed to want the comfort of the warmth and the lively, flickering flames. They helped make the looming stillness of the Iron Guards a little less sinister. Deina had slightly more space around her than the others; she told herself it was a coincidence.

At least none of Aristaeus's other servants had tried to enter the room so far. The doors at each end had been barred from the inside; clearly Aristaeus had wanted to make sure that only the silent Iron Guards witnessed his first experiments with the torc.

Thalius, cradling a broken arm, noticed the same thing.

'He was going to kill us too, wasn't he? Once you were dead, no one would know how he came by the torc or what it could do. At least until he used it against them.'

No one replied, and Deina wondered if they were all, like her, imagining what the future might have been if Aristaeus had succeeded in bending the torc to his will.

'It might have been better if you'd knocked him unconscious,' Theron said, between tightening a torniquet around Dendris's arm and watching Nat. 'We could have handed him over to the nobles and priests and so on who are supposedly waiting outside. They could have put him on trial.'

'It's a bit late to worry about that now,' Aster observed. 'Our only plan when we were brought in here was to avoid dying.' He dabbed at the gash across his forearm, wincing. 'You should go out and claim the throne, Theron. It's yours for the taking.'

Theron shook his head.

'I never wanted to be a king.'

Dendris squeezed his hand.

'You don't have to be, at least not forever. But if the throne of Thebes is left empty, you know what will happen. The archon of every city will seek to claim it. There will be a war. A huge and terrible war. No one will be safe.' Theron, still watching Nat, didn't answer. 'You should go out,' Dendris continued, 'and tell the nobles of Mycenae that you defeated Aristaeus and that you're taking your place as the rightful heir.'

'Except I didn't defeat him, did I?' For the first time, he looked across at Deina. 'She did.'

Suddenly self-conscious, Deina put her hand up to cover the torc; the warm metal vibrated beneath her touch, almost like a cat purring.

'We all defeated him. Archis too.' Something about the way Theron was staring at her sent a flash of irritation prickling across her skin. 'Dendris is right. The crown belongs to you. Go out there and show them Aristaeus's body and claim it.'

'Is that an order?' Theron asked quietly.

'Don't be ridiculous. And stop looking at me like that.' She wrapped her arms around herself. 'I'm not in charge.' She nodded towards the younger Spell Caster. 'I'd no more order you to become king than say to Siderous there, oh, go throw yourself onto the fire.'

Siderous's face went blank. He got jerkily to his feet, his arms snapped out in front of him, and he began bending towards the fire. Theron grabbed him and tried to pull him back.

'What's happening?' Thalius got his good arm around Siderous's waist; even together, he and Theron were struggling to keep the young Spell Caster away from the flames.

'I'm not doing anything,' Deina protested.

'You're clearly doing something,' Theron yelled through gritted teeth. 'So if you could just stop . . .'

'But I'm not . . .' Deina pleaded. She turned to find Nat just behind her; he shrugged his shoulders. 'All right – Siderous, stop! Wake up!'

The Spell Caster stopped straining towards the fire and went limp. He, Theron and Thalius all toppled backwards. There was a muffled grunt.

'Why are you on top of me?' Siderous asked. He sat up, rubbing his hands over his face. 'What happened?'

'I don't know,' Deina murmured, staring at the fire. It was easier than looking at her fellow Theodesmioi. Theron came and sat next to her; she felt his hand on her shoulder.

'Your left eye, Deina. The brown one with the gold ring around the pupil.'

'What about it?'

'There's no brown left. The iris is entirely gold. Nat,' Theron asked, 'what's happening?'

Deina looked over her shoulder at the former god of death. *Please, Nat, don't tell him about the nectar. Not yet.*

Nat gazed down at her for a moment before gesturing to the torc.

'Thalius was right. The torc gives the one who wears it the power to control spell-cast metal. That includes spell-cast weapons, as Aristaeus realised. But it also includes the Iron Guards, because their armour is spell cast, and the Theodesmioi, because they wear spell-cast torcs.' He squatted down between Theron and Deina. 'You remember the story I told you. That was how the king to whom Hephaestus gave the torc came to control the Theodesmioi.'

'I forgot,' Deina said, clutching Theron's hand. 'I wanted to stop Aristaeus getting it back, so putting it on seemed like the right thing to do. I just forgot.'

I definitely forgot, she tried to reassure herself. *I wanted the torc. I didn't want this.*

She tugged at the torc. Its response was to tighten about her neck.

'I don't think it's going to come off.'

Dendris and Aster and the Spell Casters were watching her.

'You have to believe me. I'm not going to order any of you to do anything. I promise.' At least Theron was still holding her hand. 'And if you don't want to be king, you don't have to be.'

Theron sighed, got up and went to fetch the crown of Thebes from where it had rolled after Archis attacked Aristaeus. He held the circle of golden leaves in his hands.

'I can't believe she killed Critos. I'm not sure I can forgive her that, even if it was an accident.' He sniffed. 'Critos thought I should try, so I suppose I'll try.' Slowly, he lifted the crown and placed it on his head. 'How does it look?' He grinned, and for

an instant he was his old self: confident, fearless, unburdened by the past.

Everyone got to their feet. All the Theodesmioi knelt briefly before him. Even Nat, Deina noticed, bowed his head.

'This is the right thing to do,' Dendris said, embracing Theron. 'And Deina's power is good too. She's not Aristaeus. She'll use it to help people.' Deina flushed with gratitude at Dendris's words and tried to ignore the tremble in her friend's voice. 'She can order the Iron Guards to break the torcs of all the Theodesmioi here,' Dendris continued, 'just like they did to us. Then they can be sent to other cities.' She swung to face Deina, excited. 'And maybe you could try to free the Iron Guards too, like you freed the Bronze Guards. Surely, we should ask them if they are willing to fight for Theron. Otherwise, we're no better than him.' She jerked her thumb over her shoulder towards Aristaeus's corpse. 'No better than the gods.'

'Of course,' Deina replied. 'I'll try.'

Someone started knocking on the doors at the far end of the room – the doors through which they'd entered.

'Your Majesty?' a voice called. 'Is everything well?'

They were out of time.

'We should arm ourselves with some of these spell-cast weapons,' Aster suggested.

'Good idea. I'll order one of the Iron Guards to carry Aristaeus's body. People were forced to fight for him when he was alive; I'm hoping now he's dead they won't care.'

She turned away from them and began issuing orders to the Iron Guards, trying hard to ignore the voice whispering inside her head.

Free the Theodesmioi. Free the Iron Guards. Just not yet. Use them to destroy the gods first . . .

Deina's prediction about Aristaeus's human guards was right. As soon as they saw the body of their former king slung over the shoulder of an Iron Guard, as soon as they realised that Aristaeus's creatures now took orders from someone else, they threw down their weapons. Many begged to be taken into Deina's service. She told them all that it was Theron's decision. By the time they reached the portico of the megaron with its huge columns, the small group had turned into a procession, including one of Aristaeus's generals. Noise erupted from the crowds when Aristaeus's body was held up in front of them, and they saw the crown of Thebes on Theron's head. However, since Aristaeus had ordered the perimeter of the courtyard to be lined with more guards – Iron and human – no one within the precinct dared try to escape. Deina pushed Theron forward.

'What do I say?' he hissed, waving an arm towards the crowd. Aristaeus had been thorough: the courtyard was filled to bursting point. To one side were a large number of priests dressed in brightly coloured clothes with ornate headdresses. Next to them were what looked like the Mycenaean nobility, or what was left of it after Aristaeus had claimed the citadel, some wearing robes of office. The rest of the courtyard was dominated by the Theodesmioi of the Houses of Zeus, Poseidon and, at the far edge of the courtyard, Hades. With the exception of the Spell Casters – who Deina guessed were still locked up inside their House – Aristaeus had summoned everyone with any rank or official position within the city to witness the execution of the young prince of Thebes and his friends.

'Tell them everything. Who you are, and where we're from, and what we've done. What Aristaeus has done. Tell the Theodesmioi that you're going to free them.'

She gave an order to the Iron Guards, to start breaking the torcs of the Theodesmioi when Theron told them to. As he began addressing the crowd, she slipped into the shadows at the back of the portico where Nat was lingering.

'Why has my eye changed?' she whispered and tugged at the torc. It tightened, just as it had before. 'Why can't I get it off?'

Nat gazed down at her.

'Do you really want to?'

Deina didn't answer. She tried to imagine herself handing the torc over to someone else – to Nat, or Theron. Or breaking it up into fragments again. Or going to Hephaestus and asking him to completely destroy it. Every image made her recoil, caught between fear and anger.

She realised she was clutching the torc tightly, and forced herself to let her hand drop.

'This is the nectar, isn't it?' Not really a question. She knew – had known as soon as she'd slipped the torc around her neck. The spell-cast, god-wrought metal had completed her transformation from mortal to god. Something part of her had wanted. Something she'd dreaded for even longer.

'I'm scared, Nat.'

Nat's hand found hers. His touch felt warm to her now.

The sound of excited voices came from the courtyard: the first of the Theodesmioi had been freed of their torcs.

'Don't be. You'll grow accustomed to it all in time. Your power has already put an end to Aristaeus. Maybe you will be able to stop the Theodesmioi becoming blood hunters.' He gazed at her. She saw compassion in his eyes. 'If that's what you really want.'

Destroy Hades. Take her throne. Claim Olympus itself.

The same voice she'd been hearing since she'd escaped her cell in the Underworld with Nat. Her voice, or the torc's? Perhaps there was no longer any difference. Perhaps, given her heritage, she was merely recognising what she'd wanted all along.

For a little while they stood together, watching the Iron Guards work.

'There is something else I should tell you,' Nat said. 'The dead are not passing into the Underworld.'

'I don't understand.'

'There are too many ghosts lingering here. Archis's ghost was still in the room where she was killed. This place is filled with the shades of those who were slaughtered when Aristaeus took the city. Do you not sense them?'

Deina looked out into the courtyard. For a moment, the daylight dimmed, and the figures of the listening Theodesmioi seemed subsumed in a dark mass of shadows. She blinked, and the scene returned to normal.

'Why?'

'Hades. She may have taken my powers, but she does not know how to use them.' He grinned suddenly. 'I told her she couldn't manage without me. This is perfect. The realms will be out of balance. Zeus and Poseidon will soon accuse her,

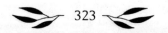

especially when they realise the other old gods are not willing for Hades' treatment of me to go unchallenged. Zeus will restore my powers to me. Perhaps more.'

'Really? When he realises you helped me gain this?' Deina tapped the torc.

Nat's smile faded. 'I would do it again, Deina. For the first time in longer than I can remember, you've given me a reason to exist.' Nat put his arm around her shoulder and pulled her close, dropping a kiss on her forehead. The excitement from the crowd in the courtyard was growing; it reminded Deina of a festival day back in Iolkos. The Iron Guards were working quickly.

'You won't be able to conceal what you are for much longer, Deina,' Nat murmured. 'The marks on your skin are fading.'

Deina glanced down at the rite-seals that swirled across her collarbone and down beneath her tunic.

'I'll tell them. I just . . . You saw, back there. When I accidently ordered poor Siderous into the fire. The way they looked at me. They were scared. Even Dendris, despite her words. They were frightened of me.'

'Gods inspire fear. And with good cause. We are capricious, vengeful, selfish. The worst of us are like small children who've suddenly been given power over life and death and have no thought in their heads apart from their own pleasure; they harm because they can. There may be nothing you can do to stop your friends fearing you. You've changed. You can't expect them to stay the same.'

They lapsed into silence. It was getting darker, strangely, even though the day was not far advanced. Deina gazed at the gathering clouds.

Vengeful, selfish, sadistic. Nat's description of the gods – and he, surely, would know. Archis had been wrong. Mortals did not have the gods they deserved. They deserved so much better.

Deina realised she could give it to them. Elated, she couldn't help grinning. This could be her purpose – this could give meaning to her craving for power, meaning that Theron and the others would understand. They wouldn't blame her for taking the torc or drinking the nectar, not when they saw how she was using her new abilities to benefit them. Deina began to pace, thinking rapidly, planning.

She'd strip the gods of their powers – not just Hades, all of them. And maybe she'd shut them up in Tartarus. And she could swear not to use her powers against mortals. Deina nodded to herself. If she did all these things, her friends would be pleased. They wouldn't resent the steps she'd taken because they would truly be free. That would be her gift to them. And then, surely, they wouldn't fear or distrust her, not any more. But she would need the power of the Theodesmioi to achieve it.

I will free them of their torcs. Just not yet.

The Iron Guards had removed the torcs from nearly half the Theodesmioi in the courtyard.

'I have to stop this. There's a better way. I need to –' She broke off as the hairs on her arm and the back of her neck stood up. Next to her, Nat stiffened. 'What's happening, Nat?'

'Oh, this isn't good. They're coming.' He sounded as panicked as he had when she and Theron had surprised him by suddenly appearing in the Underworld.

'Who's coming?' Deina demanded. 'Hades?'

Nat shook his head.

'I'm not sure . . . Her siblings, though, for certain.' He flung out his arm, pointing towards the wall that formed the far boundary of the courtyard. 'There.'

Two figures had appeared, standing on top of the wall. Huge, larger by far than any mortal man, even though they had the outward form of men. Deina recognised Poseidon from the vision she'd had in his palace; even here his attention was divided between watching the courtyard and checking out his muscles. Zeus appeared just as he had in Olympus, only now he was not smiling. Deina stiffened. Yet no one else reacted.

'Why doesn't everyone else see them?'

'A god may be revealed or not, as he chooses.' He swore. 'Zeus doesn't look happy.' A lightning bolt appeared in Zeus's hand. Deina tugged Nat forward to where Theron and the others were standing.

'Theron, watch out!'

He didn't respond. He couldn't. Before Deina reached him, the Theodesmioi, the nobles and priests who had stayed to observe the removal of the torcs, the Iron and human guards – every mortal within the courtyard had been frozen in place. The two gods, reduced to more normal proportions, appeared in front of her. Before Deina could do more than think about hurling the spear she held at one of them, Zeus addressed her.

'What are you?' The god did not raise his voice. Still, his words beat against her mind like a storm. His gaze, as he fixed her with eyes like liquid silver, seemed to fasten on to her, to make her limbs sluggish.

'I am Deina.' She had to force herself to answer.

Zeus made a sound that might have been a laugh. 'I do not require your name.' He gestured at Thanatos. 'Here we have a creature that used to be a god. So I ask once again: what are *you*?'

Deina gripped her borrowed weapons more tightly.

'I am a Soul Severer of the Order of Hades.' She lifted her chin. 'A thief. A woman. I am the daughter of Hades. What other descriptions do you require?'

'Hades?' There was a slight note of suspicion to Zeus's voice that had not been there before, quickly smoothed over. 'And that is why you dare claim what does not belong to you?' He laughed as Deina's hand went protectively to the triple-stranded torc. 'Why you dare threaten the order of things by breaking the torcs of my Theodesmioi?'

'And mine,' added the so far silent Poseidon. 'And those of Hades.' The sea god nudged his brother. 'Where is Hades? Why isn't he here?'

'Hades is having some difficulties,' Nat interrupted. 'Your brother has taken my powers, but he clearly has no idea how to use them. People are dying, but they aren't going anywhere. Look around.'

Zeus and Poseidon turned their attention for an instant to the courtyard.

'Hmm,' Zeus growled. 'It is over-full of ghosts. What did you do, Thanatos?'

'I didn't do anything, I swear. This is all Hades' fault.'

'Well, we will deal with that problem shortly. First, I will take back that torc. These creatures –' he tapped a fingernail on the armour of an Iron Guard who was frozen in position nearby, causing it to topple over – 'will no longer obey you.'

He lunged towards Deina. She dropped into a crouch and brought up the sword and the spear, aiming at Zeus's chest. The god paused.

'Deina,' Nat murmured, 'you're going to get us all roasted . . .'

Zeus smiled. 'You really think you can thwart my will with any weapon wrought by man?'

'These weapons were wrought by a god,' Deina snapped back. 'Which I think you know, or you wouldn't be hesitating.'

'I never hesitate,' Zeus shot back. 'One touch of my lightning bolt will incinerate you completely.'

And yet, he hadn't incinerated her. A fragment of the memory Nat had shared with them resurfaced: Zeus, ordering Nat to take the life of the king to whom Hephaestus had given the torc. Deina began to wonder. Zeus claimed he was too important to carry out the task himself, but maybe the truth was different. Zeus didn't obliterate the king because he didn't want to risk damage to the torc. Even now she could see the lust in his eyes as he looked at it.

'What I wish to know, before I destroy you, is why.' Zeus gestured at the Theodesmioi. 'What do you hope to achieve by releasing these mortals?'

'I wish them to be free in this life, even if their fate in the next is unavoidable.'

'Their fate in the next?' he questioned.

'The blood hunters,' Nat explained. 'These Theodesmioi have been promised Elysium in return for their service, but in fact . . .'

'Oh, yes. I had forgotten.' He smiled coldly. 'A waste. Your destruction of their torcs may free them from the control of their Houses, but as long as they are marked by our sigils, they will never escape the control of their gods.'

Zeus clicked his fingers. The Theodesmioi and the others who were in the courtyard began moving, carrying on as if nothing had happened. This time, though, the gods had revealed themselves. Panic began to ripple through the mortals.

Theron turned to her.

'Deina, what's happening?'

Before she could answer, Zeus clicked his fingers again. All the nobles and the priests who had been part of the crowd had vanished. The Theodesmioi of Zeus's order – their faces strangely blank and their weapons at the ready – stood square, facing the portico.

At least, some of them did: those whose torcs had been removed.

Poseidon struck the floor with his trident and the same happened. The Sea Singers without torcs appeared to be stripped of all emotion and awareness – to have become no more than vessels for the god's will. Deina was grateful for Hades' absence. She could not have borne to see Theron, Aster and Dendris taken over in the same way.

The other Theodesmioi were trying to waken their comrades, calling to them and shaking them. Nothing worked.

'What's happening, brother?' Poseidon asked anxiously.

'Hephaestus's torc,' Zeus growled. 'It interferes with our control over those who wear the spell-cast bronze. No matter.' He and Poseidon both began to swell in size. 'Theodesmioi, and others here present,' he boomed. 'Submit, or I will order

those within our power to attack, and you will be slaughtered like cattle. Kneel before your gods.'

Some of the torc-bound Theodesmioi started to kneel.

'No,' Deina cried out, 'we have to fight them. We have to destroy these Olympians, or we will never truly be free.'

More of the Theodesmioi knelt. Zeus laughed.

'You.' He touched a nearby, blank-faced Battle Wager with the flaming tip of his thunderbolt. 'Bring me her head.'

20

A wall of silent flame erupted, encircling Deina and the Battle Wager, trapping them inside and stopping anyone else from approaching. Deina could hear Theron's shouts, but she forced herself to ignore them and focus on defence. The Battle Wager was already circling her, his spear at the ready. He lunged. Deina sliced through the spear's wooden shaft. The Battle Wager threw the ruined weapon down and seized his axe, pivoting for another attack.

'Wake up,' Deina yelled, kicking his legs and knocking him off balance. 'He's using you.' The sigil of Zeus on the Battle Wager's forehead was glowing. Deina spun, slashing the tip of her sword across the mark. Though the skin around it split and bled, the sigil seemed impervious to her blade. And the Battle Wager was still coming for her, heedless of the blood dripping down his face.

'Please, stop. I don't want to hurt you!'

The Battle Wager ignored her. He drew his right arm back, ready to throw the axe at Deina's head. She spun round and

brought her sword down across his wrist. The spell-cast blade sliced through the bone as easily as an oar passing through water. Yet the man didn't even cry out. Just stooped, seized his axe in his left hand, shaking off his own severed fist, and prepared to attack again. Aghast, Deina hesitated. Too long – even as she leaped out of the way, the corner of the axe blade caught her earlobe. Pain and fury mingled and she screamed out a challenge, spinning and ducking beneath the axe swing to thrust her sword up through the Battle Wager's ribcage. He spasmed once and was still. Deina slid her sword free and let the body drop to the ground. The surrounding flames went out. Zeus shrieked with rage.

Theron raced forward and grabbed her wrist as the god-possessed Theodesmioi raised their weapons and began to advance. Some of the other Theodesmioi ran for the gates, those already kneeling started to plead for mercy. Only a handful looked ready to stand their ground.

'Come on,' Theron urged, 'we have to get out of here while we still can. Order the Iron Guards to open the gates.'

Deina yanked her arm from his grasp.

'Escape how? Everyone here who still has a torc is trapped in this city. There is no escape. Not as long as the gods exist.' Deina turned to Aster and Dendris. 'We have to fight. We have to destroy them, or this will never end.' She pointed at one of the Theodesmioi kneeling in the dirt. A Sea Singer novice as far as she could tell by his clothes, hardly more than a boy. 'You – get up and draw your weapons. Get ready to fight.'

It was just like what had happened with Siderous. The Sea Singer became as blank as the Theodesmioi who were controlled by the gods. He stood and readied his sword and spear.

'All of you,' Deina cried out, 'Theodesmioi and Iron Guards, obey me! Get up. Get ready to fight.'

Every one of the Iron Guards, every one of those Theodesmioi who were still wearing torcs, responded to her command. Those who were kneeling, stood. Those who were fleeing, stopped and turned to face the god-possessed Theodesmioi advancing towards them. A fierce excitement flooded through Deina's body. She felt her power growing stronger. It rippled beneath her skin, enfolding her, caressing her. She swept her sword up and aimed it at the watching gods.

'I'll not kneel before you. None of us will.'

The lightning bolt in Zeus's hand grew brighter and brighter until, with a clap of thunder that shook the citadel and sent a cloud of dust eddying through the air, both gods vanished.

'What – what just happened?' Dendris asked, looking around the courtyard. 'Have they gone? Have we won?'

Deina knew the answer was no. The Theodesmioi who had been possessed by the gods had stopped moving and had lowered their weapons, but they were just as still, just as vacant as before.

'They'll be back,' Nat said. 'They've gone to summon reinforcements, that's all. And to find Hades.' He smiled grimly. 'That, they might find a little trickier than they're expecting. My visit with Hypnos to the other old gods was productive. Hades will find that we –' He broke off and glanced down at his arms. 'Hades will find that they are not as powerless as she believes.'

'Don't worry,' Deina said, wanting to cheer him up. 'This

is going to work. I'm going to destroy the gods. I'm going to kill Hades, and give you your power back.'

For an instant she was back in Iolkos, sitting with Chryse outside the temple of Poseidon.

If gods could be killed, I'd hunt them down and slit their throats and smile while I was doing it . . .

She laughed and turned from Nat, wanting to share her excitement with the others, because she knew they had to be as happy as her.

Yet not one of them was smiling.

Theron looked . . . horror-struck. That was the only description Deina could think of. He was staring at the ranks of silent Theodesmioi, those with torcs and those without, facing each other, waiting to be ordered to kill. The only other Theodesmioi who were unaffected, the Soul Severers who had already had their torcs removed by the Iron Guards, began to gather round Deina and the others.

Theron knelt by the side of the dead Battle Wager.

'What are you doing, Deina?'

'I'm setting them free, of course.'

'Setting who free?' Aster asked softly. 'If this battle goes ahead, everyone apart from us –' he gestured at the Soul Severers looking on – 'will be dead. If Hades shows up, we'll be dead too. Release the Theodesmioi under your control. Let them go. There's no dishonour in admitting you've made a mistake.'

A mistake?

'No, you don't understand. I think there's a way to use the Theodesmioi to fatally weaken the gods. I haven't worked it out exactly yet, but –'

'Use?' Theron half lifted a hand towards her. 'We're people, Deina, not weapons. If you treat others like things, how are you different from Aristaeus? How are you different from the gods?'

Deina could feel her grip on her temper ebbing away. Why could she not make them understand?

Aster shook his head.

'What's happened to you, Deina? I know you're a demi-god. I know you're stronger than the rest of us. But this?' He gestured helplessly at the Theodesmioi within her control. 'You're my friend – or you were. I thought I knew you. I thought you were better than this.'

The triple-stranded torc around her neck pulsed like a heartbeat. Deina swallowed. Was it anger that was choking her, or grief?

'How can you say that? How can you stand there and judge me, when you were willing to kill Theron just because Orpheus asked you to.'

'Deina, you're not being fair.' Dendris's tone was gentle, for her. 'You know that . . .' Her scrutiny shifted from Deina's face to her neck. 'What's that?' She reached out and brushed her fingertips across Deina's skin. They came away smeared with something that glittered when Dendris held her hand flat. 'What's happened to your blood? Why are you bleeding gold?' She lifted her gaze. 'It's ichor, isn't it? Oh, Deina – what have you done to yourself?'

'Nothing. I've done nothing apart from trying to save you. To save everyone.' How could they treat her like this? Deina itched to shake them, to force them to see her point of view.

She backed away, searching for words that would make her friends hurt as badly as they were hurting her. 'I understand what's happening. You're all scared. Theron's scared of being king. Aster's scared of the gods. And Dendris –' she glared at Dendris, ignoring the shock she saw in her beautiful face – 'you're scared that Theron will choose to be with me instead of you.'

Aster cursed and flushed angrily.

'Leave her alone.' He beckoned to the others. 'Let's go. She's not one of us any more. If she wants to fight, she can do it on her own.'

'Wait – it's not Deina. It's the torc.' Theron, still holding his sword, was edging closer to her. He appealed to Nat. 'You've got to do something. Get that thing off her.'

'I can't. I've no power, Theron, you know that. And even if I had the power, it wouldn't make any difference.' Nat's blue eyes held Deina's gaze for a moment. 'She drank nectar in the Underworld. Even without the torc, she would still be a god.'

The word hung in the air between the five of them, as invisible as poison, and just as ruinous.

'I knew, I think,' Theron murmured eventually. 'I knew something had changed, before we reached Thebes. But you said you hated the gods. You said you'd rather die than become one of them.' The sorrow in his eyes made Deina writhe. It wasn't fair – she didn't deserve to be forced to feel like this. Every decision she'd made – she'd made it for them, as well as for herself. What did they think would have happened to them without her? She could have gone with Nat the very first time he asked her. Gone with him and left them all wandering in the Underworld.

'What was I supposed to do, Theron? I had no choice. You couldn't help me – you couldn't help yourself!' Theron flinched from the force of her rage, but Deina didn't care. 'I had to drink the nectar. It was the only way for me to free myself of the seeds and to escape the Underworld, and I guessed that if I wanted to use the torc, I'd have to –'

'So this was always just about the torc?' Dendris gripped her axe in both hands, confronting Deina. 'That was why you insisted we should keep searching after we'd found the first fragment. Stopping Aristaeus wasn't enough for you.' Her gaze swept Deina disdainfully. 'You wanted power. You wanted power and you didn't care who died along the way.'

Nat shuddered.

'They'll be back soon – Zeus and the others. I can feel it. You don't have time for this.'

'Theron,' Aster hissed, grabbing Dendris's arm and pulling her away. 'Let's go.'

'No.' He moved a little closer to Deina again. 'I won't leave you, Deina. I've told you that enough times. Please, set them free.' He gestured to those Theodesmioi bound by her power. 'I still trust you. Together, we can find another way to fight. Another way to defeat the gods. Come back to us, please.'

Deina found herself clutching the torc again, caressing the three strands and the strange, secret signs carved into the metal, her mind in turmoil. Could Theron be right? As she had done before, she tried to imagine herself wrenching the torc from her neck. Snapping it into fragments. The thought of its loss sent pain stabbing through her chest, strong enough to make her shudder. No – she couldn't give it up. She wouldn't! She needed the torc. It was helping her, sharpening her power, forging it into something strong. Something that combined the strength of all three realms. She could feel that strength now, ready to blossom within her, poised to obey her commands. Deina let the spell-cast sword slip from her hand. She knew she would no longer need it.

Theron's shoulders sagged.

'That's right.' He edged closer still. 'Now, order the Theodesmioi to put down their weapons too, Deina. Please.'

Deina glanced beyond Theron, to where those Soul Severers who'd been freed of their torcs were gathered. They were armed, all of them. Some of them held their weapons ready, as if they were about to attack her. Her – when she'd been the one to order the Iron Guards to rip the torcs from their necks. Yet instead of offering gratitude, they were staring at her as if she was a monster. Deina's palms itched as power trickled across her skin. None of them could be trusted. Not even those she'd counted as friends. There was Aster with his spear in his hand, and Dendris with her axe, both of them on Theron's side, not on hers –

Theron, who was still wearing the crown of Thebes on his head.

Suspicion rose like a mist into Deina's mind, colouring all her thoughts. Theron loved her. Theron was lying. He wanted to save her. He wanted the Theodesmioi and the torc for himself.

'No.' Deina shook her head, backing away from Theron. 'You can't have it, and you can't have them. I can't do this without them. Some of you have to die, Theron. It's necessary. The gods have to be destroyed!'

'Some of *you*?' he said. 'Listen to yourself, Deina. Is that what you really want? To destroy the gods so that you can rule in their place? Queen of Olympus, while those of us who survive bear your sigil and sacrifice our lives in your name?' He dropped his head for a moment, covering his face with his hand. When he looked back at her, Deina saw a new resolve in his eyes. 'I love you, Deina.' His voice broke on her name. 'Or I loved the person you were. I think she's gone. Still, for her sake, I can't let you do this.' He shifted his grip on his sword and strode forwards.

No. He was dangerous. He couldn't be allowed to get near her. 'Stay away.'

Her words had force. Theron yelped and staggered back, his nose bleeding, as if he'd walked into a wall. Dendris cried out in fear; she and Aster ran to Theron and tried to drag him further from Deina, as the other Soul Severers either scattered or launched spears towards her. The weapons fell to the ground before they even got close. Theron shook Aster and Dendris away and tried again.

'Theron,' Nat called to him, 'give it up. It won't work.' He held out his hand. Did Nat want the torc too? 'Please, Deina, come away. Leave the Theodesmioi – leave all the mortals and come away from here.'

Deina ignored him. So did Theron. Leaning forward, like a man forcing a path through a gale, he took a step towards her. And another step.

'Stop, Theron. Stay back!' She could see the effort it was costing him to fight her will. Every tiny movement made him grunt with effort. 'No further – I'm warning you!'

Yet he kept coming. And he still had his sword in his hand.

He was going to try to kill her. He'd try to kill her, then he'd try to take the torc. Anguish and fury built, swallowing every other impulse, until Deina couldn't stand it any more. She shrieked and flung out her arm.

'I told you to get away from me!'

Black flames, burning with cold, erupted from her palm. Theron screamed.

As quickly as they had appeared, the flames vanished, leaving nothing but a smell of ash. Deina's rage evaporated, replaced by regret.

'I'm sorry – I didn't mean to –'

Theron wasn't looking at her. He was bent double, clutching his stomach and gasping with pain. Blood started to splash into the dirt below.

Cold fear paralyzed Deina's limbs. What had she done?

'Theron, let me help you.'

She forced herself to move towards him, but he tried to back away, and as he did she saw his whole abdomen was nothing but a mess of charred flesh. He was holding his entrails in his own blood-soaked fingers. Deina clapped her hand to her mouth to stifle a cry. Theron began trembling violently and collapsed. Nat caught him in his arms.

Deina took a step forward. Stopped, afraid to make things worse.

'I never meant to hurt him. I just wanted to stop him. That was all.'

Nat lowered Theron gently to the ground. Aster and Dendris hurried to kneel next to him. Theron's eyes were glazed. His breath came in short, rasping gasps. A trickle of blood ran from the corner of his mouth.

'Can't you save him?' Aster asked. There were tears in his eyes. 'Please, Nat.'

Nat shook his head.

'I have not the power. I never did – I was the god of death, remember?'

'No!' Deina approached as close as she dared. 'No, there has to be a way. He can't die.' She gripped the torc around her neck with both hands. 'I order you not to die.'

Nothing happened, except for Theron's breath becoming more laboured.

'He's not made of spell-cast metal,' Nat said. 'You can't save him.'

Deina gasped.

'The armour – the iron armour that Aristaeus had prepared for me. We can put him in it, keep him alive –'

Aster stood and barred her way.

'You would torture him by condemning him to such a fate? Let him go, Deina. It is too late. You've killed him.'

Dendris was weeping.

Deina pressed the heels of her hands to her eyes. No tears. Maybe gods couldn't cry.

Remember who you are, Soul Severer . . .

Someone had said that to her once. She couldn't remember who, but that didn't matter. The only thing that mattered was that Theron shouldn't die. Not today. Not because of her.

She pushed past Aster, dipped her fingers in the blood pooling beneath Theron's body and used it to mark both his forehead and her own, smearing the sticky liquid across their sigils.

'What are you doing?' Dendris demanded. 'Haven't you

hurt him enough? Leave him alone.' She clutched at Theron's hand. 'You can't save him.'

'I can,' Deina insisted, talking more to herself than Dendris. 'I will.' She began muttering the Song to summon the Threshold. She had to keep Theron from dying, and she had to protect Aster and Dendris, Nat, and the rest of the Theodesmioi. She had to protect them from Zeus and Poseidon, and she had to protect them from herself.

'Deina, don't do this.' Nat's voice was low, urgent. 'I can't follow you there. Not any more. You'll be alone.'

That was the point. Deina looked around the courtyard, seeing the frozen Theodesmioi, poised to tear each other apart. The terrified Soul Severers. Not the gods' fault. Hers. She had to shut herself away forever in the only place that no one would be able to find her.

Theron let out a long, agonised groan. His eyes rolled back in his head.

Out of time, Deina gabbled the last few words of the Song and willed the Threshold into existence. The cold crept over her skin. Gathering Theron into her arms, she pressed her forehead to his, closed her eyes, and let the darkness take them.

That sweet sound again – one of the melancholy melodies Theron had made up, she thought, or something very like it. Deina lifted her head and scanned her surroundings, searching for the source. She'd no sense of how long she and Theron had been here. However long it was, she'd still not been able to decide whether what she heard really was music, or just a breeze playing among the trees. Not that it mattered. She shifted position again. Theron's head was resting in her lap. From this angle, she could almost pretend he was just sleeping; drowsing in the heat of a summer afternoon before they both returned to the House in Iolkos. His lifeline was still held in her right hand. She hadn't cut it, so he wasn't dead. He was caught here, between life and death, but not dead.

Not dead. She'd prevented that, at least.

Would it be safer to make the lifeline more secure? Deina studied it a while, then looped it tightly around her wrist. Bending lower, she kissed Theron's forehead. The faint melody caught her ear again. Despite its sadness, it made her smile a little. This Threshold, this space in which she had sealed them – with its weather-worn boulders and scrubby grass and wind-twisted olive trees and the faint scent of thyme – it looked very like a spot high up on the hillside above the House at Iolkos. Theron had told her once that he used to climb up there to practise his singing. Music had been such a part of his life. Why would it not also form part of the Threshold she had created around him, using his memories and his blood?

There was no time in this place. Still, Deina had a sense that she and Theron and everything around them were gradually freezing into immobility; skin and hair and bone transmuting slowly into stone, caught forever in the same moment. And yet, she would not leave him. She could not bring herself to sever his lifeline and watch him slip away into the Underworld. To think of him becoming a blood hunter . . .

Better for them both to stay in the Threshold forever than to let that happen.

Deina shuddered and her free hand went to the torc, the weapon she had hoped would somehow show her how to free the blood hunters from their cursed existence. She'd lost too many to that fate. Leida, Chryse, Drex, Anteïs, Critos.

Only heroes stand a chance of evading fate.

Nat had told her that, one of the first times she'd met him in the Underworld. She'd told him she wasn't a hero. Events had proved her right. She loathed the gods – now she was one of them. She'd decided she had to save all the Theodesmioi – she'd slaughtered the one she loved above all others, and ruined Nat's existence into the bargain. She'd tried to fight the gods – the gods had destroyed her. Had helped her destroy herself.

Deina's lips twitched. It was so terrible, she almost wanted to laugh. She should have stopped after she'd saved her friends from Neidius. Or after they'd returned from Poseidon's realm. She should have let them sail away from Iolkos with the torc fragment, away from her, and returned to the Underworld. She should have drunk the nectar and submitted to Hades. Maybe she could have been happy there with Nat. Instead, she'd pushed her luck.

And her luck had, finally, run out.

Tyche, goddess of fortune, if you can hear me, I ask for your blessings upon Aster and Dendris and Nat. They still need luck. If you can hear me, send them your blessings.

Lifting Theron's head, she laid him on the springy grass, stood up and stretched. Lie down next to him – that was what she should do now. Lie down and close her eyes and perhaps, even though she was a god, she would be able to sleep. She knelt and cupped Theron's face in her hands.

'Don't be scared,' she whispered. 'We'll sleep away eternity together.'

'You could do that.' The voice shattered the quiet. A girl's voice. Deina leaped up and stood protectively in front of Theron.

The girl watching her was perhaps twelve or thirteen – the age of an older apprentice, if she'd been a member of the Order. But there was no sigil marring her bronze skin. This was no Soul Severer.

'Who are you?'

The girl laughed, her amber eyes crinkling with humour.

'I'll give you a clue. I know where you found the fragments of the torc that sits around your neck, because I hid them in the first place.'

Deina stared.

'Tyche? Goddess of fortune? But – but –'

'But you saw me as an adult woman in the vision you had in Poseidon's realm? You should know by now, Deina, that things are not always what they seem. Especially the gods.' Tyche shrugged and shook her long black hair back from her shoulders. 'I like this particular age.' Her smile became more calculating. 'I like the unpredictability.' Deina remembered being around that age, and how quickly contentment could give way to rage. The goddess pointed at Theron. 'You could lie down next to him and go to sleep, but it would be a shame. The game is just getting interesting, if you still want to play.'

They were sitting on two boulders, a little way away from Theron. His lifeline stretched glittering across the space between.

'How is this possible?' Deina asked. 'We were told that gods could not enter the Threshold.' The memory of Thanatos, dark and silent, came back to her. He had haunted the Thresholds Deina called into being long before she knew who or what he was. Long before he'd first tried to speak to her during the Punishment Rite only a few months ago. And yet he too was a god. 'Another lie we were told? Just like the promise of Elysium?'

'Not a lie,' Tyche replied. She had her feet up on the boulder and was clasping her arms around her knees. 'Just not the entire truth. Most gods *are* prevented from entering this space that exists between life and death; your elders ordered it so. Most gods, but not all. You, a god, are here. I am here because you invoked me. And as you well know, Hecate, the goddess of those places that lie between, of crossroads and choices, she may enter here.' Tyche looked amused. 'The Soul Severers who first served in your Order could no more keep *her* out than a wrecked ship can keep out the sea. Thanatos, god of death, spends so much time traversing the boundaries between death and life that the Threshold is no barrier to him.' She sighed. 'Poor Thanatos. There is much anger amongst the old gods about Hades' treatment of him. That's why we agreed to help: to frustrate her search for you and to keep her from Mycenae as long as possible. I feel sorry for him. His fate, at the very end, is to be utterly alone. Yet he fights against it.'

Fate, again.

'Thanatos has always existed and will always exist, until there is no more life for him to consume,' Tyche continued. 'Until time itself has faded away. Despite our claim of immortality, he will come for the gods too, one day. Perhaps sooner than we might wish.'

Poor Nat. Deina's heart, silent though it was, broke for him. Tyche leaned forward.

'Since you called on me, tell me what you want, Deina.'

Deina hesitated. She'd spoken to gods before. She'd tricked them or tried her best to force them into a promise they wouldn't be able to escape. Yet Tyche seemed different. Deina wondered whether she was different enough.

'I want Theron to live,' she answered. 'To be healed. Even better – I want not to have hurt him at all.' Deina stared into Tyche's face. 'Can you do that? Can you change time?'

'No. I cannot alter what has already passed.' The goddess stretched out her legs and leaned back against the boulder, closing her eyes and tilting her face up to the sky. 'Tell me what you want.'

Deina sighed.

'If you can't change what has happened, can you at least help me change the future? I want to finish what I've started. I want to destroy the gods. The Olympians, at least. That is the only way we can be free.' She took a deep breath. 'It's the only way I can be free.'

'Tempting.' The goddess's appearance altered, becoming a reverse image of what it had been: alabaster skin, hair white as snow, silver eyes. Still a girl, though. 'I am Nemesis, as well as Tyche. The good fortune I deal out with one hand, I must check with the other. The Olympians have much undeserved good luck, are more deserving of retribution than most.' Tyche returned to her original form. Beneath the goddess's gaze, Deina felt as if her skin were being stripped away, as if she were being sliced through, allowing Tyche access to everything that lay at her very centre – the foul as well as the fair.

'Tell me what you want,' Tyche said a third time.

The words came unbidden to Deina's lips.

'I want to kill the part of me that belongs to the gods. I want to – to rip it out.' Deina's fist thudded into the centre of her chest. 'That's what I need to be free of – that part of me that craves power, that took control of the Theodesmioi and the Iron Guards, that secretly wished that Aristaeus had slaughtered both houses of Spell Casters so there would be no one left to make torcs.' She gripped the torc that was wrapped around her own neck and tried to wrench it off.

Tyche reached out and gripped Deina's wrist so tightly it almost hurt.

'This torc is a tool, nothing more. You know the torc itself is not to blame.'

Deina slumped as the rage that had coursed through her faded.

'I know. The curse runs deeper than that. Even before Cronos gave me nectar to drink, there was poison coursing through my veins.' Her voice sunk. 'I am Hades' daughter, and my very blood is tainted.'

Deina wondered whether Tyche could destroy her. Perhaps, if the destruction was complete enough, she would at least be put beyond caring, or feeling, or wanting anything any more.

'Come, Deina,' Tyche commanded, releasing her hold on Deina. 'We'll take a walk. There is more you must be told.'

More? Doubtful, Deina allowed the goddess to lead her

around the Threshold for a little while. Every so often Tyche stopped to pluck a leaf or a blade of grass, seemingly with the sole purpose of pulling it apart. Deina started to get impatient.

'Tyche, what is it I need to know?'

'I was planning how to tell you, that's all, but I think perhaps it might be easier just to show you.'

'Show me what?'

'You'll see.' Tyche turned abruptly, lifted her hands and pressed her fingers to Deina's temples.

The Threshold vanished.

21

Deina found herself in a gloomy space lit only by the soft glow of a fire. As her eyes adjusted, she saw she was in a forge: in the distance, a figure was standing over an anvil, working on something amidst showers of red sparks. Tyche was next to her. She took Deina's hand and, without seeming to move, they were suddenly much nearer to the anvil. The figure was revealed as a man, russet-haired and strikingly handsome. Hephaestus, the smith god. Deina recognised him from the memory Nat had shared with them. From this distance, she could see that the thick loops of gold that criss-crossed his legs were beautiful: engraved and studded with jewels. The elegantly crafted crutch he held beneath one arm didn't impede his work in the slightest. So far, he didn't seem to be aware of her or Tyche. She glanced down at her arms.

'The lifeline –'

'– is still there, in the Threshold, just as you are.' Tyche smiled. 'You see the past, through my memory. A long time past, as mortals would count it. I must play my part, but you need do no more than watch.' The goddess grew into a woman, with the same bright, mischievous expression in her eyes.

Someone else was approaching.

'A little light would be welcome, Hephaestus,' the newcomer snapped. 'Or do you wish your guests to stumble over the detritus of your forge?'

Hades' voice. Even though she knew her mother was not really there, Deina couldn't help withdrawing further into the shadows.

Hephaestus muttered a word Deina couldn't quite hear. A golden light spilled from dozens of milky globes strung on chains across the ceiling of the forge, and Deina realised the size of the space in which he was labouring, more like a great hall than a blacksmith's workshop.

'There is no detritus in my forge,' Hephaestus rumbled, 'and you are not a guest. I did not invite you.'

Hades, having sashayed up to the anvil, waved a hand dismissively. 'I would have thought you'd enjoy having a visitor. I asked Tyche to join us too.'

Tyche stepped out of the shadows. 'Greetings, Hephaestus of the skilful hands.'

Hephaestus nodded. 'Tyche. What does Hades want with us, do you know?'

'I have a project you might be interested in being part of,' Hades purred.

Hephaestus rolled his eyes.

'In other words, she needs our help.' He sighed and put down his tools. 'What do you want, Hades?'

Hades bit her lip, weighing her audience for a moment.

 351

'None of us have any cause to love Zeus. Or any of the others who dwell on Olympus. Tyche, you are a Titan, only allowed to retain your power by Zeus's favour. And you, Hephaestus – the other gods laugh at you, and make it clear you are not welcome in their golden halls. No wonder you're lonely. No wonder you listened to Eris and created the torc that you have since been forced to destroy. That plan failed, but I have another plan. A better plan. One that truly considers my brothers' weaknesses.' Hades picked up the item Hephaestus was working on – a shield that had been polished into a mirror-like finish, and smiled at her reflection. 'I want you to create a woman as you did before, a second Pandora. One that Zeus and Poseidon will not be able to resist. But this woman will not unleash ill on mortals. With Tyche's blessing, she will take power from the gods.'

Hephaestus glanced at Tyche.

'She'll take power from the gods and give it to you, Hades. That's what you mean, isn't it?' Without waiting for her to answer, the smith god shook his head. 'No.'

'You can't do it?' Hades demanded.

'I won't do it. Once was enough.' He snatched the shield out of Hades' hands and picked up a large hammer that was leaning against the anvil. 'Now get out of my forge before I come up with a way to trap you, like I did to Hera, and Aphrodite . . .'

The sound and the image blurred. Deina rubbed her eyes. Now, she and Tyche were standing on a mountainside, bright and cold with drifted snow. Hades was also there, a little ahead of them.

'Another memory,' Tyche murmured. 'I followed Hades from the forge.' She hurried nearer to Hades. 'Wait.'

The god turned, shifting into his male form as he did so. 'Well?' he growled.

'I am willing to help you, even if Hephaestus is not.'

'If he refuses to make the vessel, your help is worthless to me.' Hades began to stomp away across the snow.

'There is another way,' Tyche called after him. 'It would involve a mortal, but it can be done.'

Hades stopped and glanced back over his shoulder.

'A mortal?' His lips twisted with disgust. 'How?'

'You need to have a child. A demi-god with your power flowing through their veins. Create the child, then I will do the rest. I existed long before you, Hades. There are ways and means. Trust in my knowledge, even if you do not trust me . . .'

The scene became hazy, its elements scattering and reforming as a place Deina recognised: the throne room in Hades' palace. Hades, female again, was seated on her throne. A nymph in a flowing, plum-coloured tunic – one of the Lampades – was standing next to the throne; she held a bundle in her arms.

'Well, Tyche?' Hades beckoned, and Tyche left Deina's side to approach the throne. She bowed to the other god. 'Here is the child,' Hades continued. 'A girl, half mortal, half divine. I have fulfilled my part of the bargain. Now you must fulfil yours.'

Tyche took the bundle from the nymph; it squirmed and whimpered, and Deina's heart raced even as she felt rooted to the spot. The bundle was a baby.

It was her.

Tyche was smiling at the child. 'A pretty little thing. I need a place to set her down.'

Hades got up from the throne, dismissed the nymph and

led Tyche through a door that opened off the throne room. Deina followed.

The room beyond was smaller but just as opulently furnished, with ornately carved couches and tables and overlapping furs softening the gleaming marble floor tiles. Open archways along one side gave a view onto a landscape of green, rolling hills. Hades clicked her fingers and the view changed to a sun-dappled ocean, casting shifting sunbeams across the painted ceiling.

Tyche laid the baby on one of the tables and pulled out a soft pouch from beneath her cloak. Inside were some dried herbs, two small vials and a knife. A spike of panic knotted Deina's stomach.

'What are you doing?' she demanded.

Tyche turned her head, leaving a ghostly image still bent over the table, busy with the herbs.

'What I thought I needed to do to balance the playing field. To prevent Hades sweeping all before her. To give others a chance to play the game.' The goddess winked, turned back and became one with her remembered self. She began to sing in a low voice, sprinkling the dried herbs across the baby's head and chest as she did so.

The squirming, gurgling infant stilled. Her translucent eyelids fluttered and closed.

'There, little one,' Tyche crooned. 'You may sleep while I must work.' Swiftly, she pulled the swaddling clothes away, exposing the baby's chest, and picked up the knife. She uncorked the two vials and passed them to Hades. 'Hold these.'

'Ah . . .' Hades eyes glinted. 'You obtained the ichor.'

The divine equivalent of blood. Now Deina understood why the vials glimmered with a faint golden light.

'Of course.' Tyche raised an eyebrow. 'You doubted me? This comes straight from the veins of Zeus and Poseidon. Strengthened with the spells I've obtained, the ichor will bind to what already flows through the child's veins. She will draw power not only from the Underworld but from the heavens and from the sea too.'

Hades smiled.

'Proceed.'

Tyche picked up the knife, a wicked-looking thing with a long, tapered blade, more like a needle than a weapon. Singing once more, words that had no meaning to Deina but which resonated with dark power, she held the blade for a moment just above the sleeping child's heart – Deina held her breath and pressed one hand to her chest, even though it had been so long ago, even though she did not remember the pain – and plunged it down into the baby's flesh. She drew it out instantly. A single drop of blood welled up from the wound. Laying down the knife, Tyche picked up a blade of grass, pinched it between her fingers to form a funnel and inserted it into the hole left by the knife. Deina had to force herself to keep watching. Hades was leaning forward, fascinated. Drop by golden drop, singing spells all the time, Tyche gradually emptied the two vials of ichor into the sleeping child. Finally, it was done. The goddess removed the grass and placed her hand over the wound. When she took her palm away, the skin was whole. Uninjured. Somehow, though, Deina seemed to feel the ghost of the narrow blade and the unwelcome chill of the liquid being forced into her body.

'I am in your debt, Tyche,' Hades said, picking up the child, who was beginning to stir, and gazing down at her. 'Strange: her eyes were both brown. Now one of them is grey-green.'

Tyche nodded.

'The ichor of Zeus and Poseidon already marks her.'

'No matter. No one will see her to comment on her beauty, or lack of it. I will raise her here and teach her all she needs to fulfil her destiny. She will be the perfect weapon. My weapon.'

Horrified, Deina turned away, planning to run somewhere. Anywhere. But before she'd taken more than two steps her surroundings shifted again. The luxurious room melted like sun-struck snow, and she was in the Threshold again. Theron's lifeline was still looped around her wrist, and Tyche, a girl once more, was sitting on the boulder next to her. The goddess waited in silence as Deina fought to overcome the disgust that made her want to be sick, and the anguish that was choking her. Anguish for the child she had been. For what the gods had taken from her. For what they'd forced her to become.

'A weapon?' she said eventually. 'Is that what I am?'

'Yes,' Tyche replied. 'But it is not *all* you are.'

'And what of my memories of my father?' Deina heard her voice trembling. 'All lies? If Hades raised me in the Underworld then –'

'She did not. I persuaded her that keeping you there would risk your existence being discovered by the other gods. She agreed to allow you to grow up among mortals, your own father included, as long as she was able to claim you as a Soul Severer, the better to protect and nurture your emerging power.' The goddess picked at a patch of lichen growing on the boulder. 'Hades' plans are deep and well laid.' Tyche glanced sideways at Deina. 'However, Hades' plans are not as well laid as mine. Who do you think it was who nudged you into the path of someone dying of the plague – more than two years ago now, as you would count it. Who hid your sickness from Hades? Who made sure that Thanatos himself came to claim your life? Who prodded you enough so that your power – your nature – would be revealed to him?' Tyche shrugged happily. 'My plans always work out because I always have the best luck. In fact, it worked out even better than I had hoped. He fell in love with you.'

Deina drew back a little. For all her good humour, for all her seeming honesty, perhaps Tyche was really no different to the other gods. Treating mortals, and even the god of death, as mere playthings.

'I don't understand why you cared what Hades was doing. Are you that devoted to Zeus?'

'Oh, no. I despise Zeus as much as you could wish. But at least he leaves mortals to their own devices, for the most part. Hades, if she had her way, would strip you of all choice, all freedom. She would see every one of you marked with her sigil, forced into silent acquiescence.' Tyche patted Deina's hand. 'Whereas I prefer mortals as they are now. Surprising. Unpredictable. And often, despite our best efforts, uncontrollable. I love how they constantly throw the plans of my sisters, the Fates, into disarray.' She gave Deina a brilliant smile. 'It's fun. So, once I heard Hades' request to Hephaestus, I knew I had to act. She would have cajoled or driven him into assisting her eventually, so I suggested using a mortal child. A mortal child that could then be raised among mortals. I knew that Hades would find such a child far more difficult to control than she anticipated. That her perfect weapon might turn out to be someone with a mind of her own.' The goddess giggled. 'I wish I had been there to see the moment she realised that you had come to the Underworld unbidden, before she was ready to summon you.'

'She didn't seem surprised to see us,' Deina replied.

'Believe me,' Tyche said with a sly grin, 'she was surprised.'

A small red butterfly fluttered past, resting briefly on one of the tiny flowers that studded the grass. Strange – Deina had never seen a living creature recreated in the Threshold before. It reminded her of the pendant Theron had made for her, the one she'd lost to Aristaeus. A copper butterfly, symbol of the soul. Between the ichor that Tyche had forced into her as a child, and the nectar that Cronos had given her to drink, did she even have such a thing any more?

'You put the ichor inside of me. Can you take it out?'

The goddess sighed.

'I told you: I cannot alter what has already passed. Hades and Zeus and Poseidon are part of you, for better or worse, and so is your father. It is the mingling of the divine and mortal that makes you what you are. It is what makes you . . . unique.'

'Unique?' Deina sunk her head into her heads. 'A creature that fits in nowhere. A monster.'

'The choices you have made are no more monstrous than those made by others, both gods and mortals. You have strength and power from the gods, but what you have from your weak, mortal father may be even more important. Compassion. Mercy. Love. Those are qualities that the gods lack. But despite the ichor now flowing in your veins, you still have each in abundance. And that, Deina, gives you a power that the other gods could never have nor understand.'

How could Tyche speak of mercy? Deina turned away. She hadn't shown much mercy to that Battle Wager she killed. Or to the Theodesmioi she'd been prepared to sacrifice. She felt the goddess's hand on her shoulder.

'Two natures war within you. You must control both. Reconcile both. Or eventually their conflict will destroy you.'

Hadn't Nat said something similar to her once?

'How?'

'Fulfil your destiny,' Tyche replied. 'Do what you were born to do.'

Destroy the gods? Deina knew the old stories. The child deposes the parent and becomes ruler in his place. Cronos and Zeus had both done it. Was that the only path open to her: to destroy Zeus and Poseidon and Hades, the three most powerful Olympians, and take their place as ruler of all three realms, as queen of the gods?

'You have the power already within you. Hades and I made sure of that,' Tyche continued. 'You just need to learn how to channel it.' She reached across to touch the torc, still warm about Deina's neck. 'The torc will help, I think. Though I have to admit, I wasn't expecting it to play out in the way it has.'

'What do you mean?'

'I used the same method to help Hephaestus create the torc as I used to help Hades create you, though I did not tell *her* that. I stole ichor from her, and both her brothers, and Hephaestus bound it into his spell-cast metal using the sigils he carved into it.' Tyche leaned closer, peering at the torc. 'Such fine work. That is how you – and the king he loved – were able to control the Theodesmioi.' She caught her bottom lip in her teeth, looking a little embarrassed. 'However, using the same method for both you and the torc has, I suspect, created a link between you and it.'

Deina placed a hand over the torc, feeling its vibrations. They calmed her, somehow.

'It talks to me, I think. Whispers to me.' She let her hand drop. 'It spoke of power.'

'Ah. Well, it wants to be used.'

The torc wanted her to control the Theodesmioi. To use them by compelling them to carry out her wishes.

No.

She'd tried that, and it had led to disaster. But perhaps . . . perhaps there was another way.

'I think I need to talk to Hephaestus. Can I do that?'

'This is your space,' Tyche said, gesturing to the Threshold. 'What do you think?'

This time, Deina hadn't needed to use a rite of any sort to bend the Threshold to her will. She simply thought about Hephaestus's forge, the way she'd seen it in the memory Tyche had shown her, and ordered the Threshold to produce a doorway. When she stepped through, Theron's lifeline still glowing around her wrist, she and Tyche found the god leaning on his crutch, hammering something on his anvil – a sword blade, Deina thought. He paused in his work, held up the blade to squint along its length, put it down and nodded to Tyche.

'You're welcome as always, goddess of fortune; may your

blessings be upon me. To what do I owe this pleasure?' Without waiting for an answer, Hephaestus picked up the sword and moved to a workbench, shifting as he did so from male to female, just as Deina had seen Hades do. The god sat down on a stool, laying aside the crutch and picking a small wooden-handled tool and drawing a pile of gemstones nearer. Glancing up, Hephaestus seemed to notice Deina for the first time. She smiled. 'Both forms have their advantages and disadvantages. You are welcome also, Khthonia.'

'I prefer Deina.'

'As you wish.'

'Though I'd like to know how you know my name.'

'The peaks of Olympus echo with reports of your misdeeds. Freeing Cronos. Threatening Zeus. Stealing the fragments of my torc.' Hephaestus grinned. 'Watching it unfold has been the most fun I've had since the sack of Troy.' She sniffed. 'I was the one who gave Odysseus the idea for the giant wooden horse, whatever Athena claims.'

'Will you help me, then?' Deina asked. 'I know the torc can control the Theodesmioi and the Iron Guards and things made out of spell-cast metal, but what if I want to use it differently? I'd like to use it *with* the Theodesmioi. Against the gods.'

The god shifted back to male form, took up his crutch and came closer, studying Deina and the torc.

'I remember making it. I remember destroying it too.' He smiled at Tyche. 'You did a good job hiding the fragments, old friend.'

'It was amusing. All three of them tried to persuade me to reveal the hiding places. I pretended I couldn't remember. "Oh,

Zeus, you silly!"' Her voice, sounding for a moment like that of a grown woman, swooped and soared. '"I probably hid it in the treasury, or somewhere like that! I can hardly remember! You know what a scatterbrain I am!"'

Hephaestus roared with laughter.

'Oh, I'd have like to have seen that.' The god dabbed at his eyes. 'To return to your question, though, Deina – the answer is that I believe the torc could be used differently.' He folded his arms and rested his chin in one hand. 'There was a song, a long time ago. Something the Spell Casters made up . . .'

Deina tried to recall the phrase that Thalius had used.

'Slaughter to seal. Slaughter to seal, sacrifice to secure.'

'Yes, exactly.' Hephaestus nodded. 'Now, it looks as if you did the sealing. That part is easy enough. Gods have no hesitation in taking a life, and too many mortals are the same. That will have unlocked the ability of the torc to control spell-cast metal. But the greater power that I tried to bind into it with the interlinked sigils –' the god used his little finger to point – 'that would require a sacrifice. That's harder. The king I intended the torc for, he had no conception of sacrifice. I was besotted with him. Yet beneath his beauty was nothing. He was shallow, cruel, careless.'

'He was not worth your time,' Tyche added.

'I don't understand.' Deina looked from one god to the other. 'Isn't a sacrifice just more slaughter?'

'Not in this case. To make the torc respond fully to your will, you must give up something you love. That sort of sacrifice.' Hephaestus looked down at his strong hands. 'I built it into the torc as a test for the one I loved. A test he was not capable of understanding, let alone passing.'

'You, however,' Tyche murmured, 'you could make such a sacrifice.'

Deina looked down to where Theron's lifeline was still wrapped around her wrist.

'You know what you need do,' Tyche said gently. 'You need to let him go.'

Deina shook her head. A lump formed in her throat.

'No. He's still alive. As long as I keep him in the Threshold, he's still alive.'

'Yes, he is alive, but is he living?' Tyche reached for Deina. 'If you could ask him, what would Theron say?'

Deina stepped back.

'Better alive in the Threshold, whatever that's like, than roaming the Underworld as a blood hunter. That is what I condemn him to if I cut the lifeline.' She turned to Hephaestus, pleading. 'There has to be another way. Something else I could offer.'

'Your sacrifice of Theron was inevitable from the moment you put the torc around your neck,' Tyche insisted. 'You've already killed him. You just have to let him die.'

Deina glanced back through the doorway to where Theron lay, pale and still on the grass of the Threshold. They had grown up together, and she had so many memories of him. Some bad: how he'd attacked her, the last time they fought together as children, or the violence in his voice when he cornered her the day of the Punishment Rite. More good: the way he'd sung to save her from Cerberus. How he'd tried to pull her back when Thanatos dragged her to the Underworld. His irresistible lopsided smile.

Even if she stayed here in the Threshold forever, guarding Theron's lifeline, he would never smile at her again. Never hold her hand, and never sing for her. He'd never do or feel anything again. Not joy, nor happiness nor sadness. Not even love.

She couldn't undo what she had done to him, and she couldn't save him. But she could at least make sure that he hadn't died for nothing. She could free the Theodesmioi, break the hold that the gods had over them, once and for all. Just as Theron had wanted.

She swung back to Hephaestus.

'If I do this, how will it work? How will I use the torc and not harm the Theodesmioi?'

'The Theodesmioi act as a channel for the power of the god they serve, drawing a fraction of that god's power. They were created to act as a living symbol, to encourage the belief that feeds our strength. Yet their existence also makes us vulnerable. If all my Spell Casters were suddenly destroyed, it would drain enough of my power to weaken me. I realised this long ago. As far as I'm aware, Zeus, Poseidon and Hades still haven't worked it out.'

Deina thought about the way Zeus and Poseidon had vanished, after she'd taken control of the rest of the Theodesmioi. Perhaps they were starting to realise the risk. In destroying the Theodesmioi who defied them, they might destroy themselves.

'Now, I think you could use the torc like a lodestone,' Hephaestus continued. He picked up a hammer and started tossing it casually in the air, watching its arc until the handle slapped back into his palm, throwing it up again. 'I think – I think you could draw the power wielded by Zeus, Poseidon and Hades, the power of their realms, through the Theodesmioi to yourself. Drain the gods' power without harming the Theodesmioi.' He grinned. 'Zeus and the others will not even realise it is happening. Not at least, until it is too late.'

She was a Soul Severer. She knew how to wield the power of the Underworld, at least. Hints of a plan began to emerge from the bleak sorrow that was blanketing Deina's mind. She would need Nat, though.

'And when each of the brothers' power is exhausted –' Hephaestus smacked the hammer down onto the anvil – 'you will drain them of their very life force. And when they are no more, their power will become yours and you will rule over their realms.'

'I'm always rooting for those who try to fight their fate,' Tyche added. 'However, this does feel almost . . . inevitable.'

Deina didn't answer. Nothing in her life had prepared her for what seemed to lie ahead of her. A world where the three most powerful gods were gone, where she had taken their place – she couldn't begin to imagine what such a world might really look like. Dendris's words to Theron came back to her: *You would be the kind of king the people deserve.* Could she also be the kind of god people deserved? There was no way of telling. Yet what other choice did she have now?

Hephaestus limped back to his worktable, transforming into his female form again.

'When Zeus is no more, Deina, remember the help I've given you. A new forge on Olympus would be welcome.' As the god took up her tools and bent over the hilt of the sword, Deina led Tyche back into the Threshold. The doorway vanished behind them.

'Are you ready to cut his lifeline?' Tyche asked.

'No. I'll never be ready, but I – I'm going to do it anyway.'

And then back to Mycenae. To see if she could put things right.

'Two more things, before I leave you,' Tyche said. 'Your father. Hades believes he is dead; he is not. He had a lucky escape from the fire that ravaged the shipyard –' Tyche winked – 'and lives still. As for your mother, the spells and tricks the old gods have been using to keep her in the Underworld won't last much longer. She's too powerful. She'll come for you, Deina. Soon.'

For the first time in what felt like forever, Deina smiled.

'I hope so. In fact, I'm counting on it.'

22

Had Tyche been telling the truth about her father? The news didn't really make her feel anything. Her father belonged to her past, and at the moment, the possibility that she might have any sort of future seemed remote. All that mattered, all that existed, was here and now: her friends in Mycenae, the torc around her neck and Theron.

Alone again, she knelt by his body and took his cold hands in hers. She still hadn't been able to weep for him. There were no oils and herbs here to properly prepare his body, no shroud to conceal the extent of his injuries, no coins to place over his eyes. Those things could wait; there would be time later, she hoped. All she could do now was sing for him. A threnody. A song of lamentation. She would sing the time-worn phrases and mourn for his life cut short. For all they had both lost.

Deina cleared her throat. She could sing well enough to carry out the rites, but she knew her voice had no beauty. A mercy, perhaps, that Theron probably couldn't hear it.

'*Here we linger, the left behind,*

Grieving one who goes before
Honouring his passing as
We weep, still trapped on mortal shore . . .'

The old melody wound through the still air of the Threshold. Deina sang unhurriedly. She reached the end, and the final note died away. It was time.

She kissed Theron gently. Stood, took his lifeline in her hands, and tore it in two. Theron's ghost rose from his body, almost solid in the in-between space of the Threshold. He turned slowly, looking around. His gaze fell on his ruined corpse and he lifted his eyes to hers. The grief and shock Deina saw there struck her like a knife to the heart. She reached out for him.

'I'm so sorry – I never meant to hurt you. I love you.'

'Deina . . .'

Their fingertips brushed against each other. Deina grasped Theron's hand as a fierce wind sprang up.

'I wish we'd had more time. I wish –' The gale ripped Deina's words from her lips: the Threshold was breaking apart. Theron's hand slipped from hers. Deina stooped and gathered his body into her arms as the mortal realm began to reclaim her. Theron cried out to her, but she couldn't hear him over the roaring of the storm, and they were already too far distant for her to be able to guess what he'd said.

'Theron!'

Too late. And yet, what more did she deserve? It was right that she didn't get to say goodbye, that she didn't get to soothe her guilt by asking for his forgiveness. She'd killed him. Whatever pain she suffered from here on, she'd earned every drop of it.

As if in response to her thoughts, searing agony flared across her forehead and around her neck as the fragments of the Threshold tumbled away, becoming mere spots of light amidst an enveloping darkness. Deina gripped the torc with one hand and gasped at what she felt. It was as if the spell-cast metal had sprouted roots – roots that had burrowed into her skin, binding the torc firmly into her flesh. She tugged against the metal. The action sent a wave of pain deep into her neck.

Sacrifice to secure.

She'd made her sacrifice. Now the torc was secured. For better or worse, she and it were woven together forever.

The darkness itself shattered, light flooded into the fissures and the courtyard and the megaron of Mycenae sprang into existence around her. She was on the top step of the flight of stairs that led from the courtyard to the portico of the megaron. Theron's body was still in her arms. She laid it gently on the marble flagstones and held her hands out towards the Theodesmioi and Iron Guards she'd forced into a fighting stance.

'Be free. Do as you wish.'

Though the god-possessed Theodesmioi were as immobile as ever, Deina was relieved to see the others reanimate. They began to mill around, confused, as Nat, Aster and Dendris raced up the steps towards her.

'Deina!' Nat cried. 'You came back? I thought you'd gone forever.' He frowned. 'What happened to you in the Threshold?'

'How long was I gone?' Deina asked.

'Only a few moments.' Aster glanced at Dendris. 'We were about to leave.' He looked back across the courtyard. 'You set them free.'

'I should never have taken their liberty in the first place.' Theron's mangled body lay at her feet like an accusation. 'I'm sorry,' Deina blurted out. 'I'm sorry for everything: for what I said, and for what I did.' Aster started to speak, so she ploughed on. 'I'm not asking you to forgive me. I can't forgive myself. If you can bear to, though, I'd like you to stay with me. If we can see this through together, I won't ask anything more of you.' She looked at Nat. 'Of any of you. I swear. I swear by the Styx.'

She'd done it: acknowledged that she was a god. For what felt like ages, no one replied.

'Stay with you where?' Aster asked eventually. 'What is it you think we can do?' He didn't sound persuaded by her words, and Dendris was still staring silently at Theron's body. Deina wondered whether it too late for her to regain their friendship.

'What felt like a few moments to you felt very different to me. I learned a lot in the Threshold – about the torc, and about myself. I understand, finally, what I was meant to be. But I also know that I can choose to be something else. Something better.' Deina hesitated over her words. She knew she would only have one attempt at convincing them. 'I also learned that there is a way to defeat the gods that doesn't involve compelling the Theodesmioi to act against their will, or forcing them to fight. I could do it alone, but I don't want to.' She clasped her hands together. 'We started this as a team. Despite what I've done, I'd like us to end as one. Please.'

'Well? What is this new plan?' Dendris said. Her voice was still cold.

'All Theodesmioi draw on the power of the god whose sigil they bear. The torc, now its power has been fully unlocked, should allow me to draw all that power to myself. The more I draw, the more the Theodesmioi will draw, fatally weakening the gods.'

'Won't they stop you? Won't they just destroy the Theodesmioi?' Aster sounded doubtful.

Deina told them about the weakness built into the gods' creation of the Theodesmioi, adding that Hephaestus himself had pointed it out to her.

'The gods will be hesitant to risk losing large numbers of Theodesmioi. And I'm going to tell Zeus and Poseidon exactly what Hades has been planning. If I can take her out first, and weaken the other two, they might be willing to meet our demands. Of course –' Deina looked out across the courtyard at all the Theodesmioi still assembled – 'I'll have to convince them first. I understand that now. I can't seek permission of all the Theodesmioi throughout the Dominion, but if those who are here today agree, as representatives of their Orders, that I might draw the gods' power through them . . . do you think that would be alright?'

'Maybe, in the circumstances,' Aster said. 'If we do this, we'll be facing a fight for more than our lives. The blood hunters – that has to end too.' He raised an eyebrow at Dendris.

'I agree.'

'You'll stay then?' Deina said eagerly. 'We'll do this together?'

Aster and Dendris looked at each other. Both nodded.

'Together,' Aster sighed. 'It's what Theron would have wanted.'

'It is,' Dendris agreed. She glanced at Deina sharply, though there was some sympathy in her eyes too. 'I hope this is going to work.'

'So do I,' Deina replied. Success might be the only way to guarantee that they truly forgave her.

Nat slipped his hand into hers.

'I'll stay around too. I don't have anywhere else to be.' His gaze shifted to her forehead. 'That's new.'

Deina prodded the spot where her sigil was. The skin was still throbbing slightly from the pain that she'd experienced leaving the Threshold. The sigil itself was different. She traced her fingertips over it and tried to make sense of the outline.

'What is it?'

'It is the same mark imprinted into the three strands of the torc,' Nat told her. 'The sigils of the Orders of Zeus, Poseidon and Hades combined, with the sigil of Hephaestus above.'

Aster and Dendris came closer too.

'That looks painful.' Dendris peered at the way filaments from the torc had tunnelled into and beneath Deina's skin. She gave a slight smile. 'No more than you deserve, probably.'

'Probably,' Deina acknowledged. 'It doesn't hurt so much now, though. As long as I don't try to take it off.' She pressed one hand to the torc. Beneath her touch, the metal sang. Three strands of music, all different but all intricately and seamlessly interwoven, spilled into her mind and spread through her veins. Despite her sorrow, her body hummed with power. She felt stronger than she had ever felt before. 'Will you help me explain to the other Theodesmioi?'

'We will.' Dendris replied. 'And then what?'

'And then, we get the gods' attention. It's our turn to play. Let's not wait around for them to make the next move.'

Persuading the free Theodesmioi to agree to her plan was just as hard as Deina had expected. Between their fear of the gods, and their fear and distrust of her, many simply demanded to be allowed to leave. The Soul Severers in particular, so far spared possession by their god due to Hades' absence, were anxious to escape the palace complex. Dendris was a member of their House, but all the arguments she advanced were ignored. Confronted with Deina's mismatched eyes, their leader made the sign to turn away the evil eye. She didn't even trouble to conceal the gesture.

'If you were really a god, you'd simply force us all to stay,' the woman said, having previously complained about Deina using her power to do just that. 'Since you won't, I doubt you'll be strong enough to resist mighty Zeus –' she glanced anxiously at the sky – 'when he does return. I am an elder.' Her gaze raked Deina, Dendris and Aster. 'You are only adepts. I insist you open the gates now. And Dendris, I order you to come with me.'

'No,' Dendris replied. She hefted her axe over her shoulder and stared at the leader until the woman exclaimed and turned away.

'Be warned: if you survive this, there is no place for you in Mycenae. If we find you within our territory, you'll pay for it. Open the gates!'

Frustrated, Deina gave the order to the Iron Guard. There was nothing she could do. She wouldn't compel them. But if the other Theodesmioi followed the Soul Severer, if they all refused their help, her plan would fail.

'Don't worry about her,' Aster murmured. 'She reminds me

of Mistress Kalistra back at the House. As sour as bad wine and just as unwelcome. I'm sure most of the others will stay.'

The Soul Severers began marching toward the gate as it swung open, but a host of people coming the other way forced them to stop. Thalius, the leader of the Spell Casters, determined despite his injury to follow the one who had freed them from Aristaeus, cried out with joy.

'My Spell Casters – I thought Aristaeus's men must have slain them all!'

Deina was flooded with relief. As the Spell Casters approached, she saw that all of them were armed. All of them, even the youngest, wore a look of determination. One of those leading the host saluted Thalius.

'Those guarding us deserted, Thalius. They heard the rumour of Aristaeus's defeat and the arrival of the gods and fled. People are abandoning the city, but we want to fight.'

Deina noticed that many of the Soul Severers, despite the urging of their leader, had paused to see what was happening. She quickly explained her plan to the Spell Casters.

'Will drawing the gods' power through us not result in our deaths?' one of the Spell Casters asked. 'And what about them?' He pointed to those Theodesmioi who had been freed from their torcs and were still under the control of Zeus and Poseidon.

'I don't believe the gods are willing to sacrifice so many. Doing so will weaken them. They'll try to destroy me first, and I hope that you – that all of you – will be safe.'

'But you're not certain.'

'No. I am, however, certain of this.' Deina let her gaze sweep

the courtyard, trying to reach everyone who was watching her. 'If we do nothing, we condemn more children to the life we wish to escape. Worse, we condemn them and ourselves to the awful eternity that awaits us as blood hunters – pathetic, miserable creatures, neither fully alive nor fully dead. I do not choose that future, for us or for them.' She held herself up as straight as she could and raised her voice. 'I choose either death or freedom.'

'Death or freedom!' repeated Thalius. The cry was taken up by his Spell Casters and spread through the courtyard on the lips of the Theodesmioi of the other Orders.

Aster leaned forward to whisper in Deina's ear.

'Their fear at last turns to anger. Seize the moment and you will carry them with you.'

Deina nodded.

'I don't know exactly how this is going to work, but I hope that by the end of this day none of us will be marked by the gods. No more torcs. No more Theodesmioi.'

Her words passed from person to person; Deina could hear the hope rising within the courtyard. She glanced at Aster and smiled.

'We should act quickly, before their ardour cools,' Nat suggested.

'Agreed. Dendris, this statue of Zeus –' Deina pointed to an enormous representation of the god carved from marble and brightly painted, just beyond the portico of the megaron – 'do you think getting rid of it might send the message we want?'

Dendris grinned.

'I think it might.' She paused, surveying the statue and its

surroundings. There were two venerable oak trees planted either side of it. 'I think those oak trees could do with a bit more space to breathe.' She ran down the steps and stopped a few strides in front of the statue and held her arms out to the trees. As always, Deina only recognised a very few of the words Dendris used. On she sang, as the other Theodesmioi, realising something was imminent, tried to prepare themselves. She sang until the ground around the trees erupted in a shower of dirt and roots and branches reached for the statue. They swarmed over it, tightening until the stone cracked and broke. Zeus toppled from his pedestal. A ragged cheer went up from the watching Theodesmioi.

Aster tapped her on the shoulder.

'Here. A peace offering.' He held out a large round shield of shining bronze. 'I went back to that room with all the stuff made by Hephaestus. This is the shield of Achilles, if Aristaeus is to be believed.' He shrugged one shoulder and gave her a quick smile. 'I thought you might find it useful.'

Deina gazed in admiration at the finely wrought scenes covering the shield's surface.

'It's beautiful. Thank you, Aster.'

'Smashing up a statue of Zeus – I think that worked,' Nat said, his voice strained. 'You've got their attention.'

Deina closed her eyes and reached out with her other senses. Nat was right: beneath the mortal sounds of the courtyard an awful, brooding silence had bloomed, heavy with the promise of suffering. The air tasted of blood. It made the skin on her scalp crawl. When she opened her eyes again, Nat was watching her. He looked worried.

She reached up to kiss his cheek.

'Let them come. I'm ready.'

The gods arrived not singly but together, stepping into the mortal realm and onto the dusty paving stones of the courtyard, larger than life, facing down those Theodesmioi who were gathered opposite them. Not just Zeus and Poseidon this time, but others. Athena, armed for war, stood next to Zeus. Apollo was at Poseidon's side, his golden bow gleaming. Hera and Demeter and Ares. More than Deina had hoped, but fewer than she'd feared. Perhaps some Olympians were awaiting the outcome of this confrontation. There was no sign of Hephaestus. Hades, though, in his male form this time, was between his brothers. The god's gaze caught the torc around Deina's neck, and Deina saw his eyes widen with greed.

Zeus held out his palm and a shaft of lightning coruscated into the air.

'I will give you one last chance, mortals, since you are marked with our sigils. If you beg forgiveness, and if you willingly destroy the one who is leading you, then I may consider being merciful, despite the urging of my brothers.' The smile disappeared. 'As for you, Thanatos,' Zeus snapped, scowling, 'we will deal with you later.' He sent the lightning flaring across the sky. A crash of thunder followed, so loud that Deina and every other Theodesmioi ducked and covered their ears. 'Do as you are bid, mortals. Otherwise, I myself will strike down the one who protects you. Once the torc is mine, we will possess all of you, and with your own hands you will be compelled to pluck out your eyes and cut out your tongues and slice your frail human bodies open to spill your guts into the dirt.'

No one replied, though Deina could see some of the younger Theodesmioi trembling, and caught more than one anxious glance.

'I told you so, brother,' Hades said. 'They are weak minded, and my daughter has persuaded them not to give her up. We should destroy them all now.' Poseidon was nodding vigorously. Hades raised his bident and stepped forward, but Zeus put a restraining hand on his arm. Zeus's gaze kept flicking back to the torc encircling Deina's neck. Deina saw for the first time something else beneath the bravado – uncertainty.

Not an emotion, she suspected, with which many of the gods were familiar.

'What say you, Hades' daughter?' Zeus raised an eyebrow. 'Are you willing to let others of your kind suffer on your account?'

Deina stepped forward.

'Perhaps I am. After all, my mother is willing to let others of her kind suffer. Or did she not tell you of the suffering she planned to inflict upon you? And upon Poseidon too.'

Hades bellowed in rage and drew back his arm to hurl the bident into Deina's chest.

'Wait!'

The god of the Underworld seemed unable to disobey Zeus's order. He growled with frustration. 'But, brother –'

'I wish to hear what she has to say before we destroy her.'

'She will tell you nothing but lies!'

'Even so.' Zeus's voice was cold. 'Tell me, Soul Severer – what plan are you talking of?'

'The plan to create me, and to use me as a weapon against you. The plan to take your place as ruler of the gods.'

A murmur arose from among the gathered gods. Poseidon edged a little away from Hades.

Hades scoffed.

'I lay with a desirable mortal and she was the unfortunate result. Which of us has not given into the temptation to seize and enjoy that brief flowering of human beauty?'

Hera crossed her arms and glared, but Hades ignored her.

'I should have drowned the brat at birth. This is the result of too much mercy – let me dispose of her now!'

'Not yet,' Zeus replied. 'It may amuse us to hear more of her claims.' He bared his teeth at his brother in a parody of a smile. 'Speak, niece.'

Deina cleared her throat.

'My birth was no accident. Hades wished Hephaestus to create a second Pandora, to unleash disaster upon the gods. When he declined, my mother lay with a mortal to obtain a child that might grow into the weapon she desired. She compelled Tyche to assist her and filled my veins with your ichor. Yours too, Poseidon.'

The god of the sea looked outraged.

'I did not consent to such a thing!'

Deina couldn't help herself.

'Did Medea consent? Gods take what they want. They don't ask. Isn't that how it works?'

As Poseidon spluttered, Deina crashed her sword and shield together.

'Enough words, Mother. Prove I'm lying. Defeat me in single combat.'

Hades struck the floor with the end of his bident.

'I've had enough of these lies. Brothers, sisters – we must act now to silence this whelp.'

Silence, for a heartbeat.

'Very well,' Zeus replied.

Hades shot Deina a look of triumph. Deina braced herself to meet an attack, reaching out with the power of the torc, feeling her connection with the other Theodesmioi scattered across the Dominion and beyond, ready to gather their power.

Yet, although the gods readied their weapons, no lightning bolt appeared in Zeus's hand. 'Brother?' Hades questioned.

'You may destroy her if you wish.' Zeus shrugged. 'Destroy all of them. If you can. It will be a trial by combat. If she lies, if she is merely a demi-god, she will not be able to defend herself.'

'But – but she has the torc –'

Another shrug.

'So, she has the torc. It will not help her if she has not the power to truly wield it.'

He clicked his fingers. A huge golden throne appeared, piled with cushions and studded with gemstones that glittered despite the overcast sky above. Zeus sat down and made himself comfortable. The other gods hurried to group themselves behind the throne.

Hades was left standing alone. He glared coldly at his siblings, shifting back into the female form that Deina had first encountered.

'Very well.' Hades was wearing her favourite blue, but this tunic was short, ending just above the knee, and her jewels had gone, replaced by a bronze breastplate and helmet.

Next to Deina, Aster moaned softly.

'I can feel her. She's trying to get inside my mind, to control me –' Aster was gritting his teeth, the tendons in his neck and arms standing out as he tried to resist the god. Other Soul Severers were clutching their heads with their hands. Two, who had already been freed from their torcs and lacked the protection of the spell-cast metal, that extra link with the torc forged by Hephaestus, had turned to face Deina. Their faces were blank as they drew their swords.

Deina clenched her fists.

Stay calm. She's sending more of her power into them. That means there's more for you to draw out.

The torc was warm and heavy around her neck. She could feel the slivers of metal piercing her skin. For an instant, Deina was afraid. Afraid of the power she was about to claim, afraid of what the torc might do to her. Afraid that this thing Hephaestus had created had some will and desire of its own. She pushed her feelings away. No time for doubt, not when several of the Soul Severers had raised their weapons and were walking jerkily towards her. She could feel the energy building within the torc. All she needed to do now was open herself to it. To stop resisting.

The combined power of all the Theodesmioi swept through her on a wave of intense pain that faded almost as soon as it had begun. The Soul Severers who had been controlled by Hades stopped and dropped their weapons as Deina, gripping tightly the sword and shield of Achilles, screamed out her defiance and raced towards her mother.

23

From nowhere a blade appeared in Hades' free hand. She lunged at Deina, blocking Deina's own blow with the bident. Deina used the shield to protect herself and thrust upwards, only for Hades to dance out of the way. Back and forth they went: parry, thrust, lunge. Hades was able to use the length of the bident to keep Deina too distant to land any blows. Still, Deina felt Hades' own strength flowing into her, mingling with the power she was drawing from the Theodesmioi of Zeus and Poseidon. If she concentrated, she could taste the difference: Hades' power was bitter, carrying the tang of smoke and damp earth. Deina stared down at the sword in her hand, focusing on the unique quality of Hades' power, holding it tightly inside her. The hilt twisted. The blade elongated and divided into a bident, mirroring Hades' own weapon. The shift shocked the god. Deina took advantage of the moment of hesitation. She darted forward and plunged the bident's sharp prongs into her mother's calf.

The god screamed and stumbled and shifted shape,

transforming in to a huge, rearing serpent that hissed and struck at Deina with venomous fangs. Deina dropped to one knee and brought the shield up above her head. Just in time – the fangs scraped across the spell-cast bronze. Holes began to appear in the shield as the venom ate into the metal. Deina hurled the shield away from her. Risking everything on one last throw, she drew back her arm and propelled her bident with all her strength into the serpent's body. It stuck fast. The serpent thrashed and squealed and reared up to strike again, but even as it bore down upon Deina the god's shape shifted from snake to woman to snake to man to snake – until Hades, back in her female form and bleeding golden ichor from her leg and abdomen, still pierced by Deina's bident, fell flat on her back on the paving stones of the courtyard. The god lifted her head long enough to drag off her helmet then fell back again.

'You've weakened me, but you can't kill me. I'm a god.' Hades tugged fruitlessly at the bident, groaning with the pain of it. 'What now, Khthonia? Are you going to follow his example?' She glanced at Zeus. 'Or will you choose Cronos's path, and cut pieces from your parent's body to prove you own strength?'

'You think I can't kill you?' Deina replied. 'Are you sure? I think I can kill you. I think I can drain you of power until you are nothing more than a husk, a whisper on the wind. Is that enough of a death for you?'

Hades writhed in pain, and as she did so, something slipped from beneath her armour. A silver chain with a large, teardrop-shaped pendant hanging from it. Deina recognised the pendant as the thing Daedalus had held up for inspection as they'd passed him in the Underworld. It glittered strangely, as if its surface was boiling. Deina lunged forward and ripped the chain from Hades' neck. Up close, she could see the pendant was filled with infinitesimally small silver lines. Just like the silvery lines that had once wound about Nat's arms. Even as Hades struggled to reclaim the pendant, Deina dropped it to the floor and smashed it beneath her heel.

A black fume lit with flashes of silver poured from the remains of the pendant and gathered about Nat, obscuring him completely. When the mist dissolved, he was Thanatos again. The god of death was as beautiful as when Deina had first seen him. The symbols that spiralled across his bare arms glowed silver against his pale skin. The whites of his eyes had disappeared, and he gazed haughtily at the Olympians with orbs of blue fire. And his wings . . . They swept the sky, and seemed to Deina to be formed of the same impenetrable velvet darkness as the wall of night that bordered Hades' court: razor-edged black feathers that might cut the stars loose from their moorings. Thanatos drew the sword that hung at his waist: a blade forged not of iron but of elongated tongues of twisting flame all the more terrifying for their silence.

His wings shrunk to dark shadows at his shoulders, his eyes returned to normal, and he laughed, spinning round and grinning at Deina, Aster and Dendris.

'I'm back! Ah, there's nothing like being mortal to make you appreciate being a god. Everyone should try it.' His smile faded. He struck the sky with his flaming sword and there was a sigh like the crashing of a mighty wave. The dark clouds above the courtyard lightened a little. Nat came to stand behind Deina. He glanced at Hades dismissively and gave his attention to Zeus.

'I have fixed the problem that Hades created. The souls of the dead have passed into the Underworld.'

'Get your sword ready, Nat.' Deina summoned some more of Hades' power, making the god groan faintly. 'I'm guessing my uncle wishes me to complete my task.'

'No – you do not need to do anything further,' Zeus said hastily, rising from his throne. Perhaps he didn't like the idea of gods being as vulnerable as mortals. He nodded at Deina. 'You have proved yourself worthy of Olympus, Khthonia. Now, leave her, and take your mother's place as ruler of the Underworld. Hades may join the other traitors in Tartarus.'

Deina could hear the undertone of fear that Zeus was trying very hard to conceal. Were he and Poseidon feeling it yet – the subtle draining of their power as she slowly drew it through the Theodesmioi that bore their sigils and absorbed it? Poseidon's power was cold. It reminded her of sea breezes and saltwater. Zeus's power was like snow and honeysuckle and wet grass warmed by the sun. The king of the gods was smiling at her, or trying to, but Poseidon had grown pale beneath his golden tan.

'Well?' Zeus prompted, beckoning Deina to join him and the other gods. 'Come, Khthonia.'

Deina shook her head.

'That's not my name. And ruling the Underworld – that is not enough.'

Zeus's forced smile faded.

'You dare challenge me? Foolish girl. You have the torc, but there is only one of you. I have a host of gods at my back. If I give the word, you will be annihilated. You and this handful of mortals who stand with you.'

Deina felt for the trickle of power flowing into her from the Theodesmioi of Zeus, and tugged. Zeus flinched a little. The gods around him glanced at each other uneasily.

'There are many more who stand with me,' Deina observed, 'although you do not see them. You have the gods at your back, I have all the Theodesmioi of the Dominion and beyond. Will you listen to their demands?'

Zeus snorted.

'I will listen.' He turned to Hermes. 'Where is Hephaestus? There are god-marked mortals who bear his sigil. He should be here for this.'

The messenger god hesitated.

'Well . . . he said that –'

'Get him here, now!' Zeus thundered. Hermes vanished. Zeus turned back to Deina, trying to smooth his anger. 'I will listen. Then I will destroy you.'

Deina understood. Zeus was playing for time. He hoped to force or persuade Hephaestus to somehow rip the torc from Deina's throat.

'These are the demands of the Theodesmioi. That you remove your sigils from our foreheads. That no more Theodesmioi are created. That the Orders are disbanded and that all of you cease interfering in the lives of mortals.'

'You don't demand much, do you?' Zeus snarled. 'Out of the question. We are your gods. Your belief is our right. You will bow to us, or we will destroy you.' His expression became one of derision. 'Without you, the rest of this little rebellion will soon be on their knees begging for our forgiveness.'

Deina found the flow of Poseidon's power and imagined

herself breathing it in, absorbing through the Sea Singers faster and faster. The sea god cried out, stumbled and sagged into the arms of Apollo. The Sea Singers who had been paralysed by the god's power began to wake.

'We cannot wait for Hephaestus, Father!' Athena cried out. 'She stands there alone, unprotected. You must act.'

Deina reached for Zeus's power and drank it down. The ruler of the gods fell backwards onto his throne and sat there, clinging to the arm, shaking.

'Nat, can you fill this courtyard with shadows – make it so they can't see us?'

'Of course,' he said smugly. 'Easy. Now?'

Athena bellowed a war cry and lifted her spear.

Deina nodded.

'Now.'

Nat's wings flared back into solidity. He threw his arms wide and cast a veil of shadow across the courtyard, swathing the gods and stealing their vision. Deina beckoned Dendris and Aster towards Hades. She pulled the bident from the god's abdomen, ignoring her groans, and tossed it away. Sitting at her mother's head, Deina dipped her fingers in the ichor still dripping from the god's wounds. Smearing the ichor across the sigils on her forehead and those of Aster, Dendris and Hades, she began to sing the words to summon the Threshold. Aster and Dendris joined in. Before long, the song was taken up by all the other Soul Severers present in the courtyard. The bitter cold arose quickly, chilling the air and turning the persistent rain to sleet and then to snow. With the cold came a deepening darkness that swallowed the paving stones near Deina's feet and spread outwards. This was a Threshold unlike any Deina had ever summoned before. She took the hands of her friends.

'Are you both ready for this? I can go alone.'

'No.' Dendris tightened her grip on Deina's hand. 'I want to see it through.'

'So do I,' Aster added. 'We need to finish this together. For those we've lost, as well as for ourselves.'

Deina wasn't about to argue. She pressed her forehead to Hades'. The surrounding darkness reared up and crashed down upon them.

They were standing on black sand surrounded by the darkness of night, lit only faintly by distant stars. It was the same space she'd seen before entering Tartarus.

'So you've brought me here to kill me,' Hades wheezed. 'Coward. You should have destroyed me up there. Or do you fear that you lack the ability?'

Aster answered.

'Don't worry. We're not going to kill you.'

The scowl melted from Hades' face.

'What do you mean? What are you going to do?'

'We are Soul Severers of your Order. What do you think we're going to do?'

He sounded more confident than Deina felt. She reminded herself of what Tyche had reminded her: Severers had created the Threshold and could make of it what they wished.

'What now?' Dendris muttered. 'The Deathless Trees?'

That had worked for Orpheus, but Hades was no mere mortal.

'No. I think we need to sing something else into existence. A prison to hold a god.' Deina glanced around them. 'We need to bend this place into a sphere. Something that can't be linked to the rest of the spaces that make up the Threshold. Remember that Song for laying ghosts – the one that was used to confine a spirit if it was too troublesome? And the Song for sealing a house against ghosts?'

'And the Song for funerals, to stop the dead returning to the mortal world,' Aster added, getting the idea. 'I understand.'

'Any phrase that seems to fit, we'll weave it into a new song, and imagine the details.'

Dendris nodded.

'Those vines she used to confine us when we first met her – I'm going to add those in.'

They held hands again – it seemed appropriate – and began to sing. Deina started, Aster then Dendris followed; as each phrase ended, one of the others extended it. Gradually, the space around them began to warp. The sand dunes curved up to meet the inky sky as that curved down. Only a shrinking patch of paler space indicated the way back to the courtyard. Black vines snaked out of the sand, wrapping themselves around Hades' body before diving back into the sand once more, pinning the god to the ground.

'No,' she cried, 'don't leave me here. You can't leave me here – I'll give you anything, I'll do anything you want!'

Together, still singing, Aster, Dendris and Deina turned their back on the struggling form of Hades and walked towards the gateway.

'Please,' Hades begged. 'You can't leave me here forever. Promise you'll come back!'

Aster and Dendris stepped through the darkness. Deina followed them into the courtyard. Behind her was a dark globe, shrinking fast. The hole in its side was almost gone. Hades' voice was still just audible.

'Khthonia, please, I beg you!'

Deina sang the final phrase of the new Song she and Aster and Dendris had made together.

'Khthonia, no!'

The aperture closed, cutting short Hades' scream. The globe had shrunk to no bigger than an apple. Deina picked it up. It was heavy and its smooth surface was cold, black and studded with what looked like tiny flecks of crystal: the distant stars of another realm, held in the palm of Deina's hand.

'What's that?' Dendris prodded at a bracelet that had appeared around Deina's wrist. 'That wasn't there a moment ago.' She stepped back. 'And where did that come from?'

Deina glanced down. Her dirty, torn tunic had gone. Instead, she was wearing a dark green pleated tunic of some fine fabric, cut to the knee, and held in at the waist with a silver belt. A pair of knives in jewelled scabbards and a beautifully embroidered pouch hung from the belt.

'Deina has usurped her mother's power, so the Underworld has recognised her as its god,' Nat observed. He curved one wing protectively around Deina's shoulder. 'That –' he pointed at the bangle – 'is Hades' sceptre and bident. As for the outfit . . .' He threw his hands up. 'The Lampades, the nymphs who attend to the gods of the Underworld, are extremely good at their job. And very quick. What's next? I can't keep the Olympians blinded indefinitely.'

'You won't need to. There's one more thing we need to do. And now I've got my mother's power, I think I'll be able to do it.'

'What?' Dendris asked. 'Another Threshold? Are we going to trap the other gods too?'

'No. Not a Threshold. I want to open a gateway to the Underworld, right here. I want to show the gods exactly what happens to the Theodesmioi after they die.' Deina rested one hand on her torc, allowing its power to soothe her for a moment. 'We're going to show them the blood hunters.'

Deina thought for a moment, then took the bracelet from her wrist. Without any conscious order, it grew into a bident. She frowned at it. 'Not quite what I need.' Drawing on the power within her that she identified as belonging to Poseidon, she closed her eyes and imagined. Not a bident, but a trident, the central prong longer than the other two. When she looked down again, the weapon in her hand was exactly as she wished. Quickly, she drew the sigil of Hades in the dirt of the courtyard. With one of her new knives, she slashed her palm open. The wound healed almost instantly, but not before a few drops of golden ichor had fallen onto the sigil. Finally, Deina drove the trident down into the centre of it. The ground split open, just as the gateway at the Caves of Diros had opened when she – and Theron and Aster and Drex and Chryse – had first tried to enter the Underworld. Deina forced herself to let go of the memory and turned to Aster.

'I think we might need some regular mortal blood for the next bit.' She held out her knife.

He rolled his eyes, smiling, held out his hand over the Threshold and ran the blade along the back of his hand.

'I'm honoured to oblige. Just as long as you keep those things away from me.'

Blood began to flow, dripping from Aster's fingers into the darkness.

'Nat, can you get the blood hunters' attention? Put them on the trail of Aster's blood?'

Nat vanished, taking the mist with which he'd filled the courtyard with him. Zeus and Poseidon were still too weak, but the other Olympians, spotting Deina and the others, raised their weapons.

'Stop her,' Zeus wheezed. 'Get the –'

The unmistakable wail of the blood hunters, echoing from the portal, silenced him. Another moment, and Deina could see the green glow that lit their empty eye sockets. She reached out to them with her mind, trying to use the power of her blood, amplified by the torc, to touch the mortal part of them that yet remained and remembered, to make it strong enough to drown out the voracious clamour for fresh blood. Gradually, the screeching faltered. By the time the vast crowd of blood hunters emerged into the fading daylight of the courtyard, they were silent. Skeletal creatures they were, some with bones picked clean, some still draped in ribbons of rotting flesh. Many of the Theodesmioi nearest the portal drew back in horror from this vision of their future. Aster averted his face. Yet there was pity in his eyes too.

The blood hunters turned to face Deina, but she gestured them towards the Olympians.

'Here are those who made you what you are.' She drew again on the power of Zeus and Poseidon. Both gods moaned. Poseidon sank to the ground next to Zeus's throne. 'Surround them. Let them see what they did to you.' As the blood hunters swarmed towards the gods, who shrank from the mangled creatures, Deina and the other Theodesmioi followed them.

'Do you see the horror to which you condemn those who are supposed to be honoured to bear your sigils?'

None of the gods answered. None of them looked her in the eye.

'If you attack the blood hunters and destroy them, they will simply reform. You cannot win against them. All you can hope for is to be locked in an eternal cycle of battle. And I believe I'd have no difficulty in opening a gateway to the Underworld on Olympus itself.' Deina paused, waiting for her words to sink in. 'I'd also like to show you this.' She held up the dark, silver-flecked globe.

'Hades is trapped in here. I will do the same to you, Zeus, and to you, Poseidon, unless you agree to our demands. You will still be gods. You will be free to do as you wish, as long as you do not interfere in the mortal realm.'

'Without the Theodesmioi, belief in us fade. We will die a long, lingering death,' Zeus snarled before sinking back onto the throne.

'Yes, you'll die,' Deina agreed. 'Though you know that is inevitable eventually whatever happens.' She tossed the globe in the air and caught it. 'It's no more than mortals face every day. So, what is it to be?'

Nat clicked his fingers and a papyrus roll materialised in his hand.

'I've drawn up an agreement with all the clauses, just to save time.' He smiled cheerfully at Zeus. 'Swear by the Styx that you will abide by its contents, and we can all go home.'

Zeus looked coldly at Deina.

'I swear by the Styx that I and all the Olympian gods will abide by the content of that document. But only because you leave me no choice.'

'Think of it this way,' Deina replied. 'Perhaps this was meant to happen. Perhaps it's simply fate. As my mother once said, no one can fight that. Now, remove the sigils. The torcs, too.'

Zeus's eyelids fluttered.

'It is done.'

Deina checked her own forehead – the skin was smooth and unblemished. Dendris's and Aster's sigils were gone too. She turned to look at the other Theodesmioi. Not a torc, not a sigil remained. Then she saw something she'd hoped for but hadn't dared to expect. Freed from their sigils, the blood hunters were turning back into the ghosts of the people they had been in life. A breeze blew across the courtyard; the ghosts drifted into no more than eddies of cloud, and slowly faded from view.

'They're free,' Nat observed. 'I'm glad.'

'What about the Theodesmioi in other cities?'

'Hold on . . .' Nat vanished, then reappeared almost instantly. 'The same, everywhere. The sigils and the torcs are gone.'

'Not the rite marks though,' Aster added, inspecting his shoulder. 'I don't mind. They are part of who I was, though I'm relieved they won't be part of my future.'

Deina glanced at her own skin. Her rite marks had not

394

reappeared. Perhaps, for her, there really was no way back. Zeus and Poseidon were looking stronger; she realised she could no longer sense the power that had been flowing through the Theodesmioi – not surprising now the sigils were gone. Zeus got up, snapped his fingers and the throne disappeared.

'Farewell, Hades' daughter. We will abide by the oath we have sworn, and you must live with the consequences of your actions. You are god of the Underworld now. I expect you to take your responsibilities seriously.' He smiled maliciously. 'After a few hundred years you might cease to regret your life in the mortal realm. You may even grow used to the eternal darkness. I'm sad to report, though, that Thanatos does not improve with acquaintance.'

He turned to face the gathered Theodesmioi.

'Remember our deal with your forefathers, the bargain that created the first Theodesmioi. A tithe of children, god-marked, in return for our protection. That was what enabled your civilisation to survive the threats it faced. Now, you will have to do without our help. I hope you may not live to regret your choice.'

The gods disappeared, leaving the courtyard – and the world – to the mortals. They'd won. Elated, hardly daring to believe it, Deina turned to share her delight with Theron.

Except, of course, he wasn't there.

From where she was sitting on the bottom step of the portico, the celebrations seemed muted. Deina wasn't surprised. She had the sense that the Theodesmioi, overjoyed though they were to be free of their torcs and sigils and of the horrible destiny that had awaited them, were also at a loss. Their whole lives had been planned out for them for so long, controlled by rules drawn up in the distant past, that it was going to take them a while to decide what to do next. They were gathered in small groups around the courtyard, the different Orders mingling. Deina heard snatches of conversation. They spoke of homes they'd been taken from, only distantly remembered, or far distant lands they wished to explore or – especially the Sea Singers, she thought – of finding a small piece of land where they might settle in peace, far from Orders and elders and war.

Deina herself, with the torc weighing around her neck, and the Underworld waiting for her, and a ragged wound where Theron should have been, felt only the onset of the grief she'd been holding at bay.

'Deina?' Aster said hesitantly.

'Yes?'

'The day's wearing on. We were thinking we should do something about the bodies.' He jerked his head towards Dendris and Nat, sitting nearby. The god of death didn't seem to be in a rush to get back to the Underworld. He was probably, Deina realised, waiting for her. The thought of descending into the gloom made her shudder. Aster was frowning at her. 'Are you alright?'

'Yes. Sorry.' Deina sighed. 'The bodies.'

'Theron deserves a proper funeral. Archis too, I suppose, and that Battle Wager who was forced to attack you. Dendris suggested we should take the bodies down into the crypt for tonight and have the burials tomorrow.' He gulped, and Deina knew he was trying not to weep. 'And then there are the Iron Guards. Are we – are you – not going to set them free?'

'Well . . .' she trailed off, wondering. She'd freed the Bronze Guards from Orpheus's spells by removing their face plates. Even after decades sealed inside their armour, they'd still known they were human, but they'd all been Theodesmioi of the Order of Zeus. Battle Wagers, drawing on the god's power. Aristaeus, however, had selected ordinary men like Archis's brother to be made into Iron Guards. Deina stared at the figures still scattered motionless around the courtyard, like so many statues. What had been following the orders she'd given – the people inside, or the spell-cast armour itself?

'Come with me.'

Aster, Nat and Dendris followed her to the nearest Iron Guard. As far Deina could tell, there was no hierarchy as such; depending on the exact words used, an order given to one guard would be carried out by all of them. Hopefully, the choice she was about to offer would be shared in the same way. She stared up into the dark shadows that lurked behind the eyeholes of the creature's faceplate. Even though it was surrounded by identical beings, Deina had an impression of crushing loneliness.

'I hope you can understand what I'm saying. I wish you all to be free. I wish you to make your own choice: to stay or to go. To remain as you are, or to remove the armour that you wear.'

The Iron Guard tilted its head fractionally, as if listening more closely.

'I do not know what will happen if you remove the armour,' Deina continued. 'You might become ordinary mortals once again, but you might not. You might die.' On impulse, she reached up to rest her hand on the creature's shoulder. 'The important thing is that the choice is yours. Aristaeus took your bodies. I give them back to you. Do you understand?'

Was it a trick of the light, or was there a glint in the depths of the eyeholes, something that could be a tear?

'All of you – you are free.'

None of the Iron Guards moved. Deina turned to Aster.

'What else should I say? I don't know how to –'

Aster gasped and took her hand.

'Look.'

24

The Iron Guard had lifted its hand to its faceplate and hooked two fingers into the eyeholes. The metal began to buckle and complain as the guard tore the faceplate slowly away from the helmet to which it was attached. Until suddenly, with a crack that echoed around the courtyard, the faceplate came free. The features revealed were still human – just. The nose and mouth were barely distinguishable amidst the deep folds of discoloured flesh. It took Deina a moment to realise the guard was trying to speak. He pitched forward onto one knee. The man's voice was no more than a rough whisper and Deina had to lean close to hear his words.

'Better to die free than . . . than live another moment imprisoned in this. Thank you.' He struck his armoured chest with one fist even as he slumped to the ground. Deina drew back, barely supressing a cry of horror – the man's face was collapsing in on itself. Disintegrating.

Nat drew his sword, its fiery blade glowing fiercely. As the man crumbled into dust, the god of death swung his weapon.

There was a glimmer of something rising from the Iron Guard's remnants, then that too disappeared.

The armour settled; there was no longer a body within it. Deina swallowed her shock and sorrow and turned to the remaining Iron Guards.

'Now you see. The choice is yours. Stay as you are, either here or wherever else you wish to go, or remove your armour and leave this realm behind.'

Before much more time had passed, there were no Iron Guards left. Every one of them chose the release of death. Given what they had been subjected to, Deina knew she would have made the same choice.

Dendris put her hands on her hips, surveying the courtyard.

'We should ask some of the other Theodesmioi – former Theodesmioi – to help us do something with the armour. It doesn't seem right, to leave it lying here.' She eyed a party of nobles and priests who were cautiously making their way through the main gate. 'I wonder who is going to claim the city? And the Dominion. It should have been Theron.' Tears welled in her eyes.

'I don't know,' Deina replied. 'And there's Iolkos too. Aristaeus's army might still be besieging the city. Perhaps we should –'

'Deina,' Nat interrupted. 'They. Perhaps *they* should. These decisions are for the mortals now. Not for us.' He spoke with certainty, even though his voice was gentle. 'The Underworld awaits.'

Deina clutched at his hands.

'But I don't want to go, Nat.' Hurt bloomed in his eyes. 'I'm sorry,' she said quickly. 'I care for you. I care for you far more deeply than I ever thought possible, but I belong here. I want the joy and sorrow and hurt and chaos and wonder of the mortal realm. This –' she picked up the silken fabric of her gown and let it slip through her fingers – 'this isn't enough for me.'

Nat's dark wings shimmered at his shoulders.

'Even without Theron?'

Deina nodded.

'Even without Theron.'

Nat hesitated.

'You're the ruler of the Underworld. You know you could bring him back, right?'

It had occurred to her. She shook her head.

'I wouldn't trust myself. Not after what I did. I don't –' She broke off, aware of Aster and Dendris watching her, and tried to find the right words. 'If I brought him back, I would worry that I was only doing it to force him to forgive me. That he'd feel like he owed me his life. That everything would be different between us.' The torc around her neck shivered. 'It wouldn't be equal. He might start off loving me, but he'd come to fear me. I've learned enough about myself and my power to know that.' Deina smiled slightly. 'I can't bring him back because I'm a god, and if I'm not a god, I can't bring him back.'

Aster reached out and gripped her shoulder.

'Nat, you're an honourable man. God, rather. Is there nothing you can do?'

Nat looked up at the sky for a moment and sighed.

'I can't believe I'm saying this, but I love you too much, Deina, to want to be with you in the Underworld if you've no

wish to be there.' He pointed a finger at Aster and Dendris. 'I blame all of you for this un-godlike behaviour. Your humanity is –' he pulled a face – 'infectious. Give me a moment.'

He vanished, reappearing again almost before they'd had time wonder where he'd gone.

'I've spoken to Hephaestus. There is a way you might be freed of the torc and your responsibilities, and he's willing to help. You might not survive the process, though.'

'Why not?' Dendris asked. 'What would have to be done to her?'

The god of death shrugged.

'For a start, I'll have to try to kill her.'

Aster and Dendris stood close together, gazing nervously round the cavernous, flame-lit interior of Hephaestus's forge. Deina had been forced to use her power to bring them with her to the smith god's home; Nat had pointed out that she had more power than him and reminded her that ferrying mortals – either living or dead – had never been one of his abilities. Unlike her human companions, the god of death was wandering about examining his surroundings with interest. Even as Hephaestus was talking to her, Deina could tell that he was paying almost as much attention to Nat.

'It's because of the way the torc has threaded itself into your body, you see,' the god was explaining. 'You are so closely linked, that if you are attacked, your body will automatically draw on – Thanatos, will you please stop touching things!'

'Sorry,' Nat called.

Hephaestus growled.

'Where was I?'

'My body being attacked,' Deina nudged.

'Oh, yes. So, if we can get your body to draw enough power from the torc, the spell-cast metal –' the god tapped the torc – 'will eventually wither and disintegrate. At least in theory. A pity,' he sighed. 'It's some of my best work.'

'And if I'm free of the torc, does that mean I'm not god of the Underworld any more?'

'No. You became god of the Underworld because you rendered your mother powerless. The Underworld needs a ruler, so it instantly switched its allegiance to you.'

She'd won the game, and the Underworld itself was the prize. Deina glanced down at the bident, still masquerading as a bangle around her wrist. She'd tried throwing it away; each time it had instantly reappeared.

'So, Nat needs to render me powerless? And then he'd become ruler of the Underworld?'

'Yes. But it's a fine line. He'll need to weaken you almost to the point of death. If he misjudges it . . .' Hephaestus winced and reached down to make an adjustment to the gold bands that encircled his legs. 'I don't know whether this will leave you a mortal, a god, or something in-between. You could end up dead. Worse, you could end up still immortal, but alive and in constant agony. And as I said, I've never done anything like this before.' He gestured to his forge. 'I experiment. I try to create more beauty, more utility. It keeps me sane and stops me from ending up like Zeus and the others, fixated on jealous squabbles and meaningless liaisons. From my experiments I come up with theories, but that's all they are. So, I make no promises. The choice is yours.'

'I want to try,' Deina said quickly.

Hephaestus looked surprised.

'You don't want to think about it?'

'There's nothing to think about.' Deina touched the torc. 'I can hear it, you know. It's very seductive. Even now, it sings to me of the joy of absolute power, of what I might achieve if I take my mother's place on the throne of the Underworld.'

Hephaestus dropped his gaze as if he was ashamed of what he'd created. Deina felt sorry for him – for a god, Hephaestus seemed like a decent person.

'That king you were in love with – it might not have been entirely his fault that he ended up the way he did. Perhaps he did care for you, but the torc was too strong for him to resist.' Hephaestus brightened a little. 'I checked with Nat,' Deina continued. 'The contract Zeus signed does not bind me. And that being the case, I know how this will end. The Underworld won't be enough, not for long. I'll fight Zeus, and I'll win. I'll conquer the heavens and the seas. Then I'll come for the mortal realm. I'll leave a trail of death and destruction in my wake, and I won't care.' The smith god was staring at her with a sort of fascinated horror. 'I won't stop, you know. I have all my mother's craving for power, and that of Zeus and Poseidon, and the human will to dominate others, to win. The only chance to stop me is here and now. Besides –' she smiled at Hephaestus – 'I don't want to be a god. I never did.'

'Well . . .' Hephaestus nodded. 'In that case, let us begin.' He looked around to locate Nat and swore loudly. 'Thanatos, will you put that chisel down and get over here right now.'

Making a visible effort to calm himself, Hephaestus turned to Deina. 'You should say goodbye to your friends. I'm guessing you don't want them to watch you suffer.'

Deina beckoned Aster and Dendris nearer.

'Hephaestus has explained what he needs to do. I don't know if I'll survive, but if I do, I think I'd like to go somewhere quiet for a while afterwards. To rest. Tyche told me that my father is still alive. I'd like to find him.'

'Of course.' Aster hesitated. 'We'll see you again, though, won't we?' He held out his hand to her. 'I've lost Theron. I've probably lost Melos too. I don't want to lose you.'

Deina hugged him tightly.

'And I don't want to lose you. Either of you.' She pulled Dendris into a quick embrace. 'I just need some time, that's all. If I survive, I'll be weak, from what Hephaestus says. And you – you have so much to do.' She tried to smile at them. 'And now you have the freedom to do it too. We did that. Together.'

Dendris, still clutching Deina's hand, gave Nat a look.

'Do try not to kill her.'

'I'll do my best,' he replied. 'And I'll come and find you afterwards and let you know. Whatever happens.'

Aster's stomach rumbled. The reminder of ordinary mortal life made Deina smile.

'It's time for you to go – you need to eat. Stay safe, my dear friends.' She closed her eyes. When she opened them again, Dendris and Aster were gone. 'I've sent them back to Mycenae.' Her voice trembled, but at least that meant she was still human enough to be scared. She straightened her shoulders. 'Shall we begin?'

Hephaestus cleared his worktable and Deina lay down on the pitted wooden surface. There wasn't much for the smith god to do, but Deina asked him to stay and hold her hand, so he pulled a chair up to the table and sat down.

Nat drew his sword. The silver flames that formed the blade flickered all the more brightly against the shadowy forge and the even darker shadows of his wings.

'Are you sure you won't change your mind, Deina?' he asked softly, with no trace of his usual humour. 'It's not too late. Come with me to the Underworld. Let me love you for eternity.'

'You have to trust me, Nat. It's better this way. Better for you as well as me. I've been talking to Hephaestus about the torc. About what it will turn me into, eventually. He'll explain.'

Nat was silent for a long moment.

'Please, Nat. Do this last thing for me.'

The god of death bowed his head.

'As you wish.'

Deina closed her eyes tightly. The thrust of the blade was quick: like an icicle driving up beneath her ribs. The fierce cold spread, and in its wake came pain. So much pain that it forced her back to arch off the table as she dug her fingernails into its surface. So much pain that she had no breath left to scream. She could feel the fire of Nat's sword eating away at her power, yet the torc kept feeding her more. On and on it went. Deina lost track of time. The freezing agony consumed without being sated. It grew and spread until Deina's entire universe contained nothing but this endless, excruciating torture. She forgot why she was there. She forgot Nat and Hephaestus and the forge. She forgot Theron. She forgot her own name. The torment stripped away layer after layer until there was almost nothing left apart from the will to keep existing, as fragile as a snowflake. On and on it went, until a flare of heat forced Deina to remember the torc, to become aware of her body, to realise that the burning smell was the result of her own skin blistering and charring and falling away. The torc grew hotter still, searing her. The cold of Nat's blade was stronger, though. There was a sound like something shattering. The ring of fire around her neck faded, and all that was left was ice.

'Deina?'

The voice sounded far away. Deina became aware of a hard surface beneath her. She tried to move; a sudden ache sent her hand to just below her ribs. There was something there. A thick pad, tied to her body with a strip of material.

'Deina, can you hear me?' Something was prodding her. No – it was coming from inside. Stuttering – irregular at first – a slow pulse emerged through the chaos of her thoughts.

Her heart, that had been still for so long, shuddered back into life.

With a gasping in-breath, Deina pushed herself up to sitting.

'You're alive.' Nat was in front of her. The worry in his face changed to delight. 'You're alive! Thank . . . me, I guess. I really thought I'd killed you. Hephaestus said we should wait, that you might still come back, but I was certain I'd finished you off.' He grimaced. 'I almost did, to judge by the look of you.' He turned to speak to someone over his shoulder. 'Her neck is a mess.'

Hephaestus prodded him out of the way with his crutch.

'I haven't finished yet,' the smith god grumbled. 'This would all be much easier if you would just stop talking!'

Deina turned her head towards him. The movement sent a ripple of sharp, stinging pain across her skin, making her feel sick and faint.

'The torc?' she rasped.

'Gone.' Hephaestus plucked at something, making her yelp. 'Sorry – there were fragments of metal lodged in the wounded area and I had to pick them out by hand.' He peered closer. 'I think that was the last one. The bleeding has stopped, and though you lost a lot of blood, there is good news: the blood was red. Sort of. Red with gold streaks. How do you feel?'

'Tired,' Deina murmured. She winced as Hephaestus started smearing some sort of ointment onto her burns. 'In pain. Weaker than I remember feeling for a long time.' Or maybe this was just what it felt like not being a god. She couldn't recall. Deina glanced at her wrist. The bident bangle had gone.

Nat held up his arm and pointed.

'Look who's the new god of the Underworld.' His irrepressible grin was back.

'It's a bangle for you too?'

'Why not?' He inspected the gold bracelet. 'I think it looks good.'

'You should take this too.' Trying not to move too much, Deina pulled Hades' prison from the pouch hanging from her belt and handed the glittering orb to Nat. 'Keep it safe.'

'Don't worry, I will.' He threw the orb into the air and it vanished. 'I found out where your father is, by the way. He lives by the coast a little way south of Aulis.'

'And can you take me there?'

'Now that I'm god of the Underworld, yes. Yes, I can. There's one more thing I want to do first, though. A gift, from me to you. You've given me an entire realm. I'd like to give you something in return.'

Deina smiled wearily.

'You've given me my life back, Nat. You don't need to do anything else.'

'You'll like this present.' He winked. 'Trust me. Let me just concentrate . . .'

As Nat closed his eyes, hope built in Deina's heart, despite everything she could do to suppress it.

Nat took a deep breath and clicked his fingers. The wall of night appeared, the same dense black rectangle that had dragged Deina from Olympus back to the Underworld. This time, though, a figure seemed to be approaching from the other side, as if from a very great distance. Closer and closer it drew, until Theron stepped through the darkness and into Hephaestus's forge.

Deina put one hand to her mouth, not trusting herself to speak.

Theron was standing, staring at his hands, turning them back and forth. He pressed his fingers to his wrists, then to his neck, then put his hands on his abdomen. To Deina's relief, there was no sign of the damage she'd inflicted upon him. Theron spotted Nat.

'Thanatos . . . I'm – I'm alive?'

'Yes. Fully restored. Better than fully restored. Deina and I – and the others – freed the Theodesmioi and banished the gods.' Nat shrugged one shoulder. 'Most of the gods. I'm god of the Underworld now, by the way. We got rid of Hades.'

Theron touched his forehead and his eyes opened wider. Deina lifted her fingers to her cheeks. The pockmarks were back, and so were the rite-seals, but she didn't care.

'Where am I?' Theron asked.

'Hephaestus's forge.' The smith god, already busy with some other task over by his anvil, waved. Theron hesitantly waved back. 'I'll take you back to Mycenae in a moment,' Nat continued. 'Aster and Dendris are still there. First, though, there's someone else here you'll want to see.'

As if a veil had been lifted from his sight, Theron saw Deina and flinched.

Was he recoiling from her wounds, or from her? Deina tried to smile, gesturing to her blood-soaked tunic.

'It's not as bad as it looks. Nat got rid of the torc, but –'

In two strides Theron closed up the space between them. He lifted his fingers towards her face, bit back a gasp as he took in the ruined skin around her neck, and settled for taking her hands.

'I'm so sorry, Theron.' Deina struggled to speak through the tears that were choking her. 'It was an accident. I never meant to hurt you.'

'I know you didn't.'

Deina stared into his dark eyes.

'I watched you die. I cut your lifeline and I watched you die.'

'I remember, I think. Everything was shadowed, except you. You were so bright. Like a star in the darkness.' He swallowed hard. 'Are you still . . .'

She knew what he wanted to ask.

'I'm mortal, I think. More or less.' She squeezed her eyes shut against a sudden wave of pain.

'Deina –' Theron gripped her shoulders, steadying her.

'I'm alright. I just need to explain – though I'm not expecting that an apology will set everything right again. I should have told you about the nectar straight away. And about how much I wanted the torc.' She dashed a tear from her face. 'I'm so happy Nat's brought you back, Theron. Happier than I can put into words. You've got a second chance at life, and you should use it as you wish.' Deina forced herself to look steadily at him. 'After what I did, if you don't want your life to include me, I'll understand. You don't owe me anything.'

He just looked at her.

'Say something.'

Theron smiled. The same lopsided grin that she'd grown to love, even if the old arrogance wasn't there any more.

'I owe you everything, Deina. You defeated Aristaeus. You saved the Theodesmioi, just like you always said you would. More than that, you saved me from myself. You forced me to confront the kind of man I was becoming. You forced me to do better. You can ask anything of me, and I will give it to you if I can. You've given me more than I can ever repay.' Tenderly, he pushed her matted hair back from her face. 'Even when you almost killed me, I never stopped loving you. I never will.'

He kissed her so gently his lips barely brushed against hers, but it was enough to reignite the fierce desire that Deina feared had gone forever.

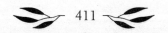

'I love you too, Theron.' She pressed one of his hands to her chest. 'My heart beats again. And it beats for you.'

The mingled amazement and relief and joy in his face was enough to make her laugh and cry at the same time. She leaned forward to kiss him again, even though every movement hurt like hell. Even though she couldn't completely stifle a cry of pain.

'You need help,' Theron said, his eyes full of concern. He swung round to find Nat. 'Can you take us to Mycenae? There are healers there.'

'No,' Deina said quietly. 'Not Mycenae. I want to go somewhere quiet. And my father is still alive – Hades lied. I'll go to him. You should go to Mycenae, though – the others are there.' A wave of exhaustion sent Deina slumping into Theron's arms. He helped her lay back down on the table and leant over her, one hand caressing her face.

'There'll be time for Mycenae. And for Thebes too.' At Deina's questioning glance he nodded. 'Critos was right. I'm going to claim the throne and try to be the king that the people of the Dominion deserve. That can wait, though. I'm not leaving you again.'

Deina didn't have to strength to argue, even if she'd wanted to.

Nat appeared in her vision.

'Two to transport to your father's house, then.' He glanced across the room. 'I think Hephaestus will be relieved to have his forge to himself again.'

Deina yawned.

'I'm so tired.'

'Sleep, my love,' Theron whispered. 'I'll be there when you wake up.'

The weight of Deina's eyelids grew irresistible. The last thing she saw was Theron, smiling down at her through his tears.

Birdsong and sunlight, and the sound of waves in the distance. Deina turned over, wincing. She was lying on something soft – a mattress of some sort – and there were warm blankets over her, but her neck was stiff. She lifted her hand and felt a bandage wrapped tightly around her throat and across the upper part of her chest. The mattress was comfortable . . . How long was it since she'd slept in a proper bed? There had been that shepherd's hut near Thebes, and the stable in Mycenae, but she'd not really slept in either . . .

Her memories came back in a flood. She opened her eyes.

The room, from what she could see, was plainly furnished but clean and neat. Though the shutters were closed, enough bright sunshine crept in round their edges for her to spot Theron asleep on the floor nearby. Deina checked she was clothed – a worn tunic that smelled faintly of lavender – and sat up. As quietly as she moved, it was enough to rouse him. He hurried to get up and swaddle her in a blanket.

'Careful – it's cold, and you've been running a fever.' He sat next to her on the bed, giving Deina a chance to study him. His face was drawn, there was stubble on his chin and dark shadows beneath his eyes, but he was smiling.

'How long have I been asleep?'

'Twenty days, more or less; you were awake some of the time, but not aware, then finally the fever broke. We were worried. We've been taking turns to sit with you.' He took her hand and kissed her palm. 'You've not been alone.'

'We?'

Theron's smile turned into a grin. He helped her get up, placing one arm protectively around her shoulders.

'Come and see.'

Together they went through to the next room. A living space: a fire was crackling in the hearth. The sound of the sea was louder here, and Deina could smell the salt tang of seaweed. The entrance to the little house was just ahead. Theron stopped, wrapped his arms around her and kissed her.

'I'll wait here.' He nodded towards the door. Her heart racing, Deina opened it and stepped out onto the springy turf. There was a man standing there, looking out over the storm-tossed waves. Chestnut hair, streaked with grey, tied at the nape of his neck. He turned. Darker skin and eyes than hers, but the same oval face. And when he smiled, she knew.

'Father . . .'

She was home.

Epilogue

Spring, having arrived late, seemed determined to make up for lost time. Overnight almost, the hillsides around the little house had burst into bloom. Their colours blazed in the late morning sun. From a distance, it looked as if some careless nymph had scattered her jewels across the grass. Deina lay on her stomach among the flowers, her chin propped in her hands. She was at the edge of the turf. From here, she could watch the progress of a striped lizard that had started a cautious descent down across the rocks that separated the grass from the beach below. In the house, her father was singing. A working song, the melody kept in time by the rhythmic swish of the plane he was using to smooth the wood. Deina listened, singing along under her breath, until the song was interrupted by a spasm of coughing. That was one of the few dark spots in her existence at the moment. As her wounds had healed over the winter, and she'd grown stronger, her father had caught a sickness from which he'd not yet fully recovered. Every so often the old whispers came back. *If you were still a god, you could help him.* Yet with the destruction of the torc, the voice had lost its persuasiveness. The part of her that craved complete power no longer threatened to overwhelm her.

A shadow fell across her and she pushed herself onto her back, squinting up at the sky.

'Nat.' He never had got the hang of waiting to be invited into someone's space. Her heart raced. 'You're here for my father?'

The god of death – the god of the Underworld, she corrected herself – smiled and shook his head.

'I'm not. This is just a social call.' As she sat up, he settled himself on the grass next to her. 'I could tell you when your father is due to die, but –'

'No. I don't want to know.'

'Wise. Though I will tell you that he's going to recover from his current illness.'

Deina sighed happily. Her father had spent the winter planning. He wanted to travel through the Dominion and visit the great cities, and she wanted him to get his wish.

Nat was looking at her searchingly. Although four or five months had passed since she'd last seen him, Deina hadn't forgotten the startling sapphire blue of his eyes. 'How are you?' he asked.

'Better.' Automatically, Deina's hand went to her neck. The scars left by the torc were still there, but no longer painful. 'I'm strong again. Though not everything has returned to normal. If I prick my finger, I still bleed red with gold streaks.'

'Well, you're still a demi-god. Removing the torc didn't cancel out your parentage, or undo what Tyche did to you. You'll probably age and die in the usual mortal way, like most demi-gods, but I'm not by any means certain.'

'That's alright.' Unless she'd succeeded in earning out her

indenture – so unlikely as to be almost impossible – Deina's entire future at the House would have been mapped out for her. A life of rites and rituals, spent as much among the dead as the living, every day virtually identical. She'd come to value uncertainty. 'What about you?'

'Oh, keeping busy.' Nat flashed her one of his brilliant, confident smiles. 'Being ruler of the Underworld does have some advantages. They have to invite me to the parties on Olympus now. I don't often go – they're actually surprisingly dull – but it's nice to feel included.'

'There's no danger, is there? Zeus isn't going to try to come back?'

'No. Well – he'll try. As you'd expect, he already has. However, I doubt he'll ever succeed in finding a way around the contract he agreed to. Tyche had the terms and conditions already drawn up, and apart from the sections that meant the contract doesn't apply to her or me, they were extremely comprehensive.'

Already drawn up? Deina couldn't help smiling. Had Tyche known how things were going to work out, or had it just been a lucky guess? She lent her head on Nat's shoulder.

'I'm glad to see you again. I've missed you. I've missed everyone.' After waiting to be sure that she was truly recovering, Theron had left for Thebes. He'd promised her messages, as soon as he could find a clerk to write them, and he'd kept his word. Thanks to the messengers who had brought his words and read them to her, she knew that, with a little help from Nat, Theron had been crowned king of the Theban Dominion and was easily wining the hearts of his people. She'd learned that Aster was now archon of Iolkos, ruling with Melos at his side. Dendris, meanwhile, had been representing the Dominion in negotiating a treaty with the queen of the Amazons. They were all busy, and she was proud of them. And messages were something. Just not enough.

Nat laughed softly.

'They all miss you too. Theron in particular.'

Deina turned to frown at him.

'Are you reading my mind?'

'No. But I know you, remember? We're linked by the Underworld, you and I. We always will be.' He slipped his cold hand into hers and grinned. 'Or I could be making a lucky guess, based on the fact that a small fleet of Theban ships is sailing into the bay.'

Deina jumped to her feet, scanning the sea.

'Ships? There aren't any –'

The top of a white sail came into view beyond the headland. Another moment revealed the prow of a ship, long and low in the water, built for speed. Another two ships were just behind.

Deina felt Nat's hands on her shoulders. He kissed her cheek and whispered in her ear. 'Tell Theron hello. Until next time, Deina.'

'Nat –'

He'd gone. Deina stood for a moment with her fingertips pressed against her cheek, then began hurrying down to the beach. The lead ship had already breached the surf; its sailors were dragging it up onto the sand. Guards leaped from the prow and stood to attention. A tall figure walked past them, spotted Deina and raced towards her.

Deina ran into Theron's open arms. He picked her up and spun her round and set her on her feet again.

 418

'Oh, Deina.' The passion of his kiss made Deina melt and tremble. She felt she would have fallen to the ground if his arms hadn't been around her, holding her close. 'I've missed you so much. I came as soon as I could. As soon as I knew things were settled enough for me to ask you.'

'Ask me what?' Deina said, smiling up at him through her tears.

Taking her hands, he knelt in the sand.

'Come to Thebes with me, Deina. Be my queen. Or I'll stay here with you. I don't care, as long as I can be with you. The choice is yours.'

'You'd give up your kingdom for me?'

'My kingdom, and my life. You're worth more to me than either.' He looked up at her anxiously, and Deina saw their history in his dark eyes. Friendship and fighting and desire and betrayal. Yet through all of it, in different ways, she'd loved him. She still did.

'Of course I'll be with you.'

With a cry of joy Theron swept her back into his arms.

'And,' Deina added, 'I'll come to Thebes. On two conditions.'

'Name them.'

'My father comes with us. I won't leave him again.'

'Of course. I'd never ask you to. And the other?'

Deina glanced at the ships.

'I'd like to take our time going back. I'd like to see how fast these ships of yours can fly.' Theron gave her one of his gorgeous lopsided grins and sent the blood raging through her body. 'You'll be busy when we reach Thebes, so I want you to myself for as long as possible.'

Somehow, between laughter and tears, they kissed again.

'I'll go and tell Aster and Dendris – they're both waiting on the ship. We'll stay here tonight and sail in the morning.'

'Bring them up to the house – I must tell my father.'

Another kiss and Deina tore herself away, racing across the rocks and grass to share her happiness.

That night, she dreamed of standing in the prow of a ship, its sanded deck beneath her bare feet, the open sea glittering in front of her, just waiting for her to explore it. She'd had the same dream many times before. Only this time, when the dawn broke over the Aegean, her dream came true.

The end

Acknowledgements

At RCW, for unflagging support as always, our agent Claire Wilson, assisted by Safae El-Ouahabi.

At Hot Key Books, we owe a huge amount to our brilliant editor Ruth Bennett and super assistant editor Tia Albert, both of whom constantly pushed us to be better. Also on the editorial side, a big thank-you to Talya Baker, Melissa Hyder and Eanna Webb for keeping Deina and our prose on the straight and narrow. Our appreciation goes to Emma Quick, Isobel Taylor, Eleanor Rose, Pippa Poole and Molly Holt for all their hard work in getting our books into readers' hands. Thanks also to Marina Stavropoulou and narrator Kristin Atherton for the wonderful audiobook of *Queen of Gods*.

Great covers sell books, so we're hugely appreciative of the work of Micaela Alcaino (artwork) and Dominica Clements (design) in giving *Queen of Gods* a cover that Zeus himself would be delighted with.

Writing can be very lonely (even though there are two of us!) so we are extremely grateful to all our author friends for their company and support. Particular shout-outs to Perdita Cargill, Kristina Perez, Holly Race, Bex Hogan, Josh Winning,

Alexia Casale, Chris Moore, Mary Watson, Sinéad O'Hart and to everyone in the screenwriting gang. You're the best!

Stories are written to be shared, so *Queen of Gods* wouldn't be anything without all the booksellers, bloggers and readers out there who have been so supportive of the House of Shadows duology. We appreciate you all so much.

Finally, we owe a massive debt as always to our family, spread across the UK and the US. We love you all.

Katharine and Elizabeth Corr

Katharine and Elizabeth Corr are sisters originally from Essex, now living in Surrey. When they both decided to write novels – on account of fictional people being much easier to deal with than real ones – it was obvious they should do it together. They can sometimes be found in one of their local coffee shops, arguing over which character to kill off next. Katharine and Elizabeth are authors of the enthralling *A Throne of Swans* duology and the spellbinding trilogy *The Witch's Kiss*.

@katharinecorr
@lizcorr_writes
Instagram: katharinecorrwrites / lizcorrwrites
www.corrsisters.com

Thank you for choosing a Hot Key book.

If you want to know more about our authors and what we publish, you can find us online.

You can start at our website

www.hotkeybooks.com

And you can also find us on:

We hope to see you soon!